STARGATE
ATLANTIS™

NIGHTFALL

JAMES SWALLOW

FANDEMONIUM BOOKS

An original publication of Fandemonium Ltd, produced under license from MGM Consumer Products.

Fandemonium Books
PO Box 795A
Surbiton
Surrey KT5 8YB
United Kingdom
Visit our website: www.stargatenovels.com

S T A R G A T E
A T L A N T I S ™

METRO-GOLDWYN-MAYER Presents
STARGATE ATLANTIS™
JOE FLANIGAN TORRI HIGGINSON RACHEL LUTTRELL JASON MOMOA
with PAUL McGILLION as Dr. Carson Beckett and DAVID HEWLETT as Dr. McKay
Executive Producers BRAD WRIGHT & ROBERT C. COOPER
Created by BRAD WRIGHT & ROBERT C. COOPER

ISBN: 978-1-905586-14-1
Printed in the United States of America

This book is dedicated to the memory of Barry Swallow,
for tales of rocketships and distant worlds.

The events depicted in *Nightfall* take place during the fourth season of *Stargate Atlantis*, between the episodes "The Seer" and "Miller's Crossing".

CHAPTER ONE

He had disobeyed before.

He had done it so many times that it had become a joke among many of the adults in the settlement. He saw it, in smirking asides or quick grins, in comments made that they thought would fly above the head of a youth. *There's Laaro,* they might say, *the reckless boy who climbed atop the grain silo roof on a dare and fell in. The careless boy who tried to swim the shallow lake where the root-taps grow.* And then they would shake their heads at his folly, as if they felt sorry for him. But no, not for Laaro. For his mother and father.

He paused in the undergrowth and crouched low. His heart was hammering in his chest, so loud in his ears he would have sworn they could hear it all the way back to the lodge house. Larro chanced a look behind him, through the snarl of twisted scrubland, off in the direction of home; and he immediately regretted it. Rods of faint yellow lantern-light bobbed and shifted, sweeping this way and that across the grasslands, coming closer. On the cool, still air of the night he could hear the grunt and spit of mai cats on their leashes, pulling at his scent. With them, the rumble of adult voices, most distinctly the dry snap of the Elder Aaren's words.

A tremor of fear shot through the boy's body and he let it go, for one moment wondering how he might be treated if he turned back and went to them. He studied his bare arms, his thin shirt. Perhaps, if he bit himself, drew blood, ripped his clothes, he might sell them on the idea he'd been chased by a wild mai.

Laaro's teeth bared in a smile. *They would never believe me.* He had told tales too many times to be trusted now. He could come home with the head of a Wraith in his back pocket and Aaren would be the first to claim he had made it from sticks and mud.

The smile became a grin. Somehow that seemed funny to

him. Somehow, that was enough to push him back to his feet, from the undergrowth, back to running. Laaro's bare feet pat-pat-patted across the earth, as he zigzagged wide of the well-worn hunting trails.

I will not go home. Not yet. The boy's jaw set firmly, but his outward defiance was weakening by the moment. He had been out here in the savannah since second sunset, moving in the pattern that his uncle Haafo had taught him, the way that a tracker would loop back and forth, as they searched for animal signs before a hunt. The quarry he tracked was the most important he had ever hunted; his father Errian.

Laaro's mistake had been to speak of this idea to his mother, and in turn she had told Aaren, her face all pinched and sad as it had been since Errian's disappearance. Aaren, blunt and grace-less like a mud bovine, made stern rebukes and waggled his fat fingers at the boy. Aaren told him it was not the business of a youth to interfere in the order of things; and then he had forbid-den Laaro to leave the settlement.

All of which showed how little Aaren understood Laaro. Why else had he climbed the silo, swum in the lake? Because he had been told *not* to do it. Someone slow and ugly and old like an Elder couldn't understand that challenge was what Laaro looked for every day of his life. It was that or boredom—the tedium of schooling and housework had to be broken by something.

But still he felt his resolve faltering. If Aaren was out here, then his mother knew he'd fled. He saw Jaaya's pinched face again in his mind's eye and felt a stab of guilt. Laaro didn't want her to be sad; he wanted to come home having rescued Errian, and reunite his parents. To be the hero for real that he was in his games and play.

Fear seeped into him, pushing aside his boldness. He was caught between two compulsions; what scared him more? The thought of the punishment he'd get if he let himself be caught, or the fear of what lay out in the night? Not the mai cats or the arachs, but the bigger, less definite things. The Giants that hid in the stars. Maybe even the Wraith.

Reflexively, he looked up and saw the glittering ring of the sky river that bisected the night above, from horizon to horizon; and beyond the great moon with its smaller brother peeking over its shoulder. Laaro shivered and moved on carelessly, his foot catching an exposed root.

The boy grunted and stumbled, turning in place as a strange new sound reached his ears. It was like thunder, it was like the roar of a great cat, it was like the crash of a cloudburst. It was all these things and none of them.

Panic seized him. Suddenly, he felt lost. Laaro looked around, abruptly aware that he had gone beyond the limits of his own explorations. His gaze found motion and light, down in a shallow vale where pillars of old brown rock five times the height of the boy stood sentinel.

The light was a cool silver, glittering and shifting. It reminded him of moonlight cast off water; and in a swift, dizzying rush, Laaro realized where he was.

The Gateway.

There were many rules Laaro was happy to break, many adult edicts he would ignore without a care in the world—but the Gateway… To come here without the blessing of the Elders was said to mean death. Uncle Haafo had told him stories of the ghostly guardians there that allowed only the chosen, the know-ers of the symbols, to approach the great ring of grey metal. Some said that voyagers could come and go through the centre of the Gateway, to other places—even to the stars, although Laaro doubted that could be possible. He had never seen voyagers; only the Elders had, in the years before his birth. Everyone knew how long it had been since the Gateway had opened; ever since the coming of the Aegis and the Giants.

And then there were the other stories. The old, terrible stories of the Wraith, the monsters that ate men like an arach would kill a click-beetle.

With a shriek of sound the shimmering light vanished, plunging the vale into darkness once more. Laaro blinked furiously, his night vision lost to him for a moment where he had been staring at the brightness in the ring. In his fascination he had meandered further down the shallow incline, almost to the shadow of one of the outermost pillars. The boy hesitated, the

question on his lips; what had come through the Gateway? He
backed off, staying low, desperately trying to look in every
direction at once—

—and bumped into something soft, covered in cloth.

Laaro spun about and found himself staring at figure a good
head taller than he was, clad in a dark, matt clothing that seemed to
suck in the faint light from the night sky; and the face…

Pale skin and wide eyes caught the lunar glow, and Laaro
glimpsed a mouth open in an 'O' of fury. The intruder howled
and the boy screamed back at it, unable to stop himself. *Wraith!*
his mind cried, and he threw out his hands, swatting at the
alien.

Laaro hurled himself away and broke into a full-pelt run,
charging toward the lip of the shallow valley as fast as his legs
could propel him. Sharp beams of light stabbed out after him,
trying to fix Laaro in their centre. He clawed at the ridge as he
pulled himself up it, frantic to escape. The question as to what
he was more afraid of had been answered for him, and now all
he wanted was to get away, to find an adult even if it was Elder
Aaren.

But on the lip of the ridge there was another one; this figure
was larger, and for a second Laaro thought it might have been
one of the Giants. The chasing lights caught up to them both
and he saw clearly a man. He was broad across the chest, his
face a dusky shade a little lighter than Laaro's, and his hair was
wild in thick locks that cascaded down over the shoulders of his
leather jerkin. In one hand he held a weapon that dwarfed the
spindly rodguns used by the Elder's watchmen.

The warrior—and Laaro knew without question that the
man could be nothing else but that—threw him a look of grim
amusement and holstered the pistol with a flick of the wrist.
Then, without pause, he rocked off his feet and grabbed Laaro
by the scruff of the neck, lifting him clean off the ground.
Before the boy could argue, he was being carried back down
into the valley of the Gateway. The warrior dropped him to the
dirt, and Laaro landed hard, smarting.

"Take it easy, Ronon," said a woman's voice, her words
pitched high with concern. "It's just a little kid."

Anger pushed Laaro back to his feet. He tried to make his voice firm, but it trembled slightly at the end of his words. "I'm not little," he snarled, looking up to see four more figures emerging from the shadows to join the warrior.

"Ah," said another female, coming closer. "He has fire in him." Laaro saw a woman with auburn hair and a careful, measuring gaze. She had the same look to her as the warrior did—he imagined she would be a keen fighter if pushed to it—but where the big man was all feral energy, she was calm and metered.

Laaro swallowed hard. Were these people from another settlement, perhaps from the northern tribes? He had to warn them. "I... I saw a Wraith!" He managed, the words tumbling from his lips. "Over there!" He pointed at the stone columns.

"Oh, hardly." The strangers all carried small metallic lanterns that cast a powerful pool of light, and another man stepped into the glow from the direction Laaro had indicated. The boy flinched, recognizing the face he had seen lit by moon-glow only moments before. "That was me." The man looked down his nose at Laaro, as if he thought the youth might be poisonous.

He felt foolish. The new arrival was not Wraith at all, but just pale of face in a way that the boy had never seen before. Glancing about he saw that only the warrior and the auburn-haired woman had skin like his; he looked beyond the lantern glow and saw there the other woman, the one who had called him little. She had long hair the color of straw pulled back in a tail, and on her face there was an expression of apologetic kindness.

Along with the one who had screamed and frightened him so, there was the last of them, who had had spiky black hair and a wry smile playing about his lips. All three of the pale-skinned people wore similar clothing, all in jackets the color of berrywater.

The one who smiled stepped forward and offered Laaro a hand in greeting, looking him in the eye. The boy understood immediately that he was being measured, but the man's gaze didn't feel like the accusatory glares of Elder Aaren. When he spoke, the dark-haired man didn't use the tone of voice that most adults did when conversing with a child, as if being younger somehow meant you were an idiot. He talked to Laaro as if he were speaking to an equal.

"Hi there. You're out a little late, aren't you? Isn't this a school night?" His smile deepened. "My name's John, John Sheppard. What's yours?"

The kid took the colonel's hand and shook it firmly, not giving in to the fear playing around in his eyes. "I'm Laaro. Are you... Northerners, John-John-Sheppard?"

Sheppard smirked. "Just John is fine. And, uh, no, not exactly. We're from a bit further away than that."

"A lot more," added Ronon, earning him a look from the boy.

"You're... From the stars?"

McKay frowned. "He catches on quick."

Laaro fixed him with a hard state. "I'm very clever."

"Then you two should get on fine." Sheppard gestured at his team. "Laaro, these are my friends. This is Teyla and Jennifer. These guys are Rodney and Ronon, who you already met. We're, uh—"

"Voyagers?" asked the boy.

He nodded. "I guess that's as good a name as any."

The boy nodded back at him, thinking for a moment. Then he cleared his throat, speaking with the kind of careful formality that only a child could muster. "Um. Then, uh, welcome to the planet Heruun."

"Thank you," said Teyla. "We're sorry if we scared you."

"I wasn't scared," the kid lied immediately. "I was just... Surprised."

Rodney made a *Yeah, Right* face and Ronon caught it, pointing at the boy "You screamed louder than he did, McKay."

"That wasn't a scream, all right?" Rodney sniffed. "It was an exclamation." He waved at Laaro. "He could have been anything."

"A Junior Genii?" Sheppard offered mildly.

Keller chimed in. "Maybe a pint-sized Replicator?"

"Why were you out here all alone?" asked Teyla.

Laaro's face creased and Sheppard saw immediately that the emotional rollercoaster this kid was on was threatening to throw him off. "I… Wanted to track him down. Rescue him."

"Rescue?" Keller repeated the word with a frown. "Rescue *who*?"

The answer came out in a rush. "My father. After the wanenight of the greater moon, when he disappeared—"

But the boy never got the chance to finish his sentence. Sheppard saw Ronon's expression shift in an instant from watchful amusement to a warning glare. He knew that look from experience; it meant trouble was coming.

"Hear that?" The Satedan's particle magnum pistol was already clear of its holster. "We got company," he grated, panning his gun upward toward the valley ridge.

Sheppard brought his P90 submachine gun up to his shoulder, aware of Teyla doing the same at his side. He heard the mutter of voices and an odd sound that reminded him of growling engines.

A heartbeat later, harsh lanterns from the ridge were sweeping the ground around them and the colonel saw men with spindly rifles being led forward by animals straining against heavy leashes. He blinked in the light, his thumb on the gun's safety catch.

Keller's voice came from behind him. "Those are lions," she said evenly, in a way that suggested she didn't believe her own eyes.

The doctor wasn't far off; the growling wasn't from motors, but the big cats themselves, pawing at the earth and spitting. There were three of them, and as Jennifer had noted, they looked a hell of a lot like lions, but with sharper, more triangular skulls. They had the same kind of teeth, though. Lots and lots of teeth.

"Nobody said anything about us gating into the middle of *Wild Kingdom*," said McKay with a grimace.

"Take it easy," Sheppard retorted, making the casual words into a command.

"Laaro? Laaro!" A woman called out the boy's voice,

and John guessed that she had to be his mother. By the
way the kid's shoulders sank there was no other person it
could be; the big cats didn't seem to faze him at all, but the
ire of his mom... Well, Sheppard could relate. He'd heard
his own namè called in just the same way when he'd been
Laaro's age.

Figures detached from the main group and came scram-
bling down toward them, but the cats remained where they
were, snarling and pulling on their leashes. Like the boy,
they were regular humans, all of them with the rangy look
of people who lived off the land and worked it hard in
return. There wasn't a fair face among them, their skin-
tones ranging from warm browns to deep ebony; they
looked on Sheppard and his team with suspicion.

A man with a stern expression shot the boy an acid glare
and then turned the same look on the colonel. At his side
was a woman wearing her hair in a high top-knot; Sheppard
saw the family resemblance between her and Laaro immediately, confirming his earlier thoughts.

"Who are you?" demanded the man. "We saw the flash
from the Gateway..."

"They're *voyagers*," said Laaro, putting emphasis on the
word, "from the stars. They... Perhaps they can help me!"

The kid's mother came to him, her face a mix of elation
and anger. "Why did you run away?" she asked him. "If
you had only waited until morning—"

The stern guy—Sheppard had him pegged now as
some kind of authority figure, a guess based on the number of bangles jingling up and down the length of his right
arm—waved her into silence and approached the group.
"Is the boy right? You came through the portal of light?"

"The Stargate," said McKay. "That's right."

"I'm Colonel John Sheppard and this is my team. We're
from a place called Atlantis, maybe you've heard of it?"
added Sheppard. "We're not invaders, we're just here looking for... For information." He gestured to the others to
lower their weapons.

"I do not know this 'Atlantis'. I am Elder Aaren. And

I must ask you, what do you seek on Heruun? If you're here to trade, I warn you we want for very little." The man moved carefully, and Sheppard was aware that the men on the ridge with the tubular rifles were following his every move, ready for a signal to open fire; but his team knew how to play these kinds of confrontations from mission after mission in the field. No sudden moves, just nice and easy.

"We seek information about the Wraith," said Teyla. The reaction from the locals was the same one John Sheppard had seen a hundred times across the Pegasus Galaxy; cold, hard fear.

"The Wraith." Aaren said the name and then spat in the dirt. "Thank the Aegis that they have been banished from our world. You will find no trace of them here."

Sheppard and McKay exchanged glances. "Is that so?" said Rodney. "Banished, huh? You guys are lucky, then."

"Luck has no bearing on it," came the reply. "The Aegis protects us from their predations." Aaren beckoned the colonel toward him, with other hand waving down the guns of his men. "Come. See for yourselves." The man's manner changed from wary mistrust to smugness in a heartbeat.

"What about Laaro?" said Ronon. "He said his father is lost. You people were out looking for him?"

"We were looking for my son!" said Laaro's mother. "His father... He..." She broke off and shot a look at the elder.

Aaren leaned closer to speak to Sheppard in a low voice. "The boy is...troublesome. He brings nothing but worry to poor Jaaya, here. He doesn't quite understand how things work."

"Right," Sheppard replied carefully. To be honest, he was having trouble understanding how things worked around here as well, but he kept that to himself for the moment.

"His father is well. He'll be coming back tonight."

"From where — ?" Keller started to ask the question, but Aaren was already moving off, beckoning once more.

Laaro was being alternately hugged and scolded by Jaaya, and he trailed her up toward the ridge, throwing Sheppard and the others a glum, defeated look.

"So, we're going with them, then?" said McKay.

"I guess so," said the colonel, his eyes never leaving the boy's.

The walk back to the settlement took a while, but the trail was easy going and the two groups moved in a wary lockstep. Rodney McKay kept pace behind Sheppard, half so he could listen in on the colonel's conversation with Aaren, but also so he could keep someone between himself and the guys handling the lion-cat-things.

The pre-dawn light was emerging at the horizon, an orange-pink band pushing blue into the dark sky overhead.

"Their clothes," began Keller, apparently thinking out loud as she studied the locals. "Some of them, they're like a burnoose, those wrap-around things. All lightweight stuff. Kinda Arabian-looking."

"Maybe," offered McKay. "This is a savannah region, probably similar to, oh, Southern Africa back home. Figures that they'd have similar dress sense to folks from those places." One of the animals made a grumbling snarl and pounced on something at the side of the road. Rodney heard a squeal and the crunching of bone as its handler pulled it off its kill. "Oh. Snack time. How nice."

Keller blinked. "That's a big kitty, all right."

"Just as long as it doesn't want me to pet it," he replied.

"Ah, lions don't bite you. Not unless you annoy 'em, or something."

McKay arched an eyebrow. "You're from Wisconsin. What makes you a safari expert all of a sudden?"

"Hey, I must have watched *Born Free* about a million times when I was Laaro's age." She grinned. "You know? *Born Free, as free as the—*"

"I know how it goes," Rodney retorted, cutting her off in mid-flow. He sniffed and glanced up.

Keller followed his gaze, staring at the fading glow of the

glittering banner in the sky. "What is that up there?"

"Ring system," he explained, "like Saturn has. Ice and dust particles, mostly, held in check by gravitation and—"

"Huh." Jennifer smiled slightly. "Guess you must have been more a *Star Wars* kind of kid."

Rodney shrugged. He didn't see what bearing that had on anything. "I owned a light saber," he admitted.

"Owned, or still own?"

He glanced away. "It's *mint in box*, okay? And quite rare." A few steps ahead, Sheppard was walking in conversation with Aaren, and Rodney found himself listening in once more.

"So, this 'Aegis' that you spoke about. You said it protects you. It's a device? A person?" McKay could imagine the direction the colonel's thoughts were taking. Were the locals using Ancient technology of some sort to drive off the Wraith? The Atlanteans had seen that kind of thing before, on other worlds like the Cloister planet, Proculus and Halcyon.

"It's not our place to question the nature of the Aegis," said Aaren, politely but firmly. "It simply *is*."

McKay rolled his eyes. So it was another gods-in-the-sky thing then. *Great*. That was the problem about traveling around this galaxy, where the feeding patterns of the Wraith made sure that hardly anyone ever got their civilization up past their equivalent of the Middle Ages. Nine times out of ten, every new world they went to was just like a visit to the Renaissance Fair. The thing was, every time they *did* meet people with a tech level closer to Earth's, they usually ended up being very unfriendly.

"Your people don't mind being defended by a mysterious benefactor?" Sheppard pressed the point a little more.

Aaren smiled and shook his head. "That is like asking what holds up the sky or who built the moons. These things exist. And we are grateful for them."

The colonel changed tack. "So, what happened with Laaro's father?"

"Ah, Errian, yes." The Elder glanced up the road and his voice dropped; Laaro and Jaaya were only a few meters away, at the head of the party. "The boy lacks discipline, you see. He has no patience to wait."

"He's a kid," said Sheppard. "Kids aren't real big on waiting for things."

"Just so," nodded Aaren. "Errian is one of the Taken. He has been graced several times now. It comes to me as a surprise that the boy has not made his peace with it."

"Taken." Sheppard repeated the word and shot a warning look at Rodney.

Aaren was still nodding. "Like all those so chosen, Errian went from his bed in the night, while the settlement slept."

The man's words chilled McKay, in their matter-of-fact manner. His thoughts raced; in his book *taken* was just another word for *culled*, a nicer term to cover up the cold horror of being captured by the Wraith. "But you said the Wraith don't come here," Rodney pushed forward, and Aaren glanced at him.

"Not for a long time, no, not since before the Aegis came." He gestured at Laaro and his mother. "Jaaya has tried to impress upon her son the reality of the matter, but he resists all good sense. Against my words, he still came out here all alone, as if he thought he could bring his father back himself." The Elder shook his head, as if the idea was the height of idiocy.

"Then where is Laaro's dad now?" Sheppard said sharply.

Aaren blinked at the colonel's tone, but said nothing of it. "The dawn is coming," he noted, "and Errian will come with it." The Elder quickened his pace and pointed ahead down the trail. "Come now. We have arrived."

McKay looked in the direction Aaren was pointing and his mouth dropped open. "Whoa."

Rising up from the middle of the grasslands was a stand of trees that were broad and wide around the base like giant redwoods reaching skyscraper-high into the air. The trunks exploded outward in vanes of thick branches, each one ending in a fan of lush green and smaller boughs. For a moment, Jennifer thought she saw hordes of glowing fireflies in among the leafy canopy, but then she realized her perspective was off. Keller raised a hand to shield her eyes from the rays of the fast-rising sun and got a better look. The trees were massive, tightly packed and meshing into one another like interlaced fingers; and in between every branch there were platforms and great big woven pods that reminded her of low-hanging fruit. What at first she thought were aerial roots were actually tethers and ropes extending out and down to the ground, leading up to clusters of egg-shaped huts and long, tubular lodges connected by wooden catwalks and byways.

"There's a whole town in there," she said. Even as she looked, Keller saw the first white puffs of smoke from chimneys as someone stoked a morning cook fire. There were dirt track roads snaking around the bases of the trees and their hanging gardens, and the Herunni led them on, into the shadow of the woods.

"Who does their decorating, the Ewoks?" said Rodney, incredulous.

"That's some tree house," agreed Jennifer. "I had one just like it. Only smaller."

McKay shook his head. "Not me." He made a vague gesture in front of his face. "Nosebleeds. And Hay fever."

Along the road, a man was walking with difficulty toward their group, another younger man helping him to find his way. Keller was wondering who he was when a cry from Laaro answered that question for her. The boy exploded into life and bolted the distance between them, barreling into the figure with such force that he almost knocked him down. Jennifer threw a look in Jaaya's direction and saw tears on her face, tears of joy.

Aaren nodded smugly. "There, you see. As I said. The Aegis protects."

"That's Errian?" Sheppard asked.

Ronon folded his arms, unconvinced, while Teyla watched the reunion. "But did you not just say that this man was *abducted*?" The Athosian woman put hard emphasis on the last word; she had been listening grimly to Aaren's words on the journey from the Stargate, and Jennifer had no doubt that she was dwelling on thoughts of her own people, who had recently been spirited away from her by unknown forces.

"I said he was Taken," noted the Elder. "And now he is

Returned."

"He doesn't look…" McKay faltered, trying to find the right word. "Uh… old."

"Keller?" Colonel Sheppard nodded towards the family group.

He didn't need to say it out loud. *Go take a look.* Jennifer skirted around Jaaya and came to Laaro's side. The boy's face was lit brilliantly from within, and he was talking a mile a minute, babbling on about his adventure that night, about his search for him, the Stargate, and more.

He saw her coming and grinned even wider "Father, look. This is one of the voyagers. Her name is Jenny-far!"

"Hi," Keller said, feeling a little self-conscious. "Uh, would you mind if I took a look at you, just to see if you're okay?"

"I…" Laaro's father gave a wan nod. "Of course."

The man who had been helping Errian to walk gave her an up-and-down look. "You are a healer?" He had wavy hair, intense brown eyes and a dark scattering of beard. He reminded Jennifer of a cute Indian geneticist she'd known at medical school.

"That's right."

He pursed his lips, considering. "As am I. My name is Kullid. And I assure you that Errian is well."

Keller accepted this with a nod, but pressed on anyway. "No doubt. But it never hurts to have a second opinion."

The Atlantis team stood in a loose knot in the shade of the tree-settlement. Teyla looked to the horizon and saw the sun finally emerging from behind a range of distant hills. In the moment's pause, she had removed her jacket and stowed it in her gear pack, sensing the day's coming heat on the wind. The air felt good on her arms and the freedom of movement she gained made her feel more comfortable still. Ever since the boy had appeared and spoken of his father in such a frightened manner, Teyla had sensed something amiss on this world. It was nothing preternatural, just a deep-seated instinct that gnawed at her. She looked to Ronon and saw that he felt the same thing as well. Unease. Suspicion, even.

She turned back to find John Sheppard watching her intently. "I know that look," he said. "Are you getting a…" He trailed off and made a fluttering gesture near his head. "A *sense* of something?"

"There are no Wraith nearby," she said flatly. "I would know it."

"Define 'nearby', Teyla," said McKay.

She eyed the scientist. "Forgive me, Rodney, but my psychic connection to the Wraith does not come with a precise read-out." She failed to keep an edge from her words.

"Just asking…"

Teyla frowned, chiding herself for reacting with irritation to the question; but there *was* an undeniable tension within her that seemed to be growing worse with each passing week. She sighed. Ever since she and Jennifer had returned from New Athos, ever since her own tribe had vanished like vapor, Teyla found it harder and harder to maintain her focus on the here and now. Every stray moment found her thoughts returning to her lost kindred, her mind conjuring up terrible thoughts of who might have taken them, and for what reason….

And then there was the *other* concern. Teyla's hand slipped toward her belly without conscious volition. She looked away and found herself meeting Keller's gaze as the doctor walked back to the group. A silent communication passed between them.

"So?" Sheppard jerked a thumb at Errian and his family. "How's Daddio?"

"He's a bit disoriented and dehydrated. Very fatigued. I'd say he probably hasn't slept for a couple of days, maybe more. He told me he doesn't remember where he's been."

Ronon grunted. "I've had mornings like that. Mostly after too much beer."

"Amnesia?" Sheppard's lip curled. "Aaren said the guy had been missing for a couple of weeks. He said all of the 'Taken' are gone for at least that long."

"How many are there?" said Ronon, half to himself.

Keller's brow furrowed in a frown. "Without doing a full medical work-up, I can't say much more at this point—"

McKay waggled his finger. "But what about the big question?"

Keller shook her head. "No, Rodney. The answer is no."

"Errian was not fed upon by a Wraith?" Teyla had to say the words aloud to fix them in her thoughts.

"As far as I can see, the man's never been anywhere near a Wraith." Keller replied. "No organic decay like we see in the premature aging they cause, no bone thinning that I could detect and most importantly, no sign of a feeding wound." She opened her hand and held it up, mirroring the pose the aliens used when they attacked.

"That makes no sense," Ronon retorted. "Wraith don't take people, keep them up all night, then send them home with hole in their memory. They're predators. They only want prey."

"So Aaren was telling the truth, then," said Teyla. "But if this Aegis he spoke of drives away the Wraith, then what happened to Errian? Who took him?" She nodded in the direction of Laaro and his parents.

"What do you say we find out?" Sheppard asked, as Jaaya approached them.

"Voyagers," she began, smiling. "Now my husband has come home to us, there will be a celebration. Perhaps, if you would wish, you could join us? My son... He finds so little to keep his attention these days, and now you are all he can speak of."

Sheppard made a face. "Well, uh—"

Teyla spoke before she was even aware of the words leaving her mouth. "We would be honored, Jaaya."

"Yeah," echoed the colonel. "Honored."

The woman bobbed her head. "And we have much room in our lodge. You are welcome to think of it as your own while you visit us. The celebration of the Returned will be a great feast!"

"The *Returned*," echoed Teyla. "There are more than one?"

"As it always is," Jaaya answered, her smile faltering a little. "Twenty are taken. Twenty are returned."

CHAPTER TWO

Sheppard's team knew the drill; this wasn't their first rodeo, after all, and together the Atlanteans had encountered their fair share of places that seemed nice enough on the outside but nasty underneath. Isolated communities, strange goings-on, unexplained disappearances—it was all another day at the office for them. Leaving Laaro and Jaaya to put a weary Errian to bed, they elected to do a little bit of informal recon around the perimeter of the village.

The team split into two groups, McKay going with Ronon and Teyla joining Sheppard; only Keller was new to this. Her off-planet experience was minimal and it had been on Colonel Samantha Carter's insistence that he'd taken Jennifer along on this mission. It wasn't that John didn't respect the young doctor or anything like that, but she was an unknown quantity. He wasn't sure how she'd react in a given situation…and that was why he'd brought her with him instead of letting her tag along with Ronon.

And there was something else. Something going on between Keller and Teyla. Sheppard knew that recently the two of them had shared a dangerous experience when they were trapped by marauders on New Athos, and not for the first time he found himself wondering if something was being kept from him.

He dismissed the idea with a slight shake of his head. Keller didn't seem the type for keeping secrets, and Teyla… Sheppard trusted Teyla implicitly. If there was something the Athosian woman had to tell him, she'd get to it soon enough.

Keller walked with them, her head turning this way and that as she tried to take in all the sights around them at once. "This place is so cool," she said. "Can you imagine how much work it took to build something like this? A whole community, homes and a school and a market, a hundred feet off the ground."

John nodded. He had to admit, he'd never seen the like himself. Broad wooden walkways curved around the main trunks of the giant trees in shallow spirals, with smaller avenues radiating off like the spokes of a wheel. The homes Keller talked about clustered to the sides of the spokes, held there by rope, wooden trestles and big fat gobs of what had to be some sort of natural resin glue. At first glance, the Heruuni settlement had a ramshackle, shanty-town look to it; but on closer inspection it became clearer that the folks who had constructed it knew a hell of a lot about engineering, and probably about just as much about ecology. They were walking through the *greenest* town they'd ever seen, in more ways than one.

"We're being followed," said Teyla quietly, darting her eyes behind her.

Sheppard nodded. "I had noticed." It was hard not to. A troupe of bronzed kids, a mix of them maybe eight to twelve years in age, were pacing the three Atlanteans a little way behind them. Every now and then, a new child would slip out of a side avenue and join the bunch. They talked among themselves, pointing and giggling. "We're like the circus come to town, I guess." He smiled to himself, amused by the idea of how Ronon and Rodney would be dealing with the same thing.

It wasn't just the children that were interested, though. Adults studied them from slat-windows or through half-open doors, but with an altogether more watchful and wary manner. For his part, John continued to smile a tight-lipped, neutral smile at all of them, and kept his hands away from the P90 strapped to his chest. He gave one man a jaunty nod and a "Howdy!" In return, the guy turned away and set off at a pace along a connecting rope-bridge. Sheppard shrugged. "Something I said?"

"They've never seen voyagers in the settlement before." Laaro emerged from the lee of a overhanging branch up ahead and approached them. He nodded at the children. "It's all new to them."

"Not to you, though," said Keller wryly.

"No," Laaro agreed, playing it nonchalant in front of the other kids.

Sheppard had to hold down a smirk at the youth's air of studied coolness. "You got over this side of the town pretty quick."

"I know all the short-cuts," he explained airily.

"How is your father?" Teyla asked.

A shadow passed over the boy's face. "He's resting now. But I…"

"What's wrong?"

"I just wanted to make sure he was going to get better. Kullid knows all about that sort of thing."

"The healer," explained Keller, off a look from the colonel. "He was with Errian when we found him?"

Laaro pointed up along the curving thoroughfare. "The sick lodge is just ahead. He'll be there. He'll know what to do."

Sheppard threw Teyla a level look. "Let's go introduce ourselves, then."

The sick lodge was a wide wooden disc wedged between two large tree trunks, held up by a fan of saplings cut from the living tree itself. Rattan window shades had been propped open to let in the morning air, but the place still had the faint scent of illness about it. Clockwork fans extending from the walls chattered slowly as they rotated, and all around Teyla saw low cots arrayed in circles. Many of them were occupied, mostly by men and women of a similar build to Errian. The Athosian woman found something about the place slightly disturbing; the quiet. The people in the beds did not moan or cry out. They seemed hollow and drawn, bereft even of the energy to do any more than lie dormant and breathe. One of them caught her eye—a man around her own age, or so she assumed—as he reached for a lacquered cup of water. Every move he made seemed like a huge effort, and she saw a twitch of palsy in his fingers as he eventually took his drink.

Teyla looked to Keller. "What is wrong with them?"

The doctor's eyes narrowed. "I'm not certain…"

"There is no special name for it," said another voice. "We just call it 'the sickness' and leave it at that." A striking young man emerged from behind a hanging muslin curtain. "Jennifer…" he said, with a wan smile, the woman's name sounding odd in his accent. "These are more of your people?"

"I brought them here," insisted Laaro, as if that fact would entitle him to something.

"Colonel Sheppard and Teyla Emmagan," said Keller, indicating them in turn.

He bowed slightly. "My name is Kullid. How can I help you?"

Jennifer's manner changed before Teyla's eyes. Outside on the walkway she had seemed enraptured by the alien world around them, almost enthusing over every new sight and sound; but the moment they had entered the sick lodge she became focused and intent, her medical training taking over by instinct. *She reacts to this the way I would react to the sight of an enemy; her skills come to the fore.*

"Actually, maybe we can help you," Keller began. "If there's a disease here, we have a lot of medicines where we come from. We might be able to find a cure—"

Kullid shook his head. "It's not a disease, not in the manner of something that can be spread by infection. This malady is inflicted upon our people." His manner grew grave and Teyla saw him shoot a look at Laaro, as if he didn't want to say too much in front of the boy.

Keller's mind was working as she studied the patients in the room. "Disorientation? Chronic fatigue, physical weakness?"

Sheppard frowned. "The same as—"

"My father," Laaro broke in, swallowing hard. Abruptly the deliberate bravado the youth had shown outside melted away and all at once he was just a scared little boy. "He's worse. Worse than he was the last time. I knew it would happen if he went to the Aegis again… I knew it…" He trailed off.

Kullid put a friendly hand on Laaro's shoulder. "I'll come to your lodge later, before the celebration, see to him, yes?" Laaro looked at the ground and nodded. "But you should go home now." He ushered the boy out toward the door.

Laaro composed himself and looked at Sheppard. "If you need a guide, I can do it. Come find me."

"Will do," said John.

The moment the boy was gone, Keller shrugged off the medical pack she was carrying. "His father has this… 'Sickness' too?"

Kullid nodded. "At first it was only one or two of the Taken and Returned who had it, and then they would recover in a few days. Now…" He spread his hands, taking in all of the sick lodge. "More."

"Laaro said *the last time*," noted Sheppard. "How many times has his dad gone missing?"

"This is the fourth Returning for Errian," Kullid replied grimly.

"I want to draw some blood," said the doctor. "Maybe run an analysis?" She pulled a syrette from her pack.

The Heruuni healer held out a hand to stop her. "It… You must not."

"She's offering to help. We all are," Teyla told him.

"I can't let you." Kullid was shaking his head, making dismissive gestures with his hands even though the tone of his voice said the exact opposite of his words. "I'm sorry. You must go. Laaro should never have brought you here."

Keller held out the injector. "If this is some local taboo thing, then you do it. Just put the needle in the vein."

"No!" he snapped. "Please don't ask me any more!"

Teyla felt the tension in the room jump a notch as one of the less listless patients around them reacted to some new arrivals. She turned, her hand dropping by reflex toward one of the fighting spars sheathed on her thigh.

Elder Aaren and a trio of men bearing similar golden bracelets of rank filled the sick house doorway; Teyla recognized one of them as the man who had disappeared in the street after Sheppard had greeted him.

Aaren's expression shifted from annoyance to suspicion and then finally settled on a forced geniality. "What brings you here, Colonel Sheppard?" It was less a question, more a demand. "This really isn't a suitable place for voyagers." He gave Kullid an acidic glance.

"I'm a doctor," Keller replied. "A healer. We have a lot of experience with infections, and we could help—"

Aaren cut her off with a tight, false smile. "No need. The Aegis will provide, and our friend Kullid has everything else in hand." He beckoned them with the same gesture he had used before, out in the grasslands. "Come now. Elder Takkol would be most distressed to learn you were in this place."

"Who?" said Sheppard.

"The settlement leader," explained Kullid. "Elder Aaren's superior."

Aaren nodded. "He asked me personally to see to your well-being. He looks forward to meeting you at the feast…" At a nod from the elder, the three larger men standing silently behind him took a step forward; a thinly-veiled threat lay beneath their manner and Sheppard saw it, stepping into their path.

"Hey, how you guys doin'?" he asked mildly. The colonel's eyes said something very different, however.

Keller spoke again, her tone rising. "I'm not going to stand by and—"

"*Jennifer*," Teyla silenced her. "Perhaps we should respect the elder's request. We are guests on his world, after all."

"You are, certainly," Aaren insisted.

The doctor looked down at the syrette in her hand, and then returned it to her pack with a frown. "Okay," she said at length, clearly unconvinced.

"My men will escort you back to Jaaya's lodge," Aaren insisted, before any more words could be spoken. In a silent line, they followed the elder's guardians out and back into the bright sunshine of the morning. As they walked away, Teyla caught the sound of two men arguing; the words were indistinct, but she knew it was Aaren and Kullid.

"That was… Interesting," said Sheppard, in low tones that didn't carry to the ears of their erstwhile new companions.

"Some of those people were dying," hissed Keller, drawing a sharp look from Teyla. "We can't just walk away from that!"

"We're not walking away," John insisted.

"Looks that way to me, Colonel," Keller retorted. "It looks *exactly* like that."

"The direct approach is not always the best one," Teyla explained. "We cannot afford to disaffect these people. Your actions may have angered them. They may have cultural strictures against alien intervention."

Keller sniffed. "What kind of strictures do they have about letting sick people die?"

Sheppard threw her a look. "Look, Doctor, I know your heart's in the right place, but trust me, you try to bulldoze these people and they'll dig their heels in. I know Aaren's type, I've dealt with them before." He sighed. "Too many damn times."

The other woman lent in closer and when she spoke, she said the words that John Sheppard had been thinking. "That wasn't about any 'taboo' thing back there. We stuck our nose in the wrong place and the people in charge didn't like it. We saw something we weren't supposed to."

"Maybe so," he agreed, "but still, we're supposed to be playing this sortie on the down-low. We're not here to mount a humanitarian mission. This is a reconnaissance."

"I think the mission has changed, Colonel," Keller replied. "It changed the moment we stepped through the Stargate."

Sheppard blew out a breath. "Story of my life."

They walked in silence for a while before Teyla spoke again. "John…" She said his name like a quiet challenge.

He didn't look at her. "Go ahead, say it."

The Athosian grimaced. "I think Doctor Keller is right. We should consider being more… Candid about our purpose here on Heruun. If only to build some trust with these people. We cannot expect them to be open with us if we keep things from them."

Sheppard eyed her. "I'm not ready to do that yet. We've only just got here. There are still too many unknowns…" He stopped and gave a dry, humorless chuckle. "Like that's a change from the usual."

But the fact was, John didn't like it any better than she did. He thought about the reasons they were here, and for a moment, he was back there in Atlantis's control room, his arms folded across his chest as he watched Zelenka and McKay give an animated briefing in front of one of the big screens.

Radek pointed at a single star out at the edge of a nebula. "M9K-153, according to the Ancient database, an Earth-normal world with a planetary Stargate." The Czech scientist adjusted his glasses.

"Ordinary and uninteresting, rather like my colleague here," added McKay, ignoring the affronted look his comments brought him, "or at least it was until recently." Rodney worked a datapad and remotely toggled a series of sensor overlays, placing one on top of another. "We've been monitoring Wraith activity as far as the city's sensors can scan, keeping a check on the battle lines in the fight with the Asuran replicators..."

Sheppard nodded. He knew all this; heck, he'd been instrumental in kicking off the whole Wraith-Replicator punch-up. "The more of them that wipe each other out, the better it is for the rest of us. What does all that have to do with some backwater planet?"

"There's been some unusual activity around 153," said Zelenka.

Standing opposite from him, Colonel Carter ran a hand through her blonde hair and studied the display. "Define 'unusual'."

Zelenka nodded. "I will. We didn't catch it before because we weren't looking for it. But a few weeks ago this happened..."

"This is a playback of a real-time feed from the sensors," added McKay.

Sheppard watched as the scanner showed the appearance of what was definitely a Wraith scout vessel at the edge of the star system. The glowing target glyph drifted closer toward planet M9K-153, and then vanished without warning.

"Gone," said Rodney.

"Destroyed," clarified Radek. "There was an energy release consistent with a reactor explosion, but no sign of any enemy craft in the area. It seems to have just... Blown up."

Carter shrugged. "A Wraith scout suffered an engine malfunction. So what?"

"That was my first assumption, too," said McKay, "and just as incorrect as yours. Look at this." He tapped the datapad and Sheppard watched a replay of what he had just seen.

"That's the same thing. Why show it to us again?"

"Aha," McKay grinned. "That's just it. It's *not* the same display. Check the timestamp. This is months before."

"And here's another. And another." Zelenka pulled up four replays, all of which showed a Wraith scout ship entering the 153 system and coming to an untimely—and baffling—end.

"We dragged all this data together from dozens of different places, the city sensor logs, astronomical records, even material we salvaged from Wraith ships." Rodney tapped the screen. "Something weird is going on out there, something that can apparently swat starships out of the sky just like *that*." He snapped his fingers for emphasis.

Carter nodded slowly. "Well, I'm interested."

"And so are the Wraith," added Radek. He worked the controls to zoom out from the nearby stellar group to a wider zone of local space. "We've been picking up increased chatter between vessels in one of their clans."

"It's encrypted, so we can't read it," said McKay, "but combined with pattern matching of their ship movements and we've got a pretty good idea of what's going on."

On the screen, a single glyph detached itself from a larger fleet and followed a course toward a white dwarf star several light years distant from M9K-153. "That's a Hive Ship," said Carter. "They're bringing in the bigger guns."

John mulled it over, trying to imagine how he would have addressed the same problem. "They've had their nose bloodied. They wouldn't just send in a capital ship, not if there's a chance it'd go the same way as the scouts."

"Yeah," sniffed McKay. "*Kaboom*."

"The Wraith are staging here," said Carter, pointing at the dwarf star. "Waiting for something."

"But we don't know what," admitted Zelenka.

John looked over at his commanding officer. "So, what do we do about it?"

Carter nodded at the screen. "We go to M9K-153 and take a look."

"And if there are people living there? What do we tell them? Hey, how are you, nice to meet you, don't want cause a panic but there's a Wraith warship floating around one hyperspace jump from your front door…"

"Atlantis has had enough problems with Wraith sympathiz-

ers, Genii and Replicators…," She met his gaze. "Until you find
out for sure what's going on, this information remains classified
among our personnel, Colonel."

Sheppard blinked away the moment of memory. Carter's
orders made sense on one level; if his team had come through
the gate spouting doom-laden warnings about a Wraith invasion, there was no way of knowing how the locals would react.
At best they'd cause a panic, at worst they might end up burned
at the stake, or something equally unpleasant. But still… He
didn't like keeping secrets. It cut against his grain.

John was aware of Teyla watching him. "How are we to proceed, Colonel?" She asked the question with careful formality.

"Same way we always do. Figure it out as we go."

The sun had set by the time the celebration for the Returned
got under way, and it seemed as if the entire population of the
tree-village was packed into the central town square, along with
braziers and big iron griddle troughs laden with food.

Of course, the *square* was actually *oval* in shape, and the
whole idea of having naked flames burning in a place that was
made almost entirely of wood did not sit well with Rodney
McKay, even if the locals seemed unconcerned by it. He followed the rest of the Atlantis team into the open area, all of
them in turn moving under the hawkish gaze of one of Aaren's
so-called 'assistants'. Sheppard had told him of his encounter with the elder at the sick lodge; apparently the leaders of
the settlement didn't like the idea of outsiders—*voyagers*, as
they insisted on calling them—wandering around unsuper-
vised. There hadn't been a threat, per se, but it had been clearly
implied that this wasn't the done thing. Ronon, typically, didn't
react well to that. Rodney could almost hear the Satedan bris-
tling at any suggestion of being told what to do.

"Huh," said Keller quietly. "A few beer coolers and this could
be a tailgate party." The whole celebration-feast-whatever-it-
was had the manner of a summer barbeque to it, informal and
relaxed, although McKay had to admit he wasn't feeling any of
that at all. He never liked parties. It was a deep-seated disdain

for them he'd developed as a teenager; they always seemed so staged, so false, just a place to parade yourself around and *mingle*. Well, Rodney McKay did not do *mingling*. It wasn't his thing.

"So what happens?" he asked, glancing at Teyla. "Do you think they bring out a big 'Happy Returned Day' cake with candles and frosting?"

She shot him a look. "I think everyone here is just happy their loved ones are back with them."

"Oh. Yes." He immediately felt like a heel. *Way to go, McKay. Why don't you remind her* again *about her people still being missing?*

Aaren approached them, and with him came an imposing bald man in a long toga-like robe flanked by two more well-muscled flunkies. Like Aaren, this new arrival had an impressive number of metal bangles up his arm, but unlike him there were more hanging from a leather necklace about his throat. He was a few years Aaren's senior and he had enough decorations on him to snap a Christmas tree. This had to be the guy in charge.

"Voyagers," began Aaren. "Let me introduced Elder Takkol, our community leader."

Takkol gave a shallow bow and he studied each of them in turn. The man had a square face with deep-set, searching eyes and a thin mouth. He smiled a little, but it seemed perfunctory, as if he had something better to do than to be talking to them. When he spoke, it was like he was giving a lecture. "Aaren has told me much about you and your friends, Colonel Sheppard. I welcome you to Heruun on this special day. I hope you will enjoy our hospitality."

"I'm sure we will," Sheppard replied. "And I hope you and I could speak later."

Takkol hesitated; Rodney could see the man was already mentally moving on, about to dismiss them, and John's comment caught him off-guard. "I'm sure Aaren can deal with any questions you might have."

McKay sensed Keller shifting impatiently, her hands knitting together. She hadn't been the same since they had returned from the sick lodge, withdrawn and quiet. Once or twice, Rodney had spotted her working on her laptop, paging through the medical database stored on the computer's hard drive, frowning as she looked for answers that weren't there.

Sheppard must have noticed as well. "We'd like to offer the help of Atlantis," he continued. "With your medical problems? Consider it a gesture of goodwill from us."

"Really?" Takkol gave Aaren a sideways look. "That is a most generous offer. I will certainly take it under consideration." Keller opened her mouth to speak, but Takkol cut her off. "But if you will excuse me... I must circulate. It is expected of me." The elder drifted away, giving Aaren another glance. In turn, his subordinate put on that same fake smile he'd worn before.

"There is a meal for everyone tonight, including our visitors," he explained. "Please partake. It is our way of thanking the Aegis for its protection."

"And for letting you have your people back?" Ronon asked, an edge of sarcasm in his words.

Aaren gave no sign of noticing. "Of course." He wandered away, leaving the Atlanteans to their own devices.

"That was productive," Keller deadpanned.

Ronon folded his arms. "Can we eat now?"

Sheppard nodded. "Yeah, go ahead. But mind your manners."

"I'm the picture of politeness," replied the Satedan.

McKay drifted after Ronon toward the food trays and watched the other man hunt and gather his way though a spread of different dishes. Rodney was more careful; after all, the ex-Runner could stomach just about anything even remotely edible, while McKay had the whole citrus thing to think about and a marked aversion toward even mildly spicy food. He could never understand the appeal of eating something that actually *hurt*. He got some rough flatbreads and what appeared to be cheese, and found himself at the end of the troughs where warm and savory meat-smells filled the air. A large pot caught his eye.

"That's whole roast mai," said Jaaya, walking up to his side.

"Would you like to try one?" She opened the lid and Rodney spied a hairless animal torso bobbing in some thin soup. It looked like...

The woman continued. "Laaro was in the party that caught them. These are the young of the hunter cats, so it's very tender."

He thought of the big lion-things that had stalked around them out in the grasslands and swallowed hard. "You're saying that's a roasted...kitten?"

Jaaya nodded, and McKay blanched. He had no doubt one of the feline beasts would have little qualms about eating *him*, but doing the reverse suddenly seemed unpalatable. "Uh... Could I just get a green salad instead?"

He left Jaaya at the server and found Ronan and the others in the shadow of a leafy branch. Keller studied her food with a similar look of doubt to Rodney, while Sheppard and Dex ate like they hadn't had breakfast. Teyla sipped water and pushed her food around its bowl, looking distracted.

"You see Errian?" said the Satedan, around a mouthful of something. "Over there."

McKay glanced over and followed Jaaya back to her table. Laaro was with his father, talking intently to the older man, but he seemed unaware of the distant look on Errian's face. "He looks a bit... I don't know, spaced out."

"He's not the only one. See the others? The Returned?" Sheppard indicated with the jut of his chin.

Chewing on a bit of rind, Rodney let his gaze wander across the whole distance of the oval, and one by one he picked out the people who didn't quite fit. Here and there, men and women, some younger, some older. He thought back to what Jaaya had said. *Twenty are taken, twenty are returned.* All of the Returned had the same look about them, a weariness that seemed bone-deep, like each one of them had just come off a fifty-mile hike. Suddenly McKay became aware of something in the mood of the celebration. He hadn't noticed it at first, but the more he looked the more he saw it; for all the smiles and jocularity, there was something strained about it all. Like the parties of his youth, it all seemed like a big show. *For us?* he wondered. *Or are they just trying to convince themselves that everything's okay?*

Teyla sighed and drew back. "Colonel, if I may, I would like to turn in early."

"Sure," said Sheppard. "You okay?"

Rodney saw Keller pause in mid-bite, watching the Athosian. Teyla gave a wan smile. "It's the heat. It's quite tiring. And the food, it's not to my tastes."

"There's ration packs in the gear back at Jaaya's lodge," began the doctor.

Teyla nodded. "If you'll excuse me." She gathered up her tunic and left them behind.

After a moment, Ronon leaned over and pointed at her unfinished meal. "Any of you going to eat this?" He didn't wait for an answer, and helped himself.

When McKay turned to Sheppard, he found him looking directly at Keller. Jennifer broke off and went back to her food.

Ronon licked some gravy off the second bowl and set it down, missing the moment entirely. "So do we just get one helping, or what?"

Teyla walked back through the winding avenues of the settlement, having memorized the route on the way to the celebration. The lanterns were lit on every intersection, and warm glows spilled from homes on either side of the street; but there were few people around, and as she moved further away from the central oval, the sounds of life grew fainter until all she could hear was a distant murmur of voices and the chorus of some sort of insect life. The little nightflyer bugs haloed the street lights, settling now and then to make a *chit-chit-chit* drone before humming away again. The noise added to the drowsy feeling brought on by the close, humid air of the evening.

She frowned as she walked, the expression marring the pleasant lines of her face. Teyla did not deal well with weakness in herself, as much as she strived to, but in all truth she had been feeling her energy drop far faster than was usual for her. She did her best to make no issue of it, but privately she wondered how much longer she would be able to keep her secrets. Soon she would begin to show, and then… Then they would all change in the way they treated her. Teyla knew what would happen; John, Samantha, Rodney and all the others, they would mean well but they would treat her as if she were made from spun glass. And above all, Teyla Emmagan despised the idea of being treated like a invalid.

While at once she was elated by the prospect of a new life growing inside her, she could not help but be afraid of what changes a pregnancy—and indeed, a child—would wreak on her life. She remembered the compassionate expression on Jennifer Keller's face when she broke the news, and for a moment experienced again the strange mingling of joy and sadness she had felt. Joy at such great news, sadness that she could not share it with the father of her unborn. Kanaan's face rose to the front of her thoughts as it did so often these days, and for a moment Teyla wished that she could have him return to her so easily as Laaro's father had come back to him.

The apprehension in the young boy's eyes found its mirror in Teyla. He feared for his parent, for his father's health, just as she was so afraid of what unkind fate had befallen her people on New Athos. Teyla paused and gripped the careworn rail of a balcony, staring out into the night, looking up at a sky of alien stars. Somewhere out there, her people waited for her to rescue them, and she vowed she would, even if it meant going into battle with a weapon in one hand and her newborn in the other—

A dash of light in among the thin clouds caught her eye and Teyla turned to study it; but no sooner had she looked than it was gone. *A flash of lightning, perhaps?* But there was no thunder, no distant stormhead on the horizon.

"Hey."

She turned to see Ronon Dex walking purposefully toward her. Teyla's eyes narrowed. "Colonel Sheppard sent you after me." It wasn't a question. "I can take care of myself," she began, her tone more defensive than she would have liked.

The big man shrugged, apparently unconcerned. "Ah, I was getting bored anyway. Food was good but the portions were small. Then that Takkol guy started making a speech and all of a sudden I felt restless." He smirked slightly.

"You would prefer a less pleasant evening?" She raised an eyebrow.

Ronon nodded; he had no artifice about him. "We're not here to play nice with people, Carter said as much. If there's something going on here, Wraith or otherwise, we need to find out, drag it into the light…" He hesitated, looking over Teyla's shoulder, out across the balcony.

She instinctively turned to follow his gaze. "Did you see something?"

The Satedan came to the edge of the balcony and looked down. Arranged in radiating rings beyond the canopy of the massive tree were curved plots of cultivated land turned over to crops and herd animals. He pointed. "Something moving down there. Like a… A shadow dropping out of the sky, black against black."

Teyla opened her mouth to speak again when she saw the flicker of light again; but this time it was low to the ground, a quick-blue white flash out by the edges of one of the farm sectors. The light was strobe-bright and it faded just as fast as it came, leaving a purple after-image on her retina. A triangular shape, hovering slightly above the ruddy brown earth.

"I saw *that*," Ronon growled.

Then a woman's scream reached them, thin and faint but still distinct.

Dex moved quickly. There was a rope ladder-pulley affair close to the balcony, extending down through a square hole cut in the decking. He gave it a hard tug to check it, and then looped the guide cord around his hand. It was rigged for a fast-decent, maybe for use as some kind of fire escape or emergency egress; it would get him down to the ground in seconds.

Teyla had her radio raised to her lips. "John, do you read me? Colonel Sheppard, I think—" She stopped and stared at the device. "It's not working. The radio has gone dead." The woman paused. "Perhaps they would have heard the cry." She glanced around, but there was no-one about.

"Not from out here." Ronon felt a sudden, strange chill on

the skin of his bare arms, and for a moment there was a metallic scent in the air like ozone. It seemed harsh and out of place among the warm odors of the trees. Then there was the scream again; a pure, animal sound of primal fear. "I'm going out there," he snapped.

"Not alone," she began, but he had already kicked off and was dropping toward the ground in a swift, controlled fall.

Ronon hit the dirt ready, his gun hand coming up with the brutal shape of the particle magnum. Teyla was a heartbeat behind him, and the defiant look she gave him dared the Satedan to suggest that she remain behind. He nodded. "Don't slow me down," he offered. It was as close to an assent as she would ever get.

They moved in quick, loping bursts of motion, staying to the edges of the farming tracks, dodging around low-lying huts and the stubby pillars of grain silos. The light flashed again, and Dex hissed in annoyance as the actinic blaze of color robbed him of his night vision. In the moment of brilliance, he saw the sharp-sided shadow of a barn and figures moving around it. He wondered if the light cast some kind of optical illusion; the man-shapes he saw were out of scale, too big to be humans.

Teyla kept pace with him, panting in the silence. "It could be raiders, perhaps from another village…"

"Or not," Ronon said in a low voice.

And then the scream came a third time, chilling his blood as it suddenly ceased in mid-cry.

He broke from cover, leading with the pistol, and sprinted the rest of the distance toward the barn. The warrior's battle-honed combat sense took in a dozen impressions at once; he saw a dozen stumpy herd beasts all fallen on their sides, as if they had been knocked down by a stun beam; he tasted the bitter ozone stink again, strong and acrid on his tongue; and out beyond the curved roof of the barn, lying in the long grass on a halo of muted green light, the shadow he had glimpsed from the balcony.

It was a craft of some kind, triangular, featureless and matt black. It hovered silently, drifting slightly from side to side like a boat at anchor.

"Not Wraith…" he said aloud. In fact, it was like nothing he had ever seen before, not in his service to Sateda, not in his time with the people of Atlantis.

"Ronon!" Teyla's warning cry snapped him back to battle-ready and he spun in place as gangly humanoid shapes emerged from inside the barn. The first of them had a woman cradled gently in its arms, in the manner an adult would use for a small child. The Heruuni female was slack like a rag doll, and her sightless eyes stared into the distance.

The next two walked in military lockstep, heads turning as one to stare at the Satedan and the Athosian. They were giants; a full head taller than Dex, they were dense with planes of muscle that shifted beneath grey-green flesh. Long, whipcord arms raised from their sides, each ending in fingers with too many joints; and their features were strange parodies of human faces, less than sketches really, with inky, dark eyes that he could not read. They studied them while the one carrying the woman walked carefully toward the grounded flyer.

Then they came at them, and they were *fast*. Ronon saw something in their hands, a glassy egg that had to be some kind of weapon. His gun came up in an arc and he squeezed the trigger; but to no effect. The energy pistol was inert, the glowing power cell behind the beam chamber suddenly dark. Dex had a moment of shock; he had fully charged the weapon before leaving Atlantis, and not fired a single shot since they exited the Stargate.

One of the hulking figures threw a blow at him that he almost didn't escape; the creatures moved too rapidly for something of their size and mass. Ronon spun, ducking low, and landed a punch on the meat of his attacker's torso. His knuckles scraped dry, powdery skin, but the force of the impact had no obvious effect. No moan of pain, no reaction, nothing.

He was aware of Teyla sparring with the second creature, her fighting sticks in her hands, each one a blur as they spun in the light from the craft. She too landed blows, and like Ronon's, any effect they had was invisible.

His adversary turned the egg-device on him and it glowed within. The Satedan felt a strange chill wash over him and without warning his muscles bunched and locked in paralysis. It became hard to breathe, as even his chest refused to move to push new air into his lungs. Something dropped from his fingers into the grass at his feet; his useless pistol.

Teyla! He wanted to cry out, wanted to warn her, but his body would not obey him. He stood there, trembling, a statue of meat and bone.

Ronon could not turn his head to look in her direction; so it was that he only saw her again when one of the giants carried her past him, following in the footsteps of its predecessor. He saw her face, her eyes blank and empty just as those of Heruuni woman; then his foe came closer, filling his sight with its strangely unfinished features. The glassine ellipse came up and he heard a whining from inside it move through the bones of his skull. The sound grew and grew, blotting out everything, every thought he could form, washing away every last trace of awareness.

Ronon Dex tried to bellow his defiance; he tried and failed.

CHAPTER THREE

"Get out of my damned way," snarled Sheppard, barely keeping his temper in check.

The guard was a thickset man, his head shaven except for a queue of black hair extending down from the back of his scalp, and the light robes he wore rustled as he turned to block the colonel's way, one hand dipping into the folds, reaching for a weapon. "You cannot enter here, voyager," he grunted.

"Colonel—" Behind him, Keller started to speak but McKay silenced her with a shake of the head.

John stabbed a finger at the great lodge in front of him; it was the largest collection of woven pod-huts they'd seen so far in the settlement, something like a cross between a village hall and a townhouse. "This is Takkol's place, right?" he demanded. "I want to see him, right now."

"You cannot enter here," repeated the guard, eyes darting around, looking for assistance. It was the early hours of morning and the walkways were deserted, the people all retired to their beds after the celebration.

Sheppard glowered at him, for one moment his hand wandering toward the grip of his P90; but then he shook his head. "You know something? I don't have time for this. I apologise."

The guard asked the question before he had even thought about it. "For what?"

The colonel's free hand shot out and hit the man in a nerve point just above the clavicle; the guard howled in pain and clutched at himself, his arm suddenly going dead. "For that," he replied, and shoved the man out of the way, taking the steps to the lodge door in two quick strides.

"Where'd you learn to do that?" said McKay.

"You spar with Ronon long enough, you pick up some things." Sheppard shouldered open the wooden doors and advanced into the entrance hall. Other guards—the same ones who had been their 'escorts' earlier—appeared from side doors, each of them hoisting a short, spindly rifle, drawn by the yell from their comrade.

McKay clutched the butt plate his P90 to his shoulder, blinking, and at his side Keller moved nervously from foot to foot, not quite ready to draw the Beretta pistol that Sheppard had ordered her to strap to her leg.

"Takkol!" called Sheppard. "We need to talk."

"What is the meaning of this?" From the upper tier of the hall came a grumbling, terse voice. The senior elder came forward on bare feet, angrily knotting the belt of his nightgown around the waist. "You cannot enter this lodge without my sanction, Colonel Sheppard! It is the dead of night! What do you think you are doing?"

"Where are they?" Sheppard demanded. "What have you done with our people?"

"Your people?" Takkol frowned and rubbed his face.

"Ronon Dex and Teyla Emmagan," said Keller.

"I have no idea what you are talking about." Takkol made a dismissive gesture.

At the door there was a commotion and Aaren entered, still dressed in his day clothes, his expression anxious. "Elder, I heard the noise, I came as quickly as I could…"

"Where are my people?" Sheppard turned the full force of his fury on the other elder. "Teyla left the celebration early, and I sent Ronon after her. Neither of them ever arrived at Jaaya's lodge out by the tree's edge. Where did they go?"

"Back through the Gateway, perhaps," offered Takkol with a snort. "If you cannot keep track of your own people, that is your concern, not ours, Colonel!"

"They wouldn't just leave," insisted McKay. "Not without contacting us first."

Takkol came down a line of wooden stairs, fixing the Atlanteans with a baleful stare. "You come here in the middle of the night to accuse us of misdeeds? You, visitors to our world, those who we have shown hospitality and openness?"

"The hell you have," Sheppard's voice was low.

Takkol's eyes narrowed. "I will forgive your impertinence

on the understanding you leave now and let me return to my
rest..."

Aaren cleared his throat. "Elder, there has been a misun-
derstanding here. The missing voyagers… I know where they
are."

"What?" said McKay. "Where?"

The other elder nodded to himself. "There was… A sighting
this night."

A ripple of surprise moved across the faces of all the Heruuni in
the room, throwing Sheppard off a little. "A sighting of what,
exactly?"

Takkol's manner changed immediately, his annoyance turning to understanding. "Of course. I should have realized…" He
paused, thinking. "But still… So soon? It is unusual." With an
off-hand wave he gestured to his guards to lower their weapons.

"A witness said they saw the Giants out at the edge of the
farmsteads. Perhaps they came early because of the arrival of
the voyagers?" offered Aaren.

"Hey!" Sheppard barked, irritated at being ignored. "I asked
you a question. I want an answer."

Aaren favored him with that fake smile again. "Your friends
Ronon and Teyla are well, Colonel."

Rodney's face fell as comprehension caught up with him.
"Oh no."

Sheppard felt ice forming in the pit of his stomach even
before Aaren spoke again. "They have been given a gift by the
Aegis. They are among the Taken."

"You mean… Like Errian and the others?" said Keller.

"They will not be harmed," Takkol said lightly, turning to
walk back up toward his bedchamber. "The Taken are always
returned safely within a span of two weeks. You will see them
again."

"Unharmed?" snorted Sheppard. "Like those people we saw
in the sick lodge?"

Takkol rounded on him and glared down at the group. "There
are some, it is true, who cannot support the great burden that the
Aegis gives them. We do what we can for those souls who have

STARGATE ATLANTIS: NIGHTFALL   45

been too close to the light of its protection."

"That's it?" Rodney shook his head. "You just let your people be kidnapped for who knows whatever reason and do nothing about it?"

"We didn't sign up for this," said Sheppard. "Two of my team are abducted and you knew all about it. In my book, that's an attack on all of us."

"There is no attack!" Aaren insisted. "The Aegis protects, it does not destroy!"

"It also does not ask permission," said Keller.

"I'm sure they went of their own free will," Takkol added.

Sheppard shook his head. "Trust me, I'm sure they didn't."

"How often does this happen?" McKay walked further into the room, talking directly to the senior elder. "Every month? Every week? Have you ever even *seen* this Aegis you keep talking about?"

"You have no right to come here and judge us," Takkol folded his arms. "The Aegis has kept us safe for generations. It has turned the scourge of the Wraith from our skies, it has let our planet prosper. Do you understand that, Doctor McKay? Since the coming of the Aegis, there has been no conflict on Heruun! We are united under our great protector!"

"Yeah," snorted Sheppard. "I can see how fear of being kidnapped from your house while you sleep would make you more worried about keeping awake, than picking fights with other settlements."

"You do not understand our ways, this is apparent. Because of that, I will overlook your rash behavior here tonight. If there is no repeat of it, you are welcome to stay until your friends are counted among the Returned. But you will not interfere here or question our society." Takkol shot Aaren a look and in turn his guards brought up their weapons once more. The message was clear. *This conversation is over.*

But that wasn't enough for John Sheppard. He took a step forward, every gun in the room tracking him. "You know something? It's clear to me *you* don't understand *our* ways, either. Where we come from, we don't turn our back on our friends." He spun on his heel and strode out of the hall, Keller and McKay following along behind.

Rodney jogged to keep up with the colonel. "Boy, is he pissed off," he told Jennifer out the side of his mouth. "Sheppard? Sheppard!"

"Colonel!" called Keller. "What are we going to do now?"

He shot them a look. "I tell you what you're going to do. You two are going to go back to Jaaya's place and stay there. Radio me if anything even remotely freaky happens, got it?"

McKay's head bobbed. "Where are you going?"

"Stargate," came the reply. "This has just become a rescue mission."

The three of them rounded a thick trunk, passing out of sight of the guard on the door, who watched them go as he nursed the spreading bruise on his shoulder. He worked the muscle to get a little feeling back into it, and as soon as he was certain they were gone, he found a shadowed corner and removed a small roll of message paper and an ink-stone from his robes. He listened carefully at the window of the lodge, and then, taking care to be certain he was not seen, he scribbled quick, careful sentences on a length of the tissue-thin paper.

When he was done, the guard crossed the walkway to a non-descript lodge facing to the west. He tapped on a window blind and it was opened by an elderly woman, her tanned face like old leather. She gave him a nod; they knew each other well. "Here," he said, handing her the slip of paper. "Soonir must see this, before high sun."

The old woman nodded once and plucked the message from his fingers.

The metallic-electric rattle of the gate chevron sequence cut right through the web of thoughts in Samantha Carter's mind. Without even pausing to think, she was out of her chair even as Chuck's voice called out over the tower's intercom.

"*Unscheduled off-world activation!*"

She still had the datapad she'd been reading and the coffee mug she'd been sipping from as she crossed the short skybridge from her office to the control tier. Carter glanced down into the gate room below and saw the third, then fourth chevron illuminate in clusters of brilliant blue dots.

"We're not expecting anyone back," she began. It wasn't a question, but she got an answer anyway.

"Not for another few hours." Radek Zelenka was at the main screen at the back of the room.

Carter put down her burden, frowning. She'd been around to see more spontaneous gate openings than anyone else on Atlantis, and still every time it happened there was a tightening in her chest that never went away. It was like the sound of your telephone ringing at three in the morning; unexpected and alarming, with that little voice in the back of your head telling you *This isn't going to be good.*

The wormhole coalesced and thundered into shimmering solidity, the flash of the city's iris field hazing over the Stargate a split-second later.

The technician looked up from his console. "I have Colonel Sheppard's IDC, ma'am."

Carter leaned over him and spoke into the radio. "Colonel? You're early."

If Sam suspected that something was amiss, then the tone of John Sheppard's voice over the open channel confirmed it for her immediately. "*More like too late, Colonel. We got a situation here.*"

Zelenka gave her a worried look as he came closer. "Is everyone all right?"

"*Teyla and Ronon are M-I-A. We think they've been kidnapped.*"

Her lips thinned. "By the locals?"

Sheppard paused before answering. "*Not exactly. It's a little more complicated than that.*"

"It usually is…" murmured Radek.

Carter spoke quickly to the technician. "Major Lorne and his team are on standby alert, get them up here, double-time." Off his nod, Sam keyed the radio again. "Tell me what you can, Colonel."

She could almost hear him frowning. In a lot of ways, Sheppard reminded her of Jack O'Neill; both men had their own casual, unconventional ways of command, both inspired loyalty and respect among their people, and both officers took the safety of their team personally. His voice was laced with frustration and annoyance as he gave a terse report on the situation on M9K-153. Carter listened with growing concern as Sheppard laid out his impressions of the locals, these Heruuni, and their stories of a mysterious guardian force, of ritualized abductions.

By the time he was done she had dozens of questions pressing at the front of her thoughts, but she held them back. "What's your evaluation, John?" she asked, giving Major Lorne a glance as the officer came up the stairs in full battle gear, ready for deployment.

"Takkol and his elders aren't going to give us any help," said Sheppard. *"And every second we waste, the trail goes colder. If we're going to find Teyla and Ronon, we need to do it ourselves."*

Lorne's eyes narrowed as he caught the last of Sheppard's words. Carter knew without having to ask that the major would understand what was expected of him. "I concur," she said to the radio. "I'm sending a support team through the gate now. Sweep the area and report back as soon as you have anything."

"Roger that," Sheppard replied. *"I'll be waiting."*

"Should we take a Puddle Jumper?" Lorne asked.

Sam shook her head. "Let's hold off on that option for a moment. If we come through with too much firepower, there's no telling how the locals—"

"Or this *Aegis*…" broke in Zelenka.

"…Will react," Carter concluded. "You have a go, Major."

Lorne saluted and rejoined his men, snapping out orders as he went.

Zelenka pushed his glasses back along his nose with a finger and frowned again. "Colonel Carter… Do you think an aggressive posture is the best one?"

"One squad of men isn't aggressive, Radek," she replied. "It's prudent. If you have a better suggestion, I'd be happy to hear it."

He hesitated, then nodded. "Of course. I didn't mean to suggest otherwise." But she could read the unspoken addendum in his eyes; *he's wondering how Elizabeth Weir would have dealt with this*.

Sam's civilian predecessor cast a long shadow over Atlantis; the woman had guided this place with intelligence and compassion through that difficult and lonely first year, and then for two more, facing challenges from all sides. And while Weir had never been one to shy away from making the hard calls, Carter still felt, even after weeks in that office, that there were some of the non-military staff who saw her as less a scientist and more a soldier. In truth, she was both, and Sam would have been hard-pressed to chose between which calling meant the most to her. Not for the first time, Carter wished she'd had more of a chance to get to know Elizabeth before the woman had been lost to them, if only for any advice she might have shared.

From below, the gate murmured as Lorne's unit stepped into the ripples, and for a long moment Sam felt a tingle in the base of her feet; she was almost rocking on her heels, drawn by the glow of the open conduit. *I want to go with them*.

Outwardly, she was impassive, but inside Sam tried to push the thought away without success. It felt odd to stand here and send her people through the Stargate on mission after mission, to stand here and watch and wonder what they would be confronted with. Carter was no stranger to the burdens of command, but her duties had always taken her *out there*. Atlantis was the first time she found herself with the responsibility of staying behind, and with each passing day in that role she had new respect for Hammond, O'Neill and Landry, her former commanders; officers who had done what she did now, sending men and women into the unknown, silently hoping that each order they gave would be the right one.

Lorne was the last to step to the gate, and he paused on the threshold, glancing up at her. He gave a curt nod, and Carter returned it.

"Bring our people home, Major," she told him.

"You can count on it, Colonel," he replied, and vanished though the event horizon.

In the blood-warm darkness of the craft, the air was close and heavy with the sharp scent of sweat. Each footfall was light and difficult, the gravity generators beneath the bone plates of the deck working at their lowest setting, just like every other primary system aboard the ship. The vessel's commander moved up to the cockpit using handholds formed from ropey sinew, placing each step with care. If he had stopped and listened carefully, he would have heard the labored rasp from the atmosphere processor's lungs. They were working the craft hard, beyond its normal capacities and durations.

The gloomy interior of the ship took in light from a viewing slit across the bow and the pale blue-white glow of two monitor lenses; these screens were the only ones in active mode.

Two of the six other crewmembers stood at their stations; one, a drone, impassive and motionless, the other, a worker, hunched over a chiming console. The latter looked up at him as he entered the broad cockpit.

"There has been a change?" he asked, absently smoothing the front of his combat tunic.

The worker—a member of the scientist caste—nodded, his pale face shining in the screen-light. "A detection from the planet's surface. Another activation of the portal. More new arrivals." His voice was low, almost a whisper.

"Show me," demanded the commander.

"See here," said the scientist, working the console. "The energy release plume corresponds with the formation of another wormhole. And these lesser peaks?" He traced a long-nailed hand over a digital mountainside of readout spikes. "Transit outputs. Several humans left the portal only moments ago."

He considered this for a moment, playing with a tuft of white, wiry hair on his chin. "More humans. Off-worlders."

"Likely," said the scientist. "Should we... Intervene?"

The commander glanced out of the viewing slit. Faint color from Heruun's yellow-orange sun reached them through the mass of dust that was the planet's ring system; hidden in the shadow of it, drifting over the night side, they were virtually invisible. "And how could we do that?"

The scientist licked his pallid lips. "Perhaps, if we tried a gravity descent—"

He turned and glared at the scientist. "Why do you whisper?"

His crewmate cocked his head. "I do not understand."

"You speak so quietly. As if you are afraid." The commander pointed at the curving bone walls around them. "As if you think your voice might carry out there, through the void. It's a foolish conceit."

The scientist considered this for a moment, then nodded self-consciously. "Perhaps so. It is a natural reaction, considering the…" He swallowed. "The threat."

"The threat," echoed the commander. "A threat your suggestion would rouse, if we were to *intervene*." He put sarcastic emphasis on the final word. "I have no desire to be blasted from space as our other scouts have been. This ship has survived in this system longer than any other of our vessels, and that is because we have been careful." He considered the commanders of the other scoutships that had come here and been obliterated; they had been rash and slow to control their baser impulses. He, on the other hand, was patient. It had taken them days to close to orbital range, drifting in from above the plane of the ecliptic without motive power, letting the gravity of Heruun snare them, pull them in. Now they were perfectly placed to fulfill their mission.

"We will remain, then? And do nothing?" An edge of challenge entered the scientist's voice.

The commander studied him, slightly amused. The tension of the past days was clearly difficult for him to tolerate; the scientist was in danger of becoming aggressive. Still, as objectionable as he might have found him, the scientist was vital to the duty at hand. "We are doing something," he hissed, showing a mouth of pointed teeth. "We are observing, and what we learn in that will lead our hive to victory. We will wait for the new arrivals to depart, and we will remain in silent mode until they do. The smallest mistake, the faintest glimmer of unmasked energy, and our lives will be forfeit. This planet's protector will kill us without hesitation." He loomed over the scientist. "Your caste is one of thinkers. Think on that." He turned away, toward the cockpit's iris door.

"There is another matter." The scientist called after him.

He paused. "The hunger, yes?"

"Yes," came the reply, and with it a hiss of raw need. "It's been so long since we fed, and with a planet below untouched, filled with prey…"

The commander sneered. The subordinate castes did not have the fortitude of their warrior kindred. He too had not fed in some time, but he kept his hunger in check, containing it.

"There is no sustenance here," concluded the scientist. "I do not know how much longer I can go without…"

"You are hungry?" he asked, drawing a stunner pistol from his belt. With a flick of his wrist he turned the weapon on the silent warrior and shot him at point-blank range. The drone-soldier collapsed to the deck. "Here. Feed, then. Take your fill, but do not dare question the orders of the Queen again."

He waited a moment for the scientist to answer, but the other Wraith had already descended on the fallen warrior and jammed the feeding maw on his hand into its chest. With a sneer of disgust, the commander left him to his meal.

"*McKay?*"

Jennifer saw Rodney react with a start and pull the radio from the pocket on his gear vest. "Sheppard?" he replied.

The colonel was terse and clipped. "*Carter's in the loop. Lorne came through the Stargate with some backup. We're doing a search-and-sweep of the area.*"

"Have they found anything yet?" she asked.

Sheppard heard her question over the open channel. "*One of Lorne's boys spotted some scorch marks in the scrub…*"

"Radiation burns?" said Rodney.

"*Negative, we scanned 'em, they were cold. The only trace we found was Ronon's gun. He must have dropped it, maybe during a struggle.*" The colonel blew out a breath. "*The power pack's dead, but he never even got a shot off. It's like it was drained.*"

Keller said nothing. She'd seen Ronon Dex sparring in the gym, and Teyla fighting off four men at once on New Athos. An enemy that could take down both of them together had to be a formidable one.

Sheppard was still speaking. "*So, in the meantime I need you and Keller to stay put until you hear from me, got it?*"

McKay rolled his eyes. "Yeah, okay, *mom*."

It was the wrong thing to say. "*Don't give me any static, Rodney, now's not the time. Just sit tight and don't screw around. We've got enough to deal with as it is.*"

"We'll be fine," insisted McKay, gesturing around at the walls of Jaaya's lodge. "I think later we're even going to have some tea."

There was a pause. "*I'm sending a couple of men up there.*"

"We don't need babysitters," retorted the scientist, throwing Keller a wan look, which she returned. "And you need every pair of eyes you've got. We're fine. Honestly. You're not the only one who knows how to handle a P90." McKay nodded to himself.

"*Whatever,*" came the reply. "*Ask Keller if you forget which end the bullets come from. Sheppard out.*"

Laaro entered the small anteroom where they were sitting with a wooden food tray. "Your leader… He speaks like he mocks you," observed the boy.

Rodney gave a weak chuckle. "He's such a kidder."

"We're just anxious," admitted Jennifer, breaking a small ball of baked bread that Laaro placed before her between her fingers. "Teyla and Ronon are very important to us." She ate a little; the bread was tangy and flavorful.

Laaro sat and chewed on something leafy. Behind him, a dual sunrise painted the whole interior a warm golden hue. "Your friends… You are worried that they will return with the sickness."

"We're worried that they'll ever return, period," admitted Rodney. "Trust me, this kind of thing never ends well."

Jennifer chewed her lip. "There could be another explanation. This might be nothing to do with the… The Aegis."

Laaro shook his head. "No, it was the Giants who took Ronon and Teyla, and they serve the Aegis."

"You know that for sure?" said Rodney.

The boy nodded. "I talked with Yuulo, who lives in the tall branches. It was he who saw the chariot come to the western farmstead. He told Elder Aaren."

"Chariot? What is that, some kind of ship?"

"The Giants come and go in it. It is like a great shadow that moves over the ground." Laaro held his hand flat and moved it in a slow, circular motion. "It is silent as a cloud, and dark like an ink-stone. Sometimes it rides in on rods of lightning, even though no rain falls." He brought up another hand and crossed the thumbs, bringing the index fingers point-to-point, making a triangle. "This is its shape."

"And these giant men?" Keller leaned closer. "What do they look like?"

Laaro shrugged. "I have never seen them. My father spoke of them…" He trailed off, his gaze turning inward. "He sometimes dreams poorly, and they haunt him in his sleep."

Jennifer and Rodney exchanged looks. Laaro and his family were the closest thing to friends the Atlanteans had inside the settlement, but both of them were well aware that pushing the boy to say too much could make him clam up altogether.

"Do you know why the Aegis takes people?" said McKay. "Does your father ever speak about that?"

Laaro shook his head. "When the Taken become the Returned, they sleep a long sleep and remember nothing. Elder Takkol says this is for the best. He says that we are not ready to know all the secrets of the Aegis yet."

"Do you agree with him?" Keller said gently.

Laaro stood abruptly, gripping the tray so hard his knuckles drew tight. "I think the Aegis should leave my father be. Take me instead, not him. He is not well."

"Laaro…" began Jennifer, not sure what to say to make the youth feel better.

Jaaya's voice called out from another room, and he followed it to the doorway. "I have to go. I will be back later."

When they were alone, McKay turned to her. "Did you get

all that? Are you thinking what I'm thinking?"

"Probably not," she admitted. Keller found McKay's thought processes pretty hard to keep up with, truth be told. He had this tendency to bounce from idea to idea, concept to concept, with no apparent train of logic between them. Her grandmother had called that having a 'mind like a grasshopper'.

"That stuff he described, the 'chariot' and the 'giants'? Black triangles, weird lightning, people being kidnapped, missing time experiences?" He gestured with his hands. "What, you've never watched an episode of *The X Files*?"

"We didn't really watch the Fox Network—"

McKay kept talking. "This is a classic alien abduction scenario!"

"Take a look around, Agent Scully," she retorted. "*We* are the aliens on this planet."

Rodney shook his head. "No, no. *You'd* be Scully, *I'd* be Mulder. Anyway. That's not important." He tapped a finger on his lips, warming to the subject. "We should check the abductees for implants or unexplained markings on their skin…"

"You want me to look for evidence of probing, too?" Keller asked; then she chuckled without humor. "And strangely enough, that wouldn't be the oddest thing I've done since coming to Atlantis."

McKay nodded in agreement. "It's not science fiction if you're living in it every day—"

There was a rattle and crash from elsewhere in the house, and Jennifer heard Errian's voice, gruff and angry. Heavy footsteps came closers, and Laaro called out her name in a warning.

McKay dove at the rattan floor where he had laid down his P90. "Jennifer, get behind me, quick!"

Her heart thudding in her chest, Keller's eyes darted left and right, searching for an exit route and finding none. *The window slats, maybe?* But then she remembered they were in a mammoth tree house hundreds of feet off the ground. *Maybe not.*

Rodney had the gun up as the sliding door was roughly forced open on its tracks. Two locals, who had all the thuggish bearing of Takkol's guards but none of the uniform robes or bangles, entered with a wiry man following on behind. The skinnier guy was clearly the one in charge. He had a tight cut to his hair and it had been deliberately stained yellow with some kind of earth dye.

"Where's Laaro?" McKay demanded. "Who are you people?"

"The boy isn't hurt," came the reply. The man had a clear, frosty voice. "And Errian knows better than to stand in my way." He nodded toward one of the bigger men, making the warning against such foolishness clear. None of the men seemed to be concerned that Rodney was pointing a submachine gun at them. "My name is Soonir. I want to talk."

"About what?" said Keller.

"The Aegis. The things that Takkol refused to speak of." He said the elder's name like a curse word. Soonir beckoned them. "Come with me. I know you seek information, I know about your friends among the Taken. There are things you need to see." He paused. "You may bring the weapons you carry if you feel better protected with them."

Keller shot McKay a quick look, both of them remembering Sheppard's clear and unequivocal order to *sit tight*.

"We're not going anywhere with you," Jennifer told him.

Soonir let out a slow, measured breath. "Ah. Now, that's not the best reply to give me." He stepped back, giving his men room to work. "You see, voyagers, I will not take no for an answer."

CHAPTER FOUR

He didn't awaken slowly; instead Ronon Dex jerked from his induced slumber as if he had been seared by fire, hissing through his teeth. He rolled from where he lay and his feet hit the metallic floor with a dull ring.

The first thing he saw was Teyla, sitting opposite him on a pallet made of spongy white material. She frowned. "Are you all right?"

Ignoring the question, he got up, taking stock of where he found himself. A small room with a low ceiling and curving walls, all arches and smooth lines. Two sleeping pallets seamlessly extruded from the floor, no windows. Diffuse, directionless light seeping in from panels in the ceiling; and an oval doorway sealed shut by a striated metal panel. *A prison cell.*

"How long have we been here?" he said, moving to the rear of the chamber. The Satedan's hands ran down his tunic, his trousers, searching his pockets.

"It is difficult to be certain," said Teyla. "I came to shortly before you did."

He shot her a look. "You should have woken me."

The Athosian woman gave him a wan look. "I saw little point in doing so."

Ronon chewed his lip, his fury burning cold and slow. All his weapons and tools were gone. The gun belt hung empty at his hip, as did the numerous blade scabbards in his leggings and boots. The secret pockets in his tunic were vacant; even the needle darts in his wrist guards and the chain concealed behind his belt had been taken. At another time, he might have been impressed by the thoroughness of his captors in so completely disarming him, but instead his face set in a grimace as he weighed the thought in his mind, asking himself what it revealed. His hands contracted into fists; if they were all he had to fight with, it would have to be enough.

"They are clearly very careful," offered Teyla, seeing the train of his thoughts.

"Not careful enough," he rumbled. "They let us wake up." He dropped into a crouch and ran his hand along the place where the wall met the floor. There were no signs of a weld or any manufacturing marks. The construction appeared flawless, almost as if it had been carved. Ronon began a careful circuit of the cell, probing at every part of the walls, looking for a blemish, a flaw, anything.

"I have already checked," said the woman.

He nodded, but didn't stop. Dex needed to look for himself, just to be certain. Presently, he came to the inset door and rapped on it with his fist. A dull report sounded. He pressed his ear to the cold metal and heard nothing. "Where did they take us?"

"We have no way of knowing how long we were unconscious," Teyla noted.

"Had to be a few hours, at least. I'm hungry."

"You are always hungry," she said, forcing a thin smile.

"True," he admitted. "And I can measure it like a clock. Less than a day." Without warning, Ronon suddenly hauled back and slammed a punch into the door. Teyla blinked at the sound of the impact and the Satedan bared his teeth. "Not made of steel," he hissed. "Something else."

"One thing is certain." Teyla gestured at the walls around them. "This place, whatever it may be, was clearly created by a science far too advanced for the locals on Heruun."

"Those creatures," he began, "the humanoids. I've never seen anything like them." Ronon turned away, flexing his hand. "They're not our usual breed of enemy."

"And this cell was not built by Wraith technology."

He eyed her. "You say that like we should be happy about it. Those things… They may not be Wraith, but they're still a threat. "

Teyla nodded slowly. "They must be this 'Aegis' that Aaren spoke of. The protectors of the planet."

"How does kidnapping people protect them — ?" Ronon's terse retort was cut off as the door abruptly opened. The metal panel retracted into the wall, revealing one of the towering humanoids. Without pause, it stepped into the cell, stooping slightly, the door whispering shut behind it. The Satedan caught a glimpse of a long corridor beyond before it closed. The creature's head turned, dark eyes studying Ronon. It aimed one of the glassy paralysis devices at him. The meaning was clear.

Dex raised his hands slowly and backed off a step; he had no desire to experience the horrible effects of the alien weapon again.

The humanoid had a different device in its other hand, spidery fingers curled around it, operating a display with tapping motions. The second object was an orb the size of a child's ball, shimmering with a pearly glow. It pointed the device at Ronon, and a series of chimes issued out. The Satedan caught Teyla's eye and she mouthed the word *scanner?* at him.

It turned the orb toward Teyla and did the same; for a moment, there was a glimmer of something close to a human expression on its sparse features, a thinning of slit-like nostrils and a motion of the head. It took a step closer to the woman, holding the sensor globe higher. Teyla's gaze met Ronon's for a brief instant, and a silent communication passed between them.

Ronon willed himself not to move, not to give away even the smallest flicker of muscle-motion. He watched the alien and waited for his moment; and as he did a faint scent touched his nostrils. It was odd, almost sour-sweet like rotting flesh or an infected wound. It was coming from the alien, a meat-odor oozing from its pores.

As the creature turned, Ronon spotted an ugly purple-black bruise on the creature's torso, where the stomach would have been on a man. *An injury*; and suddenly it was clear to him. This was the same one he had fought with outside the farmhouse, the one he had punched. Ronon remembered the dry texture of the flesh where he struck it, how the epidermis had powdered on his knuckles. *Almost as if... As if it were decaying.*

He had little time to process the thought. The alien's head turned toward Teyla and the moment was upon him.

He reacted without hesitation, launching himself off his

heels. He drove his fist straight into the bruise and the human-oid staggered, a thin gurgle escaping its lipless mouth. It spun back toward him, the sensor globe falling from its hand, raising the paralysis device. Ronon advanced, blocking and pushing the creature's arm away. It was difficult; against the Satedan, the difference in the height and mass of the giant alien made the fight unbalanced. It hissed and grabbed him by the collar with its free hand. For a moment, they struggled against one other, strong versus stronger.

Then from nowhere Teyla slammed the sensor globe into the humanoid's shoulders, drawing out a strained grunt of pain from the alien. The device fractured and cracked in her hands, knocking the creature off-balance. Ronon struck out again, punching the livid injury once more; the alien crumpled to the deck, its breathing shallow, a drool of watery purple fluid leaking from its mouth. The dark eyes fluttered closed and it became still.

"Did we… Kill it?" Teyla asked.

Ronon nudged the creature with his boot. "Maybe. I don't think we should stick around to find out." He scooped up the glass egg and turned it over in his hands. "Any idea how to use this?"

Teyla took it from him and examined it as she walked toward the door. "There are glyphs carved into the surface of—" The ellipse gave off a pulse of color and the door slid open. She moved it away and it closed again.

"It's not just a weapon, then."

"Apparently so." She opened the door once more and took a cautious glance outside. "I hear no alarms."

"That doesn't mean there aren't any," Ronon replied, step-ping out boldly. He looked up and down the corridor. "This way," he said, pointing to the right.

Teyla frowned again. "What makes you think that is the way out?"

He flashed her a feral grin and started walking.

Sheppard ran a hand through his hair and came away with his palm covered in sweat. The heat of the day was heavy, a deadening layer over the landscape that drew out the moisture in his throat, the constant rays of the two suns beating down on the colonel and his men. Haze shimmered on the horizon, off toward the direction of the Stargate. Pausing to take a swig from his canteen, he followed movement in the long grasses, where some nimble deer-like animals were pawing at the dry earth. Sheppard thought about McKay's earlier '*Wild Kingdom*' comment and wondered if the scientist had something there. The data they had on M9K-153 (or *Heruun*, Sheppard amended mentally) described a world of burning deserts about the equator, but with rich tropical grasslands in the habitable zone—a lot similar to the African veldt back home on Earth. On any other day, he might have taken a moment to savor that; but not today. Right now, he had people missing, and until Ronon and Teyla were back and safe, all other concerns were secondary. Sheppard swirled the lukewarm water around his mouth and swallowed it, grim-faced. He was liking this mission less and less with each passing hour.

All they had to show for a day of searching was an inert Satedan beam pistol and lines of blackened, dead grass. Something about this whole situation was setting off every alarm bell in his trained soldier's mind. John Sheppard wasn't someone with much tolerance for being played, and he couldn't escape the feeling that was exactly what was going on here. It made him feel powerless, and that frustrated the hell out of him. Every moment they wandered around in the scrub turning up nothing but dirt was a moment more some enemy force had two of his team—*two of his friends!*—as their prisoners. He glared up at the suns, squinting behind his sunglasses, looking for somewhere to focus his annoyance.

"Colonel?" He turned as Lorne called out. The major approached him, his t-shirt dark with patches of sweat. "We got a visitor. Says he's 'a friend of the voyagers'…" The other man gestured at a young boy trailing at his heels.

"Laaro," said Sheppard, his eyes narrowing. "Look, I'm sorry buddy, but I'm real busy right now."

The kid nodded, ignoring the brush-off. "Searching for your friends, yes." He was panting, as if he'd been running. "But there is news. I had to bring it to you as soon as possible."

Lorne raised an eyebrow. "This is your local contact, sir?"

"Something like that," Sheppard replied, keeping his eyes on the boy. "What news?"

"You won't like it." Laaro said sagely.

Sheppard's face twisted in a grimace. "McKay." He said the other man's name with a growl of annoyance. "What did he do?"

Laaro shook his head. "Rodney was quite brave, actually. But he had little choice. They had already threatened my parents."

"Are they all right?" demanded Lorne.

"I'm sorry," the boy went on, "but Rodney and Jennifer have gone."

Lorne immediately toggled his radio. "Doctor McKay, Doctor Keller? Respond please." He got nothing but static hiss in return.

"Gone where?" Sheppard crouched and took off the sunglasses, so he could look Laaro in the eye. "Gone as in *taken* gone?"

He got a head-shake in reply. "The Aegis only come after second sunset. These were the men who work for Soonir. He used to be an elder, until Takkol took away his status." Laaro nodded solemnly. "My uncle says Soonir is a bad person."

Sheppard straightened up and made a face. "I told McKay to *sit tight*."

"So now we're four people down?" Lorne shook his head. "Is kidnapping a national sport on this planet?"

"I'm starting to wonder." He grimaced. Was this all part of some greater plan, whittling down their numbers, picking off the stragglers? "New standing orders. From now on, no teams of less than four people. I'm damned if we're going to lose anyone else around here!"

A crackle from their radios hissed out into the air. "*Colonel Sheppard? This is Rush, sir. We may have a situation here.*"

Sheppard irritably snatched the walkie-talkie from his vest. "Go ahead, Sergeant. I could use some more good news." He turned to the west; Rush and his team of marines were sweeping the edge of the search zone closest to the farm where Teyla and Ronon were last seen. He could just about make out a knot of figures over there, men in indigenous dress among the dark-clothed soldiers from Atlantis.

Over the radio, he heard raised voices in the background. *"We intercepted a group of armed men and, uh, lions, I think."* Rush's voice was wary. *"There's a local guy throwing his weight around, calls himself Aaren."*

"Is that so?" Sheppard put the glasses back on. "Keep him there. I'll be right over." He nodded to Lorne. "I think its time we moved to a more proactive form of intelligence gathering, don't you?"

Lorne gave a cold smile in return. "Oh, yes sir."

"These corridors seem to go on for miles," said Teyla quietly, "and I have yet to see a single window."

Ronon nodded, hesitating at an intersection. "We could be in some kind of bunker complex, maybe deep underground." He glanced at her. "You saw the landscape when we arrived. All that scrubland, the hills in the distance. Plenty of space to hide all this and more. For all we know, we could be right underneath that tree-settlement."

She considered that for a moment. "You believe these people are like the Genii?"

"A high-tech culture hiding underneath a low-tech one? It's good camouflage. But I haven't seen any locals around here yet."

Teyla had to agree. "Those humanoids bare little resemblance to the natives. I find it hard to believe they are a related species." The aliens were nightmarish things, with bodies like corpse flesh and expressionless faces with the eyes of some deep-ocean predator. There was something unnatural, something unnerving about them that the Athosian couldn't quite define.

Ronon paused at an open panel in the wall. "Look. Another one," he noted. "How many does that make?"

As they moved through the corridors, here and there the two of them had come across places where the featureless metal had been peeled back or cut away, revealing incredibly complex layers of mesh, a weave of strange glowing filaments that formed a dense lattice pulsing with energy. In some places, the lattice appeared to be damaged, parts of it removed or in the process of being patched. Repair work, she guessed, but left unfinished. Down some of the corridors that radiated off this one, they saw areas where the overhead lighting was inactive, and some that were sealed off behind the faint blue glimmer of a force-field.

"Perhaps the complex is still under construction," Teyla wondered aloud.

Ronon's more martial instincts led him to a different conclusion. "No. This place has seen combat." He ran a finger along a torn edge. "This is battle damage."

But from a battle with what? she wondered.

"Company!" hissed the Satedan. He beckoned her sharply, into the shadow of an archway.

Teyla and Ronon pressed into the pool of darkness beyond the reach of the corridor's illumination and waited. A pair of aliens passed by them, intent on some mission that they could only guess at. It was the fourth time they had hidden from the creatures; so far their luck was holding.

She watched them go, disappearing around a corner. "Strange…" Teyla mused. "You see that they do not communicate with each other. There is no…" She struggled to find the right word. "No informality between them." There was no evidence of connectivity between the creatures at all; even a species that had evolved beyond the need for vocal speech, telepaths perhaps, even they would exhibit some form of outward awareness.

Ronon nodded. "They're like machines. Even the most tightly-drilled combat soldiers will speak among themselves. The Wraith are more talkative than these things."

The mention of the word *Wraith* made something in Teyla's thoughts twist; she grimaced and pushed the sensation away.

The Satedan was rolling the glass egg in his hand. "And this thing. I'm not even sure what it does." He held it up between his thumb and forefinger. "No buttons, no dials, nothing to manipulate. What good's a weapon you can't fire?"

He tossed it and Teyla caught it with a flick of her wrist. "This object seems to share more in common with the devices created by the Ancients than it does with human or Wraith technology."

"Those creatures can't be Ancients, not unless the stories McKay told me about them are way off."

"No," she shook her head. "They are something else…" Her voice trailed away. There was a tingling sensation along the nerves of her arm, reaching up toward her shoulders, the back of her neck. It was getting worse by the moment.

"Teyla?" Ronon stepped closer, seeing the look on her face. "Talk to me."

An unpleasant and horribly familiar awareness gathered in her thoughts, a sickening feeling like spiders crawling inside her skull. She was moving before she realized it, drawn toward one of the dozens of featureless metal doors that appeared at regular intervals along the corridors. "Over here…"

"A way out?" he asked.

Teyla wasn't listening to him; she was caught, part of her wanting to stretch out and hear, another part desperately wanting nothing but silence. "Those creatures," she said, giving voice to her thoughts, "they are not Wraith…"

"Yeah, got that already."

She moved closer, gesturing with the device. The door whispered open, revealing another corridor beyond, this one rising upwards in a gentle slope. A chilling certainty settled on her, and she suppressed a shiver.

Teyla hesitated on the threshold, and sucked in a breath. "But I can sense them now. Yes. Close by."

Ronon's manner hardened. "There are Wraith down here with us?" He grabbed her arm, his jaw set "You're certain?"

Teyla's mouth was suddenly dry. She nodded once. "This way."

"I'll take it from here, Sergeant," said Sheppard, not waiting for Rush to give him an explanation. The marines from Atlantis stood in a wary line, their P90s and G36 assault rifles off the straps and ready, pointing at the ground but ready to snap up to firing position at a moment's notice. For their part, the Heruuni men milled around, kneading the grips of their spindly weapons. The guns they carried didn't look too impressive—tubular things like a collection of plumbing supplies connected to floppy bandoliers of ammunition—but Sheppard wasn't going to take any chances. The last thing he wanted was someone with an itchy trigger finger on either side.

Elder Aaren stood among them, squinting out from under a sun parasol held by one of his flunkies. He had a resentful glower on his face, maybe from having to come all the way out here in the heat of the day. Sheppard's lip curled. The colonel was feeling very short on sympathy right now.

Aaren didn't waste time with any lengthy preamble. "Elder Takkol sent me to express his most grave concerns, Colonel Sheppard." He gestured at Lorne and Rush and the other men. "We understand your concern for your friends, but you have brought an army on to our soil and—"

Sheppard cut him off with a shake of the head. "This isn't an army, Aaren. Believe me, if we'd brought an army, you'd know about it. What we have here is a rather pissed-off search party." Maybe it was the heat, but his tolerance was already wearing thin. He found himself wondering how the Heruuni would have reacted to a Puddle Jumper buzzing their tree-top village. *Maybe that's what we need to get some co-operation, show a little 'shock and awe'.* Sheppard frowned and dismissed the thought.

"With respect, colonel, Takkol asks that you send your soldiers back through the Gateway."

"Not gonna happen. Two more of my people have been taken, Keller and McKay. I'm going to do what I have to do to get them back."

A look of genuine shock flashed across Aaren's face. "That cannot be… The Aegis does not come in the daylight."

"The voyagers were taken away by Soonir's men," Laaro offered, hovering by Lorne's side. "They came to my mother's lodge and forced them to go with them."

Aaren's expression went from surprise to annoyance and

back again. Sheppard saw the moment and took it. "So who is this Soonir guy, then? And what is he doing with my team?" The colonel aimed a finger at the elder. "You say Teyla and Ronon were taken by this Aegis thing, and you had nothing to do with it. Maybe that's so, but McKay and Keller were captured by one of your people, and that makes it Takkol's responsibility."

"Soonir…" Aaren hesitated, clearly unwilling to speak in front of the Atlanteans. "He is a criminal, a man who has broken many taboos, ignored our laws. But he is our concern." The elder nodded to himself. "Takkol has decreed it so. We shall deal with him."

"And how long is that going to take?" demanded Lorne. "What reason does this man have to take our team-mates in the first place?"

Aaren's aide, the one with the parasol in his hand, leaned closer to his master. "Elder, Takkol would not wish you to speak of this."

"Takkol is not here," Aaren retorted. "He sent me in his stead, Dayyid!"

"I'm going to ask you this one more time," Sheppard began, his tone firm. "Who is Soonir and what does he want with Keller and McKay?"

Aaren's glower deepened. "There… Is a militant group among our people, Colonel. Men and women who oppose the old ways that have kept our world free of the Wraith and living in harmony. They keep themselves secret from us, but they take every opportunity they can to oppose the veneration of the Aegis. Soonir leads them." The local called Dayyid shook his head, looking away.

"The kid said he used to be one of your top guys," said Lorne.

The elder nodded. "He was one of our leaders, until his views brought him into conflict with Takkol. Soonir was banished from our settlement, but he still has many sympathizers there. He remains a constant impediment to our society." Aaren paused, thinking. "He may have seen your fellow voyagers as an opportunity… To take them would embarrass Takkol and ensure your enmity."

"Will he hurt them?" said Sheppard.

"I do not know. It is more likely that he will ransom them in return for some demand."

"A demand he knows Takkol will never meet!" Dayyid added.

"My people aren't part of your disagreements," said the colonel, "and I'm sure as hell not letting McKay and Keller become someone's bargaining chips. Where does this Soonir hang out?"

"You cannot approach Soonir without sanction from Takkol!" snapped Dayyid. "The great elder will never allow it!"

Lorne shot Dayyid a look. "You know where he is, don't you?"

"We...suspect," Aaren admitted. "Soonir has several bolt-holes, but there is a disused river-farm in the lake shallows he favors. But he has many men at his command." The elder sighed. "Takkol has, to date, been unwilling to draw our guards from their duties in the settlement so that we may mount a sor-tie against the militants and arrest Soonir. Takkol fears it will leave the lodges unprotected."

"Not to mention him," Rush said quietly.

"How many?" said Sheppard. "How many men has this guy got?"

"At least twenty militants," said the elder. "But they are all armed, and we could not take them without significant blood-shed."

The colonel glanced at the major. "Lorne, how many stun-ners does your squad have?"

"Six, maybe eight at the most." He nodded, seeing Sheppard's plan as it formed in the other man's eyes. "Also some noise-makers and stun grenades."

Sheppard turned back to Aaren. "Here's the thing. I want to rescue my people and frankly, given your attitude to security around here, I don't trust Takkol or you to get it done. So you're going to show me where this farm is and I'm going to get Keller and McKay back myself."

"That will not—" Dayyid was silenced by a sharp gesture

from Aaren.

The elder gave a slow nod. Sheppard could guess what the guy was thinking; even from the first moment he'd seen him, John had pegged Aaren as an opportunist, as someone unhappy in his role as second-string lackey. He had no doubt that Aaren wanted Takkol's job, and certainly arresting a major criminal—if that's what Soonir really was—would help that agenda along. Finally Aaren looked up at him. "This shall be done. A temporary partnership with the voyagers, to ensure that their missing friends are safely returned to them."

"Takkol should be informed of this," Dayyid grated.

"Then go and inform him," Aaren replied, newly emboldened by his decision. "Inform him that Colonel Sheppard and I are about to do what he has been afraid to."

Dayyid grudgingly thrust the parasol into the hands of one of the other Heruuni and set off back toward the settlement.

Sheppard found Lorne watching him and crossed to where the major stood, lowering his voice so that it didn't carry. "I know that look. If you've got something to say, let's hear it."

The other officer was silent for a moment. "I'm not sure about this, sir. A reconnaissance-in-force, that's one thing, but putting together a joint military operation on the fly?"

"Technically, it's a police action," Sheppard noted.

"Whatever you want to call it, Colonel, it's a direct intervention in a local disagreement."

"You're gonna start quoting the IOA rulebook at me? You, of all people?"

Lorne frowned. "Nope. But it's got to be said. This is an escalation."

"That's why I'm ordering non-lethal weapons only."

The major nodded. "Roger that. But with respect, I still don't like it."

Sheppard's eyes narrowed. "What, and you think I do? You think I want to get in the middle of some religious or tribal argument? I wish I had the option, Major, but this Soonir has cut down all our choices to one. We leave this to the locals and we got no guarantee of seeing Keller or McKay alive again. Like it or not, we're involved."

"Colonel Sheppard!" Aaren's voice cut through the air. "Are you ready to proceed?"

He looked toward the elder and his men. "Lead the way."

"Takkol is a threat to the lives of every man, woman and child on Heruun," said Soonir, leaning forward on the wide cushion. "The matter is no less grave than that."

"Why do I get the feeling that he'd probably say exactly the same thing about you?" Keller sat to the right of McKay, on another low cushion. The room was sparsely furnished, and it smelled faintly of damp and boiled vegetables. Rodney shifted and tried to make it look casual; in fact he was doing the best he could to figure out where they had been taken to. Hooded, after a hour of bumpy riding on the back of some kind of covered wagon, they'd been marched into this building and sat down. When the hoods came off, Soonir was there along with the muscle guys from Laaro's house. It was about that time he'd belatedly noticed that their radios were gone. The bald man had kept his word about the weapons and the rest of the kit, though, but that didn't make McKay feel any better. He got the sense that any one of these bruisers would be on him the moment he made a move toward his P90 or his pistol.

Soonir was nodding. "I imagine Takkol tells terrible stories about me, Doctor Keller." He spread his hands. "I've learned to live with it. My reputation matters little in the scheme of things."

"Yeah, the thing is…" McKay drew himself up and eyed the rebel leader. "Takkol was just a bit snobbish towards us. He didn't kidnap us and drag us out to who-knows-where for a chit-chat."

"You have not been kidnapped," growled one of Soonir's men. "That is what the Aegis does."

"Gaarin is correct. Think of it as accepting a forceful invitation," Soonir added, throwing the man a sideways look.

"What was with the hoods, then?" Keller replied. "If you wanted to speak to us, there are nicer ways."

"The hoods were necessary. For your safety as well as mine." Soonir got up and gestured around the room. "You have no idea where you are, and so when I release you, you cannot tell Takkol where you were taken to."

"You're going to release us?" McKay immediately regretted the half-surprised, near-pleading words as soon as they left his mouth.

The other man, Gaarin, eyed him without warmth. Rodney noticed that, like Soonir, he too had thin lines of inky tattoos about his temples. "Of course. If you had come here without the hoods, we would have had to kill you."

"Lucky us," Keller added, in a weak voice.

Gaarin's temper, which until now had been silently boiling away, came rushing to the surface. He turned to Soonir, his eyes flashing. "Why are we wasting time with these voyagers? We do not even know who they are. They could be agents of the Aegis, like those cursed Giants, or worshippers of the Wraith!"

"We're none of those things," McKay added swiftly. "We're just explorers. Most of the time."

Soonir glared at Gaarin until he stepped back. After a moment, the rebel leader returned to his seat. "You will excuse my friend. His mother was among the Taken and Returned many, many times. She fell to the sickness."

"Her passing was not an easy one." Gaarin spoke quietly, almost to himself.

"I'm sorry," Keller said gently. "We saw some of the…the victims of the sickness in the settlement. I wanted to learn more about it, but Aaren made us leave…"

Soonir sneered. "Of course he did. He is no better than Takkol, hiding the problem inside the sick lodge and waiting for it to go away. For the afflicted to die silently and be forgotten."

"The Aegis is the source of the sickness," noted McKay. "If that's true, then why don't your people do something about the abductions?"

"Stop them, you mean?" Soonir shook his head. "And how would we do that, Doctor McKay?" He nodded at Rodney's gun. "Even if we had weapons like yours, we could do nothing. Two of your own people were taken by the Aegis, were they not? Both of them warrior-kin, yet still unable to resist the

Giants?"

Keller nodded and McKay echoed her motion. "Do you know where the Aegis takes people? Is it somewhere nearby, on the planet?"

"The Aegis allows no memories to be retained," said Gaarin. "That is how it protects itself." The younger man's hands knitted, his angry energy seeking release and not finding it. "At least the Wraith are honest about what they are. They take and kill outright, but they do not skulk in shadows. At least they are an enemy you can grip in your hands, fight with your fists!"

"The refusal of Takkol and the other elders to admit the evidence in front of their eyes is destroying us," said Soonir, a bleak cast to his features. "They banished me for daring to oppose them, named me traitor and militant. But without a dissenting voice, they are leading the Heruuni along a path to ruin." He met Rodney's gaze, and McKay saw a cold intensity glittering there. "The elders are allowing my world to become the plaything of something alien. The malaise grows worse in the wake of every new Returning, more fall to it with each repeated Taking."

Gaarin nodded. "They eventually lose themselves in the halls of their own minds."

"The Aegis will destroy our people unless we stop it." Soonir leaned forward. "Help us, voyagers. Help us shake off the yoke upon our necks, and in return we will help you rescue your warrior friends."

CHAPTER FIVE

Ronon kept close to Teyla, following her intently as she moved down the steely corridor. She held out one hand, now and then brushing her fingertips over the walls. There was no sound in the chamber other than their footsteps and the faint hum of hidden systems, but the Athosian woman walked with her head cocked, as if she were listening to something that only she could hear.

Ronon's hands flexed, and he fought the urge to let them contract into fists. It was hard for him to resist the churning anger inside him at the thought of the Wraith; the directionless, all-consuming hate he had for the alien predator race surged up from deep inside him, a ready and all-too-familiar heat that sang in his blood. The hate he had for the creatures that had destroyed his precious Sateda was as potent and pure now as it had been on the day they had made him a Runner.

"Not far," Teyla said quietly. "Yes, several of them. Quite close." She slowed to a halt outside a metallic door. "Here."

He pushed her out of the way and took the glass egg from her hand. "Let's take a look." Ronon waved it at the wall and the door obediently retracted.

The smell of them hit his nostrils; the coppery scent of alien sweat and the stench of rotting meat. Four of them sat clustered around a fifth on the floor at the back of the cell; aside from an extra sleeping pallet, the holding chamber was the duplicate of the one Ronon and Teyla had escaped from. Each of the Wraiths turned as one toward the intruders, eyes dull with hunger and hate.

One of them, a warrior by the look of his clan sigils, sprang up and came at them. Ronon stepped forward with the ellipse in his hand, brandishing it like a weapon. "Back off!" he snapped, but part of him was daring the alien to keep coming, willing it to give him an excuse to fight.

The Wraith warrior halted, snarling at the device; clearly he knew the power of the paralysis field it could emit, unaware that Ronon couldn't use it. One of the other Wraith spat something in their hissing language, drawing the warrior's attention for a moment.

"They've been here for some time," Teyla said thickly, her brow furrowing. "Several months. They're starving."

The Wraith that lay on the deck, that the others crowded around, was if anything even more sallow and skeletal than the rest of them. It's greenish-white flesh hung off its bones, and it blinked slowly, breathing hard. With a grimace, Ronon realized that the aliens had been feeding off one of their own, perhaps off of each other in small amounts to keep themselves alive. "My heart bleeds," he growled.

"That…" replied the warrior, "could be arranged." It flexed its hand, showing the feeding maw in its palm.

"Go ahead," Dex snapped back. "Try it." His fingers tightened around the glassy egg and for a moment all he could think about was using it to beat the alien's skull in.

The Wraith turned it's baleful gaze toward Teyla. "You." He cocked his head, mimicking her manner out in the corridor. "You are touched by us. Yes." It made a gurgling sound that might have been a chuckle. "A rare thing in this part of space." His eyes flicked to Ronon. "But not here to free us, no?"

"We're not those fools who worship you, if that's what you're hoping for," Ronon told him. "We're a long, long way from that."

"A pity."

Teyla shuddered visibly. The taint of Wraith DNA in her body, the strange x-factor that gave her insight into the psychic bonds of the alien hives, was a two-way street. Ronon realized that the warrior was pushing at her mind, trying to coerce her. She gasped and shot the creature a lethal glare. "Get out of my thoughts."

"As you wish." The alien opened its hands and stepped back. "I only wished to know you."

"I saw a moment of his memories." She glanced at Ronon. "Those humanoids took them captive," she explained. "They were recovered from a sealed section of wreckage, from one of the scoutships destroyed by the Aegis."

"We are prisoners, just as you are," said the Wraith.

"We're not prisoners," Ronon retorted.

"We have attempted escape just as you do now, and we failed as you will fail…" The alien chuckled again, and the sound was echoed by his comrades. "You are from the city of the Ancients, yes? Atlantis? Our clan knows of you. And if you are here, then the Aegis has taken you as it took us. Any freedom you think you have is an illusion!"

"Where are we?" Teyla demanded, glaring at the Wraith. "Where is this place?"

"I will tell you if you let us free."

Ronon snorted. "Just open the door for a pack of hungry Wraiths? I don't think so."

The warrior gave an exaggerated nod. "Just me, then. I will help you escape if you free me."

"Didn't you say your escape attempt failed?" noted Teyla.

"I'm sure with humans as resourceful as you, that would not happen again." The Wraith's words were oily and condescending.

Teyla's head snapped up and she shot a look out the open hatch, into the corridor beyond. "I hear something…"

Ronon heard it too; the metallic whisper of another door opening.

"The giants…" whispered Teyla. A group of the towering, silent humanoids were swarming up the corridor toward them.

"They come," spat the Wraith. "Our captors." It came forward again. "Quickly. You must release me!" There was an edge of desperation and terror in the warrior's voice that Ronon had rarely heard in their kind. He had only a moment to register it before the Wraith dived clumsily at him, clawed fingers grabbing for the glass device.

The Satedan reacted with a short, sharp punch that caught the alien square in the face. He felt bone and cartilage fracture beneath his knuckles and the Wraith rocked backwards, a fan of dark, greasy blood issuing from its nostrils. "I don't think so," he grunted. "We're out of here."

Before the other prisoners could come after them, Ronon and Teyla were stepping through the hatchway, closing it behind them. The other Wraith scrambled toward the moving door, falling over each other in their wild struggle to reach it.

Teyla broke into a sprint and Ronon gave chase, angry at running from a fight, but just as angry at himself for the cold certainty of defeat that would come if he didn't flee.

There was a clatter of claws on metal as the cell door slammed shut, and a final shout from within. "You fools," spat the Wraith warrior, "you can't escape this place!"

The building was an odd collection of wood-framed huts with packed earth walls, and oval woven pods similar to the ones Sheppard had seen in the settlement. The whole thing was raised up slightly on shallow stilts from the mud plain where it sat. A low-lying lake of dirty brown water spilled away from it toward the grasslands, thin and spindly trees issuing up from the shore toward the blazing sky. On the far side of the disused farm, a long covered porch ended in a jetty where tall A-frames creaked in the hot breeze; old, neglected sheets of netting hung from them like twists of blackened lace.

"Looks like a fishing hut, or something, only bigger." The colonel peered though a monocular, slowly scanning the area. Flat against the side of a low gulley, he lay so only the top of his head was exposed.

"Once it was a place for the lake hunters to come in the colder season," he heard Laaro say. "The mudgrakes they catch are good to eat."

"Mudgrakes," Lorne repeated, giving the word a sour tone. "That doesn't sound appetizing."

Sheppard glanced down. Along the gulley to the right and the left, Lorne's men were spreading out, securing their weapons. Like him, the major had swapped his P90 submachine gun for a Wraith stunner pistol. The silvery alien guns had drawn some unpleasant looks from the locals when they were deployed—anything Wraith was to be distrusted, and Sheppard had to admit he couldn't fault them on that. He checked the glowing green power cell and holstered it once more.

Lorne looked up at him. "Evaluation, sir?"

The colonel jerked a thumb in the direction of the lake. "This could be a bear, depending on the range of those 'rod-guns' they've got. The building looks like it's abandoned, but it's not. Aaren's people were right, the place is occupied. I spotted two guys, one on an upper level balcony, another one on the ground doing a circuit in the shade."

Sergeant Rush stood nearby, studying a handheld scanner of Ancient design. "Sir, you should see this. I set it to a ther-mographic readout."

Sheppard took the unit and peered at the screen. A collec-tion of green lines showed the walls and internal spaces of the sprawling farm complex, and there were orange-red dots scattered everywhere. Human life-signs. He swore under his breath. "If this thing is reading right, there's gotta be eighty, maybe a hundred people in there." He scrolled the display around until he found two specific indicators, each blinking slowly. "Found 'em. McKay and Keller's tracers are still active, so that's something."

He passed the scanner to Lorne, who frowned at it. "They have a lot of company in there," said the major.

"Yeah . And it won't be easy getting to them. This Soonir guy? He's no fool. There's no single good approach to the building, and anything that could be cover is gone. Brush has been cut away, no trees… It's open, all the way to the front door."

"If they've got sharpshooters, they'll cut us down the moment we come over the ridgeline."

"Soonir's men are skilled," noted Laaro, a hitch of fear in his voice. "Takkol says they are all killers."

Sheppard turned to Rush. "Sergeant, take team three and follow the gulley around to the southwest, get an angle on the far side of the main building. And stay low. They may have spotters. When you're in position, give me the word."

Rush nodded. "Will do, Colonel." He hesitated for a moment. "Sir, what about the locals?" He indicated Aaren, who crouched some distance away, busy in an intense, hushed conversation with his guards.

"I'll handle them," Sheppard replied. "You have your orders."

The sergeant saluted and moved off. Lorne moved closer to his commanding officer and spoke quietly. "Sir, I don't like this. We could be walking into a meat grinder up there."

The colonel nodded. "The only way we can make a stealth approach is to wait for the suns to set, go in under cover of darkness."

"That's hours away. You think Aaren's going to wait that long?" Lorne glanced at the elder. "He's twitchy enough as it is."

"It's that or we hit the place with smoke and hope the wind doesn't carry it away." Sheppard sighed.

"Sure could use the *Apollo* right now," the major noted. "We could grab the doctors without firing a shot."

"While you're at it, wish for some lemonade too. My throat's dryer than the blacktop at Groom Lake." He turned as he heard Aaren approaching. The elder's eyes were darting everywhere, as if he expected Soonir's men to descend on them at any moment. One of the trained mai cats slinked along at his heels, panting.

"Colonel, we are prepared. You will support my guards as they launch the attack, and—"

Sheppard held up a hand. "Whoa, stop right there. A couple of things you have to understand, right away. One, this is a rescue mission, it's not an attack. Two, we go when I give the word and not before."

Aaren rocked back, as if the colonel had slapped him. "When I agreed to allow you to assist us—"

Suddenly Sheppard realized that the men standing in a nervous circle behind the elder was a lot smaller than it had been when they arrived at the lakeside. "Where's the rest of your guards?" he demanded, speaking over the other man.

Aaren folded his arms. "They are following my commands."

The colonel opened his mouth to speak, but Lorne broke

in, holding up the scanner. "Sir? McKay and Keller... They're moving."

Gaarin shifted aside a door made of woven branches and Soonir lead Jennifer and Rodney into a larger room, something that might have been a barn before the rebels had re-purposed it. There were beds in close-packed lines, most of them filled with people who seemed asleep or motionless. Something inside Keller went tense, a strange kind of anger, a sudden compulsion to do something, to help; but she didn't know what she could do, or where to begin.

Light entered through high windows that had been hastily reinforced with bars and the only other entrance was a wide wooden door at the far end. A thickset man, cradling a rifle and carrying a machete-like weapon on his belt, sat in a wicker chair. Keller saw the guard and wondered why he was looking into the room, instead of outward for any potential threats.

"He is here for the peace-of-mind of the sick," Soonir said quietly, picking up on her questioning look. "They see him and believe they will not be Taken again, that he will protect them." He shook his head slightly. "A pleasant fiction, though, to help them sleep a little better at night. If the Aegis came, he could not stop it."

"We saw people at the sick lodge," began McKay, "these are victims of the same thing?"

Soonir nodded. "The ones that Takkol and the other elders refuse to acknowledge, people denied even the most basic treatment because they or members of their family are known to support me and my views."

"How many more are there?" Keller asked.

"We have an extensive funeral ground outside," muttered Gaarin.

"We do what we can to ease their suffering," added Soonir. "Some recover. Many do not."

Jennifer pulled open the zipper of her backpack. "Will you let me help?" She drew out a sampling kit and cracked the case, removing a handful of surgical syrettes. "I need to take a few drops of blood from people with the sickness." Soonir's face stiffened; as the doctor suspected, the request she made had serious significance on Heruun.

"She's very good at what she does," insisted Rodney. "She's saved a lot of lives."

"I can take the blood back to Atlantis and analyze it. If we can understand what's happening to your people when they're taken, then maybe we can find out how to cure this sickness."

Gaarin shared a look with his leader and after a moment Soonir nodded. "Very well." He took one of the medical samplers from Keller's hand and held it up to the light. "Show me what must be done."

The deeper Teyla and Ronon moved through the seemingly endless corridors, the more she feared she would never see the light of day again. Fleeing from the confinement level, they moved upward with the alien giants dogging them at every step. They had little time to stop and consider their course of action; the humanoids did not give them the chance.

"We're being herded," said Ronon, his face showing disgust at the idea. But outmatched as they were, making a stand would be pointless. Finding a way out, to freedom, was the only viable option still open to them.

On the upper levels the corridors changed. The damage they had seen in places elsewhere was much more widespread here. Whole lengths of passageway were flame-scored, panels broken or missing, the overhead illumination inert.

In one such area, Teyla's fingers brushed something on the wall and she drew in a sudden breath.

Ronon came closer. "What is it?"

"Here..." She gingerly pressed her hands into the strange, fleshy knot of matter that wound around an exposed power conduit. "Is that what I think it is?"

He nodded grimly. "Wraith technology." He poked it with a finger, and the fatty mass recoiled slightly. It sat strangely among the blackened metal and melted plastic, utterly wrong and out of place. "A power regulator node, I think." The Satedan nodded to himself. "Yeah. I've seen these on Hive Ships."

Teyla examined the device. "What is it doing here? It makes no sense."

After a moment Ronon spoke again. "It's a patch."

"I do not understand."

"Someone has cannibalized pieces of a Wraith ship to fix this damage. They didn't have a regulator so they rigged a piece of Wraith tech to do the same job."

"Is that possible?"

He gestured at the throbbing node. "Seems so." Ronon moved on, tapping and probing at the walls. In the dimness it was hard to see, but the sound of his fist rapping on steel and then something that had to be bone, was stark and unmistakable. "More here," he told her. "Looks like epidermal plates from the hull of a dart or a scoutship. It's been welded in place over a busted panel."

A crackling hum echoed down the corridor; ahead of them, it branched at another intersection. She shot Ronon a look and he nodded to her.

Silently, they made their way forward. Teyla kept low and peered around the corner. What she saw made her hesitate. "Do you see them?"

Dex nodded. "Heruuni."

"I think you misunderstand who is in charge," Aaren was saying.

"And I think you don't understand the seriousness of what's going on here," Sheppard replied. "This is a potential hostage situation, and I don't risk the lives of my people unless I have to!"

The elder smirked. "Then perhaps you need a lesson in boldness."

The colonel's jaw set. The man was letting his bravado run away with him. "Now just a damn minute," he began, but it was already too late. Aaren punched his fist in the air, and with a ragged shout, his guard surged forward, up the ridgeline.

Major Lorne scrambled to block their path, but there were too many of them. The Heruuni dashed out across the open space, shouting and firing their rodguns. Aaren went after them and Sheppard gave chase, cursing the man's stupidity to his back. He saw a flash of movement off to the right and there were the rest of the elder's men, boiling up from the gulley in a crude attempt at a pincer movement.

"They'll be cut to pieces…" Lorne snarled.

Sheppard shouted a command. "Pop smoke!" The airmen did as ordered, and a rain of cylindrical grenades arced through the air, trailing thick jets of white mist. Furious, he grabbed at his radio and snarled into it. "All units, we're going in now! Deploy, deploy, deploy!" He shot Laaro a severe look. "And you're not gonna move from this spot, get me?" The boy nodded sheepishly.

Sergeant Rush's voice answered him. *"Colonel, what's happening? We're not in position—"*

"Forget it, just move in!" He glared at Lorne as the rattle of rodguns reached his ears. "So much for stealth! Aaren's just screwed the whole operation!"

McKay's head snapped up as the sound of shouting came to his ears. "What was that?"

"Attackers!" The cry echoed down from the upper floor, followed by the distinctive *click-snap* of guns coming to the ready.

Rodney found Gaarin glaring at him with newfound anger. "Wait, no—" His next words were drowned out by the clatter and whistle of shots being fired. At his side, Keller flinched as the first salvo of crude bullets peppered the walls of the old barn with a sound like handfuls of gravel against a tin sheet.

The people with the sickness could barely stir beyond moans of fear, the more able of them stumbling out of their beds, panic in their eyes. Armed rebels raced into the room, forming a cordon around Soonir.

The rebel leader had the sampler tubes clutched in his fist, and he came at McKay, his face a mix of emotions. "Did you do this? Did you bring them to us?"

"No!" But Rodney knew that might not be true; both he and Keller had hidden microtransmitters in their gear that anyone could have located, if they knew what to look for. But surely the locals didn't have the technology for that. *Unless...* He swallowed hard.

"Was this all a trick?" Soonir shook the blood-filled syrettes at Keller. "Did you lie to us?"

"Never," she insisted. "We don't know anything about this!"

A fresh hail of rodgun rounds clawed at the walls and outside, someone screamed in pain as a shot struck flesh.

"The guards!" The shout came from the spotter on the upper level who had first cried out the alarm call. "Takkol's men have come!"

The first wisps of white smoke curled in through the barred windows and under the gaps around the door.

Sheppard went up and over, racing into the wall of haze. He didn't have to look to know that Lorne was right behind him, a pace or so back and to the left, covering him as he moved. He couldn't see much, only shadows and vague shapes, but he had the route to the farmhouse mapped out in his head. *Thirty seconds from the ridge to the wall at a full-tilt run,* he told himself, *less if I don't stop to smell the roses.*

With the Wraith stunner in a two-handed grip, the colonel moved in a quick zigzag motion, staying as close as he could to the thickest coils of the smoke; but he'd been right about the breeze. It was blowing steadily in off the lake, diffusing the smokescreen with every passing second.

He heard the snapping drone of something zipping past his ear and he ducked away as rodgun shots nipped at the dirt. Someone ahead of him shouted out in pain and crumpled to the ground. Sheppard skirted around the dead man; it was one of Aaren's guards, blown back off his feet into a snarl of robes, his face a ruin of blood and bone.

The colonel glanced up, tracking the trajectory of the kill-shot, and through a momentary break in the smokescreen he saw a rebel with a rifle aiming right back at him. On the run, Sheppard released a pulse-bolt from the alien pistol and hit his mark. The rebel shooter fell soundlessly, instantly shocked unconscious. He dropped from the upper level balcony, tumbling headfirst over a rail and through the thatched roof of a pod-hut.

Lorne raced past and Sheppard fell in with the major, pacing him. They reached the porch of the main building as gunfire hissed and buzzed around them, the chemical taint of the white vapor coating their throats. Lorne nodded at the wide wooden door blocking the entrance and Sheppard returned the gesture. The colonel planted a heavy boot right at the point where a carved lever-lock held the door closed. It splintered and broke, and the doors groaned as they fell open. Two rebels waiting for them inside were dispatched with a brace of stunner blasts.

"Breach and clear!" ordered Sheppard, and they entered, guns high.

A woman with a rifle at her side and blood on her face from a gash on her scalp bounded into the room. "Aaren has the voyagers are with them," she gasped. "The guards have already killed three of our men! They're going to overrun the farm!"

"What?" Rodney heard the pure shock in Keller's voice.

"They are here for you," Gaarin told Soonir. "They must not be allowed to take you! Takkol will have his victory!"

"No, the sick—" Soonir reached out toward the people in the beds.

"You must go!" Gaarin turned his attention to the other rebels. "Take him to the tunnels, get him away as quickly as you can!"

The rebel leader rounded on McKay and almost threw the blood vials at him. "Is this what you wanted from us, voyager? Take them, then! Give them to your master!"

"Master?" Rodney shook his head. "We're not working for Takkol or the Aegis! You have to believe me!"

Soonir was already being led away. "How can I?"

"Wait, no, this isn't what we wanted..." Gaarin stood in front of McKay to stop him following.

The other rebel shoved Rodney back with the heel of his hand. "I should kill you for this," he grated. "It would be fitting!"

"No," called Soonir. "No more death! I will not have it."

"I'm sorry!" Rodney yelled, as the rebel leader left them behind.

He looked up and found Gaarin glaring at him. "We are all sorry, voyager," he growled. "Takkol will ensure we are so."

McKay groped for something to say, but in the next second he was covering his ears as a flash bang grenade went off down the hall, the flat concussion hammering through the building.

There were four of the locals in the corridor, working silently under the glow of a lamp-globe that floated over their heads. They were patching other parts of the damaged metal walls, drawing jagged-edged pieces of Wraith bone-amour from an anti-gravity cart. One of them used something that had to be a molecular welder to bond the salvaged plating to the scorched surfaces. None of them spoke as they went about the duty.

"They move like machines," Teyla noted. She was right; their actions were stilted and unnatural.

He nodded. "No sign of any of those creatures, either."

"Shall we take the other path, then? Avoid them?"

Ronon shook his head. "No. Let's go take a look."

The four figures—three men and a woman—showed no sign of noticing their approach, and when Teyla spoke to them they still did not react.

"Hello? Can you hear us?"

"Look," said the Satedan, indicating the woman. "Remember her?"

Recognition bloomed on Teyla's face. "The Heruuni woman from the farm. The one we saw taken by the creatures."

Ronon waved his hand in front of the woman's face, snapped his fingers; nothing. "Hey," he snapped, raising his voice. "I'm talking to you."

The woman's eyes were vacant and expressionless.

"It's as if they've been conditioned," said Teyla. "Put into a waking trance…"

Ronon stepped in front of the woman from the farm and blocked her path. "Stop what you're doing," he demanded, using the 'command' tone of voice they had taught him in his combat training on Sateda.

To his mild surprise, that had the desired effect. The four of them immediately halted.

"Suggestibility," Teyla noted. "They're no better than drones in this state. Mind-controlled, just waiting for the right instructions." She glanced at him. "For someone to give them orders."

"That, I can do," said Ronon. "How do we get out of this place?" he demanded, searching their faces for any signs of consciousness; he found nothing but blank, mute stares. It was, in its own way, unnerving. Ronon turned to another of them, a man with a shorn skull and faint tattooing. "Tell me where the exit is!"

All four of the Heruuni turned as one and pointed down the corridor.

"That is progress," Teyla allowed.

"Reckon so." Ronon prodded the man in the chest. "You will show us where it is."

He got a languid nod in return, and with halting steps, the man began to wander away, off into the darkness.

Moving quickly and carefully, Sheppard and Lorne went from room to room, calling out "Clear!" each time they found an empty chamber, and using the stunners when opposition came at them. They halted at a closed door and shared a look.

"Where's this band of dangerous militants Aaren was talking about?" said Lorne. "These guys are just day-players. They barely know how to put up a fight."

Sheppard nodded. Only a handful of the rebels they had encountered seemed to have anything like a basic tactical sense. Most of them had surrendered the moment they were threatened, and some didn't even appear to be able to work their weapons correctly. These people weren't exactly the heavily-armed band of marauders that the elder had painted them as.

From the opposite end of the building came the *crash-whump* of a flash bang, and over the radio the colonel heard Sergeant Rush's voice. "*South entrance secure. Resistance is minimal.*"

"Roger that," Sheppard replied. "Hold your position and make sure that Aaren's yahoos don't shoot anyone else."

"*Wilco*," said the sergeant.

"He's not gonna like that, sir," Lorne noted.

"I don't care what he likes, Major. I've had enough of people on this planet yanking our chains. Go!" He moved up toward the door and shouldered it open.

An empty wicker chair tumbled out of the way and the two officers found themselves inside a large barn filled with beds and scared people.

"What the hell…?" Lorne halted, panning his weapon over a sea of frightened faces.

Sheppard caught sight of McKay and Keller across the room, with an armed local towering over them. "Drop the gun!" he shouted. "Right now!"

"It's okay!" Rodney replied, gingerly reaching up to take the man's rifle. "Don't shoot him."

The tall rebel's shoulders slumped and he released his grip on the rodgun. Sheppard was there in a heartbeat, the stunner still at the ready. "You okay?" He directed the question at Keller, and the doctor gave him a shallow nod; she looked frustrated and weary.

"Yes, *we* are fine," McKay added. "Thanks for asking."

"What part of the words *sit tight* did you not understand?" Sheppard glared at the scientist. "I told you to say in the settlement. Did I leave any kind of ambiguity in that statement?"

"We got blood samples!" McKay retorted, as if that was explanation enough.

"They don't call me 'colonel' because I like fried chicken, McKay. I'm the ranking officer here, and when I give an order I expect it to be obeyed!"

"They had guns," Rodney countered.

Sheppard prodded him in the chest. "So did you."

"And what would a shoot-out have done for us?" Keller broke in. "We need the trust of these people!"

He shook his head. "Yeah, well, I think that ship has already sailed." The colonel shot a look over his shoulder. "Lorne! Get your men in here, secure these people."

As the major spoke into his radio, there was a commotion at the other entrance to the barn. Aaren entered, his face like thunder, together with a knot of his guards and several marines trailing with him. "Sorry, sir," said the sergeant with them, "I tried to stop him."

"Just for once, Rush, would it kill you to bring me some good news?"

Aaren waggled a finger in Sheppard's face. "Soonir has escaped! You allowed this to happen, Colonel, with your delays and indecision!"

"You jumped the gun," Sheppard replied. "That's on your head, pal."

The elder gestured at the sick scattered around the room. "Take the prisoners back to the settlement."

"They aren't militants," said the tall rebel. "They're our families, afflicted with the sickness that you pretend does not exist!"

"You lied to me," Sheppard said, in a low, dangerous voice. He took a step closer to Aaren and the elder's men came forward; in the same moment Lorne, Rush and the other marines had their weapons raised. "This place is packed with non-combatants. You wanted me to raid a *hospital*."

"The militants escaped in the confusion," Aaren retorted. "We know they have an underground network of passages in this area. They must have slipped away..." He straightened and fixed Sheppard with a hard gaze. "You will help us track Soonir. I saw your devices. You will be able to find him for us."

The colonel grunted. "You just don't know when to quit, do you?" He turned to Lorne and shook his head. "Secure your weapons. We're done here. Assemble our people and head back to the gate."

The major saluted and moved off.

"You are going to leave?" Aaren was surprised.

"Not all of us." Sheppard replied. "Not until we find Ronon and Teyla." He nodded to McKay and Keller. "Come on."

Jennifer glanced around the room, shaking her head "Colonel, these people—"

"—Are not going to be helped by you staying here." He

spoke over her. "You're going back to Atlantis. And just in case you're not certain, that's an order, Doctor."

"John," McKay began to speak, but he was silenced by an uncompromising glare from his friend.

"We're not getting dragged into another local fight, Rodney. This has happened way too many times on my watch, and it's not gonna happen again here." He turned toward the yawning doors.

Aaren snarled. "Sheppard! I am a senior elder! You cannot walk away from me!"

He answered without turning around. "Watch me."

The bald man halted in front of a larger set of hatch doors and pointed at it. His face retained the same bland nothingness; it was impossible for Teyla to read anything from him, no emotional cues, not a single spark of self. She chewed her lip. Even the Asuran Replicators, pure machine life forms, copied human nature enough to have expressions and emotions visible on their faces. The Athosian felt a moment of sorrow for the man; was this mindless state the condition of every Heruuni who became one of the Taken?

Ronon gestured at the doors and they parted; beyond was a short length of corridor, apparently undamaged, ending in another hatchway. The man continued to point. "That way?" Dex asked. "Open it."

By way of assent, the bald man walked on, toward the other doors. Ronon followed him, but Teyla hesitated just inside the threshold. Something seemed...wrong.

Ronon eyed her. "Teyla? What is it?"

"I don't know—"

The ellipse in her hand glowed, flashing a green-red. Before she could react, the doors they had just stepped through slammed shut. She heard a faint squeal as a pressure seal locked.

A sudden and terrible thought formed in her mind. "Oh no." She launched herself toward the bald man, who was doggedly working a crystalline touchpad in the far wall. "Stop him!"

She was not quick enough. The far hatch clicked and began to open. From nowhere, a horrific tornado blasted through the chamber, knocking the three of them to their feet. The wind was made of ice and razors and it tore at Teyla and Ronon, dragging them across the smooth floor.

Panting, the very breath in her lungs being sucked out through her mouth, Teyla chanced a glance over her shoulder towards the ever-opening doors. Out beyond them, she saw a stark monochrome landscape; a mottled grey-white landscape, a black sky, and hanging in it the globe of a clouded brown world ringed by a glittering halo.

Heruun.

Then her eyes began to prickle as needles of pain lanced into them, the fluid in the soft tissues dropping toward freezing point. Teyla saw the bald man tumble silently out through the widening gap, to tumble into the white dust beyond. A stream of reddish fluid followed him down, droplets from his nostrils and mouth becoming crimson pearls as they flash-froze in the vacuum.

She tried to scream, but the wind was too loud. The terrible chill crept into her, and she was dimly aware of something holding on to her, a strong hand around her wrist. Every movement an effort now, Teyla looked back to see Ronon gripping her arm, his other hand locked around a curved stanchion in the wall. His bare arms were covered in patches of frost, and his beard was turning white. She saw his lips moving.

Hold on.

Teyla managed a nod, but it was all she could do. The sudden, punishing cold was leaching the life from her, draining away her energy. She felt icicles of blood forming on her cheeks, cutting into her. All she could think of was Kanaan and their unborn child.

Her vision fogged, turned grey.

Turned black.

CHAPTER SIX

The landscape was a rusty blur through the canopy of the Puddle Jumper, broken only by the low clumps of trees and long lines of sharp-spined hills. The heads-up display projected a ghostly grid of map lines, marking the small vessel's passage across the search zone with a blinking blue glyph.

"Coming up to the edge of zone two," said McKay. He gave a minute sigh. "No reading."

"Right." Sheppard ran his hands over the Jumper's controls and it banked to starboard. "Moving to zone three."

They'd been up for an hour or so, and the two of them had spoken little in that time. Sheppard had to admit it was actually quite a novelty to be in a room with Rodney McKay and actually have the guy be quiet for more than five minutes at a stretch.

McKay sighed again, tapping at the portable computer on his lap. Okay, so he wasn't actually being totally quiet. He kept doing the sighing thing, and it was starting to grate on Sheppard as time went on.

When he did it again, it was like the colonel's tolerance meter suddenly flipped from *full* to *empty*. He shot the scientist a glare. "If you have something to say to me, Rodney, spit it out. Otherwise, the next time you sigh, I'm dropping you off in the middle of the next lion pack I find."

McKay gave him an affronted look in return. "I can't help it if I exhale noisily. But now you mention it, yes, maybe I do have something on my mind."

Sheppard kept his eyes on the horizon. "Well?"

Rodney took a breath and launched into the speech he'd clearly been holding in since they took off from the Stargate. "Keller was right. These people need our help."

"*Our* people need our help," Sheppard countered. "Teyla and Ronon, remember them? They're the priority. Two Atlantis team members in harm's way—"

McKay broke in. "Yes, I heard what you said to Colonel Carter, you don't have to repeat it. And clearly she agrees with you, otherwise she wouldn't have authorized the use of this Jumper."

Sheppard frowned. He felt fatigued and worn out by the heat and the events of the past day. He couldn't remember the last time he slept, and it was making him irritable. He glanced at McKay again. "Don't make me out as the bad guy. Tell me you're not going to play the 'civilians versus the military' card. Keller's still a newbie out here and from her I could forgive it, but you? After everything we've been through, I thought you knew me better than that." He paused. "And for the record, Carter was *not* an easy sell about the Jumper."

"It's just… You're leaving these people twisting in the wind," Rodney went on. "They need medical attention, and someone to stand up to that blowhard Takkol."

"And that has to be us? When we moved into Atlantis, I don't recall signing up to put out every fire in the Pegasus galaxy! We have enough problems of our own, dealing with the Wraith and the Replicators and everyone else who wants us dead, without taking on the troubles of every planet we visit!" He shook his head. "I knew this mission was a bad idea from the get-go."

McKay folded his arms. "That's it, is it? You're just going to stick around until we find Ronon and Teyla, and then leave? What about those Wraith ships that imploded, what about this Aegis thing and the sickness?" He leaned forward. "What would Elizabeth have said about that, John?"

The thought of Elizabeth Weir brought Sheppard up short. "She would have agreed with me," he replied, with less conviction than he would have liked.

"That's not true, and you know it."

The colonel grimaced. "You think I want to make this call, Rodney? But if the local government here doesn't want our help with the sickness, we can't force it on them. And I sure as hell am not getting suckered into doing Aaren's strong-arm work for him, not again."

"Well, maybe it's time for a regime change…"

Sheppard eyed him. "You know that for sure, huh? You've been on Heruun less than two days and you're ready to make that judgment? We can't get that sort of thing right on our own planet, what makes you think we can do it right here?" He looked away; his tone had risen as he spoke, and the colonel had to admit a good amount of his annoyance was directed inward as well as at his friend.

"And of course there's the whole reason we came here in the first place. Hive Ship in the 'hood, remember?"

"I haven't forgotten that," Sheppard replied.

"Maybe now we should tell the locals about it?"

"Wait." On the upper range of the detection grid, something glittered and then vanished just as quickly. "What was that?"

McKay was immediately tapping at his computer. "Extending the scan envelope…" The target returned. "There! Refined metals, plastics, some organic matter…" He paused, frowning. "But it's not on the ground. It's above us."

"In orbit?"

Sheppard got a nod in return. "Seems that way. I think it could be part of a vessel…"

"Let's take a look-see." He worked the Jumper's controls and peeled off from the low-level flight pattern, into a steep climb, pouring power to the thrusters.

McKay shot him a look. "By the way, that conversation we were having? It's not over."

"It is for now," said the colonel. Outside the canopy, the dusty blue of Heruun's sky became the black of space.

The darkness went away for a while, and in pieces Teyla felt herself awaken; but not all at once. The moments faded in and out, falling from her grip like sand between her fingers.

The face of one of the humanoids loomed over her. Two more stood behind it, all of them wearing the same blank expression. The lipless mouth opened and she heard words, a rough, unfinished voice with a quizzical edge to it. "Why did you attempt to terminate yourselves?"

She forced air through her lungs, ignoring the pain. "You… Can speak…"

One of the other aliens blinked. "I have many methods of communication."

"We… Wanted to escape." She coughed, and it hurt like fire.

The closest of the creatures moved one of the glass eggs over her. Teyla flinched, tried to shy away from it, but the faint yellow ray it cast left no paralysis in its wake, only a warmth. A warmth and the absence of the pain.

"Your choice was foolish," said the first alien. Its powdery, pale skin seemed ashen and pallid, like the flesh of a drowned thing. "You acted without consideration. You did not understand where you are."

Teyla remembered the snarling words of the Wraith warrior in the cells. *You can't escape this place!* The Wraith had known exactly where they were. "A base…? On a moon… A moon of Herrun."

"A ship," corrected the third humanoid. Each of them spoke with identical tone and inflection, the words pitched strangely as if verbal speech was uncommon to them. "On the surface of the primary satellite."

"Where is my friend?" she demanded, gasping in air as the chill in her bones began to recede.

"Unhurt. The other with you who ventured outside could not be recovered." It bowed its head. "Unfortunate."

Abruptly, Teyla realized she was in motion, being carried along one of the metallic corridors on some sort of platform. She tried to rise, but her body was too weak. "Where are…you taking me?"

"Do not be afraid," came the reply. "This is necessary."

The exertion was too much, and Teyla felt the effort of everything pulling her back towards the darkness. "What are you?"

The alien touched its chest in an all-too human gesture. "This is a Risar," it explained.

The strange name followed her into unconsciousness.

Tiny particles of dust peppered the Jumper, with the occasional larger, fist-sized lumps thudding off the hull as Sheppard guided the ship toward the object they had detected. McKay leaned over the monitor of his laptop. As they climbed into low orbit, he began to see more sensor returns, a whole stream of them lying across the scanner range in a diffuse strip.

"It's a debris field," he realized. "The gravity from the planet has a hold on it, it's dragging it apart." Rodney moved his hands to illustrate, as if he were pulling on a string between them.

"Debris from what?"

The Jumper's sensor grid obediently opened another window in on the holographic HUD and text spooled down it. Rodney nodded slowly, the data confirming what he was already certain of. "A Wraith ship."

"A Hive?"

He shook his head. "No, there's not enough mass. But too much to just be a dart. It has to be one of those scouts we detected back on Atlantis.

The Jumper slowed as it approached the chunk of wreckage. It turned slowly, catching reflected sunlight from the planet below. McKay couldn't recognize the form or function of the fragment, but it was undoubtedly Wraith in origin. It looked like a broken tooth from some monstrous beast's mouth, jagged and ragged along the bony white edges, in other places blackened by carbon scoring.

"I'm not gonna cry a river over one less Wraith warship," Sheppard noted, "but it begs the question... What did that to them?" Both men knew that the hard bio-matter hulls of Wraith craft could take a pounding before they collapsed; anything capable of crushing one into pieces was not to be taken lightly.

Rodney gave an involuntary shiver. "And is it still around?" He shook off the worrying thought and worked the computer through a spectrographic scan sequence. Spikes immediately began to appear on the electrochemical analysis display. "Energy weapons..."

"That would explain the burn marks," noted Sheppard, craning his neck to get a better look at the wreckage. "Asuran tech, maybe?"

McKay gave a slow shake of the head. "No, actually." He pointed at the readout on the screen. "The radiation pattern doesn't match any known beam weapon used by the

Replicators, or the Wraith and the Travelers, not even the Ancients… In fact, it's not like anything we've encountered in the Pegasus galaxy."

"Great," Sheppard made a face. "We have a new player, then. That's all we need."

He was still poring over the data. "Decay rate indicates this happened years ago… Maybe even decades." McKay looked up at Sheppard. "The Aegis did this. There's no other explanation."

The colonel nosed the Puddle Jumper into a different attitude, and feathered the throttle. "I'm going to move us into a higher orbit. See if you can cast a wider net with the sensors, get a better angle on what happened up here."

"Are you sure that's a good idea? I mean, if this Aegis thing is blasting ships out of the sky?"

"We have something the Wraith don't—a cloaking device."

McKay blew out a breath. "Let's hope that's enough."

When she came to again, Teyla had a firmer grip on wakefulness. She became aware that the aliens—*the Risar*—had brought her to a wide circular chamber, with an arching domed roof that mirrored the design of ship's corridors. Her mind raced; she had a vague recollection of being taken from the surface of Heruun and transported the distance to the lunar surface, some faint impression of a silver craft, a cramped interior…

She shifted, moving carefully. They had left her on the floating platform used to bring her here; and there, across the chamber, was an identical platform and on it, Ronon Dex.

He was still, only his chest rising and falling. As she watched, one of the Risar approached him and worked the healing device over blackened patches of frostbite on his skin.

There were several of the humanoids in the chamber, some of them tending to wide, inswept consoles made of bronze and copper. They manipulated shapes and panes of light appeared in the air, showing images she did not recognize and streams of angular glyphs.

She studied the Risar for long moments, their movements

and behavior. Like those they had glimpsed in the corridors, they did not correspond with one another, they simply went about their tasks, never crossing paths, always focused on their silent intention. Yet, some of them seemed different. Two of those she watched moved more slowly than the others, in the way of an elderly man whose joints were paining him. They seemed less able than the rest, and their skin tone was not the blue-green hue of the others, but a deep slate grey. They appeared, for want of a better word, *sickly*. Teyla filed the observation away for later consideration.

As she watched, a pair from the group gathered around the console closest to Ronon. With a whisper of metallic leaves, an iris aperture opened in the floor and a grey orb atop a jointed arm extended upward until it stood over the Satedan's platform. One of the Risar manipulated a control and the orb rotated and shifted, coming around on itself until it hung above Ronon's head. Teyla felt her pulse quicken, instinct warning her that whatever was to happen next, it would not be good.

Panels on the side of the orb opened to allow a forest of needle-thin probes to emerge, reaching toward Ronon's face. He murmured in his enforced slumber, unaware of the threat.

"No!" Teyla shouted, and tried to force herself from the platform where she lay, ignoring the pain in her joints and the echo of nausea. She could not bring herself to sit up; although there were no physical restraints holding her down, the Athosian woman felt a sudden increase in gravity, a great invisible weight pressing on her chest. The Risar had some form of force field trapping her in place. Teyla mustered as much effort as she could, trying to find a breaking point, but for every ounce of strength she put against the invisible confinement, it was turned back against her tenfold.

One of the Risar detached from the group and approached her. "Desist," it told her. "You may injure yourself."

"Leave him alone!" she barked. "Do not hurt him!"

The Risar glanced in the direction of Ronon. "That has never been my intention. The male will not be harmed." It cocked its head slightly. "You are greatly concerned for his wellbeing. Is he your mate?"

"He's my friend!"

"Your friend will not be damaged by the regulation process."

Regulation? The toneless way the alien said the word made Teyla's blood run cold.

"It is a safety protocol," continued the Risar. "It will prevent any further accidents or unauthorized sojourns. It is applied to all transients."

The needles reached for Ronon, adjusting their position. *The Taken sleep a long sleep and remember nothing.* Laaro's earlier words returned to her, along with a cold, sudden understanding. The docile, drone-like abductees they had come across in the corridors—this process was the means used to bring them to that state!

"Stop this!" she shouted, unable to do anything else.

The Risar peered at her and said nothing. Teyla heard the whisper of skin being pierced and reflexively looked away.

But only for a moment. A loud, abrupt roar sounded across the chamber and she turned to see Ronon Dex crying out, his back arching in agony. The Satedan's hands clawed at the orb device, tearing at it in feral rage. *The pain*, she realized, *it must have shocked him awake!*

The Risar creatures hesitated, as if they were unsure how to proceed. "You said you would not hurt him," Teyla snapped.

"This is…irregular," admitted the creature.

Ronon punched at the orb and the device withdrew—but not quickly enough. The Satedan smashed a fist into it again and the machine stuttered. Warning chimes sounded from the console.

"Rejection," stated the Risar at the console. "Physiology mismatch."

Ronon was gasping, struggling to get up and failing just as Teyla had. She called to him and he saw her. He was pale and drawn, thin streaks of blood marking his face where the orb had injected him.

Another of the creatures, one of the less able of their number, moved closer to the Satedan. "Rejection," it echoed, "this one is unusable and should be return—"

The alien never got the change to finish its sentence. With all his might, Ronon lashed out and grabbed the creature by the throat. The sheer stamina it must have taken to press through the gravity field between them was amazing.

Dex snarled in fury and the Risar's neck gave a hollow cracking sound; the creature's eyes went dull and it collapsed, falling to the metal deck.

For a long moment, Teyla expected the other Risar to react with violence in return, but they paid little interest to the fallen one of their number.

"Neutralize," said the one at the console. It touched a control and a flicker of blue-white light enveloped Ronon. He managed to match gazes with Teyla for one final moment before he went slack and fell unconscious once again. Another Risar touched a control on the floating platform and guided Dex away, off through a low doorway across the chamber. After a moment, almost as an afterthought, one of the creatures gathered up the dead Risar and carried it into an antechamber.

Teyla glared at the alien that had spoken to her. "Where are you taking him?" The term 'rejection' carried with it the scent of something ominous and final. The Athosian woman had visions of Ronon being vented to space as if he were nothing more than waste material.

Her answer was a shifting of the platform that she lay upon. With growing apprehension, she tried to shrink back as the floating table moved to occupy the same position as Ronon's had. The orb hovered nearby, another of the Risar examining it for damage.

"I will not submit to you!" she shouted, fighting to keep a tremor from her voice. "You will have to reject me too!"

The Risar that had spoken glanced at its twin beside the console. "Deep scan. There may be issue with the female as well."

"Acknowledged," came the reply.

The orb hove into place over Teyla's head and halted. A thin slice of laser light issued from a slot on the surface of the sphere and traveled the length of her body; where it touched her she felt a peculiar tingle in her flesh. The sensor beam halted over her belly and her breath caught in her throat.

"Anomaly," reported the Risar at the console. She was certain she could detect an air of surprise in the alien's words. "Unexpected complexity detected."

The other Risar moved into her line of sight, watching her. "You are pregnant."

"Yes." There seemed little point in hiding the fact.

"There is more," continued the other creature. "Traces of genetic modification across scan reading datasets. Correlation match with alternate DNA source."

The first Risar blinked, as if it were thinking. "You are a human. Yet you possess a quanta of genetic material sourced from the species colloquially known as 'Wraith'. This is an anomaly." It leaned closer. "Explain."

She saw an opportunity. "Release me first."

The Risar didn't consider her demand worth answering. "I have never encountered this irregularity before. I wish to know more."

"As long as you hold me as your prisoner," she spat, "I will give you nothing!"

Again, the alien made the strange quizzical motion of its head. "You are not a prisoner," it explained, as if it were speaking to a particularly slow child. "You and the others have been brought here to help me. When tasks are completed, you will be returned."

"You are the Aegis, then," Teyla retorted.

"Aegis." The Risar repeated the word. "I have been addressed by the term before. It is not entirely incorrect."

A low tone sounded through the chamber, and at once every Risar in the room stopped what they were doing. Teyla shifted on the floating platform to follow them as they moved as one to the middle of the chamber.

A dash of white light flickered in the air over their heads and a holographic panel unfolded, streaming with more glyphs. The text was unlike the writing of the Earth people or the Ancients; it reminded the Athosian of the angular footprints made by birds. The writing shimmered and was replaced by an exterior view. Heruun and its rings lay to one side of the display, and beyond there was nothing but the black of space... Teyla shifted again, the gravity field pressing down hard on her as she turned in place, craning her neck.

A reticule swept across the holo-screen and circled a fast-moving dot. It had to be a ship; it was drifting right and left in a zigzag course, gradually closing on the larger moon.

Hope bloomed in her thoughts, but Teyla was afraid to form the words she wanted to say in case she was mistaken; but then the screen shimmered and shifted again, magnifying the image. There, clear and unmistakable, was the barrel-shaped form of a Puddle Jumper. Fear and elation pulled at her in equal measure; suddenly the chance for rescue was very real—but at the same time she had no way to communicate with the ship, no way to tell them where she was, or to warn them of the dangers of the Risar.

A voice issued out of the air; it was the same voice all the Risar spoke with. "*New priority task. Isolate unidentified craft and capture for disassembly and repurposing.*"

The aliens broke apart from their group, ignoring the work they had been conducting, and Teyla found herself being carried away once more, back down along the endless, featureless corridors.

The chorus of beeps from Rodney's computer drew Sheppard's attention immediately. "Got something?"

McKay gave a slow nod, his fingers dancing over the keyboard of the silver laptop. "A particle trace, leading away from the planet." The scientist's brows knitted for a moment. "Yeah, I got it. It's faded almost to nothing, but it's a trail. From a ship, most likely."

"Leading where?" Sheppard turned the Puddle Jumper to angle up and away from Heruun, the sweep of the glittering ice rings falling below the prow of the ship.

Rodney glanced up and pointed toward the larger of the planet's two moons, now drifting into the middle of the canopy's view. "Right there, in fact."

The colonel eased the throttle control up a notch and the Jumper broke orbit, crossing into cislunar space without a bump. Within moments, the ship's scanners registered something moving up from the surface of the airless moon.

"Cloaking device!" Rodney insisted, his voice rising an octave at the sight of the new arrivals.

Sheppard agreed. "Yeah, good call." He tapped a control pad and a faint ripple of warped light glittered through the canopy as the Jumper became invisible.

There were three objects, discernible as bright metallic shapes as they closed the distance. McKay's gaze flicked between the laptop and the viewscreen. "Wait. No. What?"

"I need a bit better intel than that, McKay. What are they? Darts?"

"Not even close," Rodney replied. "Scans are coming back garbled, like they're being partially reflected off of… Well, *something*." He sucked in air through his teeth. "This is a whole different style of technology."

"So unless the Wraith stole themselves some new hardware—which, knowing them, isn't impossible—we're looking at something new. The Aegis." Sheppard could see the alien craft more clearly now, moving in line formation. They were strange shapes, vaguely triangular in cross-section, but curved like an inverted dish. *Or a saucer.* He blinked as the odd thought popped up in his mind

What happened next was so quick that he almost missed it; in total violation of the laws of physics, the three ships broke apart in three different directions, each one moving away at a ninety-degree angle to its initial course with no loss of speed or any sign of a thruster discharge. A heartbeat later, great radial plumes of energy bloomed on the Jumper's HUD, expanding out from each of the craft.

"What the hell…?" Sheppard's pilot training took over and he automatically jinked, throwing the ship into an evasion pattern.

More pulses followed the first waves. The sky above the Heruuni moon was rapidly filling with the discharges. "They know we're here…" said McKay suddenly.

"They're beating the bushes," said the colonel. "Like a surface ship using sonar to flush out a submarine."

"I'd rather not be flushed by anything," McKay retorted.

"You may have a point there, Rodney," Sheppard offered, vectoring the Jumper around. He upped the throttle a notch more, navigating via the HUD, trying to thread the ship between the expanding balloons of energy. The Jumper turned as fast as he could make it, but against the staggered, irregular motions of the alien ships it was a whale among sharks.

Another trio of pulses throbbed across the darkness and enveloped the Jumper before Sheppard could turn away. The instant they touched the hull, a wash of crackling sparks raced down the length of the cabin. The colonel cursed as he snatched his hands back from the flight controls, and at his side McKay gave a yelp as his laptop vomited smoke and crashed.

"Sonar, my butt!" Rodney snapped. "That was some kind of the disruption field!" The acrid smell of flash-burned plastic filled the cockpit.

"We lost the cloak," Sheppard saw the glowing glyph on the console blinking its shutdown warning. The other systems stuttered and rebooted; when the short range scanner came up, it showed three targets converging on the Jumper's flight path at high velocity.

The alien ships fell toward the Puddle Jumper, disruption beams stabbing out into the dark, tracking like searchlights toward their target. The Jumper turned into a spiraling course, crossing through the fire zone and emerging safely by only the narrowest of margins.

The triangular craft broke apart once more, the formation shattering. A single ship continued the pursuit while the other two cut sharp-edged courses through the dark, moving ahead and to the fore of the Jumper in an attempt to box it in and cut off any chance of escape.

The Ancient ship's outriggers flared, the glow of the twin thruster grids a bright yellow-white. It twisted into a hard kick-turn, coming about to face the craft behind it. Compared to the uncanny abilities of the alien vessels, however, it was a slow and languid maneuver.

Without pause, the alien ship was suddenly moving backwards, away from the Jumper; with no visible means of determining which end of the craft was prow or stern, no obvious engine pods or other identifying structures, the vessel was a lethal enigma.

Behind the Jumper, its two sister ships came in like loosed arrows.

"They're almost on us," said Rodney. "Now's the time for some of that impressive Han Solo pilot stuff. Any time now, Sheppard. *Any time.*"

"Quiet," the colonel growled. He sent a mental command to the controls in his hands and from the rear of the Jumper came the *smack-whump* sound of the drone launchers. Twin streaks of yellow shot away, spinning along corkscrew paths toward the fleeing alien craft. The first drone closed to impact range, but suddenly found itself tumbling through empty space as the target abruptly changed from a horizontal flight path to a vertical one. The second drone looped in and detonated, switching at the last second to a proximity fuse. A globe of fusion fire expanded outward and clipped one apex of the fleeing craft; it flipped over and began to zigzag, a plume of gas crystals trailing out behind it.

"Hit but no kill," Sheppard said aloud.

"Two more—" began McKay.

"I'm on it," he replied, flinching as a disrupter beam flashed across the Jumper's blunt nose. Sheppard tuned out everything else and let himself feel the genetic connection to the Ancient ship's flight controls; at times it was almost as if the Jumper could respond to him before he had fully formed a thought in his brain, but it wasn't something he could just *force* to happen. It had to come through instinct, through pure reflex.

"Sheppard!" Out beyond the canopy, the surface of the moon was looming as the engagement brought them ever closer to Heruun's primary satellite.

"Hush." In his mind's eye he saw the two alien attackers closing the distance, the beam weapons lashing out. The colonel's hands worked the controls, letting his training take over. *Don't think about it, John, just do it.*

In a split-second he cut forward thrust and applied it in

reverse, dropping the Jumper's velocity from blindingly fast to almost nothing. The gravity generators inside the cabin whined as they tried to bleed off the energy state change without smearing Sheppard and McKay over the inside of the canopy.

The alien ships were quick and they reacted, vectoring away in opposite directions; but that was what Sheppard wanted them to do. This time, four drones were unleashed after the ship to the port and before it could jink away, the missiles bored into it and exploded. The blast wave clipped the Jumper and the ship bucked like a loosed bronco.

McKay gripped the console in front of him, white-knuckled. "Gee, do you think you could get a little closer to the fireball next time?" His words dripped acid sarcasm. "I felt that! I could have burned my eyebrows off!"

Sheppard was already applying power to the drives as the undamaged craft came back toward them; wary now, it flicked to the right and left, up and down, while still maintaining a lock at the six o'clock position behind the Puddle Jumper.

The colonel searched for the ship that had taken the near-hit and dove at it. As he predicted, it was sluggish, the sharp, gravity-defying course changes it had made before now reduced to twitching, stuttering motions that skidded across the black sky.

His eyes narrowed. "You're not going anywhere, buddy," he said quietly. At the last second, Sheppard released two more drones and pivoted the Jumper; it was a risk, but his options were shrinking by the second, and he knew that the alien ships only had to be lucky once to turn the Jumper into a drifting, frozen wreck.

The drones hit the damaged ship and destroyed it. The resultant flash of fusion discharge flared in the dark and buffeted the Jumper. Sheppard turned into a jousting head-to-head with the last alien ship, riding the shockwave. He gambled that the detonation would fog any sensors on the other craft long enough for him to gain the advantage.

He was right; but he was wrong.

The alien ship did something unexpected, veering sharply away from the blast—but not toward open space. Instead, it swept past the Puddle Jumper so closely that Sheppard had a momentary glimpse of his own face, a distorted reflection off the silvery triangular hull as it flashed by.

The alien craft blindly clipped the Jumper's port side outrigger and ripped it away with a concussive screech. Power rose and fell and the Ancient vessel moaned like an injured animal. Sheppard flinched as a spike of sympathetic pain shocked him. The enemy ship vanished behind them, coming apart from the force of the collision; the Jumper was more hardy.

Outside the canopy, the black of space became the washedout grey of lunar regolith. Sheppard cursed as the controls refused to answer his inputs.

"We're going down!" said Rodney, finding his voice again.

"Yeah," said the colonel, through gritted teeth. "I think that's a given."

The Risar remained mute as it carried Teyla back to the holding chamber. The cell could have been the very one she and Ronon had been deposited in upon their arrival; it seemed as if every chamber in the alien ship was constructed from a modular palette of identical components. The restraint field snapped off and she gasped in a breath of air, but before she could react the platform tilted to dislodge her, and she staggered to stop herself falling over. If she had considered it, Teyla might have had a chance to try a second escape attempt before the door slid silently shut, but her attention was taken by a more immediate matter.

On one of the formless sleeping pads lay Ronon Dex, his skin waxy, his breathing shallow. There was a water dispenser nozzle fitted into an alcove on the far wall and she cupped a little in her hands, bringing it to him. His eyes flickered open and he drank.

"Teyla?" He blinked at her, as if he was waking from a deep slumber. The Satedan's brow furrowed, half in annoyance, half in confusion. "Where…?"

"The cell, again." she explained. "They tried to do something to you…"

"Who?" Ronon winced, as if trying to remember was painful to him. "We… Should be on Atlantis…"

"Atlantis? Ronon, we're on Heruun. We *were* on Heruun," she corrected herself, frowning again. "The Risar captured us."

"What?" He shook his head. "I don't... I can't think straight..." Ronon's hands tightened into claws and he attempted to pull himself up to a sitting position. When Teyla helped him, he tried to push her away, but there was no strength in him. It was a troubling thing to witness; Ronon was one of the strongest, most vital men Teyla had ever met, but now here he was, weak and vulnerable, laid low by the technology of the Risar.

"Colonel Sheppard is searching for us," she told him. "He'll come for us."

Ronon managed a nod; even the effort of that seemed to drain him.

With a cloth from her pocket, she dabbed at the drying streaks of blood on his face. As she did so, a new and troubling thought occurred to her, a moment of unpleasant clarity as she realized what the Satedan's condition reminded her of; the people in Kullid's sick lodge. Weakened and disoriented, touched by the malady of the Aegis.

"Need to rest," Ronon husked. "Just a while. Tell Sheppard... I'll be there."

Teyla nodded, fighting down her fears. "I'll tell him."

McKay didn't really remember the moment when the Puddle Jumper actually hit the surface of Heruun's primary moon. Perhaps that might have been a good thing, in retrospect, maybe some basic animal part of his hindbrain taking pity on the rest of him, blotting out the bone-crushing hell of the impact so he would be spared the trauma.

But he remembered what the screeching meant. The high-pitched, screaming whistle coming from the hairline crack slowly making its way down the short axis of the canopy glass. Beside him, Sheppard was lolling over the pilot's station, blinking away the shock of what could only be called a 'landing' by the most generous of critics.

"Any one you can walk away from," he muttered.

"Congratulate yourself later," Rodney told him. "We've got a big problem." McKay vaulted from his seat, discarding his useless, still-smoking laptop, and scrambled toward the back cabin of the Jumper. He pulled at equipment lockers, snatching open doors and not finding what he wanted, panic threatening to rise up and overtake him.

And then he found them, in the long footlocker beneath the wire-frame bench. Sheppard came down the canted deck toward him, his expression grim. "Controls are a mess," said the colonel. "and the mid-hatch is off line. When that canopy breaks, we'll lose all the air in here."

"I saw. Here." Rodney thrust a hard plastic container into the other man's hands. He didn't wait for Sheppard to open it; he took another identical case and flipped the latches, dumping the contents on the deck—a plastic fishbowl helmet, a backpack and an oversuit of bright orange material.

"A spacesuit?" Sheppard asked. "I didn't think Jumpers carried—"

"Not as standard, no," Rodney was speaking quickly, talking so his mind wouldn't have the chance to catch up to the idea of how screwed they were. "But I always make sure they're on board a Jumper any time I'm on it." He made a flapping gesture with his hand. "Be prepared, right?"

The pitch of the air leak was growing deeper by the second as the crack widened, and it was enough to encourage them both to talk less and work faster. The suits were lightweight experimental models developed by Stargate Command for use aboard starships, low-duration quick-deployment rigs that had half the mass of the NASA legacy gear they typically used.

Rodney felt a flash of claustrophobia as he twisted the lexan helmet into place over his head. He didn't want to think about what 'low duration' meant in terms of how much air you got before you choked to death.

Sensing movement, he turned to Sheppard and realized belatedly that he couldn't hear what the other man was saying. The colonel grabbed him and the bubbles of the suit helmets clanked together.

"I said hang on to something!"

McKay had enough time to see the canopy become a spider web and then disintegrate; the next second they were in the middle of a hurricane.

CHAPTER SEVEN

"Come in, doctor." Sam Carter looked up from the data screen she held in her hand and beckoned Jennifer Keller into her office. Keller also had one of the ubiquitous portable screens that were in use everywhere throughout Atlantis, but she held it close to her chest as if she was unwilling to share its contents with the rest of the world.

"Colonel," Keller said, with a nod. Sam indicated a chair across from her desk and the doctor took it. Carter preferred to stand when she was thinking—something about being on her feet made it easier to get the cogs whirring, and she'd practically worn a path around her old lab back at Cheyenne Mountain—but she had to force herself to take a seat now, if only to put the doctor at her ease. Ever since Keller had returned from M9K-153 under Colonel Sheppard's orders, she'd been uncharacteristically withdrawn, remaining in the medical lab despite the fact that she was supposed to be on a mandatory post-mission stand-down.

Carter saw the look in Keller's eyes at once, and she understood. *The mission isn't over for her, not yet. She hasn't let go of it.* The look was a familiar one; she'd seen it in the mirror enough times in the past.

"Want some coffee?" She poured one for herself and offered the other woman a steel mug.

Keller gave a wan smile. "I could use a little."

They both shared a sip. "You wanted to speak to me," said Carter.

Keller nodded and held up the data screen. "I want to show you my preliminary findings from Heruun."

Sam nodded. She'd already debriefed Sergeant Rush on his return and got the high points of the situation on the planet from Major Lorne, who had remained on-site. The continued MIA status of Ronon Dex and Teyla Emmagan was deeply troubling, and it threw into question every aspect of the mission. Carter pushed aside a moment of self-doubt, as a voice in the back of her head threatened to blame the situation on her tight hold on mission security.

She had seen the images Keller had captured with her camera, the troubling stills of the makeshift hospital in the Herunni rebel camp, the sick and the dying. Doctor Cullen and her team had been ready and waiting with the gear for a full biological screening when Keller and the others had returned, but they had found no evidence of anything communicable. Carter took the screen from Keller's outstretched hand and tabbed through the pages. "What am I looking at here, doctor?" A single word jumped out at her and she took a sharp intake of breath.

"Nanites," said Jennifer, doubtless guessing from Sam's reaction what she had seen. "Molecular machines, or whatever you want to call them. That's the source of this so-called sickness on Heruun."

"The Replicators did this?"

Keller shook her head. "It doesn't match the signature of Asuran technology. I've dealt with that before, I'd know it if I saw it. Not Ancient origin, either. Whoever or whatever the Aegis is, this means they're pretty advanced."

Carter chewed her lip. "We've encountered several species out here and in our home galaxy that use this sort of mechanism," she noted. "Putting aside who made them for a moment, the more important question is *what are they doing it for?*"

"I can't be certain, but I don't think this is deliberate. The illness, I mean." Keller hesitated, as if she were uncertain about giving voice to something that was just a gut feeling. Sam said nothing and let her find her way; as a commander she had learned early on to let her people trust their instincts. "The blood I drew from the multiple abductees on Heruun shows concentrations of inert nanite devices collecting in their bodies. I think these things might function as markers of some kind, at least on one level."

"Like a radio tag on a wild animal." Carter considered this for a moment. "When this Aegis wants to abduct someone for a second or third time, it scans for the markers to locate them."

"More like taking them for the ninth or tenth time," Keller corrected, "and the quantity is much higher for those who have been taken the most often." She indicated a readout on the screen, "I think the sickness is caused by these nanites crossing the blood-brain barrier. It's causing an ongoing degenerative condition, most likely a breakdown of certain neurotransmitter chemicals in the brain."

"Okay, so it's not an infectious disease, it's the result of deliberate exposure to this technology. Could it be some sort of attack on the Heruuni?"

Keller shook her head again, brushing hair from her eyes. "Unlikely. I'd say this is an unplanned side-effect of something else. What that something else is, I can't tell you." She sighed. "We might be able to decode the nanite programming, figure out their core function but that's not my area of expertise. I have no idea how long it would take."

Sam ran a critical eye over the scans of the nano-machines; the tiny, molecule-sized devices were a double-edged sword that could be programmed just as easily to cure diseases or deconstruct matter. "I'll take a look at this. I've had plenty of up-close experience with Replicators…" She gave a wry smile. "More than I'd like."

The doctor frowned. "Colonel, I have to make this clear to you. The local healer I met on 153, Kullid. He has nothing approaching the level of medical knowledge that we do, and he's the only one working to find a cure for his people. He's a smart guy but he's going to fail without my help. Our help," she corrected.

"You're sure you could find a solution?"

"With your help and Doctor McKay's, I think there's an outside chance. I could take a medical team back to Heruun, and Rodney's already there, so—"

Carter held up a hand to interrupt her. "If what Major Lorne tells me is anything to go on, M9K-153 is in the middle of an armed factional conflict. I already have two key team members on the missing list. You're asking me to let you go back in harm's way, and not just you but other civilian staff, plus another detail of men to act as your security." She shook her head. "I can't do that. Not right now. I'm not willing to let anyone else gate back until we have better intel on what's going on there."

Keller's face darkened. "And in the meantime, people are dying. People we can save."

She met the other woman's gaze straight on. "I know that. But I'm not willing to add to the numbers. Your request is denied, Doctor. For the moment."

Keller put the steel mug down firmly on the desk. "We can't turn our backs."

"We're not going to. Take whatever people can be spared in your department. This city has some of the most advanced medical technology ever created. Use it."

They said that in space, no one could hear you scream; but in the confines of the helmet, Rodney McKay could hear pretty damned well. He could hear his own tight gasps as he gulped in breaths of air, the thudding rush of his blood in his ears. He followed Sheppard out on to the lunar surface, skidding a little on the rimes of oxygen ice that had formed on the Puddle Jumper's drop-ramp. As his boots hit the powdery grey moon dust, he had a fleeting, almost giddy thought about Armstrong's famous touchdown speech. *One small step for McKay,* he told himself, *one run-like-hell for Rodneykind.*

Sheppard pivoted ahead of him and pointed up into the black sky. Turning, the scientist saw glitters of light low toward the horizon. More ships, he realized. More of them, coming this way, looking for where the Jumper had augured in.

McKay cast around, scanning the stark lunar landscape for anything that could serve as cover. A long, shallow trench led away from him, a line cut through the dust where the Ancient ship had landed flat and spent its forward momentum scraping to a slow and ignominious halt. His eyes came to rest on a wide slab-like stone canted at a low angle away from the hard glare of Heruun's sun. Beneath it, there was nothing by black shadows.

"Sheppard!" He grabbed John's arm and pulled at him. "We can take shelter there!"

The colonel looked in the direction he was pointing and then mouthed the question *Cave?* through the gold-coated face of his helmet. Rodney nodded; okay, so it wasn't actually a cave per se, but without an operable radio communications link between the two of them, he wasn't going to stop to explain otherwise.

Running wasn't easy in the low gravity of the airless moon; twice McKay stumbled and had to hop-skip-jump to stop from falling flat on his face. His breath pounded in his chest and each cold gasp he took in tasted of stale plastic. Rodney tried not to think about how little air the emergency suit's small backpack contained. He ducked low and found space under the canted rock, in the deeps of the shade.

Sheppard followed him in, one gloved hand reaching out to steady himself against the stone. McKay caught his wrist and stopped him in time; lying in the direct, unfiltered sunlight, the temperature of the rock was enough that it could have burned through the glove's padding in an instant.

Crouching in the hollow, McKay could feel the warmth of the star-baked stone over their heads. He tapped his suit helmet against Sheppard's. "The heat from the rock might be enough to blind any sensors," he said in a rush, "we can hide until they buzz off!"

"Might?" Sheppard echoed.

"Here they come," Rodney tried to shrink back into the cover as much as he could, careful not to snag the lightweight suit on any sharp rocks. Sheppard lay flat, watching the downed Jumper.

Three more of the triangular ships came to a halt in a triad formation above the crashed vessel. They had to be scanning for signs of life, he guessed, trying to determine if the Jumper's troublesome crew had made it down in one piece or died on impact.

What are they going to do? McKay asked himself. Perhaps they would obliterate the wreck if they came up empty, or maybe one of the craft would land and whatever passed for their crew would come out to get a closer look.

But that was not what happened; instead, rods of green light issued out from the craft, connecting each to the next in a frame of glowing color. A field of exotic energy grew between them, expanding to envelop the Puddle Jumper, and in the next moment it shifted, rising into the vacuum. Glittering fragments of broken glass and pieces of litter and debris thrown out by the decompression went with it, hovering in an uncanny cloud. Moving as one rigid formation, the triangular ships carried the wreck away in silence, skimming over the pinnacles of the lunar terrain.

Both men watched their best hopes for survival vanish toward the horizon, the ungainly flight of craft homing in on a pair of tall, blade-like mesas.

McKay saw Sheppard swear silently. After a long moment, the colonel leaned closer so they could talk. "How much oh-two you got?"

Rodney looked at the oxygen meter on his wrist. "Just over three-quarters. Is that good?"

"If you don't take panic breaths, yeah."

"Oh, right," he retorted. "What kind of breaths should I take, then? Seeing as we are now in a situation to which panic would be a very legitimate response?"

"Give me a break, McKay. We're not dead yet." The two men scrambled from their concealment and stood, the full glare of the sunlight hard against them.

Rodney leaned in again as Sheppard peered in the direction that the alien ships had come from, and returned to. "What are you, uh, thinking?"

"Those ships are short range, I'm guessing. That means there's a base of operations up here." He pointed. "More specifically, over that way."

"So, what, we just start walking and hope they've left a window open when we get there? *If* we get there?"

Sheppard eyed him. "You got a better idea?"

As much as it pained him, McKay had to admit that he did not.

The scientist hunched over the scoutship's sensor console, the glow of the screen casting ghostly light over his face. "It is difficult to report with any certainty," he began.

The commander let out a low hiss of irritation from between his needle-sharp teeth. His tolerance for this lower caste fool was drawing down to almost nothing. "Tell me what you see."

"With the sensors in passive mode, there is a large margin of error." And still he did not answer. "In addition, the energy reflection from the planet's ring system—"

That was enough. The Wraith commander grabbed the scientist by the scruff of his neck and yanked him away from the console. "I did not ask for explanations or excuses. I asked you what happened out there." He gestured at the hull and the space beyond it. "Now speak!"

The scientist nodded jerkily. "Of course." He tried to compose himself as he was released. "The craft that left the planet appears to be one of Ancient design, likely from the city of Atlantis."

"You are telling me what I already know. The protectors! Did they destroy it?"

"It would seem not." The scientist's hands knit together as he framed his next words. "The ship survived an engagement with the alien craft, but it was damaged. It reached the limit of our detection as it fell into the gravity well of the larger moon."

"What is the probability that the craft was obliterated? Give me your estimate." The commander pressed a bony finger into the scientist's chest.

"Given our clan's previous experience with the Atlantean ships, I would say survivability is quite possible. The craft are resilient. Their pilots have skill."

The Wraith turned and stalked away across the deck. "We have the answer to one question then, at the very least."

The scientist nodded again. "Indeed. Now we know that this protector is not our old foe, not an Ancient."

The commander glanced over his shoulder. "And with that, our circumstance becomes more dangerous. If the alien presence here was the Great Enemy, then we would at least know how to fight them… But now? Now we are fighting an unknown." He paused, musing, wondering after the fate of his kindred, killed or captured by the threat that lurked in this system. "For the moment we must continue to observe."

"The… The Queen will wish to know what we have learned."

"And she will. But not yet." He gave a nod in return. "*Not yet.*"

Sheppard did what he'd been taught to do in desert navigation training, and chose a landmark to act as his waypoint—the two tall mesas where the alien ships had headed. He walked so that McKay was always in his peripheral vision, and he in Rodney's, in case one of them put a foot in the lunar equivalent of a rabbit hole and took a tumble. With no radio, there was no way to cry out for help. He blinked away sweat from his eyes and grimaced. If they got back to Atlantis after this little sojourn, he decided he would make a point of sending the technicians back at Vandenberg his precise opinions about the shortcomings of the low duration spacesuits.

But the closer they got to the twin towers of rock, the more Sheppard felt a crawling sensation in the pit of his gut, a feel for the not-quite-rightness of what he saw before him. Shaped like the ends of blunt blades, the two peaks were wrong. They were too uniform, too evenly cut to be natural formations. If he didn't know better, the colonel would have imagined they'd been carved by the action of wind, a pair of colossal vertical fins extending up from the pale sea of regolith.

They crested a low hill, trudging rather than walking, and Sheppard flicked a glance at McKay, who gave him a listless nod of the head. Both men stopped and took stock of where they were. A wall of grey rose up in front of them, something that at first glance would have looked like moon rock; but like the towers, it seemed out of place, too regular to be true. Sheppard had the sudden impression of something beneath the sand, his eyes picking out hard, curved lines. A wall was ranged out in front of them, camouflaged to match the terrain.

The only thing that broke the illusion of uniformity was the body lying face down in the powdery dust.

Sheppard knelt next to the corpse and a shadow fell over him, cast by McKay. The body wore the distinctive earth-toned robes of the Heruuni locals, but they sparkled where starlight caught a thin patina of ice across the sun-bleached cloth. There was no visible protection of any kind, no suit, no breather gear, nothing. The colonel turned the figure over and the bloated, flash-frozen face of the man stared back up at him, his eyes a dark mass of color where his blood vessels had ruptured. There were tiny, pea-sized crystals littering the moon dust all around him, and with a tic of disgust Sheppard realized that they had to be frozen droplets of blood, expelled from the dead man's lungs when he stumbled out into the hard vacuum.

McKay's shadow moved and Sheppard looked up as the other man crossed to the stone wall, laying his palms flat on it, feeling left and right. Doubtless the same thought had occurred to Rodney as it had to John; this poor fool had to have come through a doorway nearby, and that meant a way in... Into whatever this place was.

Sheppard glanced at his wrist and his eyes narrowed. His air meter was barely showing green anymore, almost all of the indicator band a livid red-for-empty. McKay had to be in the same boat, if not worse; and if they couldn't find a way in... *Then we'll end up like the moonwalker here.*

Rodney was down on one knee, frantically pawing at a piece of wall. Sheppard bounced over to him and saw he was digging white dust from an alcove. Inside he glimpsed an oval depression covered in symbols. A hatch control. He stepped aside to give the scientist all the light he needed, and found himself panting. In flight school, Sheppard had experienced the horrible sensation of oxygen deprivation during pilot training, and he felt the first twinges of it now. If this didn't work...

He forced the thought away. "Be positive, John," he said aloud inside the clammy helmet.

A train of lights appeared in the alcove and Rodney silently pumped his fist. When the hatch dropped away, it was the best sight he'd seen in days, and he propelled McKay through the low entrance, following him in.

It was only as the airlock door rose back again that it occurred to him he had no idea if the Aegis breathed the same kind of air as human beings.

She wasn't certain about the moment when she fell asleep; it just came upon her before she could be aware of it. One moment, Teyla was in the cell, resting her back against the steel wall, watching Ronon, and the next...

She was here. There was no sense of transition for her. She stood in a new chamber, the design little different from all the others she had come across inside the Risar complex, a hard-edged pool of light cast around her. In the shadows, a number of the aliens moved around, some carrying devices the function of which she couldn't guess at. A single creature hovered close by, curling one of the strange glass eggs in its clawed hand.

Had they waited for her to succumb to fatigue before they brought her here, let her sleepwalk to them? It was a troubling thought. From what she had heard from the Heruuni, it seemed the Risar—and the Aegis, if they were not one and the same—could take control of a human's flesh as easily as Teyla could leaf through the pages of a book.

The alien studied her openly, not with a predatory manner but with an odd mix of confusion and intrigue. They seemed fascinated by her.

She faced it head-on. "Why have you brought me here?" A sudden, chilling thought occurred to her. "Where is Ronon Dex?"

Another Risar, this one moving slowly and awkwardly, came into the halo of light. "Your companion is uninjured."

She grimaced. "Not so. Whatever you did to him, his body is rejecting it! Just like the others on Heruun!"

The aliens paused, as if they were considering this information. The first spoke again, moving around her. "Who are you?" it asked. "What are you?"

"I am Teyla Emmagan of Athos," she snapped, "and I have powerful friends. They are searching for me!"

"Athos," repeated the sickly Risar. "I do not know that designation. Filed for storage and later cross-reference."

A holographic pane hazed into being in the shadows, casting patterns of light across the floor. Teyla saw the blurred image of a Puddle Jumper there, as if captured in the middle of a high-speed turn. "Are you familiar with the design of this craft?" The Risar cocked its head. "Do you understand its operating principles?"

"I have never seen that before in my life," she retorted. The image dissipated; if the Risar was aware of her lie, it made no comment about it.

"You have hybrid bio-matter within you, sub-group racial ident 'Wraith'," continued the other alien. "I have never seen this before. You are of interest. How was this done? Will it affect your progeny?" It pointed at Teyla's belly with the elliptical device.

She shook her head, part of her wanting to push away the question the Risar asked, the very question that kept Teyla awake at night back on Atlantis. "Who are *you*?" she barked, taking the offensive. "What gives you the right to come to this world and abduct innocent people from their homes? What are you doing to them?" Her voice rose to a shout.

"I am not here to cause harm," said the second Risar. It turned its dark eyes to face her. "But it is important. Because of the work. It is necessary."

The inner hatch sighed open and Sheppard was out first, a Wraith stunner in one hand, panning it left and right down the shadowed corridor. Neither he nor Rodney had been able to grab anything more than the most basic kit before they had exited the Puddle Jumper—and that meant no P90s, no radios, just a pistol each and little else. McKay still had a handheld Ancient scanner, but that was it. He felt practically naked without his laptop.

The hatch closed behind them, the emergency suits in a discarded pile in the airlock. Sheppard hadn't waited for Rodney to run a toxicity test on the air; the colonel had just ripped off his helmet and taken a lungful. Once it was clear he wasn't going to turn blue and die, McKay had done the same. He had to admit, being able to breath freely again was a huge relief—even if the air in here did smell of ozone and burnt metal.

"No alarms," said Sheppard quietly. "Guess they don't know we're here."

McKay peered at the walls, poking at a carbon-scored swath of burn damage. "By the looks of this, there could be good reason for that. Looks like there was a fire, or something, maybe it knocked out some of the internal sensors."

"Let's be thankful for small mercies, then." Sheppard edged forward. "So. What now?"

"You're asking me?" Rodney blinked. "This was your plan. If I had my way, we'd still be on Heruun."

"I mean, which way?" He pointed up and down the corridor.

Rodney hesitated for a moment, consulting the scanner. "Readings on this are a bit wacky," he confessed. "Might be something in the construction affecting the device…" He peered at the display. "Okay. I'm reading life signs in that direction," He nodded to the right, where the corridor began a gentle rise. "One human and two that are, uh, not. I think." He amended hastily.

"That's very reassuring," Sheppard said dryly. "Stick close and keep your eyes open. We're deep in Indian Country here. There's no telling what's waiting for us around the next corner,"

"Just for once, it might be nice to find an alien stronghold that was well signposted," McKay noted as they walked. "I'm just saying. All these corridors look pretty much the same…"

"Yeah…" The colonel's voice trailed off and he halted. "You know something? I've seen this before."

"What, the lone heroes creeping into the bowels of the scary alien base? I saw that movie too." He shuddered. "Didn't the scientist guy get eaten by something?"

"The walls, McKay," Sheppard replied. "The design. C'mon, take a look around. It looks familiar."

Rodney hesitated and took a moment to study the structure of the corridor; and Sheppard's observation *clicked* in his head. "Whoa. Yes. If you look past the burn damage, all the missing panels…"

"Tell me I'm wrong. Tell me this place isn't what I think it is."

McKay's stomach knotted. "There's only one way to be sure."

"You must understand," said the sickly Risar, "everything I have done has been for a greater good. I regret any impairment that results from my intervention, and I have attempted to minimize it."

Teyla's lip curled. "I do not accept that. What you have done here is wrong. Nothing can excuse it!"

"I have protected the Heruuni in return for their assistance—" said the other alien.

She glared at the creature. "But did you ever ask their permission? You treat intelligent beings like animals!"

"There was no other option open to me," said the first Risar. "When my starship crash-landed here, I had no choice. The humans were the only tools I could use to repair the damage."

"Starship?"

The other alien touched it's chest. "These Risar have such short life spans, and they perform poorly in adverse conditions." It pointed at the other one. "That unit will soon perish. The cellular degradation cannot be stemmed, despite my attempts at hybridization."

"I cannot continue to create new Risar." The sickly one's head bobbed. "Stocks of genetic material are low. You must understand. Without the humans, I am stranded."

Teyla's mind raced. Every Risar she had encountered spoke as if it were alone; each one said 'I' instead of 'We'. Their voices were all a uniform pitch—and now, with all this talk of 'genetic material' and 'creation of units', she found herself wondering what kind of beings they really were. "You… You are all of a single mind," she breathed, the understanding stark in her thoughts. "You share the same consciousness."

"The Risar are tools," came the answer. "A basic, primitive vessel for my intention. A mechanism, Teyla Emmagan, nothing more."

She understood that what she was looking at was no more

than a proxy, a mask for the real intelligence behind everything that was happening on Heruun. "Then what is the Aegis?" she demanded.

"It is only a name, it is not who I am." The other Risar was about to speak again, but an abrupt, strident bell sounded through the chamber. Teyla recognized an alarm signal when she heard one.

"What is happening?" she asked.

The sickly Risar glanced at her with its rheumy eyes. "There are intruders aboard my vessel."

The corridor walls passed him by in a blur. Ronon pulled against his captors, but he had no energy to resist them. His legs felt like they were made of water, and it was all he could do to keep himself on his feet. Reaching deep within, he drew on reservoirs of strength, forcing every final iota of will to the surface. "Get...off... *me!*"

On any other day, the strike would have been flawless; instead it was clumsy. But he was Ronon Dex, and that meant it still worked. The Satedan's balled fist collided with the side of the skull of the Risar holding his right arm, and staggered the alien. It released him, letting him use his momentum to swing around and pull the second creature grasping him off-balance.

His head was swimming and he over-extended. Instead of laying out the other Risar, he dragged it down to the deck, and the two of them collapsed in an untidy heap. Ronon kicked out hard and struck meat and bone; the other alien grunted and stumbled, clawing at him.

Everything was an effort now, the damnable weakness in his limbs turning each move he made into a laborious task. He felt as if he weighed ten times as much as normal. He was lead-heavy, sluggish and slow. It made him furious.

Where were they taking him? It hardly mattered. All that was important was to find Teyla, rescue her. It had been his mistake before, his rash choice that had got them recaptured. But not again. This time he would do it right. This time.

If only he could just stand up.

The downed Risar had stopped moving but the other one

was returning, and he had the paralysis device in his grip. A shard of fear cut through Dex; in his weakened state, exposure to the shock of the ray from the weapon might be too much for him to take—it could mean the end of him.

He made it to one knee, reaching up to defend himself.

Then there was a screech of sound, a blaze of white fire, and suddenly the Risar was on the ground, twitching.

Dex blinked owlishly as two figures in blue-black fatigues came closer, his blurry vision clearing a little.

"Hey, Ronon… Are you all right? You look awful."

"McKay." A grin split his face and he allowed Rodney to pull him to his feet, with a grunt of exertion. "I am actually pleased to see you."

"The feeling is, ah, mutual," came the reply.

Sheppard hove into view. "Thought you could use an assist."

"I had it covered," Dex lied. "About time you got here. How'd you find us?"

"More by luck than judgment," noted McKay.

"Isn't that always the way?" Sheppard gestured with the stunner in his hand. "Long story short, we're on the moon and we don't have a ride home."

"First things first," Dex said, fighting down a wave of nausea. "We find Teyla." He extended his hand toward Rodney. "Give me your gun."

"What? Why?"

"Because even in this state, I'm a better shot than you'll ever be. *Give*."

McKay shrugged and conceded the weapon. "I guess you have a point there."

"Got any grenades?" he demanded.

Sheppard held up a single flash bang. "Just this."

"It'll do." Ronon pointed back the way he had come. "Down there. I saw the Risars taking her."

"Risars?" Sheppard and McKay exchanged looks.

"Come on," he growled, and stumbled forward.

"Easy there, cowboy," said the colonel, reaching out to help steady him. "You look a wreck, pal. Maybe you ought to sit this out."

Ronon didn't bother to grace that with a reply; instead, he fixed Sheppard with a hooded, baleful glare that could have cut steel.

"Or not," amended the colonel.

It happened very fast; as if they both heard a voice inside their heads at once, the two aliens froze for a heartbeat, then turned toward the chamber's entranceway. Teyla heard the shriek of stunner bolts, then there was a concussive blare of noise and a flash of intense light. In the next second the door was filled with white smoke and through it came Ronon, John and Rodney.

Sheppard called her name and crossed to her, keeping the creatures covered with his weapon. "You okay?"

"All the better for seeing you," she admitted.

"You cannot do this," said the sickly Risar, shifting in place. "You will disrupt my work."

"You must submit," said the other. "Drop your weapons."

"And if we don't?" Sheppard stepped closer to them, unafraid. "You might be able to scare the locals down on Heruun with the lightshows and all the flying saucer stuff, but let me tell you, on my planet that *Close Encounters of the Third Kind* garbage doesn't cut it any more."

"We know what you are," said McKay. "The Aegis is a front." He nodded at the walls. "This is an interstellar starship. And more than that, it's an Asgard starship."

Teyla frowned. *Asgard*; they were a powerful race of beings that the people of Earth had encountered more than a decade ago, during their battles with the parasitic Goa'uld. They had a fearsome reputation, and yet...

She had met one of them, the acerbic engineer Hermiod, who served for short time aboard the Earth ship *Daedalus*; and while the Risar had a passing resemblance to the slight, grey-skinned humanoids, they were only similar as much as a Wraith was similar to an Athosian. She shot a look at the creature. "But you do not look like them."

"This is a Risar," said the alien, in a matter-of-fact tone. "It is not me."

"I told you this," said the other, "the Risar are my tools."

"I'm guessing they're modified Asgard clone-stock," said McKay. "Hybrids, with more muscle mass than their normal bodies." He sniffed. "Y'know, to do all the heavy lifting, that kinda thing."

"How do you know my kind?" demanded the weaker Risar. It seemed agitated by the sudden turn of events.

"We know a lot of stuff," replied Sheppard. "But before we go any further, I'm not going to do any more talking to the monkeys. I want to speak to the organ grinder."

"Show us your true face," said Teyla.

There was a long silence; and then the holographic screen reappeared. On it was a delicate, slender being with an oval head and eyes that had no whites, only inky black pupils. A small slit of a mouth opened, and when the being spoke, the Risar echoed every word in the same hollow tone. "You are not mistaken. I am Asgard, and this craft is my vessel. My name is Fenrir."

CHAPTER EIGHT

The pop-up on the screen read 'download complete', and Carter paused to double-check the contents of the laptop's memory; in hyper-compressed and encrypted form, every giga-byte of her work and personal research database relating to the Asgard had been ported over, ready to accompany her through the Stargate. She moved around the room, gathering up the last few items she would need to take with her to Heruun.

She glanced up at McKay, who stood in the doorway, his fingers knitting together. "Go ahead, Rodney, I'm listening." The scientist was conducting an on-the-hoof debriefing; he had only been back on Atlantis for a few hours and would soon be returning to M9K-153 with her.

"He's the real deal," said McKay. "At first, I thought we might be dealing with another situation like Angelus—"

Despite herself, Carter gave a shudder. "Let's not go *there* again."

"—But no. He's Asgard, all right. From head to toe. If they have toes."

Sam recalled the first time she had met a member of the Asgard species, the warrior-scientist Thor. His kindred had turned out to be one of Earth's greatest allies, and they had given so much of themselves in the struggles to keep threats like the Replicators, the System Lords and the Ori at bay. And after what had become of them...

She frowned. *Now is not the time to dwell on that.*

First things first, she had to focus on the problems in front of her. Carter had no doubt that the International Oversight Advisory would be contacting her in short order with tersely-worded commands to 'secure' the Asgard ship and its valuable technology, and that was part of the reason she was going off-world. Partly to avoid the IOA long enough to make her own evaluation, and partly because she just had to see it for herself.

There was one other reason, of course, and it amused her a little to have McKay admit to it; of all the people on Atlantis, Samantha Carter had the most first-hand experience with the Asgard and their incredible hardware, thanks to her time in SG-1. Rodney never found it easy to confess to knowing less than anybody about anything.

"He knew what we were," McKay went on. "Humans from Earth, I mean. He knew our planet."

She nodded. The Asgard had originated in another part of the intergalactic neighborhood that included the Milky Way and Pegasus galaxies, and they were well-traveled. Like the Goa'uld, they had visited a lot of human worlds in the guise of godlike beings, but where the System Lords had come to conquer and subjugate, the Asgard had brought protection and enlightenment. Earth, Cimmeria, K'Tau and many other planets had been touched by them in the deep past, millennia later the legacy of their visitations cemented into local myth and legend.

"I think he was as surprised to see us here as we were to see him," said Rodney. "Even more so when I showed him I could work one of his computers," he added with a smug sniff.

Sam glanced at him. "I've never heard of the Asgard visiting Pegasus, but it's not beyond the realms of possibility. After all, they had colony worlds in our stellar community, as well as the Othala and Ida galaxies." She closed the laptop and placed it in her gear pack. "How were things when you left the planet?"

"Hectic," he noted. "Sheppard convinced our new friend to release all the Heruuni people he had aboard his ship and return them to the surface, in return for having us promise to fix the damage to his vessel. When all the Taken were returned at once, in the middle of the day… It was a pretty big deal."

"No doubt," said Carter. "And the Asgard just agreed to it? That's a lot of trust to put in a stranger."

"Well, I have to take some credit," he noted. "As a good-will gesture, I cannibalized some of the cloaking circuits from the Jumper One to patch the long-range matter transporter on the ship. I figured that would score us some brownie points, but to be honest, it wasn't me or Sheppard who convinced him, in the end."

Carter pulled the pack on to her shoulder and left the office, McKay walking with her. "Really?"

"No. It was Teyla. The Risar seemed to pay more attention to her than any of the rest of us."

Carter didn't comment on the point, but put it aside for later consideration. "*Risar*. You used that word before." She threw a nod to the gate technician as they crossed through the control tier.

"It's the name he gave to the... I'm not sure what to call them, his remotes, his organic drones..." McKay shrugged. "Like most Asgard stuff, it's a Norse mythology thing. Apparently the Risar were servants of the gods, or something. Giants."

As they descended the stairs to the gate room proper, the blue symbols around the edge of the Stargate began to illuminate as M9K-153's dialing address locked in, chevron by chevron.

Carter checked the pistol in her thigh holster; it never hurt to be prepared, and after everything that had happened on Heruun up until now, it seemed prudent to have the ability to defend yourself if the circumstances required it.

McKay went on. "From what we can figure, a few years ago the ship dropped out of hyperspace in the Heruun system, and by some fluke found itself in the midst of a Wraith culling fleet preparing to attack the planet."

"How long ago?"

"Decades, perhaps a generation or two. I can't be sure." He shrugged. "So. There was a firefight and the Wraith were destroyed, but not before they scored a few choice hits."

"And the damaged Asgard ship was forced down on to the lunar surface," she replied, picking up the thread of the story. "But the damage was too widespread for these Risar to fix on their own?"

McKay nodded. "Not enough manpower, and apparently the drones have a very limited lifespan. Days, at most, before they degrade and die off."

"So the Asgard kidnapped the locals to use as a labor force, keeping them for couple of weeks, and then erasing the memory of what had happened to them."

"Some sort of engineered hypnotic control, apparently." Rodney pulled a sour face at the idea of being someone else's puppet. "That's what happened to Laaro's father."

"The boy Lorne spoke about?"

"Yes. I think that's what they were trying to do to Ronon, program him the same way to act as a worker drone."

The last chevron locked and the gate plume cut through the air, shimmering into solidity. Sam paused on the threshold. "We've seen that kind of thing before. A few years back, on Earth, SG-1 encountered a rogue Goa'uld doing something similar."

"I read that file," said McKay. "Creepy."

"How is Ronon?"

McKay's frown deepened. "Doctor Keller has already gone back with a medical team. I'm sure she'll be able to fix him up. The guy's pretty tough." He didn't sound convinced.

Carter advanced through the event horizon of the gate's open wormhole and felt the strange, cold rush across her face as she pressed into the ripples. She was aware of a giddying, thunderous sense of displacement, and then suddenly she was walking down crumbling steps of brown stone, the heavy heat of a long, cloudless day enveloping her.

Standing sentinel amid the stone pillars surrounding the Stargate, Major Lorne threw her a salute. "Welcome to Heruun, Colonel."

Sam returned the greeting. "Thank you, Major. Sitrep?"

"The natives are a bit restless, but so far nothing beyond that."

"Good, keep me posted." She glanced around. "Where's Colonel Sheppard?"

Lorne jerked his chin up at the evening sky, toward the silvery ring bisecting the clouds and the distant moons beyond. "Still upstairs, ma'am. He's expecting you."

Sam felt a familiar tingle growing all around her, and nodded. "Right."

The air around them became a curtain of glowing white energy, and for the second time in less than a minute, Carter's and McKay's bodies were dissembled into their component atoms and thrust through a quantum tunneling effect, to be reconstructed at a new location. When the white glow died away, Carter was standing on the deck of the Asgard ship, the familiar curved walls arching away from her. John Sheppard waited nearby, and with him was Teyla Emmagan.

"Teyla," said Carter, a sense of relief washing over her. "You're all right."

The Athosian woman seemed troubled, but she hid it quickly. "I am unhurt, Colonel."

"I intended no harm to come to anyone," said a voice. Sam turned and found a tall, rangy creature standing next to the transporter control console.

"Risar," said McKay, from the side of his mouth.

"I guessed," she replied. Carter stepped forward. "I am Colonel Samantha Carter of Stargate Command and the Atlantis expedition. Am I addressing Fenrir?"

"In a manner of speaking," said the creature. The closer she looked, the more she could see the faint physiological similarities between the drone and an Asgard; but the humanoid was a cruder, more primitive version of the willowy, slight aliens she knew—the Asgard equivalent of a Neanderthal. "But I am not here," continued the voice, the Risar touching its head.

"Then, where are you?" Sam's eyes narrowed. "You have nothing to fear from us. Our species and yours has a history of alliance and co-operation."

"So I have been informed," came the breathy, if suspicious reply, "but you will forgive me if I am reluctant."

"We made a deal in good faith," Sheppard began. "Think of the transporter repair and releasing the abductees as the first payment. This is the next step."

Carter nodded. "We prefer to speak to those we deal with face to face."

"It's a, uh, human thing," added McKay.

The Risar said nothing, watching them with a neutral expression; finally, Teyla spoke. "Fenrir. You must trust us."

"I will," it said at length. "Follow this drone."

They did as they were asked to, and the Risar silently led

them through a series of junctions, deeper into the heart of the vessel. The humans approached a wide, reinforced hatchway, guarded by another pair of Risar armed with crystalline ovoids that resembled the control spheres from Asgard consoles.

The hatch retreated into the deck and a cold waft of air reached out from the chamber beyond. Carter and Sheppard entered first as illuminating strips came on all around the walls. The chamber was dominated by a long, low capsule covered in a thin layer of frost, surrounded by smaller control consoles. Parts of the complex machinery seemed damaged, indicator lights flickering, burn damage visible here and there. Sam saw a glassine port in the side of the capsule and glimpsed blue-white flesh inside.

"Fenrir?" she asked, her breath making a cloud of vapor at her lips.

With a hum, the holographic image of an Asgard came into being between them and the machinery. "*Greetings, Colonel Samantha Carter. I am Fenrir.*"

"Uh, no offence meant," said Sheppard, "but you're not. You're a hologram." The colonel stepped forward and waved his hand through the image, making it flicker and pixelate for a moment.

Sam studied the image. The Asgard were identical, beings born from clone stock who endured by the transfer of their minds from one living copy to another; and yet there was something about the representation of Fenrir, an unusual cast to his eyes that set him apart from the others of his kind she had known, a subtlety she couldn't fully quantify.

She pointed at the capsule. "That's really you, isn't it? Your organic body, inside that pod."

The alien nodded once. "*My flesh, yes. In cryogenic suspension. However, my consciousness remains active and connected to some of my ship's systems. Hence, my ability to converse with you through this interface, and my operation of the Risar.*"

"They are all Fenrir," said Teyla quietly.

"*From a certain perspective, that is correct.*"

"Stasis pods," said McKay, "used for long duration space flight. But that begs the question, why are you still in there?

Relatively speaking, I mean."

"*I am trusting you with this knowledge*," said the alien, "*to prove my sincerity.*" The hologram gestured at the capsule. "*Although I wish it, I cannot end the stasis cycle and exit the pod. Damage sustained to my vessel has caused a critical interrupt in the system, and any attempt to intervene could cause a cascade failure. If the deactivation cycle commences, I will perish.*"

"But you can transfer your consciousness to another cloned body—" began Sam.

"*No, Colonel Carter. The emergency genetic bank aboard this craft was also lost when the Wraith attacked me. I was only able to reconstruct the gene-code for Risar.*" The Asgard seemed to frown. "*My only chance of survival is to repair my ship and return to my homeworld, Hala.*"

Carter was suddenly aware that McKay and Sheppard were watching her intently. "We'll do whatever we can to help you," she replied, keeping her tone neutral.

A space had been cleared for Keller's equipment in the middle of the sick lodge, and in short order she had set up a folding table and all the immunobiology gear she could get through the Stargate. Kullid hovered nearby, both nervous and fascinated by the advanced technology; he was paging through a data pad filled with microscopic images of the Asgard nanites. "At last we know the face of the sickness," he had said, when she told him what they were up against. He had grasped the idea of the nanites quickly.

If anything, the lodge's population had grown since she had been here last, doubtless from new arrivals who had succumbed to the malaise after the en masse returning from Fenrir's ship. Keller scowled. How could a life form that was supposedly so advanced do something so callous to another intelligent being? The doctor had admittedly seen such behavior—too much of it, to be true—among her own species, but on some level she'd been hoping that out here in the wider universe, maybe things went a little differently. She felt slightly disappointed at her own naiveté.

"Doctor?" One of the nurses she'd enlisted from Atlantis approached, a rack of sample tubes in her hand. "We're ready to start the next series."

"Go ahead, Cathy," she told her. "You know what to do." Keller crossed to where Ronon was propped up on a low bed. The Satedan had taken a wooden stool from somewhere and was using it like a table. He had a dozen weapons spread out on the makeshift platform, and was cleaning them with a stained oilcloth.

"This is a hospital, not an armory," she told him.

He didn't look up at her. "Gotta have something to keep me occupied. Unless of course you want to sign off on me, let me go." Ronon seemed to have regained his focus after returning from the alien ship.

Keller folded her arms over her chest. "How do you feel?"

"Fine," came the reply, and with it a stifled cough. Dex grimaced.

"You're the worst liar in the world," she retorted. "I can't help you if you don't help me."

Finally he looked at her. "I don't need help. I've dealt with worse than this, come back from it." He put down the knife he was cleaning and Keller saw the slight tremor in his hand as he tried to hide it. "It's the air in this place, it's making me sick just being here."

She lowered her voice. "Don't try to sell me that tough guy stuff, because I'm not buying it. You're staying here until I say you're fit, and not before. So deal with it."

That got her a flash of annoyance. "You're enjoying this, aren't you?"

"Yeah, sure," she retorted, "I'm really enjoying watching people get sicker and sicker while I run up one blind alley after another looking for some cure that may not even exist." The heat in her words surprised her, and Ronon as well.

After a long moment, he looked away. "Send me back to Atlantis, then. Check me out there. It's gotta be easier than shipping all this kit to Heruun." He nodded at the equipment table.

"It's too risky. I'm not certain how the nanite markers will react to gate travel. It could disrupt them. I don't want to take the chance that someone will come through the wormhole and drop dead in the gate room."

"I'm used to risk," said Ronon. "It's what makes me a soldier."

She eyed him. "Well, I'm used to caution, and that's what makes me a doctor." Keller sighed. "Sorry, Ronon, but for now you're stuck here."

There was a moment of open, hard anger on his face, a dart of fury that he had nowhere to direct; but then it faded and his lips thinned. "Guess so."

Voices filtered in from outside the sick lodge, raised tones full of laughter and relief. "At least someone is having a better day than I am," said the Satedan.

"They are celebrating the Returned," said Laaro. The boy approached, carrying an Atlantis holdall that was far too heavy for him. He had insisted on helping Keller set up the temporary lab, and had taken it upon himself to trail around after her, observing everything she did. "Where should I put this, Jennifer?" He grunted as the bag threatened to fall from his fingers.

"Give it to the nurse," she told him, and he dutifully obeyed.

Kullid patted the boy on the shoulder as he walked away. "Celebrations," he mused. "Such things never reach within these walls. But perhaps it is for the better."

"How's that?" Keller asked.

"Elder Takkol called another festival day only because he had no choice. *Your* people convinced the Aegis to bring back all the Taken, but he has to make it seem as if it were *his* doing, otherwise he is weakened by this turn of events."

"Politics," Ronon grunted sourly, and returned to his weapons.

"What the elders do affects us all," Kullid said glumly.

"All that matters for now is that there won't be any more abductions," said Keller, moving back to the table. "Heruun can sleep soundly from now on. No more Giants, no more Taken and Returned."

"If only that meant the end of our problems," said Kullid.

"You and I are healers, Jennifer, and it is our way to look for the good among the ill…"

She smiled slightly. "You sound like my mom. She said I always had to find the sunny side of things, no matter how grim."

Kullid shared a warm smile. "She sounds like a wise woman."

"She was." Keller looked away. "She's been gone a while now."

He touched her arm. "Oh. I'm sorry."

Jennifer's smile returned. "It's okay."

"Your mother was right," Kullid continued. "Both of us strive to help others find the strength within to deal with whatever has struck them down. But there are some sicknesses that come from outside the body. Some things that cannot be cured. At least, not by mere humans like us…"

"What do you mean?"

"The virus of fear. Takkol knows it well. He knows that the fear of the Aegis cannot vanish overnight. Something must fill the void."

"You think the protection that the Asgard…" She halted, correcting herself. "The Aegis gave this planet is going to end, is that it? Because we intervened?"

"Some believe so. That is why Takkol tries to soothe them with another false celebration. But he cannot stop them from wondering what will happen next. And Soonir does not help matters with his rhetoric."

"Soonir?" Keller recalled the look on the rebel leader's face the last time she had seen the man. "He's in the settlement?"

"It is possible, he has hiding places everywhere. I have heard that he is rallying his supporters to have Takkol's rank and status taken from him. Without the Aegis to back his rule, the senior elder is weak." He gave a solemn nod. "Some say it is only a matter of time before the Wraith return."

Keller shook her head. "That's not going to happen."

"Can you be sure? You have crossed their paths, yes?" Kullid seemed suddenly eager to hear more.

She nodded. "That's one way to describe it."

Kullid's voice dropped to a hush. "I have heard it said they have the power of life and death in the palm of their hand. The mastery of the energy of the body itself."

"They're predators," she told him. "Believe me, you don't ever want to be face to face with one of them."

"I would imagine so," he replied carefully. "But without the Aegis, that may not be our choice to make."

Keller wanted to give him an answer, but she had no assurances to give him. The young man's dark face softened, answering her silently.

"Doctor?"

Jennifer turned to find Major Lorne standing in the doorway. "Is something wrong?"

"No, ma'am. Colonel Carter asked me to come get you. She's assembling the senior staff for a meeting at Jaaya's lodge."

Keller nodded at the radio on the table. "She could have just called me."

"After all that's gone on here, we're not taking any chances with anyone moving around unescorted." Lorne beckoned her to him. "If you'll come with me?"

Keller glanced at Kullid. "This may take a while."

"I understand."

Lorne spoke to a female Marine officer at his side. "Allan, make sure this building is secure."

"Sir!" The lieutenant saluted and pushed past Keller on her way out.

"What's this about?" said the doctor quietly.

Lorne shot a look up at the sky. "Take a wild guess."

"He doesn't know," said Sheppard, peering out through the slats of the window. The mingled scents of a cook fire and night-blooming flowers reached Teyla's nostrils as she waited for one of the others to speak.

At the doorway, Major Lorne seemed to take this a cue to answer. "If anyone is worried about talking openly, don't. I swept the house earlier today."

"I'm sure the only bugs in this place are the six- or eight-legged kind," noted McKay.

"How did Jaaya take that?" asked Keller, cradling a cup of water.

"We came to an understanding," Lorne noted. "A few MREs go a long way."

"Thank you, Major," said Carter, casting around to look at all of them in turn. "I'm sure I don't have to underline to everyone here the seriousness of the situation."

Sheppard turned to face the assembled group. "He doesn't know, Colonel. Fenrir…" He stopped, trying to frame the enormity of it. "His people… The entire Asgard race are dead, and he doesn't know it."

"We can't be certain of that," said McKay.

"C'mon, Rodney," Sheppard shot the scientist a look. "He said he wanted to go home to Hala. If I remember rightly, that whole planet was destroyed in the war with the Replicators." He stepped into the middle of the room. "Look, the Asgard committed mass suicide over a year ago to stop their technology from falling into the hands of the Ori—"

"They did give us a copy first," McKay added.

"They blew up their second home planet in the process. They wiped themselves out."

"Orilla." Teyla saw a distant look in Carter's eyes as she remembered that moment. "I was there when it happened."

"So why doesn't Fenrir know anything about that? Why wasn't he called back to the home planet before the end, like all the rest of his kind?"

"There could be a hundred reasons," said Teyla. She felt the urge to defend the alien, although she couldn't fathom where the sudden impulse had come from. "The damage from the battle with the Wraith may have destroyed his communications system. He may have been out of range…"

Carter shook her head. "This is the Asgard we're talking about here. They don't make mistakes like that."

"Maybe they thought he was already dead," offered Keller.

"The fact is, as far as we know, Fenrir is the only living member of his species. The last Asgard." Sheppard shook his head at the thought.

"We cannot keep this from him," said Teyla. "He has a right to know."

"That might not be a good idea," said McKay. "We can't be sure how he's going to react."

Teyla gave Rodney an appalled look. "Are you suggesting we lie to Fenrir, after everything it took to make an ally of him? You are all correct that this is a terrible, terrible truth, but he must not remain ignorant of it!"

"McKay is right," said Carter. "We have to chose the right moment. We can't just drop it on him."

"Hey Fenrir, great to meet you, oh, sorry about your whole species being dead and all," Rodney mimicked. "He's going to love hearing that."

Keller stared into her cup. "Shock can make people do strange things. And I'm not even sure how to begin to gauge the mental stability of an Asgard."

"So if not now, then when do we tell him?" demanded Teyla. "When his ship is ready to travel, when he sets a course home, when he reaches Hala and finds nothing there but dead space?"

"Teyla—"

"What if it were your world, your people, Colonel Carter? Would you not wish to know?"

"This isn't just about the extinction thing," McKay broke in. "This is about trust."

Carter nodded. "I have to admit, I don't get the same feeling with Fenrir I did with Thor and the others. He's different somehow."

"Yeah, he abducts people and the unlucky ones get a dose of nanites," noted Lorne.

"And then there's that name," said McKay. "I took the liberty of chatting to Professor Gudrunsdottir in the xenobotany lab on Atlantis. Turns out, she's a bit of a Norse mythology expert on the side. And let me tell you, Fenrir is a name to conjure with." He drew out his data pad and Keller took it from him.

"Fenrir, also known as Fenris or Fenrisulfr," she read aloud. "The son of the trickster god Loki."

"Loki…" Carter repeated. "He was a troublemaker."

Keller continued. "According to Viking legends, Fenrir is a gigantic wolf that will continually grow until it gets so big that it will break the chains the other gods used to bind it."

Sheppard's lip curled. "Those little grey guys never go for the low-key, do they?"

"Oh, it gets better," said McKay. "Gudrunsdottir told me that our pal Fenrir the wolf ushers in the end of world by *eating the sun*. The Norse people called it Ragnarok, the darkness and the eternal winter that destroys everything."

"The Nightfall." Teyla's breath caught in her throat. "On Athos... Some of the tribes there tell a similar story, of a monster who swallows up the stars." She gave an involuntary shiver; she hadn't heard those tales since she was a small girl, but they still held a primal power over her.

Lorne folded his arms. "At the risk of thinking above my pay grade, aren't we just talking about a bunch of stories written by crazy Norwegians, a thousand years ago, on a planet in a completely different galaxy?"

Carter smiled dryly. "Yeah, I used to think like that, Major. But I learned the hard way that myth is built on truth, at least to some degree." Her smile faded. "I contacted the SGC and had a message relayed out to the *Odyssey*, where the Asgard Core is located."

"What is that?" asked Teyla. The term was unfamiliar to her.

"Before the Asgard died, they loaded the sum total of their knowledge into a computer system that was installed aboard the starship *Odyssey*," said the colonel. "I asked them to run a search through it for anything about Fenrir."

"What did they find?" said Keller.

"Nothing."

McKay shook his head. "That's impossible. They must have screwed up the search routine."

"Maybe the Asgard forgot to upload that disc," said Lorne.

"No," Carter tapped the data screen. "That information is there. My guess is, it's buried deep, possibly encrypted."

Teyla looked away. "Why would it be hidden?"

"Why indeed..." murmured Sheppard.

"We need to get someone out to the *Odyssey* to take a look-see," McKay went on, addressing Carter. "What about your buddy, Jackson? He's good."

"He's also busy, on a covert operation chasing down one of the last renegade System Lords." She fixed Rodney with a hard look. "That's why I'm sending *you* back via the Midway gate bridge to rendezvous with *Odyssey* and recover those files."

"Oh. Right." McKay seemed a little nonplussed at the sudden orders. "Okay." A slow smile formed on his face as he realized what he would be granted access to. "Okay…"

"Colonel?" Keller leaned forward. "I'd like to add something to that. These nanites I'm dealing with, I need all the help I can get, so if Rodney can bring back everything you can find on Asgard nanotechnology…"

McKay nodded. "I'll do what I can."

"All right." Carter stood up, signaling that the meeting was over. The group began to file out, but Teyla hesitated, unsure of how she should feel about what she had heard. Her thoughts about Fenrir were conflicted; strangely, she felt a pang of sympathy for the alien. Ever since the disappearance of her people from New Athos, Teyla had harbored a secret fear that they might be lost to her, that she might be all that remained. For a moment, she saw her own darkest dread reflected in Fenrir's circumstances.

Carter was speaking to Sheppard. "Colonel, I want you to escort Rodney to the *Odyssey* rendezvous. I've seen the knowledge contained inside the Asgard Core, and it'll be like giving him the keys to the candy store. I need someone to keep him on-mission."

Sheppard hesitated. "With all due respect, Colonel, I'm on-mission here. I don't like ducking out in the middle of this."

"I've got it covered at this end, John. And that's not the only reason. I want a military officer there as well, someone who can make tactical sense of what he sees… In case we have to take steps." Sheppard nodded grudgingly as she spoke.

"Steps?" said Teyla. "Against Fenrir? You speak about him as if you have already decided he is a threat to us."

"We don't know what he is," Sheppard replied. "All we do

know it that he kidnapped people against their will, you and Ronon among them, and exposed them to toxic nanites either deliberately or by accident."

"I do not believe it was intentional," Teyla insisted. "That is my... My instinct."

Carter turned away. "I'm sorry, Teyla," she said, "but I'm going to need more than that."

CHAPTER NINE

A silent landslide began on the surface of Heruun's prime
moon. Streams of powdery stone and lunar dust shifted
and fell away in slow floods, seeping back towards the crater
basin beneath the concealed Asgard starship.

On landing, all those years earlier, the vessel's automatic
defensive systems had scanned the descent site and activated
a camouflage subroutine. Tailored gravity wave generators
drew the grey sand over the ship like a blanket, an emergency
defensive measure to protect it from cursory visual detection;
but now the vessel was shrugging off sleep, rising with stately
power from its resting place. It was a steel phoenix clawing its
way from the ashes.

Damage that would have taken years more to repair using
the Taken and the Risar had been completed in days, thanks to
the intervention of the Atlanteans, although the vessel was still
far from being fully operational; but once more it returned to the
ocean of space, the airless void where it belonged. Such craft
were not made to be shackled by the forces of gravity—the
starships of the Asgard were their art as much as they were
their conveyances—and Fenrir's vessel seemed to welcome its
freedom, the huge hammerhead prow turning to catch the light
from the sun.

In profile, the Asgard ship resembled a massive iron claw,
vertical fins extending from the dorsal and ventral hulls, and
curved wing-like sections fanning out from the main fuselage.
The light of new energy glittered through numerous viewports
along the length of the craft, and at the stern the thruster grids
of the massive sub-light engines glowed a soft honey-yellow as
they idled at station keeping. But still the ship's ascent, quicker
now, a falling feather in reverse, was marred by the lines of
damage across the steel-grey hull metal. Great scratches carved
by the burning touch of Wraith energy weapons were visible

across the bows and along the starboard side, mute reminders
of a salvo delivered by a Wraith cruiser's broadside batteries.
The enemy that had inflicted those wounds was long destroyed,
ashes and wreckage that had burned up in Heruun's atmosphere,
lighting the night as falling stars.

The moon dropped away and at last the ship was in free
space, drifting in the orbit between the satellite and the mother
planet. Turning in a long, steady arc, the Asgard ship brought
itself to bear on Heruun. The thruster glow grew brighter and
it coasted forward at a fraction of its available power, moving
toward the slow-turning world.

The ship that bore the name *Aegis* took up a high orbit above
the planet and the people it had protected, and like an animal
awakening from hibernation, it began to stretch its muscles and
test its boundaries.

"Have we been detected?" spat the commander, glowering
at the scientist.

The other Wraith shook his head, the long white streaks of
his hair plastered to his face with fear-sweat. "No... No."

The uncertainty in the words made the commander's lips
peel back, revealing his fanged mouth. "Be certain!" he snarled.
"If we are found, we are dead!"

"We are safe." The scientist turned from his console and gave
the commander a defiant look. "For the moment, at least."

The ship's master glared at the flickering image on the
viewer lens before him. The gunmetal alien craft turning, moving slowly through the darkness. It was a battleship, of that
he had no doubt. The design of it was all threat, a brute force
expression of menace. Unlike the graceful sculpting of a Wraith
cruiser, with its spindly arachnid lines, this vast craft was a war
hammer, a weapon poised to smash its enemies. As he watched
it move, the commander understood why so many of his clan
had been killed by this intruder; it radiated power. Nothing so
large should have turned so quickly... It seemed wrong that
such agility could be present in such a behemoth.

Fear was a rare commodity for a Wraith to experience; so
much of their existence was spent in the creation of that emo-

tion in their prey that they seldom experienced it themselves. And yet… A cold prickle lanced through the commander's flesh as he grasped the scope of the alien ship's power. His tiny scoutship was no match for the intruder. It would crush it like an insect.

But fear was not the only sensation that came to him. Quickly, the first was overpowered by a second, greater emotion. *Avarice.*

The scientist shared it with him. "What secrets it must hide," whispered the other Wraith. "What power. If our clan could possess it—"

The commander gave a terse nod. In the war with the hated Asuran machine-beings, a ship of such magnitude could tip the balance; and it would seal the ascension of their clan above the others of their species. "Our Queen must know of this. Plans must be drawn, and quickly. It is time for us to depart."

"Is that possible?" The scientist was fearful again. "If we move from our hiding place in the rings, we will be detected!"

"If we do not, we will be found cowering and culled like humans!" he snapped back. "Observe the alien's aspect; it has yet to reach orbital stability. Until then, we have a window of escape open to us that will soon close." The commander nodded to the drone at the navigation podium. "Set a stealth course. Follow the rings around to the far side. We will place the planet's mass between us and the intruder craft. Even if our hyperspace transition is detected, they will not have time to intercept us."

"The risk is great," grumbled the scientist.

"You are correct," agreed the commander, as he studied the alien vessel once again. "But the reward will be so much greater."

"This vessel is…impressive," said Teyla. The word hardly seemed enough to encompass the ship's quiet power. She glanced at the unmoving figure in the stasis capsule; it felt odd speaking to a holographic avatar when the real being was lying nearby in suspended animation.

The simulated Fenrir turned from the screen in front of them. "*The* Aegis *is a* Beliskner-*class starship, the mainstay of the Asgard starfleet. An old design but a reliable one.*"

She nodded. After the conversation at Jaaya's lodge, Teyla felt uncomfortable in the company of the alien, as if she feared the secret she held would suddenly slip from her lips. "I must admit, I am unsure why you invited me to witness this. Colonel Carter, perhaps—"

"*She is below, on the engineering decks,*" said Fenrir. "*She is quite intelligent for a human of her evolutionary status.*" The Asgard made a small noise in its throat. "*Ah, forgive me. I do not mean to appear patronizing. The ship would still be planet-bound if not for the help your kind have given me.*"

"I am not offended. Just curious…"

Fenrir came closer. She watched him walking; the Asgard seemed so frail, so delicate, as if a stiff breeze would blow him away like a bundle of sticks; and again she felt a pang of sympathy for the alien, of sorrow.

He looked up at her. "*I… Have had little company in the past years. The Risar are only reflections of my own psyche and the Heruuni… Those I attempted to speak to at first were unable to think of me as anything other than some form of deity. But you, Teyla Emmagan. You are the first human I encountered who challenged me, who did not fear me. I wish to know you.*"

It wasn't the response Teyla expected at all. She wasn't sure how to respond; she took a different tack instead. "Where are the other crew of the *Aegis*?"

"*There are none,*" he explained. "*Our ships are highly automated. At the most, our craft require only one, perhaps two Asgard to operate it. In the event of a larger crew requirement, Risar can be deployed.*"

"You must be lonely." The last word threatened to catch in her throat.

"*I have known that emotional state, yes. But I have had my work and the repairs to occupy my mind.*"

Teyla paused, weighing her thoughts. On the one hand, she could not deny she felt a kind of kinship to the lost Asgard, but at the same time she questioned the things that he had done to the Heruuni. "Fenrir, you spoke of challenge. I must do so again, and ask you this—why did you prey upon the natives of this world?"

"*They were not prey,*" said the alien, affront in his voice. "*I did not mistreat them. I regret what I was forced to do, but you must realize that I had no other choice.*"

"But the sickness, this malaise caused by the nanite markers you used. I saw the process of insertion, remember. I saw what you tried to do to Ronon."

The Asgard was silent for a long time, and the hologram flickered slightly. "*I am sorry for any pain or suffering I may have caused. That was never my intention, you must believe me. I had no idea that the markers would create a side-effect.*" He walked across to the stasis pod and in an odd moment of reflection, the holographic Asgard stared down at his living, dormant body. When he spoke again, it was with genuine regret. "*I have made so many mistakes in my life, Teyla Emmagan. But sometimes the course of right lies beyond our reach, no matter how hard we try to grasp it.*"

Fenrir's words cut deeper than Teyla wanted to admit. She returned to her earlier thread of conversation. "Doctor McKay spoke of how your species are from another galaxy."

"*We call it Othala,*" he nodded.

"What was it that brought you out here, to Pegasus?"

The hologram flickered again. "*My voyage... Was an extended mission of scientific research,*" explained the Asgard. "*It gave much opportunity to think.*" He was silent for a moment, his gaze turned inward. "*We Asgard are caught in a dilemma. Assailed by outside forces, we strive to endure. My species do not have the biological ability to procreate as yours do.*"

"You reproduce by cloning yourselves."

Another nod. "*Genetic duplication of a host body.*" Fenrir pointed a long-fingered hand at the stasis pod. "*Neural patterning technology allows us to transfer memories and persona from a dying body to a new one... But one must question, Teyla, if that is truly life or just a facsimile.*"

Despite herself, the Athosian's expression clouded at the alien's description of his artificial immortality. "But how can that be an existence? It is not a continuation. You are dying over and over again, each new Asgard only a copy of the last…"

"And the copies fade over time. I have observed that some civilizations believe in the existence of an ephemeral component to a living consciousness, an essence that transcends crude matter in the moment of death."

"A soul."

"That is one term for it. And if such a thing does exist, then I fear that the souls of the Asgard people were lost a long time ago."

She crossed to the capsule. "Perhaps not. On Athos, we believe that a person is not born with a soul, only the seed of one. We believe that it can only become fully formed through deeds, through work and sacrifice, through self-knowledge."

Fenrir's small mouth turned in something that could have been a smile. *"Then perhaps there is a chance for my people yet to know such a thing."*

Teyla returned a rueful smile. The Asgard continued to confound her expectations of him; she began to understand what it was about these aliens that so intrigued the people of Earth. There was a sadness about the lone being that was undeniable; and yet she also sensed something hidden, something more than the Fenrir she was being allowed to see. The hologram was as much a mask as it was the reality.

"I envy you," he said abruptly, coming closer. *"You carry a growing life within you, the merging of your genetic matrix with another of your kind, and more. It is at once such a complex and wondrous thing, and yet so simple a process. But for all the great knowledge of the Asgard, we cannot duplicate so basic a biological function. Our every attempt to stem the tide of decay has been a failure. The very process we have used to survive will eventually destroy us."*

Fenrir raised a tentative hand and held it before Teyla's belly, as if he were afraid to touch her; then the hologram flickered once more and his limb dropped to his side, as he remembered that he could never actually make contact with her, not with a mere pattern of photons and energy. *"The Asgard are fast approaching an evolutionary dead end,"* he said, *"and when that point is reached, the light of our civilization, the sum of all we are, will be extinguished."*

Teyla's silent self-reproach burned like acid in her chest. "I am sorry," she told him. It was as close to the truth as she dared to voice.

In the drive chamber of the *Aegis*, a ball of energy that looked like a piece of the sun roiled and spun inside a column of pure anti-protons. Around it orbited contra-rotating rings of systemry that turned about each other in mid-air; and beyond them were vanes made of crystalline circuits and conduits channeling enough raw power to punch a hole through the fabric of space-time.

'Cool' was the word that Samantha Carter would have used if someone had asked her to describe it. Under normal laws of physics, anyone standing where she was would have been instantly immolated by the catastrophic bombardment of exotic radiation, but inside the Asgard engine room, protected by force fields and quantum baffles, she felt nothing but the slightly-below-room-temperature ambience that the Asgard seemed to like aboard their ships.

She glanced at the data pad in her hand; confirming that the power train from the drive core was stable, she tugged on the fiber optic cable connecting it to the monitor station where she stood and detached the device. Carter stood silently for a moment, basking in the glow of a science she could only just begin to understand. From what the SGC's best minds had been able to comprehend, Asgard ships used the energy differential states in captured remnants of neutron stars to power their vessels. Just the basic mechanics of making something like that work were beyond the ragged edge of humanity's knowledge of quantum mechanics and cosmology, and Sam was enthused by the enormity of it.

"One day," she said aloud, "one day when we're not looking over our shoulders for the next invasion, I'm going to take one of you boys to bits and figure out what makes you tick."

"But not today, ma'am, right?" Major Lorne had entered the chamber without her noticing. "I mean, not that I doubt your skills or anything, but I'd hate to be stuck on this tub with the lights out."

"Not today," she agreed. "Besides, there's too much to do here. Sensors are still out, so are the weapons. We have sub-light engines and hyperdrive, though, which is a start."

"That's great, Clonel, because we might want to think about zapping out to another system for a drop-off."

Carter frowned. "I don't follow you, Major."

"We have some, uh, cargo that you might want to dump. Sergeant Rush's team were sweeping the ship and we came across some old friends in a holding chamber."

"Wraith," she said with a scowl. "Teyla mentioned that she'd encountered some in one of the cells. Are they secure?"

"I posted guards with shoot-to-kill orders outside the hatches."

"Good work."

Lorne cleared his throat. "What do you want me to do with them?"

Carter realized the question she was being asked. "We can't release them here."

"No ma'am. And from what I hear, the Asgard doesn't seem to care what happens to them." Lorne paused before continuing. "Which doesn't leave a lot of choices."

Sam's expression hardened. "I'm not issuing orders for an execution detail, Major, if that's what you're suggesting."

"I'm just outlining the options," he replied. "If things were reversed, you know how it would go."

"I do," she noted. "But we're not the Wraith. For now, keep them locked up. We'll deal with the prisoners once we get the *Aegis* up and running."

Lorne saluted. "Yes, ma'am."

The Puddle Jumper emerged from the Stargate on P5X-404 into the middle of a rainstorm. Sheppard blinked as a wall of water battered against the canopy glass and sluiced away, forced into streaks by the velocity of the craft.

"Lovely weather," noted Rodney from the jump seat.

"It always rains when you come home." Sheppard angled the Jumper upwards in a slow climb, leaving the rocky canyon they had emerged into behind, sweeping up toward the low, ponderous clouds. He caught a glimpse of strange, globe-like monoliths out across the landscape, but they were lost as the ship entered the storm bank. In a few seconds they were flying in clear blue skies, the color darkening by the moment as they rose up toward the edge of the atmosphere.

McKay watched the planet fall behind them. "Welcome to the Milky Way galaxy," he said, mimicking the tone of an in-flight announcer. "Thank you for flying Gatebridge." He grinned at his own joke. "Can you imagine the kind of air miles you'd get for this trip?

"Technically, not as many as the *Daedalus* and *Apollo* crews would get. I mean, realistically speaking, we've only gone from the hangar to the Atlantis gate room, across the Midway station and now out of the gate here."

"Wormhole travel still counts," McKay replied. "I'm keeping a record."

"What, really?"

Rodney nodded. "Bill Lee and I have been keeping a log. We're trying to work out who's the most-traveled human being in history."

"That's dumb," Sheppard rolled his eyes. "We really have to get you a proper hobby, McKay." He paused. "So, who's top of the list?"

Rodney frowned. "Sam."

"Am I on there? In the top ten?"

"Didn't you just say you thought it was dumb?"

"I just wondered." The Jumper's passage began to smooth out as the atmosphere of 404 thinned, the blue sky becoming black.

An alert tone sounded from Sheppard's radio. "*Jumper Three, do you copy?*" asked a crisp female voice. "*This is Odyssey.*"

"*Odyssey*, this is Colonel Sheppard, we read you five by five."

"*Roger that. Your vector is zero six bravo, clear to land on deck two, checkers green. And Colonel? Word to the wise, sir. Watch your separation, we have a lot of busy sky up here.*"

"I read you, *Odyssey*. Sheppard out."

"What did she mean by that? 'Busy sky'?"

"Take a look." Sheppard brought up the tactical plot on the heads-up display and it was instantly filled with moving indicator glyphs.

"Whoa, what is this, a boat show?"

"Staging point," Sheppard explained, dropping the HUD again. "The SGC's taking part in a joint task force mission."

McKay leaned forward in his seat to get a better look and his eyes widened.

Dwarfing the size of its stone-built counterparts on Earth, a towering golden pyramid drifted past the Jumper's blunt nose. Beyond it were a half-dozen more Ha'tak class motherships, the sigils of the System Lords that once commanded them now blotted out by the new pennants of the Free Jaffa Nation. Amid the fleet, smaller Al'kesh bombers moved in tight arrowhead packs, and box-formation flights of Death Gliders conducted area patrols.

A group of the ships matched pace with the Jumper for a few moments, the winged scarab shapes of the Jaffa starfighters bracketing them as the pilots gave them the once-over; then abruptly they broke off in high turns and banked away.

Sheppard glimpsed the hard lines of the USS *Odyssey* to the starboard and angled toward it. Among the sculpted shapes of the Goa'uld-designed vessels, the Earth ship looked out of place, angular and deadly among its larger companions. The colonel turned for the deep space carrier's landing pontoon, passing a lone F-302 fighter going the other way. The 302 pilot dipped his wings in a salute and Sheppard rocked the Jumper from side to side in return.

Sheppard flared the Jumper and took it in low and slow, though the atmosphere shield and down on to the deck, where an airman in a visibility vest directed the ship to a parking area.

"Down and safe," he said aloud, dropping the embarkation ramp.

Waiting for them was an Air Force major in the characteristic khaki jumpsuit worn by almost everyone aboard these

ships. He tore off a hard, sharp salute that was so firm, at first
Rodney thought it was a kind of karate chop. "Colonel, Doctor,
welcome aboard the *Odyssey*. I'm Major East, the executive
officer. The captain sends his regrets that he couldn't be here to
meet you, but he's off the ship." East began walking in quick,
non-nonsense strides across the landing bay and Sheppard fell
in with him as McKay jogged to keep up. "Tactical operations
meeting," he continued. "The Jaffa are planning this strike
down to the heartbeat."

"What's the op?" asked Sheppard.

"We have good intel about one of Baal's bases in an asteroid
belt, out on the edge of Jaffa space. The Ha'taks are leading the
fight, we're handling combat air patrol of the engagement zone.
Watching their backs, so to speak."

"A strike mission?" echoed Rodney. "Nobody said anything
about going into battle when we got here."

"You won't," said East, "you'll be gone by then."

"Major, this could take a while," said Sheppard, "I mean,
there's a whole database of Asgard learning aboard this ship
and we have to find just one little bit. "

"If it's actually in there," noted the officer. "We looked once
already."

"I'll find it," Rodney insisted.

"I hope so," said the major, "because the IOA and the SGC
want you back on your way to the Pegasus galaxy within 48
hours. That's the zero line for the mission go-no go." East gave
Rodney a measuring look. "You're lucky to get across the
bridge so fast. Normally there's a day-long quarantine."

McKay nodded. "Colonel Carter got them to waive that and
gate us straight here."

"That SG-1 rep goes a long way, I guess. You save the planet
as many times as her team did and it gets you a lot of leeway."

"We've saved planets and stuff as well," noted Sheppard.
"Not in this galaxy, but you know… Important planets."

East gave a nod. "Yes sir. I heard that." They halted at a hatch
to a corridor. "Doctor McKay, if you follow me, I'll escort you
down to the core for a security check."

Something caught Sheppard's eye and he nodded. "Yeah,

you two go on ahead. I see someone I know. I'll catch up."

Rodney watched him walk off across the deck. "What kind of security check?"

"The Asgard database is of highly critical strategic value," said East. "Obviously we don't just let anyone have access to it. The check's a formality, no big deal." He shot McKay a quick look. "Unless you have a thing about needles."

"Staff!" He called out and a soldier in British-issue BDU camos turned to face him. "Staff Sergeant Mason, how the hell are you?"

The SAS trooper snapped off a salute. "Colonel Sheppard, sir. I'm as well as can be expected. How are things on Atlantis?"

"Same old, same old. Wraith. Replicators. The usual mayhem."

Mason accepted this with a nod. "I heard you moved the city."

Sheppard shrugged. "It's a long story. But the fishing is much better in the new place."

"Sorry to hear about Weir and Beckett."

"Yeah." He frowned and nodded, then gestured at the ship around them. "I see the IOA still has you Brits knee deep in the Stargate program, though."

"Just doing our bit, boss," he replied. "It's a long way from what happened on Halcyon."

"Yeah," agreed the colonel. Mason and his squad had been part of a military exchange program posted to Atlantis almost two years ago, and during an off-world mission on a planet riven by endless wars, Sheppard had found the stony-faced spec-ops sergeant to be a dedicated and steadfast soldier. "What are you doing here?"

"We've been on the *Oddie* for a couple of weeks, along with some Spetsnaz lads. We're going in with the first wave of Jaffa to do some recon-in-force." He lowered his voice. "We're the only ones getting our hands dirty, though. To be honest, sir, the IOA has pressured Stargate Command to keep this ship well out of the firing line. If they had their way, it'd be permanently parked out at Area 51."

"The Asgard Core," said Sheppard. "It's too valuable to chance it being destroyed."

Mason nodded. "'Course, that means the Free Jaffa think we're all yellow. But me and the Ivans and a squad of SG-13's Jarheads are going to change some minds."

"Just watch your six around that Baal creep. Don't let the smooth accent fool you, he's tricky."

"I'll keep that in mind. Good luck, sir." The soldier saluted again, palm out, thumb down.

Sheppard did the same. "You too, Staff."

McKay rubbed the sore spot on his arm were the corpsman had taken the blood sample, and glared at him. "Got enough?" he said pointedly.

"We can't be too careful," said East, who stood with an armed security trooper at the entrance to the compartment housing the Asgard database. "Our enemies have played some pretty smart tricks on us in the past. The Goa'uld, the Replicators, the Ori, they've all used duplicates and spies at one time."

"Do I look like a Prior?" McKay retorted. "I mean, really. I have much better skin tone."

The medical corpsman's analysis unit gave a chime. "He's clean. It all matches up, blood, retina, voice print, the works."

Rodney clapped his hands together. "Great. Now we've established that I'm not a Cylon, can I please get to work?"

East nodded to the security guard, who opened the hatch. "Knock yourself out, Doctor. Just remember—"

"48 hours, right."

McKay's first thought on seeing the Asgard Core was of a church organ; the device resembled most of the consoles on Fenrir's ship, but it was larger, and forged from a strange hybrid of human and alien technologies. Multiple holographic screens danced in the air, projected from hidden emitter nodes in the complex metallic-crystalline matrix of the device.

His mouth went dry. Inside this machine lay the assembled secrets of a species that had been venturing across intergalactic space when mankind was still in the bronze age, a universe of knowledge belonging to a race that had shackled stars to their command, bent and twisted the laws of mathematics, quantum physics and biology… It was staggering to think of it.

For a moment, a flash of childhood memory replayed in his mind's eye; the day when he had taken his father's hand and followed him into the local public library for the very first time. The towering stacks of books reaching away from him, seeming to go on forever. *Knowledge*, there for the taking.

He blinked away the reverie. As much fun as it would be to dive into the depths of the core and find the answers to problems like the Collatz conjecture or the framework for a Grand Unified Theory, Rodney wasn't here to sightsee. He had a job to do, a target to locate.

McKay took a seat at the central console, the holographic screens orienting themselves obediently to him. "Open search engine," he told it, cracking his fingers. "Search parameters are as follows; tell me everything there is to know about the Asgard known as Fenrir."

Three words immediately appeared on all the screens. *NO DATA FOUND*.

He grinned. "You're just not looking hard enough." He leaned forward and began to work the keyboard in front of him.

There were just three of them left now, the other two nothing more than papery skin over jutting, angular bones.

One of the others bent over the last they had fed upon, placing his hand upon its sunken chest; but the feeding maw in his palm gained no purchase. There was no more life left to take.

With hard eyes, feral and hungry, the Wraith turned to face the others it shared a cell with. One was another functionary drone, but the other was the warrior. The warrior had made the decisions as to which of them would be sacrificed, as was the right of one so ranked in the clan. But now the choice of who would be fed upon next had narrowed too far. This time the Wraith drone would not accept its fate.

The warrior cocked his head, sensing the thoughts of its kindred. His lips drew back in a low snarl, daring the other Wraith to defy him, to attack.

And if he did, then what would happen? The thin veneer of control that had kept them barely sane, living out weeks and months since the alien had dragged them from the wreckage of their cruiser, that would break. It would shatter like glass and they would fall upon one another, fighting and feeding in frenzy until only one was left.

The low-ranked Wraith hesitated. No matter what happened, death was the only end point. He would either perish now at the hands of his own kind, eke out a slow and painful ending as a food source for his kindred, or—perhaps by some miracle—win out and survive to eventually die alone and starving.

Aching muscles coiled in his legs and his hands contracted into claws. So be it then; death now or death later. There was no point in waiting—

"Wait," said the warrior, a twitch on his face. "Wait. Listen."

At first he thought it was some sort of ploy, a distraction the warrior would use to blindside him and then drain him dry; but then he *heard*.

Not through the meat and bones of the audial pits on his cheeks and skull, but through the haze of his thoughts. Distant, like the sense of an electrical storm far beyond the horizon, close like the acidic stink of his own stale body fluids. He caught the eyes of the other Wraith in the cell with him and they all shared a nod of new, unshakable purpose.

It was a voice, echoing and approaching. A sweet, sweet voice dripping with promise and the raw pleasure of a feeding as yet untasted. A psychic bell tolling, the call of his clan Queen.

A single word, brimming with emotion and assurance.
Soon.

Teyla Emmagan stumbled to a halt in the corridor and put out a hand to steady herself, pressing the other to her head.
For a moment...
It was a spike of pain that lanced through her, harsh and brutal; but as quickly as it had arisen, it was gone, faded away as if it had never occurred.

I thought I heard…
She took a breath and straightened up.
Nothing. It was nothing…

CHAPTER TEN

"Jennifer?" Laaro held out a sample vial to her. "I was told to give this to you."

She gave the young boy a quick smile. "Hey, thanks." Keller turned the tube in her hand and read off the numbers written on the side. Another disappointment.

Her thoughts clearly showed on her face. "I'm sorry," said Laaro, as if the failure of the test solution was his fault.

"It's okay," she told him. "We'll just try again."

He watched her work for a moment. "Why did you choose this path, Jennifer?"

"Why did I become a doctor, is that what you mean?" She sighed. "I guess because it's what I'm best at. Sometimes, if you're lucky, you find a... A path that leads you where you need to go. And along the way you can help people." Keller paused and gave a self-conscious smirk. "Does that make sense?"

Laaro nodded solemnly. "It does. Do you think I could become a healer?"

"I don't see why not."

He nodded again, his eyes losing focus. "I... Want to help people. Like you do, like Kullid does."

Keller realized where this was coming from; Errian's condition had grown worse over the last day, and Laaro's fears for his father's wellbeing were bearing down on him. It was a lot for a child of his age to shoulder.

Kullid approached and the two healers shared a look. "Laaro," he began, "it's getting late. You should head home. Jaaya will worry about you."

"I can help here," insisted the boy, "at home I can do nothing."

"You can help your mother," came the reply. "Go on, go."

"It's okay," Keller added. "We can talk more later."

Laaro nodded dejectedly and left without another word.

Keller watched the youth go. "It can't be easy on him,"

"It isn't easy on anyone," Kullid said, his kind eyes fatigued. "The sickness touches those who are well as much as those afflicted."

"We will fix this," Keller insisted.

"I know you believe that. But I wonder if it is time to seek out another resolution..."

There was a clattering sound from the sick lodge's doorway, and the wooden slats came open awkwardly. Lieutenant Allan stood there, her face pale. "I, uh..." She took an unsteady step into the room.

Ronon rose quickly from the nearby sleeping pallet where he had been resting. "You all right?"

The officer blinked owlishly. "Not sure," she slurred. "Everything's all kinda... Colorful." Without warning, her legs gave out from under her, and Allan tipped forward, her eyes rolling back into her head, her P90 dropping from her fingers. Ronon was there to grab her before she hit the deck. She gasped and went limp.

Keller was instantly at the woman's side. "Give her some air,"

"The sickness—" began Kullid.

Jennifer shook her head. "She wasn't taken."

Ronon lay the lieutenant down on the pallet and swore beneath his breath. He turned her head and exposed a thin wooden blow dart in the flesh of her neck. "We got trouble." He went for his weapons, grabbing his gun belt where it lay across a stool.

Kullid removed the dart and sniffed the tip. "Fermented venom from the tepkay serpent. I use it myself to ease the pain of those with severe injuries. It will make her sleep deeply for a few hours."

Ronon came up with the particle magnum in his hand. "Get away from the doors and windows," he snapped, blinking away a twinge of pain.

From out of the evening shadows came a hooded figure, advancing slowly on the sick lodge. Keller became aware of more shapes through the slatted windows all around. The patients who had come awake at the sudden commotion shrank back towards the walls.

Jennifer reached out toward Allan's gun and a voice called out to her. "I wouldn't do that, Doctor. We don't want to fill this place any more, do we?"

"Soonir…" She recognized the intonation immediately.

The figure in the doorway glanced at Ronon and folded back the hood; the rebel leader gave him a cold look, as if daring him to shoot.

Keller placed a hand on the Satedan's arm. "It's okay."

"I don't think so," Dex grated. "He attacked the lieutenant."

"She will wake by dawn with an aching head but no other ill-effects," Soonir replied. "It was necessary to silence your guardian. She would have raised the alarm."

"What makes you think I won't?" Ronon stifled a hollow cough.

Soonir studied him. "You have the sickness. You can barely aim that pistol. You're more likely to injure yourself than me."

A cold smile crossed Ronon's lips. "I'm not that sick. But go ahead, try your luck. I could use something to break the boredom."

"I won't have violence here!" said Kullid. "This is a place of healing!"

"Quite so," said Soonir. "And the sickness is what I have come to speak of." He stepped inside, a pair of men emerging from the branches nearby to flank him.

With a scowl, Ronon let his gun drop away from a firing stance; but he did not return it to its holster.

Soonir glanced at Keller. "The truth is in short supply on Heruun, doctor. Takkol ensures that this is always so. I come to you because I believe you will not deceive me."

She met his gaze. "You've changed your tune. Last time I saw you, you were calling Rodney and me liars."

Soonir's face clouded for a moment. "I have since had opportunity to reflect on what took place at the lake. Perhaps I was too quick to draw conclusions."

"Or maybe you just realized that you're running out of friends?" offered Ronon.

"The only matter of importance is the freedom of my people," Soonir replied. "The events unfolding in the skies above our world have shifted the balance of our society and it is reeling! If we are to find any kind of stability, the full truth must be known!"

"And you are the man to tell it?" said Kullid.

The rebel leader shrugged off the cloak he wore. "Who else will do it? Aaren?" He snorted. "Takkol? Doctor Keller, let me ask you. Since the Returned were freed by your Colonel Sheppard, has Elder Takkol come to you, asked you to explain what happened up there?" He stabbed a finger toward the window and the night sky beyond. When Jennifer didn't reply, he smiled grimly. "No, I thought not. He does not want to know! He is afraid that the threat of the Aegis that backs his rule may be gone!" Soonir came closer, and Ronon moved to interpose himself between them. "I want to know if the rumors are more than fantasy, Doctor! Is the great power in the sky really a falsehood? Is it true that the Aegis is merely a living being like us, not some god or demon?"

Keller gave a slow nod. "What you know as the Aegis is a being called an Asgard. He's not like us, he's from a world very far from this one. But his people were extremely advanced. Their science is thousands of years beyond ours."

Soonir faltered for a moment, taking in her explanation; clearly he had not expected Keller to be so open, so quickly. "You Atlanteans are ranged far beyond the learning of all Heruun, and so if this Asgard dwarfs your knowledge, then it must be great indeed…"

"You said '*were*' extremely advanced not '*are*'," noted Kullid. "What happened to them?"

"He's the last one left of his kind," said Ronon, with a sneer. "And after what his Risar freaks tried to do to me, if I had my way he'd be as dead as all the rest of them."

"The last…" echoed Kullid, musing.

"But why did this being take our people?" said one of the rebel guards. Keller thought he looked familiar; she was sure she had seen him at Takkol's lodge. "Why did it blight us with the sickness?"

"Yes," said Soonir. "The Taken are Returned and Takkol tells us it will never occur again, but the sickness remains! The curse of the night!" He gestured at the people in the sick lodge.

"The Atlanteans aid us in the search for a cure," said Kullid. "We are close—"

Soonir waved him away. "You have searched for a treatment for years, healer, and found nothing."

"That's because he didn't have our help," Keller broke in. "The sickness is… It's a taint in the blood of the Returned. An accident. Once we can figure out how to purge it, it will never come back."

"An accident?" Soonir clearly found that difficult to accept.

"Doctor McKay has ventured back through the Gateway," added Kullid. "He will bring back new learning that will make the cure a reality."

The rebel leader was silent for a long moment. "I do not doubt your intentions, healers," he said, at length. "But until I see the sick restored, I remain unconvinced. And you should know that for all the false cheer Takkol demands, there is unrest here."

"Meaning what?" said Ronon.

"The people do not know what they should believe, voyager. Some fear Takkol and the other elders are in league with you and a new tyranny is on the rise. Others are afraid that the Aegis is dead and the shadow of the Wraith will soon fall across our world once more. There are even those who would welcome such a thing, those who believe it is fated." One of Soonir's men suddenly moved to the doorway, drawing his leader's attention. "There is confusion," he concluded, "and where that leads, violence is certain to follow."

"Guards are coming," said the man at the door. "We must go."

Soonir gave Keller and Ronon a hard glance. "Remember what I have said. Tell your Colonel Carter." He pushed past and moved toward the back of the lodge, vanishing into the darkness. "And be watchful."

Kullid shook his head. "What shall we do?"

"Keep quiet," Ronon growled, as the doorway crashed open

under the force of a boot heel.

Sheppard entered the core compartment, rubbing at the sore spot on his arm. "McKay?"

Across the room, panes of shimmering holographic text hung in the air, crowding around the sloped console of the Asgard supercomputer. "Over here," said Rodney, over the rapid-fire tapping of fingers across a keyboard. McKay gave him the briefest of looks. "Let me guess. Blood test?"

Sheppard nodded, navigating through the floating screens. "I'm surprised they didn't ask me for the fillings in my teeth and my first-born child as well."

"Yeah, I bet SG-1 wouldn't get the same treatment…" He reached up and touched a screen, making it turn in virtual space. "Look at this. I found our little grey buddy. Chapter and verse, right here."

Sheppard studied the picture of an Asgard for a moment, his lip curled. "They all look the same to me."

"That's because they are all the same, more or less."

"Why didn't these files open for the *Odyssey* crew?"

"Encryption," replied McKay, with a smug smile. "The Asgard use layered structures inside their computer architecture, and they encode each tier with a different cipher. The lower levels are so heavily coded that unless you know they're there, you'd never find them."

"Nice work,"

"Yes, I like to think so."

Sheppard stood in front of the console; with all the holo-screens around them, it was like being in a hall of mirrors; except instead of reflections, there were streaming waterfalls of dense alien text. "So, what's the scoop on Fenrir."

The momentary grin on Rodney's face slipped. "I don't think he's been entirely forthcoming with us, that's for sure. The reason Fenrir's records were so hard to find was because they didn't appear in the central registry. They were in a sub-frame belonging to the Asgard equivalent of the, ah, correctional system."

The colonel's eyes narrowed. "He's a convict?" Sheppard

had a crazy mental image of the diminutive alien wearing an orange prisoner's jumpsuit. "I thought they were too advanced for all that kind of thing, y'know, lawbreaking and stuff."

"We know there have been other renegade Asgard. There was Loki, who conducted human biological experiments on Earth…" Rodney paused. "To be honest, I think the Asgard hid these files because they were an embarrassment to them."

"What did he do, McKay? I'm guessing from the look on your face that it's something big."

"You're not wrong." The scientist got up and came around the console, bringing a data pad with him that trailed glowing cables from an interface socket on the core. "From what I can see, Fenrir was originally a bio-researcher working with some of their biggest brains—Heimdall, Sigyn, Thor, those guys—on their life-extension project. But then the Replicators became a problem and he switched majors, so to speak. After one of their main colony worlds was consumed, it says here, he began work on a crash development program."

"Military research?"

"Bingo." McKay began manipulating the pad, and the holographic projectors in the core moved the screens out across the room, the panels growing wider and larger. Sheppard saw images of a blue-white world of large oceans and massive ice sheets webbed by Asgard mega-cities, then time-lapse scans of the surface turning dark as a tide of Replicators advanced across it. By the time the short animation concluded, the planet was a wasteland. Rodney continued; "Whatever he was working on, it was big. The data is buried so deep I need a jackhammer to dig it out…" Red runes in the Asgard language flared brightly around them as McKay hacked the security codes keeping the files closed. "Wait. Wait. No. I've got this."

Like a dam bursting, all the holographic screens flooded with data as Rodney broke the lock and released the files. Sheppard picked out fleeting schematics for an Asgard warship, the complex orbital structure of a solar system, a cutaway globe showing the interior of a star; and repeating over and over was a symbol, a stark vertical line on a dark background. He pointed into the hologram. "What does this mean?"

When McKay looked up from the data pad his expression was bleak. "It's a warning. An Asgard rune. It's the character '*Isa*', it means ice, entropy...the end of the universe."

Elder Aaren and a group of armed guards crowded into the sick lodge's anteroom.

"Where is he?" Aaren demanded. Without waiting for an answer, he bellowed an order at his men. "Find him, bring him to me!"

The guards barged in and began a forceful, careless search.

"Hey, watch it!" snapped Keller, as one of the men almost tipped a table of lab gear on to the floor.

"Where is Soonir?" snapped the elder.

Ronon made a show of sitting down. "Who?"

"I know he was here." Aaren turned and glared at Keller. "Again we find you in his company, Doctor! Why does a healer collude with a militant, answer me that?"

Jennifer drew herself up. She didn't like this guy's attitude. "The only thing I am doing is trying to protect people. The way I see it, the only thing you're protecting is your...self!"

Aaren's nostrils flared in annoyance and he took a threatening step toward her. Ronon leaned forward and flicked his pistol around in a spin; the simple action stopped the elder cold. His expression changed, becoming one of false kindness, but Keller could see the fury boiling away just underneath the surface.

"Perhaps I was mistaken. Forgive my zeal." He snapped his fingers and his men returned to him; it was clear by now that Soonir was long gone. He paused on the threshold and glanced over his shoulder at the doctor. "Soonir is a dangerous man. The people need protection from someone like him. Anyone who associates with that man will be considered to be his accomplices and treated as such... No matter who they are or where they come from."

Pages of data from Fenrir's research projects hung around the walls of the compartment, mute representations of the ruthless science the Asgard had employed in his studies.

"Talk to me, Rodney," said Sheppard. "Tell me what this

stuff all means. You're the only person in the room with a PhD, remember?"

McKay's free hand turned in the air. "Several, actually," he said absently. "Oh boy. This is… Incredible."

"And not in a good way. I'm getting that."

"Fenrir's new project was a super-weapon, something so powerful it was capable of obliterating entire star systems…" Rodney shook his head, as if he couldn't believe what he was reading. "A sun killer. Good grief. He built a collapsar bomb."

"Nightfall," murmured Sheppard.

McKay waved the data pad at a graphic of a device, a cylindrical module bearing the 'isa' rune that had appeared earlier. "That's it."

"How does it work? Is it a beam, a missile?"

McKay shook his head. "It's the ultimate in scorched-earth devices. I mean, forget your nukes or your fusion warheads, those are like firecrackers compared to a collapsar device." He stuffed the data pad under his armpit and made a globe with his hands. "Every star has a finite life span, right? After so many billions of years they burn out and implode—"

"Collapse."

"Right. But some go beyond that super-compacting level, they go past the point of no return and become a singularity, a collapsar!" Rodney was speaking rapidly now, animated by the lethal power of what he was describing. "A gravitational maelstrom so powerful that nothing can escape it, not even light itself, something that is literally a death star!" He closed his hands into tight ball. "A black hole."

Sheppard turned back and looked at the solar system model he had seen earlier, a small orange star orbited by a spread of six planets. "And that would be goodnight for any planets in the vicinity."

McKay nodded. "See, that kind of stellar collapse takes a long time to come about. I mean, most species would have either evolved far enough along to leave their planet behind before this could ever happen to them, or else they'd have been exterminated in one of their star's earlier expansive phases. But Fenrir figured out how to make a sun go black *in minutes*."

"How is that possible?"

He worked the pad and brought the cutaway of the star to the front of the forest of images. "We know the Asgard have an deep understanding of cosmology, temporal physics, matter-energy transfer... This is a merging of all three." He pointed at the heart of the star where a diamond-shaped glyph had appeared. "The collapsar bomb is beamed into the middle of the star and it generates a fast-time field." Sheppard watched as a globe of white energy expanded out of the device. "Everything inside that radius experiences the passage of time at a vastly accelerated rate, we're talking a trillion years in a nanosecond." The image expanded until it was filling the room.

Sheppard nodded grimly as the enormity of what he was watching became clearer. "It eats the heart out of the sun. Turns it rotten inside."

Suddenly the graphic vanished and became a hyper-detailed image of the star and its worlds, moving about their orbital paths, turning before them in silence.

He felt giddy for a moment at the stark transition and rocked back on his heels. The colonel felt as if he could reach out and touch the glowing sun.

"And then..." McKay's voice was hushed. "Instant stellar collapse."

Silently, the star died in front of them. The glowing sphere seemed to shake, trembling like a soap bubble in a breeze, suddenly vulnerable. Flares erupted all over its surface, turning it into a furious churn of energy; the color of the sun shifted, darkening as its spectra was broken apart. Sheppard's breath caught in his throat as the orange star flickered and contracted, as if an invisible hand were tightening around it.

Then came the flash; the murdered sun pulsed brilliant white, the image throwing stark, hard-edged shadows across the walls of the compartment. He reflexively looked away, the intense light pricking his eyes.

"X-rays," said Rodney. "An output equal to billions of hydrogen bombs."

Sheppard blinked away the purple after-image from his retinas, and watched an expanding sphere of the radiation shockwave swell. It crossed the orbits of the inner worlds first, then reached inexorably toward the larger planets and the gas giants further out. He saw one desert globe as it passed within arm's length of his face; the wave kissed it and it turned black. "Nothing could survive that." His throat was dry.

McKay shook his head. "Any habitable world is burnt to a cinder. The radiation turns the atmosphere into plasma. A planet-sized firestorm."

Now the star began a final, inexorable spiral toward implosion, the wreckage of the sun and the halo of stellar material crowding it drawing back, retreating inward. The single point of light grew darker and darker, the orbits of the devastated worlds twisting as gravity grew stronger. The shattered planets coiled in, falling toward a second death.

There was a final, brief eruption of color, and then the star was gone; in its place, a featureless ball of blackness surrounded by a disc of dead matter.

Abruptly, the image froze and Sheppard gasped; without realizing, he'd been holding in his breath. "That's a pretty damned final solution," he admitted. "Deploy that in a system infested by Replicators and you'd wipe them out. The speed that happened, they'd never even have the time to jump into hyperspace." He turned to Rodney. "But this has gotta be a theory, though, right? I mean, tell me they didn't actually build this thing?"

The color drained from McKay's face and he looked up from the data pad in his hand. "John... What we just saw... That wasn't a simulation. That was a recording of an actual real-time sensor log. Fenrir's weapon killed six planets. One of them had a pre-industrial culture living on it."

A hot flare of anger struck him. "Why the hell would he do that?"

The panes of text returned, the image of the dead sun vanishing. "It was a error. A misfire."

"An error?" Sheppard snapped. "A whole star system ripped apart by mistake? That's a pretty damned big screw up!"

McKay nodded. "There's a report here, written by none other than Thor himself." He paused, reading. "Fenrir was running a test of the collapsar device's deployment system, against the advice of the Asgard Council. He had been warned that it wasn't ready, but Fenrir didn't agree. He wanted to certify it ready to use against the Replicators. It was never supposed to trigger."

"But it did." Sheppard ran a hand down his face. "Holy crap, how do we know he doesn't have more of these things on board that ship of his?" He moved to the intercom panel. "I'm calling the bridge. We'll get *Odyssey* to send Atlantis a flash traffic message, warn Carter—"

"Wait!" McKay grabbed his arm. "This is an Asgard we're talking about, remember? Don't forget, most of the cutting edge tech on our ships is based on hardware they gave us! And that includes our FTL communications."

"Meaning any signal we send Fenrir could read and decrypt." Sheppard was silent for a long moment. "We have to go back, then, warn Atlantis in person. Download everything you can pack into a hard drive. We gotta jet, right this minute."

But McKay's attention was on the screens of data. "Just a second," he said, his eyes widening. "There's more here. Another holographic file, bearing Thor's personal seal."

Sheppard hesitated; what he had seen troubled him greatly, and he couldn't get the image of the dying star from his mind, imagining the same horror unfolding inside Atlantis's sun, the same monstrous storm of boiling atmosphere engulfing the ocean planet and the city of the Ancients. But too he understood that they needed to know the whole story before they returned the Pegasus galaxy.

"Okay," he said. "Run it."

"So," said Corporal Kennedy, "you're an Asgard, then."

The tall alien creature standing across the corridor from him gave the soldier a curious, doll-eyed look. "This is a Risar," it explained. "It is a fabricated short-span genetic construct drawn from optimized Asgard DNA, retro-evolved for greater physical strength and motility."

"Right. Thanks for clearing that up." Kennedy gave a nod, and scratched at his arm. He felt a faint crawling sensation on his flesh and dismissed it. The aliens on this ship had precious little to say, and so far all his attempts at a conversation had been non-starters. He glanced away down the corridor. He still had half his shift to go before Major Lorne sent someone to relieve him, and like most guard duty, this job had nothing to break up the monotony. The interior of the Asgard ship was almost identical throughout; Kennedy idly wondered if maybe the aliens saw colors in a different way to humans, and what looked like plain metal to him was actually highly decorated to the Asgard. *Or Risar, or whatever they want to call themselves—*

The sound was so quick, so fleeting that he almost missed it. A scratching, skittering, something with too many legs running across bare steel. His hand went to the grip of his P90. "Did you hear that?"

The Risar cocked its head. "I heard nothing."

The corporal sighted down the barrel of the submachine gun, bringing the butt plate tight to his shoulder. For a moment, he thought he saw a blurred shadow at the corner of his vision. "Over there…"

Then the sound again, this time from the other end of the corridor. He spun in place, bringing the weapon to bare. Suddenly he was sweating. Kennedy thumbed off the safety catch. In the places where the glow-lamps on the walls didn't work shadows fell in deep patches. He saw movement, arachnid shapes with shiny chitinous carapaces and iridescent wings.

The Risar watched him in expressionless silence.

He glared at the alien. "Are you blind?" he demanded. "Don't you see them?"

"I do not understand what you are referring to," it replied.

The tap-tap-tapping became a rattle, then a thunder. The shadows were marching closer, thickening, growing in depth, coming at him with needle-sharp mandibles and scraping claws. Both ends of the corridor were choked with insects, a tidal wave of them, threatening to engulf him. Kennedy squeezed the trigger and fired bursts of rounds into the darkness, but the bullets whined away harmlessly.

Suddenly the Risar was upon him, strong, slender fingers grabbing at his weapon. "Cease fire," it said. "There is no enemy here."

"Get off me!" he shouted, and brought his head forward, butting the alien in the chin. It grunted and staggered from the impact, but didn't release him. "They'll kill us both!" The insect-sound was everywhere now, inside his head, echoing through his bones, and his flesh crawled with the proximity of them.

He had to escape. Had to find somewhere safe, a place where the monstrous bugs could never get inside.

On the Risar's belt was a glowing yellow-white orb. Kennedy snatched it up and brandished it at the door to his back.

"Desist," said the alien, but he was already at the hatch. With a hiss, the doors to the cell parted and the corporal stumbled inside, dragging the Risar with him. The creature clawed at his arm and he swatted it away, slamming it into the wall with a roundhouse punch.

But the sound did not abate; if anything, it grew louder. He was dimly aware of three figures standing in the centre of the chamber, hands palm-to-palm like the members of some strange séance. *Wraith*, said a far distant voice in his mind, an echo of something Major Lorne had once told him, *they mess with your head.*

"No," he snarled, forcing the sound away, trying to focus. His fingers felt slippery around the P90, and when he looked down the weapon was covered in blurry, crawling shapes, indistinct ghost-things that nipped and whispered over his hands.

He cried out in alarm, and it seemed to break the spell; the trio of Wraith turned from their circle.

In one fluid movement they fell upon him, razor-toothed maws in the palms of their hands reaching for him. Together, they tore the life from his flesh, feeding until he was ashes. The Risar, bleeding thin grayish fluid from a cut on its head, died next, caught as it stumbled away down the corridor.

Giddy with the violent pleasure of the nourishment, the three Wraith paused, listening to the serene voice in their heads.

It is time, it told them. *Do as I command you.*

She felt the pain again, and this time it almost forced her to the ground. Teyla staggered and fell against one of the control room's consoles for support. A tight gasp escaped her lips.

Fenrir's hologram materialized next to her. "*Are you unwell?*" There were a pair of Risar in the chamber, and as one they turned to face her, ready to follow any orders the Asgard would give.

"Something is wrong." She bit out the words. The agony lanced through her head, bringing tears to her eyes. Amid the pain she could sense the echo of a voice, a thought, a feeling. A cold, calculating anger. "The Wraith…"

One of the consoles chimed and a Risar glanced at it. "Warning," it explained, likely more for Teyla's benefit than any other reason. "Weapons fire detected, tier nine."

Fenrir's face stiffened. "*The holding cells.*" The holographic image froze for a split-second as processing power was diverted to some other task. When it refreshed, the Asgard's dark eyes were drawn into tight slits. "*A Risar is dead.*"

The blinding headache suddenly abated, and Teyla drew in a gasp of air. "The Wraith have escaped."

"*You seem to be certain of this.*"

She nodded. "The Wraith elements in my DNA provide me with a certain…insight." Teyla took a deep breath. "Before, I sensed something, but it was so fleeting I couldn't be sure." The moment of psychic contact she sensed had to be overspill from a communication directed to the prisoners, a telepathic message so strong it could be sent over interstellar distances. Only a Hive Queen was capable of such a feat.

"*Extrasensory perception,*" remarked Fenrir, "*a most unique phenomenon.*"

"This is not random," she told the Asgard, reaching for her radio. "They have chosen this moment for a reason."

"Attempting to isolate intruders," said the other Risar. "Scans are inconclusive. Repairs to internal sensors remain incomplete. Unable to locate targets."

Teyla raised the walkie-talkie to her lips. "Colonel Carter, do you read me? We have a situation."

Lorne gave the colonel a look; both he and his commander

heard the warning in the Athosian's tone.

"Carter here," said the colonel, raising her voice to be heard over the thrumming of the engine core. "Teyla, what's going on? Corporal Kennedy missed his check-in."

"*The Wraith prisoners are free,*" came the dour reply. "*The corporal has most likely been killed.*"

Lorne swore under his breath and ratcheted the slide on is P90. He grabbed his radio and toggled it to the all-units guard frequency. "All teams, go to alert. We have Wraith targets in the clear, repeat Whiskey-Tangos loose on the ship. Weapons free."

He had barely said the words when the chatter of gunfire sounded from the upper level of the engine chamber.

"Contact!" snapped Carter.

The hatches hissed open and a trooper fell backwards into the room, retreating along the upper gantry, his assault rifle firing bursts from the hip. A pair of ragged Wraith hurtled after him; one held a pistol in either hand and came on, blazing away with each weapon; the other marched a dying man in before him as a human shield, feeding on his fresh kill even as he moved.

The major and the colonel took aim and opened fire, their shots flashing off the metal and plastic of the raised platform; but the predatory aliens were moving fast, dodging and slashing with their claws.

The second Wraith snarled and pitched the near-dead corpse of its feeding victim into the air, off the gantry and down. The soldier bounced off the protective field around the spinning energy-exchanger rings of the drive core, and fell with a sickening crack into a heap.

Lorne saw the soldier with the assault rifle take a round in his leg and stumble. The armed Wraith dove at him, wild for new prey. He led the target and bracketed it with a full-auto discharge, knocking it down; but incredibly, the alien was still alive. The major ripped out a spent stick of ammunition and slammed a fresh clip into the breech.

"There's two," shouted Carter, firing and moving, trying to draw a bead on the other attacker. "There were three in the cell! Where's the other one?"

The door hummed opened and a dead Risar was thrown into the chamber. Teyla saw the two flash bang grenades that had been stabbed into its flesh and instinctively threw herself away from the corpse, down behind the cover of a console.

The concussion wave clipped her as she moved, the magnesium-bright flare of white light blazing through the room.

Unprepared for the shock effect, the two Risar gave off strange, low groans and touched their faces in a peculiarly human gesture. They blundered about, dazzled and stunned.

Teyla smelled the Wraith before she saw it, sensed it entering the smoke-wreathed room behind her. Snatching the stunner pistol from her belt holster, she pivoted, turning to come up on one knee.

She heard Fenrir call her name in warning. The alien warrior was already upon her, and with a savage kick, it connected with her wrist and knocked the gun flying. She staggered, stumbling backwards, trying not to lose her balance.

It was the same Wraith she and Ronon had encountered in the cells. He gave a hissing chuckle. "You again. I thought I could feel you." It tapped its head. "In here." The alien drew two blades from its belt; they were USAF-issue combat knives, and one of them was still wet with human blood. "I wonder, what will it feel like when I kill you?"

CHAPTER ELEVEN

Rodney reached out and touched a virtual tab on one of the holo-screens. The panel unfolded, panes extending and shifting, infinite boxes building upon one another until they had grown to encompass the entire room. Instead of the data cascades or the unreal images of the star system, new scenery projected itself over the walls of the compartment, building simulated ceilings and walls, sketching in metallic chairs and tables, an arching bench and an enclosed dais; he had the immediate impression of a courtroom.

The detail was indistinguishable from the real thing. McKay and Sheppard were no longer in a cramped room aboard the starship *Odyssey*, they were standing in a long vaulted chamber on the far distant—and now long since destroyed—planet Hala.

As a last touch, the holo-projectors conjured images of a handful of Asgard, each one standing at a different podium. Most were unadorned, but some wore metallic collars about their throats, ornate devices that appeared to be as much technological as ceremonial.

The last of the aliens to appear stood alone, isolated and off to the far side of the room.

"Fenrir..." muttered Sheppard. There was no-one else it could have been.

McKay glanced around. The illusion of being there was total, the actual walls of the core room hidden beneath the false reality of the Asgard chamber. As long as they didn't stray to far from where they stood, there would be nothing to break the artifice of it.

One of the Asgard took the tallest of the podia and swept a gaze across the room. "Here comes the judge," said Sheppard, from the side of his mouth. "This is like *A Few Good Asgard...*"

"This assembly is gathered to address a matter of most serious import," said the alien. "Let the record show that I, Thor, First Scientist and Commander, have opened this conclave."

"That's Thor…" whispered McKay. "He's not what I expected."

"Did you think he'd be taller?" Sheppard eyed him. "And why are you whispering? It's not like they can hear us."

Rodney nodded. "I know that," he said defensively. "I was just, uh, paying attention."

Another Asgard bowed. "I, Eldir, Healer and Biologist, second the word of Thor."

The other aliens ranged in a semi-circle bowed their heads and spoke one at a time.

"Freyr, Commander, accedes."

"Penegal, Counselor, consents to this."

"Jarnsaxa, Commander, agrees."

"Hermiod, Engineer, gives consent."

Sheppard wandered closer to the alien engineer and studied him. "Our little buddy from the *Daedalus*," he noted. "Guess this was him in his younger years…"

Thor looked right through the colonel to the podium where Fenrir stood. "You know why you have been called to this place," he began. "You must answer for your crime."

Fenrir's eyes flashed and he looked up. "I committed no crime." There was real heat in his retort. "What transpired was an accident. I deeply regret it, but it was through no deliberate action of mine."

"That is open to definition," said Jarnsaxa; the Asgard's voice had a slightly feminine timbre. "How would you characterize the action of negligence? Is that deliberate, or not?"

"Warnings were given," stated Hermiod. "On more than one occasion, as I have documented." A panel of text floated into being before him, runes filling the space. "They were ignored."

Freyr leaned forward. "Is that so, Fenrir?"

"I did not ignore Hermiod's counsel…" muttered the alien. "I merely considered it to be… Too conservative."

Eldir nodded. "The engineer's cautious nature is well known

to all of us, that is so." Hermiod made a tutting noise as the biologist continued. "But surely there were other concerns?"

"Nothing I considered insurmountable," Fenrir replied.

Thor seized on the comment. "So you concede that you were aware the collapsar device was flawed?"

"Not flawed," came the firm reply, "only untested."

McKay watched the action unfold, his head going back and forth as if he were observing a tennis match. Fenrir seemed different from the alien he had briefly met aboard the *Aegis*; this other version of him seemed more arrogant and cocksure, defiant in the face of the assembly's displeasure.

"And so you deployed an *untested* device that you were aware could malfunction, within a populated star system." Freyr's words were flat and damning. "The result is known to us all."

"I'll say," added Sheppard.

"It was an accident!" Fenrir snapped; McKay had never heard of an Asgard shouting before, but there it was. "The detonation profile was never meant to progress beyond the initial phase! But there was radiation interference—"

"Has that been confirmed?" Penegal, who had remained silent until now, addressed the question to Hermiod. Clearly he was of important rank; when he spoke, the others fell quiet.

Hermiod gave a terse nod. "Yes, counselor. But it was a known phenomena. It should have been guarded against."

"It was," insisted Fenrir, "just not well enough."

A question was forming in McKay's mind at the same moment Jarnsaxa gave it voice. "Why did you choose this system to test the collapsar device? Why not another, with no indigenous life?"

Fenrir's hands reached out and clutched the podium before him. "It was the best profile in our database. The presence of life was not an issue. I expected no complications. I was secure in the knowledge of my own skills."

"Huh," said the colonel. "Who does that remind me of?"

"Are you ever going to let that drop? I blew up one planet with nobody on it," scowled Rodney. "He destroyed a whole star system. Big difference."

Eldir was speaking once again. "Then you are not guilty of negligence. Only arrogance."

Fenrir drew back. "I have made myself clear. I am not the only Asgard to have made errors in his works."

"Loki was punished for his misdeeds," offered Thor, but Fenrir ignored the comment and spoke over him.

"I did only what I thought was right! I did what was needed to forge a way to defend us against the threat of the Replicators!"

"By building an unstable weapon of unmatched lethality?" said Freyr. "Perhaps, if you had remained within your original field of expertise—"

"The losses inflicted on all of us by the Replicators are open wounds," said Penegal, bringing silence once again. "The worlds they have destroyed, the numbers of our kindred killed..." He gave Fenrir a meaningful look. "We have all suffered great losses."

"Revenge..." muttered Sheppard, seeing the moment between the two aliens. "Is that what it was about? Fenrir lost someone he cared about to the Replicators, so he went gung ho?"

"But that forgives nothing," noted Thor. "A terrible error has been made. It cannot be undone. There must be consequences."

"Here it comes," said McKay. "They're going to throw the book at him."

"I reject the authority of this assembly," Fenrir sneered. "I reject any edicts you may make!"

Jarnsaxa nodded. "That right is yours, if you wish to be avowed as a renegade. If you wish to follow in the footsteps of Loki and all the others who renounced our ways. But if you make that choice, you will be declared lost. You will no longer be one of us."

The room was silent for a moment, before Thor spoke again. "I move we declare a punishment for Fenrir."

"Did the Asgard have the death penalty?" said Sheppard. "Did they even have prisons?"

"I don't know," McKay admitted. "I didn't think they'd ever had need of that kind of thing. They were a highly evolved and intelligent species."

Sheppard folded his arms. "Those two things don't automatically make you a saint," he replied. "Look at the Ancients. Hell, look at the Ori."

The other aliens spoke again, each one saying the same single word. "*Exile.*"

"Fenrir," Thor was solemn, "it is our judgment that you will be banished from the worlds of the Asgard for five hundred seasons."

"Your body will be placed in stasis aboard your ship," said Penegal, "and it will roam the galactic clusters, on a course set to return you to Hala when your sentence is complete."

"Your mind will remain in a wakeful state," added Thor. "On your journey, you will have time to reflect on the mistakes your haste and belligerence have led to."

"A penal cruise," murmured McKay. "That's why his ship was in the Pegasus galaxy. It would have had to drop out of hyperspace every so often to make course corrections."

Sheppard gave a slow nod. "And he just happened to find himself in the middle of a Wraith hunting party. There's a battle, his ship is damaged, he crash-lands on the moon… And the rest we know."

If anything, the pale flesh of Fenrir's face was even more pallid than usual. "And if I choose not to agree to your decree?" he demanded.

"Then your exile will be permanent," said Freyr, with finality. "You will die alone, lost to the Asgard for all time."

Fenrir looked down. "It seems that I have no choice." The Asgard's head snapped up abruptly, and he glared at Thor. "But you will not banish the Replicators so easily! They will destroy us… Or we will destroy ourselves in the fight with them."

The image froze and disintegrated, becoming grainy clusters of holographic pixels that melted away; once more McKay and Sheppard stood in the middle of the dull grey compartment, the bubble of illusion broken.

"He was right, in a way," said Rodney. "The Asgard did destroy themselves trying to endure long enough to wipe out the threat of the Replicators. It's ironic, really. Thor and the others actually used Fenrir's collapsar technology to destroy Hala's sun when the Replicators finally overran the planet."

Sheppard picked up McKay's data pad and handed it to him. The colonel's expression was bleak. "We've got the whole story now," he said. "We have to warn the others. Until we know otherwise, we have to consider Fenrir a threat."

Teyla ducked as the combat knives slashed through air. She felt the wind of the blades passing on her face and pivoted, sending a hard sweep kick out at the legs of the Wraith warrior. He dodged and gave a guttural chuckle, rebounding off a bouncing motion to come at her again. This time he stabbed and slashed, aiming at the centre of her body mass, her abdomen.

The Athosian's fighting sticks slipped from the sleeves on her thighs and into her hands. She blocked and parried, aware that the bigger, more muscular alien was pushing her back toward the Asgard cryogenic capsule. He stabbed out again, trying to draw blood.

"I know you are with child," it snarled, "I smell it inside you. It makes you hesitant! The fear makes you slow. Too afraid to exert, to fight!" The warrior laughed again.

"If that comment was meant to intimidate me," she said between grunts of breath, "then all you have proven is how little you know of Athos's daughters!" Teyla flicked the sticks around and hit the Wraith in the face with the blunt ends; the blows caught the sensitive sensory pits on the cheekbones and drew a reedy yowl of agony from the alien as it rocked backward.

"I will cut your spawn from you!" Fresh with anger, the warrior went for her once again.

Lorne used the oddly-shaped hand-holds on the plastic ladder to propel himself up to the drive room's second tier. He led with the P90 and fired off a burst; his target, the Wraith that had used one of his men as a shield, spat at him and threw itself off the balcony, somersaulting to land on its feet across from Carter. "Colonel!" he shouted.

She took aim without looking his way. "I got this," she

replied, and opened fire.

Satisfied Carter was in control down there, Lorne vaulted up the rest of the way to the upper tier. A few feet away, an airman fought face-to-face with a snarling Wraith, the two of them going tug-of-war over the assault rifle trapped diagonally between them. The airman was bleeding from scratch wounds across the face, one eye bloody and gummed shut; the Wraith was attacking in a frenzy and the fight wouldn't last much longer.

Lorne had emptied half a clip of ammo into the freakish alien and still it wasn't lying down to die. He dimly remembered something Doctor Beckett had once said about the Wraith, how they regenerated faster than anything, how their bodies appeared to secrete some kind of enzyme that made them ignore pain, set themselves into a berserker rage or something…

The two combatants were too close for Lorne to chance taking a shot; he was good marksman but he wasn't going to risk it. *If in doubt, fall back on traditional methods,* he told himself.

The major turned around the very hi-tech, state-of-art submachine gun in his hands and proceeded to use it in the manner of a weapon that his species had been employing since before they walked upright. Lorne clubbed the Wraith hard in the spine with the butt of the SMG and heard a nasty crunch of breaking cartilage. The alien howled and spun about to attack him, slamming the injured airman to the floor. The major hit it again and knocked the Wraith off balance; then before it could shake off the pain, he put the P90 back the way it was supposed to be and squeezed the trigger.

Teyla saw the two Risar that had been stunned by the flash bang grenades shake off the effects and as one, rush the Wraith. The alien heard their heavy footfalls across the steely deck and spun the combat knives about, bringing the pommels to his thumbs. With a sudden, hard strike, the warrior stabbed backward and buried the blades to the hilt in the chests of the Risar drones. Fenrir's clone-proxies spat grey foam and fell

STARGATE ATLANTIS: NIGHTFALL

to their knees with airy moans; of the Asgard's holographic projection, there was no sign.

She took the opening presented to her and slammed the sticks toward the bruises she had made on the Wraith's face; it blocked her with bone-armored wrist guards. Teyla pressed the attack, regaining some of the ground she had lost.

But something seemed wrong. Many times she had fought the Wraith, many times in hand-to-hand combat just as she did now, and she knew their ways. Wraith warriors did not play the tactical game, they did not wait for opportunity or moment, most certainly not when fighting a single, lightly armed opponent. Teyla kept waiting for the creature to claw at her, to make a pass with the fanged maw in the meat of its hand; but he did none of those things, instead defending, not attacking. Marking time. *Waiting for something.*

Sam chased the Wraith around the chamber, finding it and throwing bursts of blazing gunfire wherever it paused; she had to concentrate hard. The thing was trying to cloud her mind, to throw off her perceptions. She'd read the reports filed by Colonel Sheppard and other members of the Atlantis military contingent; no-one was quite sure how the aliens did it, the effect was some kind of natural psychic aura they gave off to confuse their prey.

Carter was damned if she was going to be *that*.

The way to beat the Wraith mind games was to concentrate, to burn through it. Fail, and it was a downward spiral; once you were convinced there were more of them, or that they were hiding in every dark corner, they had you. Sam's eyes narrowed and she focused everything into the small cone of vision down the iron sights of her P90. The fogging flickered, faded—

"Gotcha," she snapped.

A tongue of muzzle flare leapt from the barrel of her weapon, a fully automatic storm of hollow point bullets ripping into the torso of the alien, shredding the ragged leather jerkin and hammering it backwards. Carter moved up from the partial cover of a console and nudged the Wraith with her boot. The acrid smell of cordite was strong, along with the battery-acid stink of the Wraith themselves.

Black, oily blood pooling in its mouth, the alien fixed her with a glare and did something she wasn't expecting. It grinned.

"I... Can only die once," it managed, coughing. "But the Queen... Will take you to death and bring you back, over and over. Kill you a hundred times..." A spasm ran through the Wraith and it fell silent.

"The Queen," repeated Carter. Ice formed in the pit of her stomach. "Major Lorne!" she shouted. "This isn't over yet!"

The alert siren was a peculiar ululating whoop, and it reverberated through the chamber. The sound startled Teyla for a split second, and she flinched, ready for the blow that her momentary distraction would allow the Wraith warrior to inflict.

It never came. The warrior grunted with amusement and dropped its guard, clawed fingers flexing as its hands fell to its sides. Teyla held her fighting sticks to the ready, unsure of how to react. What kind of ploy was this? Surrender? A Wraith would only do such a thing if grossly outmatched, and she, as much as Teyla was sure of her fighting skills, was at best only an opponent of level prowess.

The hatchway opened and a quartet of Risar lumbered into the chamber.

"Teyla Emmagan," said one of them. "Step away from the prisoner."

"I have the situation in hand," she panted.

The Wraith chuckled again. The noise was a rattle, like stones in a can. "Nothing could be further from the truth. If you have any intelligence, you will surrender to me now."

"I see no reason to do so," retorted the woman, adrenaline still coursing through her.

"No?" It cocked its head, and Teyla felt a brief moment of pressure deep inside her skull. "Ask your friend." The warrior gestured at the cryogenic pod.

Fenrir's projection reformed in a whirl of photons. "*We*

are in danger," said the Asgard urgently. "*We must retreat. A battle cannot be won in this state against such odds.*"

"What are you talking about?" she demanded, even as a spidery sensation crawled along the flesh of her spine. "No…"

"Oh, yes," rumbled the Wraith. "Reach out, Teyla. Reach out and know that your defeat is coming."

A holo-screen sketched itself in above the consoles in the room, displaying an image of Heruun turning slowly beneath a black sky. A shape, a massive insectile form of bone and chitin, crawled inexorably up over the horizon from the planet's far side, homing in on the orbit of the *Aegis*.

"Hive Ship," she breathed, her blood chilled.

The Wraith nodded. "My Queen approaches."

In the drive core, the siren was accompanied by red-orange strobes that gave the room a hellish, otherworldly glow.

"Teyla!" Carter spoke into her radio. "What's going on up there? The power systems are ramping up to maximum. What's Fenrir doing? We haven't even tested them at half-capacity yet!"

In reply, a flash of light signaled the appearance of the Asgard's holographic avatar. "*Colonel Carter, the status of main weapons and shields remains inactive. Auxiliary craft offensive capabilities are insufficient to match threat. This vessel cannot resist.*"

"What threat?" demanded Lorne.

"At a guess, a Hive Ship…" said Carter, fixing the image of the alien with a hard glare. "Or worse."

"*Worse would suggest there is a greater extant threat to the safety of this ship at this time.*" Fenrir glanced at one of the control consoles and it lit up, streams of indicators turning a stark blue.

The spinning rings of the power train moved faster and faster, becoming a blur. "Fenrir, what are you doing?" said the colonel. "The sub-light engines may not be able to handle full thrust."

"*I do not intend to employ the sub-light engines,*" came the reply. "*I would suggest you prepare yourself. Many of the*

*required safeguards are not in place. You may find this dis-
placement uncomfortable.*" The avatar winked out, leaving
them alone in the engine room.

In that moment, Sam knew exactly what was going to happen. "No—!"

In the skies above Heruun, a skein of coruscating blue-white
energy rippled into existence, spilling out from the gap between
quantum states, bleeding icy color across the void. The hammerhead shape of the Asgard vessel *Aegis* turned in a steep,
ungainly banking turn and fell toward the phenomenon, retreating from the questing lines of plasma fire reaching out from
the encroaching Hive Ship. The vessel touched the ephemeral
interface between space and hyperspace, and vanished into it
with a silent collision of unreal forces.

Now alone in orbit over the brown and green planet, the
Hive Ship paused; then it turned to face its serrated prow at the
surface, and from its flanks fell sharp arrows of bone, primed
for the hunt.

He was dreaming of Sateda, of safety and quiet. He was
dreaming of a place where he could rest, where it was all right
for him to be fatigued and weakened, a place where he could
just let go, heal up, and forget the war.

They took that from him. The sound, in the sky, crashing
down around him, lancing into his thoughts. Ronon heard the
razor-edged keening, the nerve-shredding buzz of the enemy;
but it was just a dream.

Just a dream—

"Ronon!" He blinked back to wakefulness with a gasp of
effort. Sleep and the heavy pull of the sickness dragged on him,
threatening to draw him down again to soft oblivion. He shook
his head, and it felt like it was full of sand.

Keller pressed something to his throat and he felt a pinprick
of pain. In a moment it was gone and some vague semblance of
clarity returned to him

"What did…" At first he found it hard to form the words.

"A stimulant," she explained. Her voice was high and tight

with fear. "Ronon, we have to get out of here."

It was then he realized he could still hear the sound of the Wraith Darts crowding the sky.

Ronon threw himself from the bed, using a support stanchion to haul his body to its feet. He grabbed at his pistol and pushed his way outside, into the morning light. The gun felt good and familiar in his grip. It gave him a point of reference, something to focus his anger through. It was a lens for his revenge.

"Stay back!" he threw the words at Keller, waving her away as he staggered out of the sick lodge and on to the settlement's wide wooden boulevard. His gaze found Laaro, the boy huddled in the shadow of a tree bough, eyes fixed on the sky. White shapes with needle prows and bladed wings shrieked past overhead.

"The Wraith…" said the youth in disbelief, his trembling lips almost unable to form the words. "The Aegis has forsaken us. The Wraith have returned!"

"Get inside," he growled, and then shouted at the top of his lungs to all the Heruuni who stumbled and panicked in the street. "Get inside your homes! Don't let them catch you in the open!" He grabbed Laaro's arm and pulled him back toward the sick lodge.

Above, the Darts wheeled and turned, sweeping back and forth in patterns that cross-hatched the sky.

The healer Kullid pushed his way to the door to stand by Keller's side. "They have come back, after all this time…" He spoke in hushed, awed tones, fascination in his eyes.

Ronon shoved the boy toward Keller and hesitated on the steps of the lodge, kneading the grip of his pistol. Something was wrong. He couldn't put his finger on it, but there was something missing… Annoyed with himself and cursing the Asgard for making him sick, Dex shook his head, as if the gesture would force away the fog in his thoughts.

The realization struck him like a slow bullet. "They're not… Culling." None of the Darts weaving above them were streaming the capture beams from beneath their hulls, sweeping the settlement for prey. None of them scooped up the frightened and the terror-struck, they only moved in lines and circles.

"What are they doing?" said Keller

Ronon nodded to himself. He had seen this behavior before, on wilderness hunt-worlds when he had been a Runner. "They're searching for something."

The Puddle Jumper blew through the open Stargate and into the middle of chaos. Rodney ducked instinctively as a white streak of energy slammed into the canopy of the ship, and he saw the sparks of automatic weapons fire flash by as they swept up and away from the valley where the portal was located.

"Did you see that?"

Sheppard didn't reply; instead he turned the barrel-shaped ship around in a tight stall-turn and swept back the way they had come.

McKay saw more clearly now. The valley was being swarmed by Wraith warriors, a cluster of the steel-armored, blank-faced creatures storming forward with weapons blazing.

The colonel spoke quickly into his headset. "Jumper Three to all units, this is Sheppard, respond!"

Rodney's stomach tightened as he heard Sergeant Rush's voice over the radio. Gunfire was thick and noisy in the background. *"Colonel! They came out of nowhere, sir; we're being overrun! We're gonna lose the gate!"*

"But, the Asgard ship…" began Rodney. He picked out the figures of men in Atlantis uniforms lying sprawled out on the ruddy dirt below them.

"Rush, disengage and retreat through the wormhole! Get back to Atlantis, double-time!"

The sergeant's voice wavered. *"No can do, sir. They'll take us down before we make it ten feet! You have to shut it down! We can't let them get to the city… Tell Atlantis to shut it down!"* The hiss of Wraith blasters crackled through the air and suddenly the channel went dead.

"Sergeant? Sergeant, do you read me?" Sheppard cursed the static that answered him.

Energy pulses reached up from the ground toward the Jumper as the Wraith took aim at a new target. McKay saw alien figures break from the group and run towards the glittering vertical pool. He spoke into his headset, shouting down the base channel with frantic urgency. "Atlantis, McKay! Condition Black! Condition Black!"

The Wraith were almost at the Stargate when the wormhole evaporated, the connection cut. The code-phrase had done its job; the gate technicians back on Atlantis had severed the wormhole, and until a set of pre-determined security protocols were cleared, it would remain locked out of the dialing computer.

"Good call," said Sheppard grimly. He reached forward and toggled a control. "I'm cloaking the Jumper." A glassy shimmer hazed the exterior of the craft and rendered it invisible; the Wraith continued to fire, shooting wild in hopes of clipping the Ancient ship as it sped away.

"Rush," said Rodney, his breath tight in his chest. "And the others... Oh god, what did I just do?"

"The right thing," said Sheppard. "Atlantis has to come first. We lose that, we're all dead. Those men know that."

Rodney nodded stiffly. He knew John was right but that didn't make him feel any better. "We... We have to find the others, Sam and Jennifer, Ronon..."

The Jumper was rising high into the air. "Already on it. I'm gonna get some altitude, run a sensor sweep." Sheppard brought up the HUD overlay and swore for the second time. "Oh, that's not good."

McKay glanced up and choked on the other man's understatement. Toward the settlement, the display showed multiple glyphs moving and swooping around the tree-city. "Darts..."

Sheppard pointed at another glyph, a lone object out in low orbit. "And there's home base. A Hive Ship. Seems like they got tired of waiting."

"Long-range interstellar jump," said the scientist, "if they entered hyperspace in the shadow of a planet and then dropped out again close to Heruun, the galactic sensors on Atlantis might have missed it." He shook his head. "But to do that, they'd have needed to know exactly, precisely where they were going to emerge."

"A scout. They must have had a scoutship out here, scoping the whole damned planet." The colonel frowned. "And we never even knew it."

"Uh, Sheppard?" said McKay, scrutinizing the tactical display. "There's only one starship up there. Where's the *Aegis*?"

The Darts had been joined by more of their kindred. Ronon could see them coming, the impassive, eyeless masks of Wraith warriors marching up the ramped concourse catching the dull sunlight. Stunner bolts flared, striking any Heruuni who ran in the back and laying them down hard.

Those who tried to fight—men in the robes of the guards he'd seen with Takkol and Aaren—did little to slow the advance. Ronon saw the spark of rounds from the primitive rodguns as they ricocheted harmlessly off Wraith body amour; he heard the howl of mai cats as the aliens cut down the guardian animals.

At his side, Lieutenant Allan gave him a hard look. "We can't take them all on." Her face was still pale from the effect of the serpent venom in her system, but Dex didn't comment on it. He knew he had to look just as bad, if not worse. Every moment he stood still, the sickness pulled at him, threatening to drown him in fatigue.

"We'll see," he replied, through gritted teeth. Ronon turned and pressed a Beretta pistol into Doctor Keller's trembling hands. "You know how to use this, right?"

The woman blanched. "It's not really my thing—"

"It is now," Ronon cut her off. Without waiting for a reply, he pushed off from the sick lodge doorway and came out firing, shooting over the heads of the guards who fired from cover or bended knee. The lieutenant moved with him, her P90 at her shoulder, marking off three-round bursts into the advancing line of the enemy.

The particle magnum spat red energy, knocking every Wraith they touched into a heap; but Ronon was hissing with annoyance as he missed with one shot for every two that hit home; the creeping malaise was affecting his aim.

The Wraith squads scattered, realizing that this new enemy was a more serious threat to them. He saw them make for cover, regrouping. A larger troop of them held back in a tight cordon. *Protecting something?* he wondered.

A stun blast shrieked past him and threw a Heruuni guard off his perch on a support rail, his rodgun firing wild. Allan dodged and emptied the rest of her clip at the assailant. "Reloading—"

She never finished the sentence. Ronon saw it coming, but something in him was just too slow to react. He saw a Wraith officer point a pistol her way and even as a warning cry was forming on his lips, the white flash crossed the distance from the muzzle of the alien weapon to the woman's chest. She didn't even have time to cry out; instead she fell silently to the boardwalk.

A storm of stunner fire converged on Ronon Dex, streaking past him, snapping at his heels as he forced himself to run. All the Wraith, so it seemed, now had him in their sights. He dove for the lieutenant's fallen submachine gun, but still he was too sluggish. *Too slow!*

A stun bolt caught his arm and spun him with the shock of it. Dimly he was aware of his particle magnum turning to dead weight in the insensate flesh of his hand. The cold, numbing sensation swept down the side of his body, wiping out feeling from his nerves. He sagged, swearing a gutter oath as his legs gave out and let gravity take him.

The next moment he was prone, the instant between the hit and the fall gone to him. Ronon tried to drag himself up, toward the pistol that lay just beyond his reach. His fingers touched the warm metal; but then a heavy boot came down on the barrel, holding it in place.

He looked up into the leering face of a Wraith officer; closer now, and he could pick out the clan sigils that identified the male as the commander of a scoutship. "The Runner," it said, cocking its head. "A good catch."

"Bite me," he spat. Rough, pale hands dragged him back to his feet.

The commander grinned. "Show some respect," it told him. "You'll live longer." The alien stepped away as the cluster of warriors parted to reveal a figure standing in among them, the person they had been protecting.

She was Wraith; that was to say, she was the very essence of what they were, distilled into a single being. Lithe and sinuous, her flesh was a glistening greenish-grey the color of a bruise, and dark, oiled hair cascaded down around her shoulders. She wore a close-cut outfit made of some form of tanned hide that did not invite too close a scrutiny. But more than anything, it was the manner in which she carried herself that identified her, gave her name. The female was haughty and sinister by equal measure; she was every inch a Wraith Queen.

She gave Ronon an arch, disdainful glare, which by moments slowly transformed into a ready, fang-toothed smile. "Where is the alien vessel?" she demanded.

The Satedan gave a rough shrug. "The what?"

"I know who you are, Ronon Dex," she continued, stalking slowly around him. "I know of you and your cohorts from Atlantis. I can imagine why you are here. You want it as much as we do."

From the corner of his eye he saw movement and his heart sank. The commander was directing a group of Wraith to push people out of the sick lodge and on to the boulevard; first among them was Keller, the boy Laaro and Kullid. The healer was open-mouthed at the sight of the aliens, too fascinated by what he was seeing to understand the danger he was in.

Ronon made a play of yawning. "Let's get this over with. You wanna go straight to the threats, or what?"

The Queen gave a throaty chuckle. "I don't want you, Runner," she sniffed, offering a hand to the commander as he returned, "you are just…collateral."

The Satedan saw the Wraith commander drop an Atlantis-issue radio into the Queen's spindly fingers. She studied it for a moment, and then spoke into the mike. "I wish to speak to Colonel John Sheppard. I know you can hear me, human. Your shuttlecraft was seen exiting the portal. I know you are nearby."

There was a long moment of silence before the radio crackled into life. "*Hi, this is John. Sorry I'm not in to take your call right now, but please leave a message and we'll get around to kicking your butt just as soon as we can.*"

Ronon rocked back on his heels, grinning. "He's a funny guy."

The Wraith Queen's frosty smile became brittle. "Colonel. It is a pleasure to finally encounter your band. You have been quite troublesome to many of my race's clans."

"We like to keep busy," offered the Satedan.

The alien ignored him. "Understand me, we have no interest in this planet or its people. There are so many rich worlds to cull and this ball of dirt has so little to offer us…" She sniffed the air, as if she smelled something unpleasant. "Nor do I care about you, your Runner or the rest…" The Queen shot Ronon a glare. "What I want is information, about the alien ship. The thing these tribals call the Aegis."

A ripple of fear spread through the Heruuni who cowered in groups under the stun guns of the Wraith.

She gestured at the commander and inclined her head; in turn the Wraith strode over to Keller and the others, and grabbed the boy by the arm.

"Laaro!" shouted the doctor. "No! Leave him alone!" More Wraith crowded in, forcing her back.

Ronon took a step forward and got a rifle butt in the chest for his trouble. He staggered, wheezing. "Not… Not the boy. Me. Take me if you have to—"

"Be silent," snarled the Queen, as Laaro was presented to her. She gave him a cold, indulgent smile. "Hello, little human. Do you know who I am?"

Laaro was trembling, but he didn't look away. "I know."

The Wraith Queen spoke into the radio again. "Sheppard. Give yourself up, show me where you have sent the alien ship. If you do not, then I will let my warriors free to feed on every living being on this planet. And I will begin the cull with this child before me." She chuckled again, the tip of a black tongue flicking across the points of her teeth.

CHAPTER TWELVE

Carter entered the control chamber with her weapon at the ready, Major Lorne a few steps behind her in a similar stance. "Teyla?" she called. "Are you all right?"

Across the room, close to the cryo capsule, the Athosian woman threw her a wave. "I am uninjured."

"Where's the other Wraith?" said Lorne, panning around with his gun.

Before them, the Asgard avatar faded into being. *"The Wraith has been subdued."* It inclined its head and Carter glanced in the direction it was indicating. In the corner of the chamber, three Risar stood in a triangle around the trembling form of the alien warrior, each of them holding a glass orb in their hands. Softly glowing rays from the objects bathed the Wraith in waves of color.

"A neural paralysis beam," explained Fenrir. *"The Wraith will harm no one in this state."*

Carter slung her weapon and strode across the chamber to come face to face—or close enough—with the Asgard hologram. A nerve jumped in her jaw; the colonel was about as furious as she could be, and it took a moment of effort to keep her voice level when she spoke. "Your actions have left the entire planet Heruun open to attack by a Hive Ship. Everyone back there, the locals, my people... They could be culling them all right now!"

Fenrir cocked his head. *"You have a greater understanding of Asgard technology than any of the humans here. You know that this vessel's combat and defense systems are not at full capacity. What would you have had me do? Remain in orbit and let the* Aegis *be overrun by them?"* He pointed a thin finger at the Wraith.

Carter bit down on the first angry retort that came to mind and pushed it away. "This ship has teleportation technology.

You could have beamed people to safety. You could have—"

"*Done what, Colonel Carter?*" Fenrir's dark eyes narrowed. "*I made a tactical hyperspace jump in order to save my ship.*"

"Where to?" said Lorne.

"*Only a short distance away, Major Lorne. A few light-minutes from the planet you call Heruun, up above the star system's plane of the ecliptic.*"

"We have to go back," Teyla told him. "Fenrir, we cannot leave an entire world to the predations of the Wraith…" She faltered. "These are the people you have been protecting, the ones who helped you repair your ship. You cannot abandon them."

"You owe them," Carter added. "You have a responsibility."

The Asgard eyed her and his tone turned colder. "*The only responsibility I have is to my work. It must be protected at all costs and that means this ship must be preserved. I will not send this vessel into harm's way without shields or weapons.*"

"Fine," snapped the colonel. "You give me the access I need and I'll help you get the combat systems back on line."

Fenrir considered this for a moment, then gestured at a panel on the far side of the chamber. "*Agreed. This console will enable you to access systems directly. I will quicken new Risar to assist you.*"

Carter glanced at Lorne. "Get everyone together. Do a head count, find out who we lost in the break-out."

He saluted. "Yes, ma'am."

Without pausing, Sam went to the console and began pulling up skeins of data, submerging her foul mood in the task at hand.

She caught Teyla speaking quietly to the Asgard. "You said you must protect 'your work'. What did you mean by that?"

Carter saw Fenrir turn away. "*That is none of your concern, Teyla Emmagan.*"

"Colonel Sheppard," said the Queen, teasing each out syllable of his name. "I am disappointed in you." She cupped Laaro's face in her free hand. "Are you really willing to let a child die just to test my resolve?" The Wraith gave a sibilant hiss. "Very well, if I must make an example, I will." Cries rose up from the Heruuni captives, some of them trying to rise and being clubbed down or stunned for their temerity.

"*Wait.*"

There was a flutter of wind and a faint humming in the air; and from nothing came the shape of the Ancient shuttlecraft, floating above the wooden boulevard. Sheppard and McKay were visible through the canopy, both men grim-faced with the choice they had been forced to make.

The Queen chuckled once again. "Such a pretty ship. Not so pretty as the prize I want, however. Land your craft and exit with your weapons stowed. Do it, or the boy dies." She yawned slightly.

In answer, the outrigger pods on the ship extended from the striated hull. "*Or how about you let the kid go and I don't make you chew on a drone missile?*"

"This posturing is starting to bore me," said the Wraith, a dangerous tone entering her voice. "I see through your bluff, Sheppard. I can taste the color of your thoughts from here. You won't do it. You know what you will reap for this world if you do."

"Just shoot her," snarled Ronon, struggling against his captors.

After a moment, the outriggers retracted. "*Fine. Let him go.*" The Jumper settled to the boardwalk and the aft ramp fell open.

Sheppard exited the ship, his hands out by his sides. McKay followed on behind him, still gripping the data pad that hadn't strayed from his side since they left the *Odyssey*.

The colonel gave his team mates a wan smile. "Ronon. Doctor. Looks like we're on our own for now." He raised his eyes to the sky, hoping they'd get his meaning. Keller's face fell; she understood all right.

The Queen approached him. "John Sheppard," she purred. "I am almost honored to meet you. My clan has so much to thank you for. If not for you, we Wraith might be sleeping still.

And the wars and destruction you and your Atlanteans have fostered…" She licked her black lips. "The other Queens you have killed, the clans you left in disarray, that wake of destruction has allowed my kindred to rise to prominence where before we were denied the chance." The female bowed slightly. "I give you my appreciation."

"You're, uh, welcome." Sheppard's nostrils flared at the scent of her, the peculiar acidic perfume of Wraith he recognized from dozens of sorties aboard Hive Ships. Zelenka had once told him that was what humans could sense of Wraith pheromone output; like their insect counterparts on Earth, the Wraith Queens exuded chemical smells that trigged genetic command-obey codes in their subordinates. Apparently, the stuff also worked on some human beings. She must have been pumping it out like crazy, because the fug of it was making his eyes prickle. He felt his heart thumping in his chest and the beginnings of a fear response as his body reacted. He swallowed hard.

"Quit trying that crap on me," he told her firmly. "I'm not a believer, so let's cut to the chase."

"Such a shame. We treat those who worship us with great care." The alien female gave him a demure, toothy smile. "Very well then. You know my question. You know my offer. The ship that hid itself on the moon claimed the lives of many of my clan. I want it, and the being aboard it. In exchange, I give you my word that we will let you leave unharmed and that we will not cull this planet."

"Your *word*?" Despite himself, John let out a short bark of laughter, and then coughed. "Oh, I'm sorry. You were actually serious."

"Wraith lie," rumbled Ronon. "That's all they know how to do."

A Wraith commander pressed his gun into Dex's throat. "I warned you before, Runner. Don't speak out of turn again."

Sheppard glanced at McKay and saw the determination in the other man's eyes. He didn't need to hear Rodney say it; it would be bad enough if he actually delivered the advanced technology of an Asgard vessel into the greedy claws of a Wraith clan, but with what they had learned about Fenrir and his doomsday device… His blood ran cold just thinking about it.

"Well?" prompted the Wraith. "Your answer?"

The colonel blew out a breath. "Y'know, even if I knew where that ship was, which I don't, I wouldn't made a deal with you, not even if you threw in box seats for the Super Bowl."

The false coyness fell from the Queen's face to be replaced by cold anger. "That is so very disappointing, John," she began, putting brittle emphasis on his name. "I had hoped you would be accommodating. Association with the Wraith can be very rewarding if you work with us…"

He shrugged. "What can I tell you? I can't help you out. I'm sorry." He paused. "Wait, no, not sorry. What's that word I meant? The opposite of sorry. *Glad.*"

She turned her glare toward McKay. "And you, Rodney?" She said McKay's name like it was two separate words.

The scientist hugged the portable data screen in front of his chest in a gesture of self-protection. "What he said. Can't help. Don't know."

"That is not true!" cried a voice.

For a moment, Sheppard was thrown off-guard and he cast around, looking to see who had spoken. He heard Keller call out a warning, and suddenly Kullid was pushing his way forward, stepping out across the boardwalk.

The Wraith commander moved to intercept him, but the Queen made a guttural grunt in her throat and her warrior stood aside, allowing the healer to come closer.

He bowed. "I am Kullid, your highness," he began.

"I don't like where this is going," said McKay, from the side of his mouth.

"Long have the stories of your kind been told on Heruun," continued the healer. "In secret, passed from generation to generation. But I never…." He took a deep breath, and Sheppard realized he was willingly inhaling the Queen's pheromone aura. "I never expected to see you myself." Kullid's face was lit by something new; an attraction that knew no bounds.

"Wraith worshipper…" Ronon spat the words.

"Here?" said McKay.

"Why not?" Sheppard replied. "There's clearly a sucker on every planet."

"Kullid, no!" Keller was calling out to him, stunned by his words. "You can't possibly... These creatures, they're predators! They only exist to prey on other life!"

"But they can give it as well as take it, is that not so?" he snapped.

The Queen gave a languid nod. "It is so."

"You see?" Kullid turned and addressed the other Heruuni. "If we look past our primitive fear of the Wraith, they can save us! They can cure us of the sickness!"

"Sickness—?" repeated the Wraith commander, but the Queen spoke over him, seizing the opportunity.

"Of course we will," she said silkily. "If you in turn help us, Kullid. You said that Rodney was being less than truthful. Please explain."

"The Atlanteans have knowledge of the Aegis, I know it," he went on, moving toward McKay. "They left our world through the portal to gather it up and return here." He looked at the data screen and nodded. "Inside that device. Yes, I am certain of it. They carry the words of more texts than I have ever seen before!"

"No, that's not it at all," Rodney managed, clutching at the portable computer. "This is, uh, I just use it for playing *Minesweeper*—"

The Queen gave the smallest of nods and one of the Wraith warriors stepped forward and slammed his stunner rifle into the back of McKay's knees. Rodney howled and crumpled; Sheppard surged forward to step in and received the same blow from another of the masked aliens.

He hit the decking hard, and saw Ronon take the opportunity to rush his own captor; it was a bold but futile move. The Wraith commander spun and slammed the butt of his pistol into Dex's chest, putting the Satedan down with one blow. Keller ran to him, desperately checking his pulse. Ronon groaned and coughed.

Kullid pulled the data screen from McKay's hands with a savage jerk and turned to present it to the Queen. She inclined her head in thanks and tap-tapped a curved nail on the plastic surface, a curious smirk playing on her lips.

"Take this," she handed the computer to another Wraith, this one in a leather long-coat of the kind their scientist cadre liked to wear. "Drain it dry."

"We can translate the human language," he replied. "It will be done."

"Tell me you encoded that thing," said Sheppard.

"Of course!" McKay retorted hotly. "I'm not stupid…" He trailed off. "I just hope I encoded it *enough*."

"Well," said the Queen, flashing them a shark-toothed smile. "It appears that the advantage is mine." She glared at Sheppard. "You have won so many victories, John. I wonder if you remember what being on the losing side feels like."

"I remember," said the colonel, steel beneath his words. "I remember every man and woman we've lost to your kind."

"That is good. I would hate to have to remind you again." She nodded at the Puddle Jumper. "I think I will begin here by taking this little vessel as a trophy. You will convey me to my Hive." She walked casually toward the rear of the ship, the scientist and a cluster of warriors moving with her. "And do bring Rodney with you."

"What?" McKay piped, clearly unhappy with the suggestion.

The scientist eyed him. "He may come in useful if his data device proves…difficult."

The Wraith commander prodded Sheppard in the back. "Go, prey. Do as you are told."

"Colonel?" Keller gave him a terrified look.

Sheppard got to his feet and returned the gaze, looking at Keller and then Ronon in turn. "You two stay here. Keep safe, understand?" When the doctor hesitated, he silently mouthed something else. *For now*.

Keller nodded, fighting back her fear.

"Your highness?" said Kullid, trailing after the alien female. "And what should I do?"

The Queen gave him an indulgent glance. "Tell your people the truth about us, Kullid. Spread the word." She nodded to the commander. "Remain here. Help him understand our kind."

The Wraith officer bowed. "As you order."

Fenrir's avatar stood motionless before a panel at the rear of the chamber, above which a wide oval screen showed a cutaway display of his starship's interior spaces; many sections of the craft were dark across numerous levels where the internal sensors were inoperative.

Teyla watched him work the screen via thought, her gaze flicking between the holographic Asgard and the chilled capsule where the real flesh-and-blood Fenrir lay in stasis.

Across the room, Colonel Carter caught her eye. She nodded toward the alien, and her inference was clear. *Talk to him. Find out what you can.*

The Athosian approached the panel, as Fenrir muttered something in a low voice. "Is something amiss?" she asked.

He glanced at her. "*I cannot understand how the Wraith were able to approach my ship so swiftly, without detection. How did they locate me? I ensured the complete destruction of all their craft, blanketed this system and nearby space with a dampening field to retard subspace communications.*"

"The Wraith can communicate through other means," she noted. "They possess a telepathic ability."

"*That is known to me. But the range of that ability is limited.*"

"For common Wraith, that is so. But the Queens aboard the Hive Ships… They are much stronger." Teyla shivered as she thought of the cold psionic tendrils of the Queens she had encountered, and the scars they had left in her psyche.

The avatar nodded, accepting this. "*I understand. It was my error to preserve the lives of some of the Wraith from the last craft I destroyed. I was curious. I sampled the superior elements of their genetic code in order to…*" He paused, as if he suddenly realized he had said too much. "*Their regenerative qualities are quite incredible.*" After a moment, Fenrir looked at her. "*I believe the Wraith have been looking for me for some time, perhaps since the aftermath of their first attack on the Aegis, when I arrived in the Pegasus galaxy. Other Wraith have come to the Heruun system in the past.*"

"You fought them."

"*Yes. I deployed Risar aboard remote auxiliary craft and used my technology and skills to dispatch them. They were formidable adversaries.*"

Teyla nodded. "And in doing so, you preserved the lives of all the humans on Heruun. You protected them."

Fenrir leaned back, his expression tightening. "*Despite whatever the Herunni believe, I engaged the Wraith in combat only to protect my vessel and myself, not them. I turned the Wraith to my use as I did the human tribals. I could not construct replacements for certain elements of my ship's systems, so I used recovered pieces of their bio-technology to fulfill the same function.*" He looked away. "*I am not a guardian or a god. The Asgard have played that role all too often and it has only ever brought us difficulty.*"

Teyla opened her mouth to speak, but Fenrir's avatar moved away. "*I must ensure that the Wraith do not surprise me again. Bring the warrior here.*" The last words were directed at the three Risar surrounding the lone captive Wraith.

"Obeying," The clone creatures spoke the word with one voice, and deactivated the paralysis field. The warrior gasped and stumbled forward a step.

At the engineering console, Colonel Carter reacted by snatching up her P90. "What's going on?"

"I am not certain," said Teyla; but she suddenly had a creeping sensation across the flesh of her back.

"*I cannot risk any compromise of my work,*" said Fenrir. "*It was my error to let this creature live. To sever any possible telepathic conduit to this ship, it must be put to death.*"

The Risar raised the orb-devices in their hands and aimed at the Wraith; in turn, the warrior threw up its hands in self-defense. "Wait!" it shouted. "Wait! Do not kill me, Asgard…"

Teyla hesitated. "It knows his species…"

"It could have heard any one of us say that," said Carter.

"Fen…rir!" The Wraith ground out the name between gasping breaths. "You are… Fenrir… Asgard!"

All at once there was something else in the room with

them. It was nothing tangible or visible, nothing seen by Colonel Carter, Fenrir and his Risar or the sensors of the *Aegis*; only Teyla and the Wraith could sense it, a stygian tide of bitter thought pressing its way out through the void, and into their minds. Teyla forced the gates of her own consciousness shut, holding them fast by sheer will. A groan escaped her lips.

"Teyla?" Carter saw her distress. "Are you okay?"

"The Queen…" she grated. "She is…searching."

"Searching," repeated the Wraith warrior. "Speaking."

Fenrir pointed at the Risar. *"Terminate it, now!"*

"I have a message!" shouted the Wraith. "Hear me out! The Queen speaks… Speaks… Through me!"

The Asgard hesitated, a questioning cast to its face. *"Then speak,"* he said finally.

"This is a mistake," said Carter.

"My Queen wishes to speak to you, Fenrir… Under a banner of truce."

"Truce?" echoed Teyla, her head pounding from the psychic undertow. "The Wraith do not understand the meaning of the word!"

The warrior gave a shudder, and his body language changed as the pressure inside Teyla's skull lessened until it was a distant background throb. The alien moved jerkily, like a puppet worked by a hesitant master. "Hear me," it said, in a breathy murmur. "I speak through this instrument… I ask for truce… With the Asgard Fenrir."

"To what end?"

"The disclosure of information… To mutual benefit… Do you accept?"

"You can't trust the Wraith," Carter told him.

The warrior turned blank eyes toward the colonel. "No, human, it is… Your kind that he should not trust. The… Atlanteans are the ones who… Keep secrets… Not us."

"What secrets?" demanded Fenrir. *"Explain yourself."*

"Not yet, Asgard," gasped the warrior. "When… We meet." The puppet's telepathic strings were abruptly severed, and the Wraith collapsed to the deck, shuddering and panting.

Teyla shot Carter a worried look, the memory of the conversation in the lodge coming back to her with grave force. When she turned back the holographic avatar was staring at her.

"*What did she mean?*" asked the Asgard.

"I do not know," Teyla lied.

The two ships met in the void, Heruun a distant sphere beneath them lit dull brown by the reflected glow of the far sun.

They came together, closing the distance, prow to prow; they were a study in contrasts, two vessels built by races galaxies apart from one another, from philosophies that were utterly unlike.

The Asgard cruiser *Aegis*, heavy and armored in appearance but more agile than anything so large had the right to be, drifted to a halt, the maws of weapons tubes and the lenses of beam weapons open wide in apparent ready threat; although the reality was very different. The *Aegis* was many centuries old by human standards, and yet the enduring steel and iron of its hull was still sturdy; the marks that aged it were a handful of half-patched wounds from plasma fire.

The Wraith Hive Ship moved to mimic the motion of the other craft, the wide spear tip profile of the bony fuselage broken by the spider-leg spars of great antennae extending out behind its hull. It did not have a name, for Wraith did not give their craft appellations as other species did; Wraith simply knew their ships by the trace and the texture of them, as an animal would know its lair by the scent it had laid there. Grown from bone-seeds in vast pools of sluggish blood media and liquid cartilage, the Hive Ship was almost a living thing, made of meat and bone, nerve and sinew.

Asgard and Wraith turned slowly around one another, each taking the measure of their opposite.

"I'm warning you," said Sam, "these creatures are the most dangerous predators in Pegasus."

Fenrir's avatar did not look up from its console. "*I have faced the Goa'uld, the Replicators and a dozen other threats from five different galaxies, Colonel Carter. I am fully capable of meeting the Wraith face-to-face.*"

"Hive Ship has come to a full stop," reported one of the Risar. "Scanning."

The oval screen on the wall became a graphic of the alien craft. Carter studied it; the display showed an even power distribution throughout the Hive Ship; there was no sign of any of the telltale energy spikes that might signal weapons being charged or Dart bays about to launch their deadly payloads.

"Target vessel remains in quiescent mode," said another of the clones.

"You see?" said the Wraith warrior. His voice was still hoarse from before, when his mistress had used him as a telepathic conduit. Dried streaks of black blood marked his face about his flared nostrils. "We come in peace."

"I doubt it," noted Teyla. She gave Carter a look. "Fenrir," she began, maintaining eye contact with the colonel but addressing the Asgard. "Before you go any further, there is something you must know."

"Teyla…" Carter warned.

"Transport system ready," said a Risar.

Fenrir didn't wait for Teyla to continue, *"Engage transport."*

There was a flash of white light and columns of energy fell from the air, a curtain of lightning that flared and faded to reveal a disparate group of figures. Carter felt a moment of relief at the sight of Sheppard and McKay among them, but that quickly evaporated when she saw the look on their faces. The rest of the group were mostly Wraith warrior-drones, stood in a tight circle around a male in the garb of a scientist and a stately, angular female; the Queen. Almost out of sight at the rear of the group was a lone figure wearing manacles, face hidden in the folds of a hooded robe.

The Queen inclined her head and gave Fenrir a level look. "So you are an Asgard, then." She smiled, showing teeth. "Your kind is known to me. I have been learning so much about you recently, I feel as if I already know your species intimately."

"*I am Fenrir,*" he replied bluntly. "*Understand immediately that I will react to any assault against my vessel or my per-*

son with utmost severity." To underline his words, the Asgard's Risar disengaged from their consoles and turned to face the Wraith party, each one raising an orb device.

The Queen studied the Asgard for a moment, considering. "Real and yet not real," she remarked. "If I could smell blood or hear heartbeat I would think you a living being. Will you not show yourself to us, Fenrir? Do you fear us?"

"I show you all of myself that I am willing to. And I have no reason to fear you," he replied, *"as the number of Wraith ships I have obliterated will attest."*

Carter heard the scientist give a low growl, but the Queen shot him a hard look and he fell silent. "Just so. Clearly you have great power. I respect strength. As a gesture of that, and to show my peaceful intent, I have brought two of the Atlanteans with me as my guests, unharmed."

"Oh yeah," said Rodney, sarcasm dripping from every word, "she's really been the hostess with the mostess."

The Wraith honor guard stood away, allowing Sheppard and McKay to move across to where Carter was standing. "Colonel?" she said, in a low voice.

"We have a very big problem," Sheppard didn't wait for her to question him further. "Be ready. Things are going to go south very fast."

"And then some," added McKay. "They cut through the encryption like it was made of tissue paper."

"Encryption on what?" But Carter's question was answered when she laid eyes on the device in the hands of the Wraith scientist; an Atlantis-issue data pad. "Oh."

Sheppard leaned closer. "Trust me, however bad you think it is, it's worse than that."

Fenrir was speaking again. *"You have made claims about your peaceful nature, and yet it was your vessels that attacked me on my arrival in the Pegasus galaxy."*

The Queen shook her head. "Those were craft of another cadre, Fenrir. We Wraith are a clannish culture with many factions. I represent one of those with a less... Reactionary mindset."

"Indeed? Then tell me what it is you and your clan want

with me."

The alien female threw back her head in a basso chuckle. "I want to help you, Asgard. I know much about you. I know many things you should know."

Carter watched the Wraith scientist tap at the data pad. "They took it," she said. It was a statement, not a question. "They broke the coding."

"Kullid betrayed us," said McKay bitterly. "He's a Wraith worshipper, near as we can tell."

Sam cursed silently, her mind racing. They had lost control of the situation here, and soon it would be too far gone for the Atlanteans to regain it.

"I know about your long and brutal war," continued the Queen. "For, you see, in a very real way we share the same enemy."

"What are you doing?" demanded Teyla, but the Wraith ignored her, instead bringing the hooded figure forward.

"Who is this?" snapped Carter.

"No idea," McKay admitted, "they just dragged this guy up from the holding decks and brought him along with us."

With a flourish, the Wraith scientist tore the hood away to reveal a human male in a bland, sand-colored tunic and trousers. He stumbled forward, his face furious.

"Do you know what this is?" grinned the Queen. "No? Let me enlighten you?"

Sam and the rest of the Atlanteans knew exactly what the prisoner was, however; a captured Asuran, doubtless one of many the Wraith clan had taken during their recent ongoing battles with the artificial beings.

The holographic avatar looked on, Fenrir's alien face caught in peculiar moment of wonderment and distress. The Queen nodded at her warriors and as one they turned and gunned down the Asuran, pouring a huge salvo of energy bolts into the prisoners body. Overloaded, the Asuran screamed and disintegrated, becoming a heap of metallic powder.

"*A Replicator...*" whispered the Asgard. "*A humanoid-form Replicator.*" He shook his tiny head, blinking. "*We had always suspected they might evolve toward this level of sophistication, but never...*" He halted, gathering himself. "*How did they come to this galaxy?*"

"They're called Asurans," Carter called out. "They're not the Replicators that you know of. They evolved separately, here in Pegasus. Similar, but different."

"Different, yes," said the Wraith scientist, "but still the same in their programming. Destroying organic life, spreading like a virus."

"You speak of yourself," said Teyla. "The Asurans were made to fight the Wraith!"

The Queen snarled at her. "But now they kill everything, so what does it matter?" She took a step toward the silent avatar. "Our war is your war, Fenrir. Do you not see that simple truth?"

Fenrir nodded once, still staring at the Asuran's ashen remains. "*I ... See it.*" Suddenly he turned to glare at the humans, a new hardness in his dark eyes. "*You knew of the existence of these... Asurans, and yet you said nothing of it. You know of the Asgard's conflict with the Replicators and yet you kept silent!*" Fenrir's voice rose in pitch. "*You concealed the presence of my most hated enemy from me. Why?*" He turned to face the Athosian woman, almost pleading. "*Why, Teyla? Why would you do this?*"

The Queen's expression grew grave. "That is not all the humans have kept from you," she intoned.

"Here we go," McKay muttered.

"*Explain!*" barked Fenrir, the word echoing from the lips of every one of the Risar; his anger spilled over into the body language of the clones, turning their stances aggressive and threatening.

"That's enough, right there!" snapped Sheppard, coming forward. "Okay, we admit it, we were a little economical with the truth, but so were you!"

"The Asgard High Council didn't send you out here on any research trip," noted McKay.

The Risar crowded toward them, raising their orb-weapons. "*Silence!*" Fenrir's voice thundered around the chamber. "*No more lies, no more secrets! Tell me!*" His avatar shimmered and trembled, moving toward the Queen. "*Tell me!*"

Carter saw the Wraith female smother a faint smile with a carefully constructed look of sadness. She glanced at her scientist and the other Wraith produced a compact storage module from a pocket; Sam knew the type, the Wraith equivalent of a portable ultra-high density hard drive. Teams from Atlantis had recovered them from Hive Ships and alien bases on several occasions. "See for yourself," said the scientist.

A Risar took the device and slotted it into the console beneath the oval screen.

"Fenrir," said Teyla. "Don't look at it. This isn't the way, not like this."

The hologram ignored her and gestured in the air; the data module glowed blue and information transfer began.

"It gives me no pleasure to be the one to bring this news to you," said the Wraith Queen. "But I must."

On the screen, a wave of flash-frame images raced past; Carter registered views of the planets Hala and Orilla, a swarm of beetle-like Replicators, genetic schematics of an Asgard, a complex octo-helix of alien DNA, a dying star, and more.

"*My people...Are dead,*" said the Asgard. His synthetic voice crackled and wavered as if something were breaking up the projection.

The contents of the module sank into the memory core of the *Aegis* itself, and with his mind connected directly to the starship, into the conscious mind of Fenrir's physical body. Sam felt a sense of great empathy for the alien; the Asgard did not even have the luxury of processing and assimilating the great loss in his own time. One moment he did not know, the next he knew it all, in complete and total detail.

The diminutive, child-like body of the avatar flickered, frozen for long seconds. Then he was moving again. The narrow, sharp edges of the Asgard's face were rigid and taut with an emotion Carter had never thought his kind capable of displaying. He stared at her with real hatred in his eyes.

"*You were there,*" he husked. "*You saw my species perish.*"

"I'm so sorry," said Sam. She could find no other words to say.

The Queen gave a derisive snort. "Now she admits it. You see, Fenrir? The humans cannot be trusted. Only you and I, Asgard and Wraith have spoken in truth. Even when my kind attacked your ship, it was not subterfuge, but an honest reaction to an intrusion..." When Fenrir didn't answer, she came closer to him. "Don't you see? We have a common foe in the Replicators, no matter what their origin. We have a foundation of truth between us..." She shot a look at Carter. "Not lies."

"*Leave me...*" The words were so quiet that Sam almost missed them.

"Asgard, you must listen to—"

Fenrir turned about and the Risar surged forward. "*I told you to leave me!*"

From nowhere came a brilliant surge of white rising from the deck around them. Carter jerked as the power of the transporter took her, dragging her away from the *Aegis* along with every other human and Wraith who stood there.

All but one.

CHAPTER THIRTEEN

From the smell of it, the cages had actually been built as animal enclosures of some kind, a long line of them radiating off an enclosed corridor that ran the length of one of the tree-settlement's vast boughs. There were other people in other cages ranged around them, most of them the airmen from the squads brought through the Stargate by Major Lorne and left behind to act as security. They had been overwhelmed by Wraith shock troops; the diminishment of their numbers made it clear how many of them had fought until they fell. The doctor caught the eye of Lieutenant Allan and the woman nodded grimly back at her.

"I have really had it with being locked up," said Jennifer, testing the heavy knurled branches that formed the bars of the wide enclosure where they had been confined. Through knotholes in the planks that made up the floor, Keller glimpsed green leaves waving in the wind and far below the brown earth at the foot of the massive tree complex. They were below the main tier of the settlement, down in the underlevels beneath the lodges and the main square.

"You get used to it after a while," said Ronon, laboring his breaths. He looked pale and drawn, and he sat in the shade, avoiding the shafts of orange sunlight coming down through the slatted ceiling.

She went to him and crouched by his side; in turn the Satedan looked away, irritated. "How are you feeling?" she asked.

"Bored," he retorted listlessly, "Bored with you asking me how I feel." He stifled a cough and glared at her, as if it were her fault he was unwell.

The doctor rolled her eyes. "Tough guys are always the worst patients. You do know that it doesn't make you a wimp if you're sick, right?"

"Of course I do," Ronon snapped. "But I don't have to like it."

"How do you feel?" she asked again.

He blinked. "Light's too bright. Headache. I just need to get out of this place, that's all."

"Tall order," grumbled the lieutenant, looking around at all the dense wood surrounding them.. "I'd give my right arm for a hacksaw. They took all our weapons."

"All *yours*," noted Dex, palming two small spade-shaped throwing blades from a hidden pocket in the lining of his tunic. "Not all *mine*."

"Great, a pair of fruit knives," said Keller. "That's really going to intimidate them."

"Company coming," called the lieutenant, as movement at the far end of the corridor signaled a new arrival. One of the elder's guards, nervous and sweaty, hustled Laaro toward them; the boy had a barrow laden with clay bowls and a massive gourd the size of an oil drum filled with water. The youth moved from cage to cage, doling out bowlfuls of the brackish liquid. Allan took one and sniffed it.

"Safe to drink?" said Keller.

"The Wraith took *all* our gear, including our purification tabs."

Laaro tapped the gourd. "The water is clean, I promise you." To demonstrate, he took a deep draught himself.

Keller passed a bowl to Ronon and he sipped it gingerly. "What's going on out there?" she asked the boy. The doctor kept her voice low so the guard would not hear them talking.

Laaro's young eyes were fearful. "Everyone is very afraid," he began. "The Queen has left many, many Wraith behind, here in the settlement, some out at the valley of the gateway. Kullid has been talking for them."

"Collaborator," spat the Satedan. "I wasn't looking hard enough. Should have guessed…"

"*None* of us guessed," said Keller. She could see that Laaro was more shocked than any of them by the healer's secret allegiance. "What was he saying?"

"Kullid spoke of the old stories of the Wraith, and said that they were lies. He said that many people have known this, but they never spoke up for fear of incurring the wrath of the elders." Laaro sighed. "He was right. Kullid is not the only one to have declared himself subject to the Queen."

Keller considered this for a moment; the Atlanteans had encountered worlds before where the Wraith were feared and revered in equal measure, and reluctantly she realized that Heruun was no different. Even after all the horror the Wraith brought with them, there would always be some souls who saw such power over life or death as a thing to be venerated.

Laaro went on. "Kullid said that the Wraith have come back and freed us from the tyranny of the Aegis. He told the whole township that they must show the Queen the fealty she deserves…"

"And if they don't?" said Allan. "I bet I can guess the alternative."

"He said those with the sickness will be healed by the Wraith."

Keller stopped. "They don't heal. The Wraith kill."

"Kullid promises otherwise." There was a note of forlorn hope in Laaro's voice that cut the doctor like a knife. "Many of those who did not go to the sick lodge have now ventured there on his assurance."

"It's a lie," growled Ronon. "Never forget that."

The boy's hand trembled slightly as he passed Keller a bowl through the wooden spars. "My mother… Thinks differently."

"Jaaya?" said Keller.

"She has gone to the lodge with my father." He shot her a sudden, hard look, his eyes shining with barely-contained tears. "I told her the voyagers would save him, but she did not listen!"

"Laaro!" called the guard. "You are finished here. Come!" The burly man in robes came forward and tugged on the boy's arm.

Keller gave him a rueful smile. "It'll be okay," she told him. "We'll get through this, believe me."

"Do not forsake us, voyager," said the youth, as he pushed

away the barrow.

At the entrance, the door banged open once more and new
figures entered, pushing Laaro aside and tipping the dregs of
the water-gourd over the floor. A cluster of men in the robes
of high office were shoved forward; each of them were elders,
with their characteristic clothing ripped and torn, and their
gold circlets and bangles broken or missing. A pair of Wraith
warriors marched them in at the tips of stunner rifles, slamming the weapons into their backs when they didn't move
quickly enough.

A trio of the elders were forced into the cage next to the
one where Keller, Ronon and Allan had been placed. They fell
to the floor and scuffled, desperate to plead for their freedom.
Only one of them did not beg their new jailers for release; he
sat on his haunches, staring at the floor.

"Takkol?" Keller recognized the man from the feast of
the Returned, but he seemed a pale shadow of the proud and
haughty chieftain who had looked down his nose at the contingent from Atlantis. He seemed smaller, lost in the dark pool
of his tattered robes, his finery tainted. The elder raised his
head slightly and saw her.

With sudden animation he scrambled over to the cage
wall, reaching through the bars toward her. "Voyagers!" he
implored. "Please, you must take me with you!"

"Take you where?" said Ronon. "We're prisoners too."

Takkol didn't seem to hear him. "Please, take me with you
through the Gateway, to your Atlantis! I cannot stay here…
They will…" His voice fell to a whisper. "Cull me."

"Nobody goes back to Atlantis," said Ronon. They had all
heard McKay's use of the 'condition black' emergency code
over the radio channel, and they all knew what it meant.

Takkol shook his head furiously. "No, no. You must understand, I have been cast out, and I will be murdered before the
day is done! Aaren betrayed me, the filthy traitor!"

"How'd that happen?" said the lieutenant, with grim irony
that went totally unnoticed by the fretting elder.

"He defected to the Wraith," hissed Takkol. "I… I think
he may have always harbored a secret admiration for them…

Certain things he said, deeds he did… In the light of recent events, they take on new meaning." He sighed. "Aaren is Senior Elder now, with the collusion of Kullid and the blessing of the predators."

One of the other minor elders spun away from the bars and snarled at the Atlanteans. "You brought this upon us! You knew the Wraith were coming here, didn't you? You knew it and you did not warn us! And now we will all perish!"

Keller said nothing.

The energy wash of the teleportation effect was so strong that Teyla was knocked off balance, and she found herself leaning against a metal console, blinking away the afterimages seared on her retina. Her throat was dry and she swallowed, fearful that the first image she would see when her vision cleared was the arid landscape of Heruun or worse, the gloom of a Wraith vessel; but she quickly realized that she had not been transported with all the others.

She was still in the command chamber of the *Aegis*, still surrounded by the shambling Risar moving to and fro at their tasks, still before her the wide, low shape of Fenrir's cryogenic capsule lying in a pool of white vapor.

"Where did you send them?" she demanded, her voice echoing. "Fenrir? Answer me!"

The Asgard's holographic image was gone.

"I know you can hear me!" She moved to the capsule and beat a fist on the thick crystalline glass, beneath which slumbered the flesh of the alien being. "Where are my friends?" Her voice became a shout.

The eyes of the sleeping Asgard snapped open for one brief moment, then closed again just as swiftly. Suddenly there was a Risar at her side, firmly taking her arm and pulling her away. She spun about, ready to attack, and came face to face with a second of the creatures brandishing an orb.

"*Why did you lie to me?*" The voice came from everywhere and nowhere. "*I… Had begun to believe that I could trust you, Teyla Emmagan. I believed we had developed a rapport.*"

"If you have injured Sheppard and the others—"

"They are unhurt," came the sharp reply. *"I sent them to the Hive Ship."*

Teyla gasped. "Then my friends are as good as dead! The Wraith Queen will destroy them!"

"No," said the voice. *"External sensors register the presence of locating tracer devices similar to the one I detect upon you. Sheppard, Carter, McKay and the others... They live still."*

"You must bring them back!"

A flash of color and light signaled the formation of Fenrir's avatar. The Asgard's face was pinched and his eyes clouded with anger. *"Do not presume to tell me what I must do. I have only to form a command in my thoughts and you will be sent to join them, human."*

Teyla spread her hands. "Then do it. Send me to the Wraith, send me and my unborn child to our deaths!"

"You will not leave until I have my answer!" raged the Asgard, fury and dejection warring in his words. *"Why did you lie?"* The question resonated in the cold air of the chamber like distant thunder.

The Athosian let out a long breath. "Because I felt sorry for you. I have lost all of my people in recent months, and unlike you I do not even have the mercy of knowing what fate befell them. The pain and loss I feel... I did not want to inflict it on another living being, even as I knew that we were wrong to keep this from you." She was unable to meet the alien's unwavering gaze. "There is no excuse, Fenrir. I am sorry that we kept this secret."

The avatar paced the room. *"My people, gone forever... The Replicators dead but a new breed of their kind running wild here in Pegasus... It is all so much to comprehend. And all the work, everything I did was all for nothing."*

"The work," repeated Teyla. "When I asked you about that before, you would not speak of it to me. What do you mean by that?"

Fenrir halted, his thin fingers knotting together. *"I have created such horror, Teyla Emmagan. In the pursuit of war, such great darkness. But all I wanted was a chance to find*

STARGATE ATLANTIS: NIGHTFALL   217

redemption... And now that has been denied to me."

Teyla's blood ran cold. "What horror?"

Lorne picked at the matted, fibrous webbing across the entrance of the cell, but the pliant material refused to budge. He stared out into the corridor beyond, where four Wraith warriors stood silently on guard, stunner rifles cradled in their grips. "So," he said, turning back to face McKay, Sheppard and Carter, "forgive me for saying so, but if I understand it correctly, we have gone from our normal kind of being in serious trouble to a whole new level of how screwed we are."

"Yeah," sighed McKay. "That's about it."

Sheppard gave Lorne a hard look. "Show a little optimism, will ya? We've been in worse situations."

Carter raised her eyebrows. "Have you? Really?"

"Oh yeah."

"Like what?"

"Uh..." Sheppard hesitated. "Well, there was this one time—"

McKay made a loud, wordless sound that was half annoyance and half exasperation. "What do you two want, a scorecard? Can we concentrate on the problem at hand?"

"Which one, Doc?" Lorne said in a deceptively light tone. "We've sure got plenty to choose from." Things had moved quickly when the Asgard had done his beaming thing; one second all the Atlantis team members were on the *Aegis*, the next they were on the Hive Ship. The Wraith Queen had been ready for them—maybe she used her telepathy to raise the alarm the second before they appeared on her ship, or something—and Evan Lorne and his colleagues found themselves disarmed and languishing in Wraith Jail. *Again.*

Still, at least they weren't strapped up and glued into one of those feeding chambers along with a bunch of desiccated corpses. Not yet, anyway. He sighed; hopefully Ronon Dex, Doc Keller and the rest of the squad down on Heruun were having better luck.

"I am so sick of seeing the inside of these places," grumbled McKay. After the Wraith had thrown them in the cells and left

them to rot, it was the scientist who sheepishly added the new
and alarming pieces to the jigsaw puzzle of what was happening around here. It was bad enough the Wraith had taken the
upper hand, tactically speaking, but all this stuff about the little
grey guy being some kind of mad scientist convict was not a
welcome revelation.

Colonel Carter had not said much since McKay mentioned
the word 'collapsar'. The look of abject shock on her face had
been more than enough to worry Lorne, and Sheppard had
helpfully cemented that by explaining still further.

"Fenrir made a black hole bomb," he said bluntly. As much
as Lorne thought about that string of words, the scope of
something so destructive was just out of his comprehension.
He'd seen naquadria-laced super-nukes detonate and those
were incredible enough to behold; what Sheppard was talking
about dwarfed that by an entire order of magnitude.

Not for the first time, the major found himself wondering
whatever happened to the Air Force that he had joined out
of high school, the nicely earthbound military with jet planes
and that kinda stuff. *Just when did serving my country turn
into a science fiction movie?*

McKay held his chin in his hands. "I'm not sure how much
she gave him of the files I recovered from the Asgard core
aboard *Odyssey*," he noted, "but there was a lot of content on
that Wraith data module."

"I saw tactical plots of Asuran forces in Pegasus flash up
on that big screen," said Carter. "We have similar information
back at Atlantis."

"Showing him where the enemy is," added Sheppard.
"You saw how Fenrir reacted when the Queen did that little
show-and-tell with a captive Replicator. I've never seen that
look on an Asgard's face before."

Carter nodded "I have. Thor had the same expression when
the bug-form Replicators took down the *Beliskner*. They may
seem alien, but they have the same emotions as we do. Fear
and terror, hate and anger."

"Enough to want revenge?" said Lorne. The tech stuff was
out of his league, but understanding the simple need to take

some payback… He knew that all too well.

The colonel nodded again.

Much of what Fenrir said ranged far beyond her ability to grasp, but among the terms and complex sciences he spoke of, Teyla swiftly found a route to understanding; and with it, an icy dread deep in her chest.

She asked the Asgard to speak of his 'work' and he told her, unfettered and without concession. The old Athosian myth-tale of the Nightfall gained new power as Fenrir spoke of the weapon he had created in the war against the other strain of Replicators, this 'collapsar' device. Teyla had seen and experienced much that had challenged her view of the universe since joining John Sheppard's team; but there was little she could bring to mind that so frightened her as Fenrir's clinical, metered description of a weapon that could put out a sun and turn whole worlds to ashen ruin.

He spoke of the accident and his arrogance, of his responsibility and the pariah's mark placed upon him by his own kind, a sentence of exile that spanned generations by human reckoning. Teyla listened, unable to speak, struck silent by the enormity of it. Fenrir continued, and she sensed that for him, this was no longer an explanation. It had become a confession. In all the time he had been alone aboard this ship, crossing the void with nothing but crude reflections of himself for companionship, he had wanted nothing more than the chance for some kind of salvation. She felt a sorrow for Fenrir that matched her fear of his dark science.

"*After a time, I came to understand my mistakes. The totality of it was made clear to me. And so I rejected my works as a weaponsmith and returned to the discipline that I had known first, known best. The science of life and biology.*" The avatar glanced down at its photonic hands. "*Our people, Teyla, we had traveled so far down the road of genetic alteration that we had transformed the very matter of ourselves beyond recognition. We could no longer reproduce, only duplicate, and even then with greater and greater errors of replication in each iteration.*"

Teyla thought of the images she had seen cast from the Wraith data device. She found her voice again, in a whisper. "Your race was dying."

He nodded once, a curt gesture of utter finality. "*I made it my goal to search for a solution. And… I believe I came close to it.*"

"How?"

"*The Wraith.*" Fenrir gestured toward the oval screen, where a visual of the Hive Ship drifting nearby was displayed. "*They possess such unprecedented physical capabilities. Their capacity for cellular regeneration… It was only by chance I came here, by chance I captured them and dissected one of their kind… Or perhaps fate, if such a thing exists…*" He paused, musing. " *I believe… I* believed *that their genetic structure might provide the missing piece of the puzzle. I wanted to draw from them, weave that potential into the Asgard DNA helix and give my race the chance to live again.*"

Fenrir fell silent once again; he seemed to have the weight of the ages upon his thin, frail form. He was a digital ghost, the manifestation of a lost soul. Fenrir's terrible solitude came from him in a mute wave, and Teyla's breath caught in her throat in a moment of pure empathy.

"*But now that data is worthless,*" he said. "*And my life has no meaning. All I have left is my sorrow… And my fury.*"

"Why do you think we're still alive?" said Rodney, picking at the scabby flesh of the cell walls and grimacing. "And please don't say 'lunch'."

"This Queen doesn't seem the type to waste an opportunity," said Sam. "She said her clan was a small one. She's probably looking at the bigger picture. She wants to know what we know."

"Drain us of intel before she drains us of life," noted Lorne. "Nice."

Sheppard folded his arms. "We may have already given her way too much of that already."

"I'm sorry!" snapped McKay, feeling heat rise in his

cheeks. "How was I to know that data pad would be hijacked the moment we got here? Quadruple 128-bit encryption seemed like it would be good enough—"

"It's not your fault," Carter broke in. "We have to fix the problem, not the blame, Rodney. Don't beat yourself up about it."

Lorne nodded. "The Wraith will do that for you."

Sheppard gave the major an acid glance. "The way I figure it, Queeny and her gang here didn't come looking to pick a fight with Fenrir. You saw how she spoke to him. She knows they don't have the grunt to beat the *Aegis* in a stand-up fight."

"Lucky for Fenrir she didn't know the combat systems were damaged," Carter threw in.

"I think she wants that ship intact, or at least as in as few pieces as possible. I mean, think about it. Forget the collapsar bomb for a second, even without that an Asgard warship is some pretty heavy iron. Intergalactic hyperspace capability, transporters, advanced weapons and shields."

Carter considered this. "Enough to tip the balance in a battle, that's for certain."

McKay saw where Sheppard's train of thought was leading. "They take the *Aegis* and become Wraith Clan Number One…"

"Maybe even turn the tide of battle against the Asurans," added Lorne. "But if the Queen knows about the bomb… She's not going to let that slide. She'll want that too, the whole nine yards."

All of them were quiet for a while. McKay knew that Carter, Sheppard and Lorne were all thinking the same thing he was, imagining a war-torn Pegasus galaxy ripped open by collapsar weapons and pirated Asgard technology, set afire by the battles between the Wraith and the Replicators; and beyond that, the threat of the vampiric aliens venturing further, perhaps to the Milky Way galaxy as well.

"The Wraith cannot, under any circumstances, be allowed to possess that 'isa' device or the *Aegis*." Sam's voice was low and grim. "We have to do whatever it takes to deny it to them."

Rodney wandered over to the cell entrance and glared at the web holding them inside it. "The only question is, how?"

"A communication," said the Wraith scientist, pausing in his work. "From the Asgard."

The Queen heard his words but did not acknowledge them. She lay back in repose upon the command throne at the centre of the Hive Ship's control chamber, her subordinates working over the open incision in the flesh of her abdomen. The pain from the live cut was harsh and constant, but it focused her thoughts in a way that nothing else could. Because of the quickened nature of her species and the lightning speed with which Wraith could heal, it was necessary for one worker drone to constantly slice at the edges of the slit to stop the bleeding edges from knitting back together before the surgery could be completed. "Finish it," she hissed, savoring the pain.

He bowed slightly. "Just so, mistress. It is almost done."

She felt a slick, dense shape as it was slipped beneath the epidermis of her torso. In seconds, the matter of her flesh was meshing around it, making the implant part of her.

The scientist backed away and bowed again, oily lines of royal blood staining his fingers. "Complete," he breathed. "You shame us all by your willingness to accept this burden, my Queen."

She looked down and waved the other drones away, watching the wound pull itself tight and scab over, the flow of seeping blood slowing, stopping. "We are Wraith," said the Queen. "And no matter what caste we are born into, we still serve the greater good of the clan at day's end." With difficulty she stood up, wincing at jagged darts of agony from her abdomen. "Ah. I will bear this duty proudly."

The scientist brought his hands together. "My colleagues labor below in the egg orchard," he noted, referring to the protected chamber in the heart of the Hive Ship where knots of genetic material that were Wraith yet to be born were formed. "The pheromones have been injected into a suitable zygote. Birthing of an alternate will commence when... When..."

Suddenly the Wraith halted and gave a shuddering sigh, something akin to a human sob. "Why must you do this?" he demanded sorrowfully. "Why must it be *you*?"

The Queen reached out and cupped his chin in her hand. "Because only I can." She bared her teeth at him. "Do not be afraid. I do this for you all, for the clan." The female Wraith spread her hands to take in the whole of the chamber and all the drones and warriors working about her. "I do this because I love you all."

She stepped down from the throne's dais and stood in front of a flickering lens-screen. "Prepare the warriors and open a channel," she ordered, buttoning her tunic closed. "I will speak with the Asgard now."

"As you command." The scientist touched a fleshy nerve-control and the screen resolved into an image of the dark-eyed alien.

"Fenrir," said the Queen, noting without comment that the human female Teyla—the one whose genetic matrix had been marked by one of the other clans—stood behind him. She had been slightly disappointed when the woman had not been given to her as the other humans had; but it was becoming clear to the Queen that the Asgard viewed these lessers as some sort of pets. Perhaps this Teyla was his favorite...

"*I will hear what you wish to say to me*," said the Asgard, without preamble. "*Under truce, as you requested.*"

The Queen gave the scientist a sideways glance and he nodded. Everything was proceeding as she had expected it would. "I will speak to Fenrir," she replied. "Only to Fenrir."

"*Whatever you have to say can be heard by Teyla Emmagan*," said the Asgard. "*In the interests of balance, I will hear you both.*"

The Queen flicked at a long, talon-like nail. "Very well. But I will not address you from a distance. If I must speak to you in this manner, it will only be face to face."

"*I cannot accommodate you*," retorted the spindly humanoid. "*I can communicate only through this avatar—*"

"And I have only the word of a simulation that it is indeed the real Fenrir!" Her voice rose. "I trust nothing," she continued, "only the evidence of my own eyes. Face to face, Asgard, or you will never know what I have to offer you."

There was a long moment when the image froze, and briefly the Queen entertained the thought that she might have misread the little alien's emotional state; but then Fenrir's avatar flickered and changed, nodding once. "*Very well,*" it replied, "*but none other than you.*"

"That is all that will be needed," she noted. The screen went black and she turned quickly to the scientist. "You know what to do. No thrusters, use only—"

The rest of her command disappeared into the humming rush of a teleport discharge.

Teyla watched the Queen bow stiffly toward the Asgard and in turn Fenrir's avatar inclined its head. She stood nearby and did nothing, never taking her eyes off the alien female. Her nostrils twitched; the moment the Wraith appeared in the teleporter flash, she had detected the faint odor of blood—but Wraith blood, not human. She wondered what might have transpired on the Hive Ship and fought down the desire to shout out and demand to know the fate of Sheppard, Carter and the others.

"*Speak,*" said the avatar.

The Wraith Queen glanced casually at the Risar standing about the chamber and walked toward the cryogenic capsule. "Fascinating technology," she began. "Your flesh-form is in suspended animation, yes? And yet you are capable of communication through this instrumentality," she nodded at the holograph, "and these organic drones. Your knowledge is far superior to ours. We Wraith are utterly dormant when we enter a slumbering state."

"*I will not grant you that technology,*" Fenrir replied. "*The Asgard do not share their knowledge with strangers.*"

"But you shared it with the humans," she noted. "And 'the Asgard'? Do you mean the High Council, Fenrir?"

Teyla saw his dark eyes narrow at the mention of his peers.

The Queen continued. "They are dead, my friend. All that is Asgard exists here now." She chuckled. "You can decide what is and is not to be shared, or with whom."

"The Wraith want only to feed and to rule," snapped Teyla, no longer able to remain silent. "Anything you give them will be turned to that goal!"

To her surprise, the Queen gave a slight nod. "The human is almost correct. Yes, we do seek superiority, but only against our enemies. We wish to end our war with the Asurans, the Replicators. You could help us do that. With this ship." She licked her lips. "With the isa device."

"*How do you know of that?*" Fenrir demanded. The Risar mumbled the same words beneath their breath, coming forward in a threatening manner.

"Does it matter? The humans were careless. I know that you have the power to blind suns. If you granted that to my clan, we would be able to wipe out the Asurans in weeks." She inclined her head. "Think of it, Fenrir. The Replicators, the scourge of galaxies, finally wiped out forever! Is that not fitting?" The Queen came closer, her voice thickening with venom. "After all that they took from you, after all the destruction they wrought across the worlds of your kind, is it not right that a child of Asgard extinguishes their blighted kind from the universe?"

Fenrir's image trembled. "*I... Am the last...*"

"You cannot give them the collapsar!" cried Teyla. "Once they have destroyed the Asurans, what then? Will the Wraith stand down, or will they use your technology to plunder? The hunt... The cull is all they know!" She moved toward the avatar. "Pegasus will burn in their wake, and no life will be safe from them. They will claw across the void and pillage every world they find."

"We have no interest in empires!" snarled the Queen. "Only justice for our dead and an end to the Replicator menace!"

"She lies!"

"And she is afraid!"

"*You will both be silent,*" growled Fenrir. "*I... Have made my choice.*" He wandered to the oval screen, where a vast intergalactic map was displayed, a red line showing the course the *Aegis* had taken on its penal cruise, from the Othala star cluster, through the Kalium and Andromeda galaxies to distant Pegasus. The Asgard seemed lost in the image. "*My world is dead. My people gone. There is nothing here for me now."*

With those words, Teyla sensed some terrible fraction of the distance in Fenrir's heart, and it robbed her of her breath.

On the screen, the red line extended, moving up and away into the starless void between galaxies, projecting a course into an infinite dark. *"You will both be put off my vessel. I will leave this quadrant of space and never return."* He paused. *"I want nothing more to do with war. Perhaps I will find solace in other places… Other universes…"*

"A pity," said the Wraith, glancing at the Athosian. "That was not the answer I had hoped for. But in truth, I suspected the human cattle might have swayed you."

"Fenrir's choice was his own!" Teyla retorted.

"Do not attempt to employ force against me," warned Fenrir. *"My Risar have completed repairs on the weapons systems of the Aegis. I can disable your Hive Ship with a single command."*

The Queen gave a long, staged sigh. "Yes, I noted the damage to your vessel… I wonder what systems still do not function? Matter transporters? Force shields?" She grinned. "Internal sensors?"

"What do you mean?" Teyla whirled as the oval screen morphed into a display of the ship's interior; as before, may parts were still blacked out.

"I took advantage of your weakness, Asgard," she purred. "While we have spoken, my clan has inserted clusters of warriors aboard this ship."

"I have detected nothing. This is a bluff."

The Queen wandered toward the centre of the room, the Risar moving to encircle her. "Believe that if you wish. But the reality is, my clan will not let this ship or its bounty slip from our grasp. We are going to take the *Aegis*, with or without you." She reached down and undid her tunic as she spoke, pressing at a bulge in her stomach. "This prize will ensure our mastery of all Wraith…"

In the depths of Teyla's mind there was a sudden jolt of pure, black emotion, resonating out from the thoughts of the Queen. "No—"

"That victory," said the alien, "is worth any sacrifice." With a strangled yell, she twisted the knot of flesh in her gut and leapt toward the cryogenic capsule.

Even before she was aware of doing it, Teyla flung herself in the other direction, diving for the cover of a control console.

In the churning core of the organic implant inside the Queen's abdomen, bio-chemicals mingled with Wraith blood and triggered a catastrophic release of burning energy.

In less than a heartbeat, the alien evaporated, becoming the core of an exothermal detonation that ripped apart Fenrir's Risar and tore into the Asgard's vital life-support frame.

CHAPTER FOURTEEN

The wooden door rolled back on its stays with a groan and Ronon heard a ripple of fear sweep down the length of the enclosures. Takkol and the other elders retreated like startled animals, pushing themselves as far as they could into the shadowed corners of the cages.

The troop of Wraith marched up the central corridor with the one bearing the commander's sigils at their lead. He wore a fanged smile that was hideous to behold.

Ronon knew what would happen next. He took Keller's hand and pulled her away from the wooden bars. "Get behind me," he grated.

She could read his intentions in his expression. "You're in no condition to fight," she whispered urgently. "Don't do anything crazy!"

"Too late to play it safe now," Ronon stifled a cough and nodded to Lieutenant Allen, ignoring the stab of pain from the muscles in his neck.

The officer returned the nod; she would follow his lead.

The Wraith commander drew level with their cage. "It has been decided that your value to our clan is negligible."

"Y-you're going to let us g-go?" stammered one of Takkol's adjutants, desperation raw and pitiful on his face.

"In a way," replied the commander. "Open the pens," he ordered, and a pair of warriors moved forward to unlock the heavy iron chains holding shut the cages.

"Stay back, you fool!" cried Takkol, but it was too late for the other man. He took two steps toward the opening doorway and another of the Wraith surged at him. A thin scream echoed as the warrior ripped into his chest and fed upon him.

Cries of alarm joined the scream; if Ronon had harbored even the slightest doubt that the Wraith had come to execute them all, it vanished now.

In the first seconds, the Satedan had the advantage; there was only one way into the enclosure where they stood, and that meant the Wraith had to come in single-file. The first into the cage approached him, claws raised. The dart-daggers concealed in Ronon's palms had grown warm and sweat-slick as he had waited for the inevitable attack, and now he threw them, left and then right. He cursed as the first one went wide, his sickness-blurred vision making him miss; he was dimly aware of the small blade bouncing off the alien's chest amour and clattering to the floor

The second dagger found purchase in the hollow of the alien's throat and it wailed, clutching at its neck. Ronon went in and followed up the attack with a punch that drove the dagger still deeper; the memory-metal of the blade was designed to expand on contact with organic matter, growing to twice its width in a matter of moments. The Wraith fell to its knees, vomiting black fluid.

Chaos was all around him as the Wraith began their cull of the prisoners. There were screams and yelling, the ozone stink of a stunner discharge. He glimpsed Keller swinging a heavy clay bowl into the face of the Wraith commander, knocking him off balance.

Allan came up from a crouch with the other dagger in her fist and struck at another of the Wraith warriors, dislodging its helmet. It turned on her as the blade-tip scraped over its bare shoulder and the creature viciously shoved her back. Ronon moved to help her, but he was sluggish and his joints ached with each motion.

The Wraith planted its hand on her chest and hooted with pleasure as it began to feed off her. She screamed, the flesh of her face turning grey, becoming taut across the bones of her skull.

Ronon kicked low and connected with the Wraith's knee, smashing bone. The creature twisted and dropped, freeing Allan from the death grip. She pitched forward, wheezing, and shoved the dagger into the warrior's eye socket. The Wraith tumbled over in a twitching heap.

He caught the lieutenant and heard her gasp; in the space of just a few seconds, the Wraith had drained decades from her life. The young woman he had spoken to before was twenty, thirty years older in aspect, her buzz-cut hair streaked with grey and her face lined. "Behind you!" she husked.

Ronon turned and punched blindly. He was rewarded by a howl and the sensation of cartilage snapping beneath his knuckles. The Wraith commander spun backwards, out of the cage proper and into the confusion of the corridor beyond, blood gushing in a fan from his crushed nose.

But these were only minor victories in the melee. Ronon saw Takkol's men becoming food for the Wraith, while the former elder stumbled on his robes as he tried to flee the killing.

The Satedan grabbed Keller's arm and dragged her out of the cage, with Allan hobbling along behind. "We have to fall back," he shouted. "Find another way out!"

They pressed into the cluster of survivors, Takkol, the medical team and the last of the Atlantis airmen with them, but the further back they retreated down the corridor, the clearer their situation became.

"There's no other way out of here," the lieutenant coughed. "There's only one exit from this place, and the Wraith are between us and it!"

"They're going to butcher us like herd animals!" moaned Takkol.

"Not without a fight," said Ronon.

The smooth metallic lines of the control chamber lit by cool yellow-white illumination were gone, replaced by something dirtied with oily residue. There was a smoky, cloying burnt-meat stink that hung in the air.

Teyla shoved the sparking remains of a computer panel off her legs and struggled to her feet. She shuddered as she surveyed the room; the Queen's suicidal attack would have killed her just as it had torn apart Fenrir's Risar, had she not sensed that tiny moment of thought before the implanted bio-charge exploded. It was horrific to conceive; the Wraith Queen had willingly given her own life in order to destroy the command centre of the *Aegis*, and although she had not fully succeeded—a testament to the resilience of Asgard technology—the consoles and holographic screens all around the chamber were flickering and incoherent. The alien had done much damage.

And for Fenrir's cryogenic capsule was at the heart of it all, the impact point of the detonation. Coolant pipes spat foam, forming hazy clouds of ice crystals in the frigid air. The whole forward section of the suspension module had been ripped open and blackened by thermal damage, heat-warped fingers of broken metal twisted and bent by the force of the blast.

Teyla's hand went to her chest. He had to be dead. He could not have—

"Tey…la…" The voice was faint and labored. It took her a moment before she realized it was not a synthetic echo, but the real thing.

"Fenrir?" She rushed forward, slipping over newly-formed patches of ice and shallow drifts of broken glass. She found a foothold on the side of the ruined cryo module and pushed up until she was kneeling atop the frost-rimed surface of the machine.

From this angle, it appeared as if a monstrous blade had slashed along the length of Fenrir's capsule. The pod, sealed closed for generations, was open to the air and ruined, the fragile life within moments away from death. She glimpsed pallid flesh moving amid the smoke and vapors, and Teyla fanned them away.

A spindly, childlike hand emerged from the cold fog and grabbed her wrist. She reached down into the flickering glow of the pod's interior and found the alien there, his chest fluttering as he fought to breathe. Teyla's eyes were stinging and she blinked furiously. She tried to pull Fenrir up, but he was caught beneath a distended piece of machinery; his bird-thin limbs were atrophied and weak, so much so that she feared she would snap his bones if she pulled too hard.

The Asgard's head turned, revealing a half-coronet made of hair-like wires and smooth crystal spheres about the back of his skull. Snaking cables that pulsed with light extended away, doubtless toward the interface that married Fenrir to the systems of the *Aegis*.

"Teyla," he repeated. "I am sorry I deceived you. Perhaps now I have done my penance…" The Asgard gasped as pain lanced through him. "We should…have been open with each other… Perhaps this is fitting. I will go to be with my kindred… and be forgiven." He blinked, his heavy lids closing slowly.

"Fenrir, no!" cried Teyla. "Please, you must hold on! If you perish, there will be no-one to control this ship, it will be lost! The Wraith are already on board…"

He gave a pained nod. "I sense them. Yes. Moving. I cannot stop them."

She squeezed his frail fingers. "Then help me stop them! Hold on!"

"You…cannot do that alone." He sucked in a shuddering breath. "I will…bring you the help you require."

The crystal spheres clustered around the interface crown began to glow.

McKay followed the others to their feet as the webbing across the cell door vibrated and reeled back into the chitinous walls. The four Wraith warriors on guard had been joined by the scientist-type he remembered encountering down on Heruun. The alien glanced at them all in turn with sly, open avarice.

"My Queen has opened the way. The Asgard ship will soon be under the control of my clan. If you wish to live, you will help us understand its mechanisms."

Sheppard shrugged. "Hey, I can barely change a light bulb. Can't help you with any space doohickeys, pal."

This seemed to amuse the alien. "Not you." He nodded at Lorne. "Nor you. You are warrior drones, without the intellect required for such tasks."

"I'll have you know I'm an ace at sudoku," Lorne sniffed, moving to join Sheppard where he blocked the path toward Carter and McKay.

The Wraith scientist pointed at the others. "These two, the female and the inferior male."

"Inferior?" echoed McKay. "I resent that!"

"We won't help you," Carter said firmly. "We'll resist you every inch of the way."

The Wraith grunted. "And how will you do that?"

Carter was about to say something more, but from nowhere a white nimbus of light surrounded her and vanished with a humming crackle.

"Huh," said Sheppard, a grin forming on his lips. "*That* way, maybe?"

The alien shouted out a command, but it was too late; the transport effect flared again, and when it faded he was alone inside the cell.

The Wraith commander advanced, the corridor's floorboards creaking as he came ever closer. His head turned, lips peeling back to show wet fangs. "Surrender. It will pass quicker if you do not fight us."

Ronon Dex was aware of his heart hammering in his chest, his pulse rushing in his ears; the sickness in his blood was sapping his strength, draining his will even as he stood here and did nothing. He shook his head to dispel the miasma in his thoughts; he rejected the fatigue in his bones, the desperate need to slump to the wall and let the blackness take him.

No. He was Satedan. He would die on his feet, meeting death as he had life, head-on and without compromise.

A strange calm came over him, and he felt a smile pull at the corner of his lips. In the rare moments of introspection spared him by the world, Ronon had always suspected that his end would come in battle, and at the hands of the Wraith. No simple, quiet ending for Specialist Dex, no soft and restful deathbed. From the moment they had smashed his world and made him a Runner, Ronon had known he would die with blood in his teeth, his hands around the neck of his enemy. He nodded to himself. There was something right about it.

He glanced at Keller, her pretty face pale with fear. His only regret was the others would share his fate; they deserved better, not to die out here, thousands of light years from their homeworld.

"Surrender!" hissed the Wraith again.

"Come and make me," he snarled, spreading his arms.

But without warning Keller's hand was on his arm, pulling

back. "Ronon!" she cried. "The floor!"

He had a moment to register what she said before the slats below them shattered, as stone hammers crashed into the wood from beneath, sending storms of splinters flying.

Sam gasped in surprise as the Wraith holding chamber shifted and reformed into the command deck of the Aegis. "Huh," she managed "Well, that was unexpected."

The acrid tang of melted plastic and stale smoke wreathed the air around her and she coughed.

"Colonel!" shouted Teyla, from across the room. "You're safe!"

"Thanks to you, I imagine." She glanced around. "What happened in here?"

"The Wraith Queen destroyed herself, with an explosive device implanted in her body. She was trying to kill Fenrir."

"She…succeeded."

Carter was startled by the second voice; she immediately recognized the thin, reedy accent of the Asgard. "But the cryo pod…" She pointed at the wrecked device, still spewing icy foam.

Teyla's expression was grim. "He does not have very long."

Sam nodded and picked her way around a fallen stanchion to one of the consoles that was still operable. "You brought me back… What about Colonel Sheppard and the others on the Hive Ship?"

"There was a power fluctuation…" Fenrir managed. "They are aboard, on the lower decks…"

She moved her hands over the bowed control panel, shifting the oblate key-spheres back and forth. "The Wraith sent over boarding parties," she began.

"I am…aware," said the Asgard. "They slipped in…undetected. Pierced the hull…" He coughed, as if he felt the wounds to his ship as much as if they were injuries to his flesh.

Carter frowned as she tried to navigate the complexities of the Asgard system; parts of it were familiar to her, but others were labyrinthine, layered puzzles that she had never encountered before. She could sense Fenrir was trying to open the

Aegis to her, but he was faltering with every breath. On a tertiary hologram screen, she saw a cluster of dots indicating the trackers belonging to Sheppard and the others, in a corridor close to the main engineering decks; the Asgard had been as good as his word. But she could also see other dots clustered nearby—Wraith. The alien trace was fuzzy and indistinct, wavering between a ghost-image and solidity. Something about the aliens was making it hard for the ship's already-damaged internal sensors to read them.

She automatically reached for her radio, only to remember that it had been taken along with all the equipment they had on them when they appeared on the Hive Ship. Without any weapons to defend themselves, Sheppard and his team would be easy prey for the Wraith invaders.

A thought suddenly occurred to her. "Fenrir! This ship has a data-matter converter, right? You can construct objects from stored information patterns…"

The alien nodded jerkily. "I will provide you with… That facility."

"And access to the transporter system records," she added, thinking aloud. "When you beamed us off the ship, the matter patterns of everything we had on us would have been recorded…" Carter gave a quick grin as she found what she was looking for.

A few quick commands and an object shimmered into being on the panel before her; an Atlantis-issue walkie-talkie, synthesized from the ground up, molecule by molecule. She picked it up and turned it over in her hands. "Just like the real thing. Let's see if this works." Carter ran the converter again, this time sending a newly-formed device elsewhere.

Sheppard gingerly picked up the radio from where it had appeared on the floor before them, holding it by the antenna as if it were the tail of a poisonous snake. "Okay, that's odd," he admitted.

A short way up the corridor, Major Lorne leaned in against the side of an intersection, peering into the dimness. "There's a whole bunch of them up there, Colonel," he reported. "Half a dozen Wraith, I'd guess."

"Oh, great," said McKay. "Out of the frying pan."

"Rodney—"

"*Colonel Sheppard?*" Carter's words crackled from the walkie-talkie. "*Do you read me, over?*"

"Sam?!" said McKay. "Where is she?"

"Quiet!" Sheppard retorted, and raised the radio to his lips. "I'm here, Colonel. Are you okay?"

"*I'm a few levels above you, on the command tier with Teyla and Fenrir. He's badly hurt, John. The Queen tried to kill him.*"

His lips thinned. "Understood. We got a situation ourselves. Wraith, a whole bunch of 'em blocking our path. There's no way we can get past."

"*I have intermittent internal sensors, I see them.*"

"Feel free to beam them out into deep space, if you'd like," said Lorne.

"*No can do, Major,*" Carter replied. "*The internal sensors can't lock on to their bio-signs...*" She paused. "*Stand by, I'm sending you some ordnance. Wait one.*"

"How's that gonna work? We lost all our stuff on the Hive," said McKay. The question had barely left his mouth when a flash of transporter glow blinked in the middle of the floor, revealing a couple of G-36 assault rifles and a P90, along with a pile of ammunition.

"Never mind." The Major's face creased in a grin and he grabbed one of the rifles, slamming a twin-drum cyclic magazine into the G-36. "Merry Christmas!"

Sheppard took the other rifle and tossed the submachine gun to McKay. "Thanks for the care package," he said to the radio. "We'll deal with these creeps and then rendezvous with you."

"*Negative,*" said Carter. "*I'm plotting the movements of the Wraith from up here. It looks like they're moving toward the computer core.*"

"They could shut down the ship," noted McKay, "or worse."

"*Rodney's right,*" came the reply. "*The primary matter converter array is down there. If they take control of that, they can make copies of anything in the Asgard database.*"

"Oh crap," said Sheppard. "Like weapons?" He hefted the assault rifle in his hand.

"*Like weapons,*" Carter repeated. "*For starters.*"

Color drained from McKay's face. "The collapsar device. The blueprints will be in Fenrir's database!"

"Can't it be shut down from the bridge?" asked Lorne.

McKay shook his head. "It's a stand-alone system, like the Asgard core on the *Odyssey*. Even if you isolated it from the rest of the *Aegis*, it can still operate independently."

Sheppard spoke into the radio once again. "Colonel? I copy your sitrep, over. We'll move in and take the converter out of commission."

"*Roger that. I'll do what I can to help you from up here. Good luck.*"

The survivors reeled backward as part of the floor of the animal enclosures gave way, planks ripping and falling into space, cascading down over the boughs from the main trunk of the city-tree. The Wraith went with them, screaming and howling. Through the gaps Ronon saw men hanging from ropes of vine, swinging back and forth beneath the enclosure. Some of them had rodguns that chattered rapid-fire rounds into the aliens, knocking them off their handholds and tearing them open.

The Wraith commander was still clinging to a broken support beam, his claws digging into the wood as he pulled himself back up, inch by shuddering inch.

"Stay back from the edge," said Lieutenant Allan. "It could give at any second."

"Maybe," Ronon ignored her advice and stepped forward, feeling the twisted flooring bow beneath his weight.

The commander met his gaze and spat at him. Clinging to its handhold with one arm, it snatched at the pistol holster on its belt, grabbing at a stunner weapon. Balance lost, the Wraith began to lose its grip.

Ronon shook his head "Bad choice," he said, holding out a hand to assist the alien.

There was a moment of surprise on the Wraith's face when

he could not understand why a mortal enemy would offer to save his life; then Ronon grinned wolfishly.

"Nah," he said, the open hand curling into a fist, "just kidding." He put all his effort into a savage punch to the Wraith's face. The impact dislodged the commander's grip, and with a hate-filled snarl, he fell, down and down toward the rusty landscape below. The alien vanished into the lower canopy of trees and was gone.

The figures on the rope-vines swarmed up toward the wrecked enclosure and clambered inside. Ronon blinked as one of them pulled a thin cloth scarf from around his face.

"Ronon Dex," said Soonir, with a cocksure smirk. "We saw the Wraith coming. I thought you and your people could use the help of me and mine."

"How did you do that?" said Keller.

"The lower enclosures are the oldest structures in the settlement," he noted. "The stone hammers are used when we must demolish them." The rebel leader grinned. "This seemed the most expedient way to deal with the Wraith."

"You could have killed us all!" shouted Takkol, forcing his way forward. The decking beneath his feet gave an ominous moan and he faltered, his fury waning for a moment.

"I could have left you all to perish," Soonir retorted. "It is your idiocy that has led our world to this invasion!"

"Hey!" shouted Keller, her strident tone surprising everyone, Ronon included. "Now is not the time for this! We need to get out of here before this place comes down around us!"

Soonir gave a nod. "The healer's point is well made." He signaled to his men to draw up the ropes. "Follow the tethers. My men will lead you to a platform below this one." He offered a vine to Ronon, and eyed him. "That is, if you can manage it…" Soonir was staring closely at Dex's face, at his pale, drawn features.

Ronon ignored the pounding headache in his skull. "I can manage," he replied, and snatched the rope from the other man's hand.

Sam heard the sound and turned away from the bridge console. It was unlike any cry she had ever heard before, an alien moan from an alien throat.

"Fenrir…" Teyla tried to hold the Asgard up, but he was limp in her hands. Carter saw his chest rise and fall in ever slower stutters, his breath whispering from his tiny mouth in puffs of vapor. "We have to help him!"

Carter came closer. "I'm sorry, Teyla. There's nothing we can do."

"Humans," came the whisper. "You are so like us and so unlike us." The Asgard's expression was pained as he worked to force out every word. "We share so many things. Wonder and daring. Greatness and folly. Sorrow…and regret."

"The Wraith will not take this ship," Carter said quietly. "I promise you that."

"I believe you." Fenrir's head lolled and his dark eyes found Teyla. "You… You must survive, Teyla Emmagan. Guard the new life within you, nurture it." His thin hand fell to her belly. "It is your future."

"I will," she told him. "I can do nothing else."

And then there were no more breaths from the Asgard's silent form, no more words. In a very human gesture toward so alien a being, Teyla reached up and closed Fenrir's eyes, then gently lay him down inside the broken cryo capsule.

Sam felt the ghost of the same hollow feeling she had experienced when the planet Orilla had destroyed itself in front of her; it was a terrible emotion to consider, the raw loss of being a witness to the extinction of an entire species.

"Now they are truly gone," said Teyla quietly. "The Asgard are no more."

Sam spoke again after a moment. "If I have learned anything after over a decade in this job, it's that the universe has ways of confounding your expectations." She reached out and touched the other woman's arm. "Come on. He protected us. Now we have to do the job of the Aegis, protect Heruun and our people down there."

Teyla nodded. "In his honor, I will do so gladly."

Rodney pressed himself as flat as he could into the lee of a

support beam and gritted his teeth. He felt the numbing edge of
static backwash from the Wraith stunner blasts arcing past him,
and he was in no rush to meet one full-on. McKay was far more
familiar than he wanted to be with the highly unpleasant after-
effects of taking a hit from the alien weapons. It had happened
with enough regularity that it sometimes kept him up at night,
wondering about how many neurons the stun shots fried each
time; the very thought of losing some of his precious brain cells
made Rodney feel quite unwell.

Blind-firing, he poked the muzzle of the P90 out into the
corridor and let off a burst of rounds, but it didn't seem to slow
the return fire from the Wraiths. Across the corridor, similarly
in cover behind another pillar, Sheppard was aiming down the
barrel of his assault rifle and planting careful three-shot clusters
in the enemy line; further back, lying prone so he presented a
smaller target, Lorne laid down cover fire, trying to keep the
Wraith off-balance. It didn't seem to be working, though.

"They're dug in tight," called the major.

"Yeah, I'm getting that," Sheppard replied dryly. "We
should have asked Carter to magic us up a bunch of grenades."

McKay chanced a look around the support. Between the two
sides of the firefight, a handful of Risar stood mute and con-
fused, blinking and clutching at the air, completely oblivious
to the bullets and energy bolts streaking past them. One of the
organic drones was clipped by a blast from a Wraith warrior
and stumbled to the floor without a cry.

"What is wrong with those things?" said Lorne. "They're
right in the line of fire!"

"Fenrir," said McKay. "He's not controlling them any more.
Without any orders, they're just going around in circles." As if
to underline his statement, the lights along the floor dimmed for
a moment, and in concert the Risar reached for their heads.

At the far end of the corridor, where the passageway
branched toward a heavy hatch, the Wraith warriors had ripped
out a wall panel for use as a makeshift barricade. Behind them,
he could pick out one of the black-tunic-wearing scientist caste
working at the controls to the door. For a second he thought it

was the same Wraith they'd left looking like a fool back on the Hive Ship; but then there was no way he would have been able to get over to the *Aegis* this fast. The truth was, it appeared relatively rare to find differentiation between the different Wraith sub-groups; from the research started by Carson Beckett three years back, it seemed that each of them were formed in egg-sac pods as basic 'blanks', and then transformed in utero by the injection of biochemical triggers by a Queen. It wasn't much different from the way hive insects worked on Earth. The right mix of genetic code could create a low-smarts, high-strength warrior, a thinker for the scientist caste, a ship commander, even a new Queen.

There was a sparking and a cough of smoke from the hatchway, and Rodney's heart sank as the doors slid open, granting the Wraith scientist access. A stun bolt hissed past him and he yelped, ducking back into cover.

"We're out of options. I'm gonna rush them," said Sheppard. "On three."

"Three what?" McKay snapped back. "Bad plan! You step out, they'll cut you down!"

"Then how—?" Lorne was starting to speak when lights went out in the corridor, and for one stark moment the only illumination was the muzzle flare of the rifles.

"What the hell?" said Sheppard.

There came a sound that made Rodney's skin crawl, a weird keening moan that echoed down the corridor. With a start, he realized it was coming from all around them.

"The Risar…" said Lorne. "It's them."

The lights flickered and came back, both humans and Wraith brought to pause by the brief blackout. The moaning grew louder, more strident. The Asgard drones were agitated, clawing at themselves and stumbling against the walls.

"Oh no." Rodney felt a jolt of comprehension. "Fenrir… I think he's dead."

One of the Wraith warriors fired a shot into the shambling, directionless Risar and knocked it to the deck; it was a grave mistake. As one, the rest of the drone-creatures howled incoherently and surged toward the Wraith barricade, into the teeth of the alien weapons. The densely-muscled Risar attacked on reflex, shattering the line. Without their Asgard creator to guide them, they had become primitive and animalistic, reacting to only the most savage and basic of instincts.

Sheppard shot the others a look. "C'mon, move up! This might be the only chance we get." He broke from cover, moving and firing, with Lorne charging after him. McKay swallowed hard and followed.

Teyla placed her hands on the half-spheres of the control console as Colonel Carter had shown her, and moved them gently. On the holographic screen in front of her, a disc of color turned and flexed, showing the power train from the energy reactor in the heart of the *Aegis*.

"Careful," said Carter. "I need you to manually regulate the flux from the core while I fire up the sub-light drives."

"I understand," she replied, although she had only the most basic grasp of what the colonel was actually doing. The Asgard ship's controls were not like those of Wraith ships; there was none of the unearthly sense-connection between flesh and machinery.

Carter's hands moved over the neighboring panel in long loops, as panes of data unfolded in the cold air before them. Teyla saw an exterior view flicker into life on the large oval screen. There, blotting out the distant ball of Heruun's orange sun, was the monstrous arachnid silhouette of a Hive Ship. She saw it shift. "They are turning," she reported. "They see us moving."

"External sensors are picking up energy transfer." Carter chewed her lip. "Yes, there. The Wraith are charging weapons."

"Will they risk firing on us? Do they not wish to keep this craft intact?"

The colonel glanced at her. "My guess is they'll be more than happy to put a few dents in it if they have to. And worst-case scenario…"

"They will destroy it if they cannot possess it."

Carter nodded. "Here we go, sub-light engines to one quarter thrust."

On the screen the Hive Ship slipped away, turning even as it dropped past them.

Teyla studied her console. "The shields… The indicator ribbon here is barely a third full."

"I know. We'll have to do what we can to avoid getting tagged—"

The decking beneath their feet rocked and pitched; on the power screen, a schematic of the *Aegis* flashed up, a series of red circles appearing all along the aft of the vessel were the first salvo from the Hive Ship impacted.

"Or not," Carter frowned. "We have to get some distance, give the weapons grid time to charge up, otherwise they'll pick us apart."

Teyla's mind raced. She had been both the hunter and the hunted, on foot in the forests of Athos and on other worlds across Pegasus; but the rules of the hunt there or here in the void of space were still basically the same. *Evade your enemy. Deny them their advantage. Strike from cover.*

She nodded at the exterior view. "We should make for Heruun. The planet's ice halo. We could lose them in the clutter."

The colonel angled the ship and applied more power to the drives. "Good call. I'm taking us in."

Sheppard's rifle ran empty and he spun it about as he advanced, slamming the skeletal butt of the G-36 into the chest of the Wraith warrior blocking his path to the computer core chamber. The alien cried out as it was knocked back over a shallow railing; built for the diminutive Asgard, the safety rail only came up to the Wraith's knees, and it tumbled headfirst to the chamber's lower level twenty feet below.

The colonel threw a glance over his shoulder as Lorne and McKay followed him in, both men laying down blasts of gunfire. The few remaining Wraith outside had been mauled by the wild Risar, but in their uncontrolled state there was a chance the drones might turn on the humans as well. They had to move quickly.

The core chamber reminded Sheppard of an amphitheatre, with tiered concentric levels dropping downward to an open area in the centre. A broad column of crystalline circuitry glowing with power dominated everything, and from it extended spokes of Asgard technology that connected to other, smaller cylinders of systemry around the edges of the room. Hanging over the floor were glass maintenance platforms with no visible means of suspension.

Lorne dispatched a pair of armed Wraith left behind to guard the entrance as Sheppard dropped into a crouch, reloading his weapon. On the lowermost level the other Wraith were reacting to their presence, firing stun blasts toward them, moving into cover. The larger group of them were clustered around a cylinder of smoked glass; glowing blue vanes circled around it, humming with power. Sheppard spotted one of the Wraith leather jacket brigade working a console under the watchful eye of a senior warrior. The soldier Wraith looked familiar; he had been in the control room when Fenrir had first brought the Atlanteans aboard the *Aegis*. The colonel raised his rifle, but the angle was poor. He couldn't draw a bead on either of them from here.

Lorne voiced the question forming in Sheppard's thoughts. "What are they doing down there?"

McKay made a face. "That cylinder… It's the matter converter platform."

A sphere of white light appeared inside the smoked glass and then faded away; the panels retracted to reveal a barrel-shaped object half the height of a man. It was constructed out of the same featureless, matte grey metal that formed the walls of the Asgard starship. About the sides of it, there were rings that pulsed slowly with dull red color.

Sheppard's throat went dry. "Rodney. Is that what I think it is?"

Two of the Wraith warriors gathered up the device and removed it from the converter; in doing so they turned it, revealing an oval plate attached to the side of the object. On it was a single Asgard rune, a simple vertical line like a downward knife cut. *The symbol 'isa'.*

"Oh no," managed McKay.

"I really hate it when you say that," said Lorne. "So that's a bomb?"

Rodney nodded. "And then some."

CHAPTER FIFTEEN

Ronon emerged into a chamber formed by the natural growth of the great tree's thicker trunks, following Keller and the others. Flooring had been set across it, and a circular door had been fitted into a curved bole. Two more of Soonir's men were waiting for them there, one at a viewing slot in the door. He nodded to the rebel leader. "No sign of any more Wraith. The others may not have been alerted yet."

"Good," said Soonir. "Our luck is holding."

"For now," said the Satedan. He wondered if Sheppard and the others were faring any better.

There was a commotion behind him and Ronon turned to see Takkol barge past Lieutenant Allan. The fear the elder had shown in the cages was gone and his usual haughty mien had returned. "Is this one of your bolt holes?" he demanded, glaring at the rebel. "Is this how you moved around the settlement, to plant your seeds of sedition and plot to overthrow my rule?"

"Yes," Soonir replied evenly. "And now it has saved your life. I think gratitude would be in order."

"To you? Never! For all we know, you are the instigator of all this! Perhaps you are in league with Kullid and Aaren, perhaps you are one of the pawns of the Wraith!"

Soonir's face clouded. "I had hoped your eyes would have been opened when your precious Aegis renounced you, but I see that was too much to ask for! You are still the same blinkered fool you ever were."

The two men squared off, each a moment away from resorting to physical violence. Ronon's face twisted in a sneer and he stepped between them. "Both of you, be quiet before I beat that noise out of you." Both the rebel soldiers and the remainder of the elder's guards bristled at his words.

"How dare you threaten me!" Takkol retorted.

Soonir eyed Ronon. "The sickness has made you foolish,

voyager. You are in no state to fight."

"If you think that," Ronon glowered at the two men, each word a razor, "then you're a poor judge of character." He snorted. "Look at you. Away from the Wraith for less than a minute and you're already falling back into your old patterns." The Satedan shook his head. "Your people need help, not your damned posturing."

"You know nothing of our society," Takkol replied defensively.

"I know this." Ronon prodded him in the chest. "I've seen more worlds scoured clean by the Wraith than you can count, my own home among them." He coughed and spat. "And I know that the only way to fight the Wraith is to be willing to give everything. Even your life." He shot a look at Soonir. "So if you want Heruun to have another sunrise, put aside any rivalry you have. Fight together or die apart. It's that simple."

His grim pronouncement brought silence with it. Neither Soonir nor Takkol could dare to deny the truth of what he had said.

Finally, Keller spoke up. "The Wraith who came to the cages… There will be others. Sooner or later, they're going to do what they always do. Start the cull."

"We've gotta hit them now," said Allan wearily. "We have the element of surprise."

Ronon nodded. The lieutenant's suggestion made good tactical sense. "We'll need your help," he said, turning back to the elder and the rebel. "The Wraith must be staging from somewhere…"

"The sick lodge," said Soonir. "Kullid has given it over to them."

"If we can get close without raising the alarm, we can tip the balance."

Takkol frowned. "There are many of our people there, many of the sick who have come lured by Kullid's promises that the Wraith have a cure for them."

"Laaro's parents…" murmured Keller.

"Can you get us there unseen?" said Ronon.

Soonir paused, thinking. "It can be done. But we must move

now."

"I will come with you," Takkol added, drawing himself up.
"I should be there."

"The more, the merrier," said Allan.

Ronon felt a hand on his arm and turned. "Are you really sure
you're up for this?" Keller spoke quietly. "I've been watching
you. You can fool the others but you can't fool me, I know the
pain and disorientation are getting worse."

He shook her off. "I'll be okay."

The doctor's jaw set firmly. "I'm sure you think that. But just
in case you're not, I'm coming with you."

"No," he began, "that's not going to happen. You need to
stay out of sight, take the others and find a safe haven." Ronon
gestured towards the nurses and medical staffers who had come
with Keller from Atlantis.

"This isn't a discussion," she replied. "And besides, you're
not the reason I want to go back to the sick lodge. If Kullid is
telling the truth, and the Wraith do have a cure for the sickness, that's where it will be." She folded her arms and stared
defiantly at him.

He sighed; he couldn't muster the will to argue with her.
"Fine. Just don't get yourself killed."

"Lorne!" Sheppard shouted to attract the major's attention
and jabbed a finger toward a shallow curved ramp leading down toward the lower level of the computer core. "Take
McKay, get down there and stop those creeps from using the
collapsar."

"What are you going to do?" said McKay.

"Something daring to keep them off your asses. Now go!" If
he had paused to think seriously about it, Sheppard knew that
the recklessness of what he was about to do would convince
him to stay put; so he threw caution to the wind and just winged
it.

Yelling at the top of his voice, he burst from cover with his
assault rifle at his hip, the fire selector slotted at full auto. It had
exactly the effect he wanted, catching the Wraith off guard as
he looped around the raised walkway, laying down a fan of bul-

lets. Shots whined off the support stanchions and blew warriors off their feet. All around him were the buzzing flares of stunner bolts, some of them so close he could feel the numbing corona of energy.

Reaching another curved ramp on the far side of the chamber, he let himself fall backwards into a half-slide, coming down against one of the low safety railings. Ignoring the friction down his thigh, he rode the smooth banister toward the lower level. A pair of Wraith moved to block his path and he kicked off, spinning around to land bodily against the pair of them. Reacting without thinking, Sheppard slammed the still-hot muzzle of the G-36 into the face of one of the aliens, and sent it howling away, clawed fingers grabbing at flash-burned skin. The second Wraith grabbed a handful of his gear vest and yanked him backward; he lost the rifle and let himself drop. The warrior overbalanced and fell hard against a steel wall. The colonel mirrored a move he'd once seen pulled by a WWF wrestler and put all his weight behind his elbow, driving the Wraith's skull into the wall with a nasty crunch of bone.

More of them were coming. He couldn't spare a second to see if Lorne and McKay had made it down; instead he flung himself across the floor and snatched up a fallen stunner rifle, clutching the metallic, maggot-shaped weapon to him. He squeezed the firing pad and dispatched the aliens advancing on him.

Gunfire rattled on the far side of the chamber and he scrambled away, pausing only to snag the strap of his discarded G-36 and swing it over his shoulder.

"Sheppard!" He heard Rodney shouting his name. "Stop him!"

He didn't need to ask who. The Wraith veteran—the one from the bridge—was shoving two of his lackeys across the chamber, toward another of the room's cylindrical alcoves. The bigger warrior drones were carrying Fenrir's isa unit between them.

Unlike the matter converter, this other alcove was a shallow dais under lit by green and white strobes, pulsing in a regular rhythm. To one side, a curved panel was connected to the device and standing over it was a Wraith scientist.

Something clicked inside Sheppard's head as he suddenly understood what was going on. The other alcove wasn't another converter. It was a teleport pad.

And with that they can beam that sun killer anywhere in range. Gotta stop them no matter what—

Without warning the deck of the *Aegis* resonated like a struck drum skin and tilted wildly for a few seconds as the ship's gravity generators struggled to compensate. The lights ringing the chamber dimmed and then steadied.

The aliens were still intent on their deadly task. He saw what was coming, and he knew he was too far away to stop it. Sheppard dumped the unwieldy Wraith rifle and grabbed at his G-36, inserting the last clip of ammunition he had on him. He had to make this count.

The warrior Wraiths dropped the collapsar unit on to the pad. From where he stood, Sheppard could see the pulsing rings around its circumference. It was armed and ready to be deployed.

The colonel raised the rifle to his shoulder and took a breath; he had just one shot at this, and if he did it wrong… Hell, he had no idea what would happen, but it probably would be very, *very* bad.

The Wraith veteran spotted him, drew his pistol and took aim. Sheppard's thinking time had run out.

They both fired and moved at once, dodging away from one another; but John Sheppard wasn't aiming at the alien with the gun. He had drawn a bead on the Wraith scientist. The trigger pulled hard to the stop, the colonel unloaded a burst into the black-jacketed alien and the console before him, praying he would hit something vital.

The alien scientist jerked and spun as the discharge ripped into him; the delicate fusion of Asgard crystal-metal construction before him blew apart, even as the power of the transporter field surged through it.

Distantly, Sheppard was aware of McKay shouting out a warning. He had only a moment to register one thought. *Looks like I broke something expensive.*

Then the teleporter control panel detonated like a bomb and a shockwave of released energy flashed across the core chamber, blowing out circuits and tearing into anyone who stood in its path. Sheppard felt the deck fall away underneath him and he was carried backwards, the crackling, murderous heat searing his palms as he brought up his hands to protect his face.

Pain made him cry out as he slammed into the far wall. There were a few seconds where he teetered on the edge of passing out, but he was ready for it, and sucked in a shuddering breath. Sheppard coughed and shook his head, sending a rain of dust and tiny crystal splinters falling away to the floor. Using the rifle as a prop, he hauled himself up, ignoring the spikes of agony from his knees. Through the soles of his boots he could feel the deck of the *Aegis* vibrating constantly now, juddering like a badly-maintained engine. *Did I cause that?* he wondered. *Carter will be pissed if it turns out I bent the ship.*

"McKay?" He managed a dry-throated yell. "Lorne!"

"Still alive," moaned a familiar voice. "I think."

He lurched across the chamber, avoiding the corpses of the two burly Wraith warriors. They had unwittingly saved Sheppard from being immolated, largely because they had been standing between him and the energy surge. The front of their bodies, the silver-grey amour plate and oily, burned skin, had become molten and run together like hot wax.

Sweet-smelling chemical smoke from fried components wreathed the floor, each step disturbing it. The colonel coughed and flinched as a shape rose abruptly from the deck and stumbled away from him, toward the blackened ruin that was all that remained of the teleport pad. Back-lit by the firefly-flicker of the wounded computer core, the Wraith veteran dragged itself toward the alcove.

Resting there on its side in a snowdrift of glass shards was the collapsar device, damaged but clearly still operable. The Wraith moaned as it moved, one whole side of its body a mass of seared flesh. Driven on by hate and fury, it clawed through the thick air toward the weapon.

"Stand back!" Sheppard shouted, bringing his rifle to his shoulder.

The Wraith threw him a look over its shoulder, one eye blazing with anger, the other a ragged, empty socket. It hissed at him and stepped forward, its one good hand snatching at a control wheel on the device's upper surface.

This time there was no hesitation, and Sheppard shot him through the head.

McKay and Lorne emerged from behind a long, wide control panel. In the flickering dimness of the chamber, the two men looked like a pair of grim-faced ghosts. The major's skin was streaked with blood; his right cheek and his ear were covered in hundreds of tiny lacerations where fragments of glassine crystal had buffeted him in the blast wave.

Sheppard eyed him. "You should try an electric shaver next time," he deadpanned.

"With all due respect, sir," Lorne replied, "bite me."

McKay pushed past them and gingerly nudged the dead Wraith off the top of the collapsar device where it had fallen. Sheppard saw that the red rings were pulsing in a new configuration, growing quicker with each cycle.

"Oh no." Rodney's voice was a whisper. "Oh no. Oh no. Oh no." His fingers scrambled over the surface of the Asgard weapon, stabbing at keys without apparent rhyme or reason.

"I *really* hate it when he does that," Lorne grated.

McKay looked up, his eyes wide with horror. "They weren't going to wait. They started it up before it was even ready to deploy. Oh, this is bad. It's already building to criticality."

"But you can disarm it, right?" Sheppard leaned in. "I mean, you're Rodney McKay, genius guy. You do this sort of thing all the time. You thrive on it!"

"The thing I thrive on the most is not being reduced to my component atoms," he replied, his voice cracking. "which this thing will do, along with yours, this ship's and anything else nearby when it implodes."

"But that thing needs a star to make a black hole," insisted Lorne. "Right?"

McKay bolted back up to his feet. "Yes, but even without one it will make a hell of a mess. Like, blowing a chunk out of a planet or the aforementioned reducing-to-atoms thing." He paused, rubbing his hands together. "Oh no."

"Stop saying that," Sheppard snapped. "It's not helping."

The major winced. "How long until... Well, until it does what it does?"

"Maybe fifteen minutes, I think. These Asgard numerals all look the same."

"What happens if this thing goes off in deep space?" Sheppard nudged it with his boot. "I mean, nowhere near any planets or stars or stuff?"

"Please do not kick the alien super weapon while it is counting down to gigadeath," said McKay. "And in answer to your question, it would create a bubble of hyper-accelerated space-time around it that would instantly age everything inside a ten kilometer radius by a factor of several billion years."

"Then what's the problem?" said Lorne. "Let's just use the Asgard transporter and beam it as far away as we can."

"Great idea, brilliant solution, first class," snarled McKay, "except for the one small detail that Colonel Trigger Happy here just destroyed the central teleportation matrix!"

"Oh no," said Sheppard.

Like a hammer cast down by some mythic titan, the blunt bow of the starship *Aegis* slammed through the drifting halo of ice and dust surrounding the planet Heruun, the force field beyond the curved wall of grey steel smashing frozen shards the size of buildings into glittering pieces. Behind it, a trail of frigid gas and swirling particles spread in a sharp-edged wake. Energy cannons arrayed in omni directional turrets along the curved wings and towering fins of the Asgard vessel tracked to aim backward, and loosed a shower of lightning bolts at its pursuer.

The Wraith Hive Ship paced the *Aegis*, undeterred by the storm blazing around it, its defensive shields sparking where each hit landed. Random blasts penetrated the ethereal energy envelope and carved wounds in the bony hull, and gouts of blood-like processor fluid spat into the void where they instantly became ice. But the wounds seemed to do nothing but enrage the Wraith vessel, and it fell after the Asgard craft, vomiting back fat streaks of superheated plasma in furious retort.

In aspect, the Hive Ship's profile was like that of the blade from a spear tip, a rounded petal with dagger-sharp edges; if it had been in battle with one of its own, as the Hives of this clan so often were, the conflict would have been ended by now. But the Asgard craft, a match for the Hive Ship's speed and weaponry, was obdurate and durable. Even as it was now, injured by damage within and without, piloted only by mere humans instead of the Asgard themselves, it still resisted them.

Probing sensor scans read through the wash of radiation and discharge between the warring vessels, as the Wraith ship sniffed the void for the first sign of weakness just as an ocean predator would taste blood in the water. Thermal blooms deep inside the steely hull warned of power failures and broken conduits; there was a chance that the Asgard ship might destroy itself if the engagement went on too long. For the Wraith to have the victory they craved, obliteration was not their goal. The alien craft was to be brought to heel, not destroyed. And to achieve that, a swift and decisive blow was needed. A hard, punishing strike, enough to hobble the *Aegis* once and for all, before the humans ran it into the ground.

The Hive Ship received its command through the webs of neural fiber that coiled through the channels in the hollows of its bones, and reaction mass surged through its drives.

The Asgard vessel tried to turn away, using the fog of ice and dust as a screen, but the Wraith were too fast. The Hive came up from its position to the stern of its quarry, rolling hard to present its port edge to the dorsal surface of the *Aegis*. It powered ahead, cutting over the top of the other vessel on spikes of thruster fire. As they passed, the Wraith craft unleashed a series of pinpoint broadside shots from its cannons, targeting them at every power nexus its sensors could detect.

The *Aegis*, rendered sluggish by the damage it had suffered, shuddered and groaned. Across the top of the hull, brief spurts of flame and vented gasses signaled direct hit after direct hit.

Shredded metal forged in shipyards a galaxy away tumbled into the grip of Heruun's atmosphere, becoming brief darts of fire.

"Damn it to hell!" said Carter, the rare curse escaping her lips as a blue crackle of static charge snapped around the console and caressed her outstretched fingers. She snatched back her hands in reflex and winced, the holographic screens around her blinking on and off as the backwash from the Wraith bombardment lashed the vessel.

"Colonel," said Teyla, and her tone was enough for Sam to know what was coming next. "Power levels are dropping across all tiers. The autonomic weapons are not responding."

Carter grabbed the control spheres on her panel and manipulated them, trying to access the ship's offensive systems, but nothing seemed to work. If anything, the Athosian woman's estimate of the problem was conservative. The semi-intelligent computer systems of the *Aegis* had already begun a vain attempt to repair the damage and prevent it worsening—and to do that, power had been channeled from the guns to shields. Sam hesitated for a split-second, ready to override the machine mind's choices, but then left it to work. The energy cannons they still had operable were barely making a dent in the Hive Ship. Unlike the *Aegis*, a vessel that had only recently risen back into space and was still riven with damage from battles past, the Hive Ship was at the top of its game, fresh for the fight.

If the situation had been reversed, the Wraith craft would have already been ashes; but that wasn't how it was playing out. Sam had been at the helm of ill-fated craft before, from a gut-shot F-15 Eagle during Desert Storm to a blast-damaged Goa'uld Death Glider, and more besides. She had a pilot's innate feel for a wounded bird, and the *Aegis* was hurt bad, she could sense it.

The deck rocked and vibrated as another salvo slashed across the hull. Carter caught Teyla's eye and saw her own grim expression mirrored on the face of the warrior woman.

Sam reached for the radio on her gear vest. "Carter to Sheppard, respond. What's your situation, over?"

When the colonel replied, he sounded husky and fatigued. "*Good and bad. The Wraith in the computer core have been eliminated. But they left us a gift.*"

Carter felt her blood run cold. "They got to the matter converter?"

"*That damned thing is like a doomsday weapon vending machine. We got a fully-armed collapsar device down here, and its ticking. Well, flashing, but you get the idea.*"

"Can McKay—?"

He answered before the question left her lips. "*He's trying to disarm it, but I'm not hopeful. We need another solution.*"

"The Asgard teleportation system..." ventured Teyla, but Sam shook her head and nodded at the power grid on the holo-screen. Among other less critical systems, the network of energy links feeding the transporters aboard *Aegis* were dark.

"We can't beam anything off this ship," she told her, "not us, not the collapsar." Carter swallowed hard at the end of the statement, realizing that what she had just said was effectively a death sentence for them all.

There was a rattle from the radio as it changed hands and then Rodney McKay's voice issued forth. "*Sam, if you have any suggestions about how to deactivate this thing, they would be really appreciated.*" His tone was tight with anxiety. "*I mean really, really appreciated, because I got nothing.*"

Sam's chest tightened. Perhaps, if she had been down in the core with McKay, she might have been able to help... But she doubted it. If Rodney couldn't find a solution, Sam knew it was likely she would have come to the same conclusion. The methodical, logical Asgard were not the type to fit a star-killer with any kind of an *off* switch.

"Colonel?" Teyla gestured to one of the flickering holographic panes, an exterior view showing a fuzzy image of Heruun below them. "If the Asgard weapon detonates here, what will happen to the planet?"

"Nothing good," Carter replied, a sudden, cold sense of

certainty settling in her. She glanced down and scanned the active panels of the console in front of her, finding the energy stream she was looking for. It glowed softly, pulsing blue-green. The power train to the hyperspace drives was still active, still on standby after Fenrir had used it for his earlier short-range displacement. By some miracle, the pounding the *Aegis* had taken from the Wraith had not yet disrupted it.

McKay called out again. "*Sam? Are you there?*"

"We're all here," she said, half to herself. "Wrong place, wrong time…" Carter worked the controls, and the ship groaned as the sub-light engines throbbed with power. "I'm bringing us around. I'm going to cycle the hyperspace drive."

It was Sheppard who spoke next. "*Roger that..*" His tone made it clear he understood what she was really telling him.

"*We'll need to be at least five light-days out…*" Sam heard Rodney in the background.

"Got it." Sam's hands moved in loops as she selected the jump co-ordinates and began the process that would spin up the engines to full power.

On the exterior screen, the view was changing as the Aegis turned slowly to face the Hive Ship, the two craft closing on one another bow-to-bow.

Teyla glanced at blinking indicator on her console. "The Hive Ship is sending a signal. A call for our surrender." She cut off the communication without waiting for Carter to suggest it. "Colonel, I know we cannot let the weapon detonate near the planet, but if we depart, we will leave Heruun to the predations of the Wraith."

Sam shook her head. "Actually, I'm programming the hyperspace envelope to extend a little further." She smiled thinly. "We're going to take them with us."

"They won't let that happen."

Carter moved a control and the *Aegis* surged forward on a direct collision course toward the Hive Ship. "I'm not going to give them a choice." She remembered something another Asgard had once said to her about human ideas, about a crude and brute force approach, and a faint smile crossed her lips. Sam toggled the radio once again. "All hands," she announced, "brace for impact."

It was an unexpected and radical tactic.

The Wraith saw the *Aegis* coming and prepared for a broad-side barrage, waiting for the inevitable backlash from the Asgard ship's weapons. Too late, the sensor pits studding the hull of the Hive Ship detected energy moving not to the vessel's cannons, but into the drives and the gravity generators and integrity fields. The hammer of the *Aegis* turned in space and fell toward the hive, starlight gleaming across its surface as it loomed large.

Too late, the worker cadre crew in the Hive Ship's command nexus realized what the humans were doing, and they tried to retreat. Something like panic spiked through the aliens, and in sympathetic vibration the organic semi-mind of the great Wraith vessel shuddered. Vital seconds lost, they tried frantically to shift the orbit of their craft as the *Aegis* powered toward them, closing the gap.

Too late, they discovered that they could not flee fast enough. The thrusters flared and the vast beetle-shape of the Hive Ship began a turn, but the Asgard craft was upon them, the force fields of both craft crackling and falling as they pressed into one another, like soap bubbles meeting, distending, popping.

Too late, there was furious screaming and angered cries of alarm; but these were drowned out by the chaos of slow collision as the *Aegis* slammed into the Hive Ship, dragging its portside wing over the ventral hull of the Wraith craft, ripping it open like a massive talon.

Great chunks of fuselage from both ship were slashed apart and sent spinning away; huge plumes of gas and fluid jetted into the dark. Metal met bone in a screeching, grinding impact that resonated through the decks of both vessels, leaving ragged wounds in either craft.

The force of the impact knocked both craft into a slow spin, the two fighters now locked together in a literal death-grip. Wreathed in clouds of their own wreckage, the massive ships fell toward the edge of Herrun's outer atmosphere, the first licks of a cherry-red glow flaring across their leading edges.

Teyla Emmagan dragged herself up from the deck where she had fallen and wondered if Samantha Carter had taken leave of her senses. Ramming the Hive Ship could have destroyed them in the attempt, and yet somehow both craft were still functional, and she was still alive. Her hand strayed to her belly and she thought of the tiny life growing there. So faintly, she thought she could sense her child's weak distress, and she did her best to push back with gentle, soothing emotion; but nothing could draw away from the terrible choice that was closing around them all. With no means of escape from the *Aegis*, they would be forced to stay with the Asgard ship until it was consumed by the energies of the collapsar weapon. Her breath caught in her chest as she dwelled over that thought; *We will save the lives of an entire world, but we will perish in the void. I will never see my beloved Kanaan again, and he will not know his own child, nor will the baby be carried to its birth.* She blinked back tears. *I am sorry, little one,* she told the unborn. *I am...*

Teyla let out her breath in a gasp. The realization was so hard and fast it felt like a punch to the sternum. There *was* a chance. *Yes!* A means of escape! "I have been so blind..." she muttered, turning toward Carter.

Sam's face was dirty with smoke and among the flickering ruins of the damaged holo-screens, the colonel looked like more like a war-weary specter than a living being. Teyla could see by the expression on her face that Carter had been just as surprised that her tactic worked as anyone.

"The hyperdrive field won't initiate," she snapped. "Come on! We've got the Wraith right where we want them, come on!" Carter slammed the heel of her hand into the console before her and the screen shimmered, then stabilized. She worked the activation sequence again, her brow furrowed.

Teyla's panel showed static-laced images of the *Aegis*'s bow, rendered in simple digital frames. As she watched, a spill of blinking red indicators swarmed around the ragged edges of the ship's damaged zones, and began to penetrate inside. The hazy graphic reminded her of screens in Atlantis's infirmary, images showing viral colonies infecting healthy flesh. "The Wraith are reacting," she said, "warrior drones are massing near the hull breaches. They're coming aboard."

"I'll say this for them, they're tenacious," growled Carter. Once more the hyperdrive activation sequence stalled in mid-program and she hissed through her teeth.

The constant background shudder through the deck plates was now a steady throbbing rumble; the ships were falling into the atmosphere, doubtless cutting a fiery streak across the sky of Heruun that could be seen across the planet.

Sam shot her a look. "One way or another, we're going to end this. Either out there, or we burn up on re-entry."

Teyla shook her head. "No, Colonel, I think there is another way."

Carter blinked in surprise. "I'm open to any ideas, but make it quick."

"Fenrir's auxiliary ships, the triangular craft he used to seek out and capture the abductees from Heruun. There may still be some on the hangar level. I believe the craft possess a short-range version of the—"

"Asgard transporter!" Sam's eyes flashed with sudden understanding. "But the hangar is two decks down from here." Her face clouded as she glared at her console. "And if I leave this—"

"I was not suggesting you accompany me," Teyla said, stooping to gather up a fallen weapon from the deck. "I will go alone. If I am successful, then I will transport you away. If not…" She sighed. "It will matter little." The Athosian gestured around the wrecked command deck. "I can do nothing else to help you here, Colonel. Let me do this."

Sam saw the determination in her and nodded. "Okay, go. But I'm not having you do it by yourself. I'll get you some help."

"She is beyond insane!" shouted McKay, pushing himself off the deck from where he had landed.

The impact of the collision had sent all of them to the floor, even though they had been ready for it. Sheppard dusted himself down and recovered his rifle and a pair of Wraith stunners, nodding slightly. He had to admit, Rodney had a point. Ramming ships... Hadn't that kinda thing gone out of fashion along with Viking longboats?

"Whatever you think of Carter," ventured Lorne, "she's gutsy."

"I want my guts to remain where they are, inside here!" McKay ranted, patting his belly. "Just because this ship looks like a mallet, you don't have to use it like one!"

"My grandfather used to say, 'if all you got is a hammer, pretty soon everything starts to look like a nail'," said Sheppard. "Never really got what he meant by that until just now." He blinked and massaged a crick in his neck.

"*Colonel Sheppard, do you read?*" Carter's voice crackled through the air.

Lorne found the radio where it had fallen and tossed it to his commander. "I read you," Sheppard said wearily. "We're all still in one piece down here."

"Speak for yourself!" snapped McKay, lurching toward one of the active computer consoles.

"*John,*" came the reply, and Sheppard knew things were at their most serious. Carter didn't often call him by his first name, and the fact that she did it now meant that she wanted his full and absolute attention. "*Teyla's on her way to the hangar bay on tier three, that's a deck above you. There are Wraith swarming the ship through the hull breaches. Rendezvous with her and see if you can find a working shuttle.*"

"Got it." Sheppard's thoughts raced. Those freaky UFOs that had dragged the Puddle Jumper from the lunar surface... If one was still working, it could be their ticket off this tub. "Lorne, McKay! Gear up. We're moving out."

"No," said Rodney, in a low, serious voice. He didn't look up from his panel. "I'm not going anywhere."

"What?" Lorne blinked. "Uh, doc? Hello? Escape route?"

McKay snatched the radio from Sheppard and spoke quickly into it. "Sam. I'm at the secondary drive monitor down here. I can see the hyperdrive program... It's not initiating."

Carter sighed. *"Confirm that. I'm trying to re-program it on the go from here."*

The scientist shook his head. "That's not going to work. Too many variables. With all the damage its taken, without an Asgard to program the transition, that's never going to work. The wave-form won't coalesce…" He stopped and shot Sheppard a look. "I can help. If we do it together, Sam up on the bridge and me down here, in tandem we might be able to get the drive to accept the activation program."

"Rodney…"

A crooked, terrified smile crossed the other man's face. "Hey, look, I told you you'd need my help sooner or later. You're not as smart as you think, Carter."

"You sure about this?" said Sheppard. "We… We may not be able to come back for you."

McKay looked away and made a dismissive gesture. "Go away. Let me do my thing and you do yours."

The colonel threw Lorne a nod and the two men raced toward the chamber doorway and the corridor beyond.

Rodney called out as the hatch opened. "And you better be kidding about the 'not coming back' part!"

CHAPTER SIXTEEN

The hangar bay was a wide space with a low ceiling, supported by the same curved stanchions of steel that ribbed the corridors throughout the interior of the Asgard ship. The interior illumination was poor, most of the glow strips set in the corners of the deck dead or dying. Colonel Carter's surprise attack upon the Wraith hive had put the interior of the *Aegis* into disarray; gantries and pieces of the roof were toppled and lay in shattered piles. There were perhaps a dozen of the strange, manta-shaped Asgard shuttlecraft scattered about the chamber, most of them damaged where they had shifted in the colossal impact. Teyla saw one of them flipped over against another, the glowing coils of its drive matrix blinking and fading.

The air inside the hangar was acrid with the smell of burned plastic, and cold. Life support functions on this tier were failing, and she could see the first rimes of hoarfrost forming in white patches across the decking, the puffs of vapor from her breaths. Beneath her boots, the metal flooring creaked and vibrated.

To the far side she spotted a craft that appeared intact, the dim glow beneath it illuminating the area around it in a pool of radiant light. The sight of it gave her pause, and Teyla felt her adrenaline spike; it was a moment of primal fear-reaction, recalling the terror she had felt when the Asgard's gene-drones had captured her on Heruun. For an instant she remembered the horrible sensation of paralysis as the rays from the orb device engulfed her, her own body resisting her as the aliens gathered her up and took her away. She shuddered and forced the recollection away.

The memory had distracted her; even as she realized it, the attack came.

A giant humanoid shape threw itself from the shadows of an overhead support frame, and Teyla spun away, hearing the rush of air as it fell toward her. She was quick enough to avoid being flattened by the enraged Risar, but not quite enough to get out of its reach. It cuffed her as she turned to aim a stunner, and the impact made her howl with pain. The Wraith pistol flew from her grip and was lost in the shadows beneath another of the saucer-ships.

Landing with a heavy thud, the Asgard clone-creature went for her with its spindly, taloned fingers raised in claws. It was mumbling incoherently, staggering even as it advanced. Teyla saw it was wounded and sickly, but still she did not doubt that the Risar could kill her easily enough. In sheer body mass alone it was twice her size, and beneath its pale torso, ropey muscles bunched whenever it moved.

She backed away, raising her hands in a fighting stance. Teyla searched the blank-eyed face of the Risar for any kind of recognition or intelligence and found none. With Fenrir dead, whatever advanced technology the Asgard had used to control his towering proxies was inoperative, and now the clones had been reduced to mindless automatons, savage things that knew only madness.

There was dark blood on its fingers; the mark of kills it had already made, perhaps human, perhaps Wraith or other Risar, it was impossible to know. The creature made a gurgling sound and rushed her.

"Move forward!" Ronon shouted, pushing out from behind the shade of the nearest tree trunks. Behind him, he sensed Keller moving quickly, keeping low and going from cover to cover, and past her the mixed group of Takkol's guards and Soonir's rebels. Lieutenant Allan was at his side, firing and moving. Her face was haggard and worn, and as they both paused for breath behind an overturned cart, she threw him a glance.

"You look like I feel," she told him.

"I'm fine," he snapped back angrily. "If you can't cut it, then stay here." He ducked as pulses of stun-fire shrieked past them, answered seconds later by the rattle of a returning rodgun salvo.

Something caught his eye and he glanced up. High above,

way beyond the clouds and into the deep reaches of Heruun's sky, there were streaks of dark color and fire, crossing from horizon toward horizon. He'd seen the like before; wreckage from low orbit, burning up as it plunged through the atmosphere on re-entry. There was no way to know if they were pieces of Wraith or Asgard starship; but whatever they were, it was a grim signal that battle had been joined out in space.

Allan was looking up as well. "You think— ?"

"I think Sheppard and Carter won't go down without a fight," he rumbled. "And neither will we."

Keller pressed closer to them. She had a gun in her hand, but Ronon knew she wouldn't fire it unless circumstances were at their very worst. The doctor fixed him with a measuring stare. "Maybe we should let the locals handle this," she said, and nodded in the direction of the sick lodge just up ahead along the wooden boardwalk.

Ronon peered through a gap in the wagon's slats. "They'll get cut to pieces," he growled. From his vantage point he could see the shapes of a handful of Wraith warriors moving behind the open windows of the lodge. The odds were bad, but he'd faced worse; and inside that building were dozens of civilians who, out of foolish choice or coercion, had become prisoners—and therefore *prey*—of his old enemy. He couldn't let that stand.

Keller spoke so only he could hear her. "Ronon. On your neck there, the skin." She touched her throat to indicate the place she meant. "There are lesions… I saw them before, on the Returned. It's an indicator, a sign of the last stage of the sickness."

Ronon blinked hard. His head felt leaden and heavy, and each breath he took tasted strange, tainted. The Satedan had said nothing of this to anyone else, not of that or the shooting pains in his joints that were growing worse with every passing hour. "I can deal with it," he grated.

"Ronon—" she began.

"I said I can handle it, Teyla!" he snapped.

Keller frowned. "Ronon, it's Jennifer. Teyla's not here, remember?"

He hesitated, his head swimming. For a moment, the face of the woman before him became shadowy and indistinct. Angry with himself, he shook off the instant of confusion and gripped his particle magnum tightly, enough so the tremors in his hands were not evident. Ronon eyed Keller. "Whatever is wrong with me, I'm not going to lie down and wait for it to take me. That's not my way."

Without waiting for an answer, he grabbed the side of the wagon and vaulted up over it with a howl of effort, leading with his pistol. Ronon landed hard on the wooden deck on the other side and fired as he ran, some shots going wide, but enough of them hitting their marks to knock down the Wraith guarding the doorway.

"Follow the voyager!" shouted Soonir. "Advance! Advance!"

The pain blazed through Ronon, stinging like poison, but he cursed it and kept on going, driven on by pure fury. He kept expecting the next stun bolt that crackled through the air to be the one that struck him down; but the numbing cold of the energy discharge never came, and suddenly he was at the sick lodge's entrance, cracking the faceplate of a Wraith warrior with a slamming blow from the butt of his gun. Even as the alien fell, there came a ragged battle cry from behind him as the men and women of Heruun took the fight to their invaders.

Another wave of fatigue swept over him and he gritted his teeth. *I just need to hold on,* he told himself, *just until the fight is over.*

Teyla had nowhere to go; the Risar had backed her into a corner formed from a fallen cargo module and the canted fuselage of another shuttlecraft. She dodged, bracing herself off the saucer-ship's wing and kicking away. Teyla spun and put all her effort into a sweeping blow from her foot, connecting with the Risar's arm. Bone snapped and the clone gurgled again, ignoring the hit and slashing at the air with its good arm. The very tips of razor-sharp claws caught the front of her tunic and tore through leather and cloth, a scant hair's breadth from the flesh of her throat. She bobbed and shifted on the balls of her feet, but the Risar kept on coming, waving those gangly arms. Teyla could see no escape route that would not have her clawed and torn should she take it.

In that moment there was movement. More shapes in the half-light, behind the Risar and coming closer. For one fearful second, she thought the creature would be joined by more of its kind; but then a familiar and welcome voice cried out her name.

"Teyla!" called Sheppard. "Hit the deck!"

The Risar turned angrily, irritated that it had been disturbed. The Athosian woman did not question the colonel's command; she dropped and struck out again at the Risar's legs, this time hitting the mark.

Momentarily caught between two targets, the clone-creature snarled and hesitated, raising it's uninjured hand. With Teyla clear of the line of fire, Sheppard brought the stunners he held in either hand to bear and fired twin bursts of white fire into the Risar's torso. Incredibly, it took the first two hits without pause and staggered toward the colonel, lowing and hooting.

Teyla pivoted into a crescent kick that went up and connected hard with the clone's head. The stunning impacts finally registered in the Risar's maddened mind and it toppled, falling toward a snarl of wreckage on the deck. The creature collapsed against a broken stanchion and coughed out a final gasp of air, the metallic support beam impaling it like a spear.

Lorne extended a hand to help Teyla to her feet, but she waved him away with a thin smile. "It did not injure me."

"Glad to see you're still in once piece," said Sheppard. He sounded tired and crack-throated. "And that was a good call about these UFOs. Never woulda thought of that."

She blinked "You-eff-oh? I do not understand the term?"

"Never mind," he told her, pointing back the way they had come. "I'll dig out a copy of *Independence Day* when we get back to Atlantis, that'll explain everything. Come on, I think I found us a ride."

Sheppard led them toward the lone craft she had spotted earlier, and Teyla nodded. "I confess I have only a basic grasp of Asgard technology. I hope we will be able to operate this vessel."

"The colonel once told me he could fly anything," said Lorne. "Time to see if he was just bragging, I guess."

Another threatening rumble resonated through the decking and a segment of the steel ceiling broke away and collapsed with a ringing concussion.

"I said *anything with wings*," Sheppard retorted, stepping up to the hull of the ship, feeling across the surface with the flat of his hand. "This doesn't count." He frowned. "No seams. Where's the damn hatch?"

"There will be a touch point," Teyla noted.

"I got it." Sheppard moved his fingers over a shallow oval indent in the hull metal and part of the steel fuselage folded in on itself. "There—"

Whatever he was going to say next was lost as the Risar inside the shuttle came through the hatch and slammed Sheppard into the deck.

"Let me through!" Keller shouted, and shoved her way past the men collecting at the sick lodge's door. She felt a hand on her shoulder—Lieutenant Allan—and heard her call out a warning, but Jennifer shrugged the other woman away and kept going. Allan cursed and coughed; the USAF officer was still weak with spent effort and the aftershock of losing decades of her life to a hungry Wraith.

The bodies of a dozen dead warriors littered the floor, and a dozen more aliens were being held on their knees by rebels from Soonir's forces; the renegade leader himself and his opposite number in the elders stood close by. No-one was moving; the air was heavy with tension, laced with the smell of ozone and sweat.

She found who she was looking for; Ronon Dex stood with his gun drawn and aimed at a cluster of fearful Heruuni, who stood in a close cluster. For a moment, she couldn't understand what was happening, until she heard a familiar voice issue out from behind the trembling group.

"Get out!" shouted Kullid. "You have no right to be here! You do not believe!"

Keller's hand went to her mouth in shock. The young healer, the charming and handsome man whom she had thought might become a friend, a kindred sprit… He was using his own people as a human shield to prevent Ronon from shooting him where he stood.

"I believe this," Ronon told him. "If you don't toss out that rodgun and step away, I'll put a beam right between your eyes."

Her gaze was drawn to the Satedan's outstretched gun. It should have been rock-steady, but instead Ronon's hand was trembling with palsy. *The sickness,* she thought. *On any other day he could make the shot, but today?*

"You will not fire!" Kullid snarled. "You will kill an innocent if you pull that trigger…"

Ronon hesitated; he knew that the healer was correct.

"Kullid," ventured Jennifer. "Please, stop this. You've lost. Just tell us where the others are."

"Yes, where are the rest of the Wraith?" demanded Takkol from nearby. "The voyagers are right. Your foolish devotion to these monsters is ended! Surrender!"

"No!" Kullid shouted, and Keller saw him moving behind his wall of hostages. "I have lived a lie for my entire life! I worship the Wraith, and I am not alone in that!"

"Are you sure?" said Soonir. "Where is Aaren and the rest of your miserable adherents? They have abandoned you."

"Aaren has been granted the blessing," retorted Kullid. "The Wraith take life but they give it as well! Only gods can do that!" He was ranting now, and his hostages reacted with fear. Among them, Keller glimpsed the tear-streaked face of Laaro's mother, Jaaya. The woman met her gaze, imploring her for rescue.

"Enough of this," said Takkol, swaggering as he stepped forward. "You are like a child, Kullid! You could not defeat the sickness on your own, so rather than admit defeat like a man, you place your faith in these monsters! But they are the killers, you fool! We have known it since the beginning! Without the Aegis to protect us, we would have been culled by them long ago!"

"No! *No!*" Kullid's ire rose by the second. "You are a liar!

You have always been a weak, venial man, and you do not deserve to see their glory!" The hostages cried out as Kullid surged forward. Keller saw him moving, the thin shape of a rodgun rifle in his hands.

She felt Ronon's firm hand at her back. "Get down!" he shouted.

And then she was falling, pressed to the floor; what happened next was so fast it was nearly a blur.

Kullid took aim at Takkol and fired, the rodgun clattering angrily in the close confines of the sick lodge wardroom. She saw Soonir react and shove the other man out of the way; then in the same heartbeat a bloom of crimson flaring on the rebel's chest, a yell of pain, the stink of spent cordite.

Then Soonir falling, the hostages screaming. Kullid turning toward her, his handsome face now something ugly and hateful, animated by zealous rage.

She turned away from him and heard the flat crack of Ronon's pistol as it discharged a single, fatal pulse of red light. Kullid took the shot in the torso and was blown backwards off his feet, collapsing into a nerveless heap against the far wall. The rodgun fell from his grip, and she knew he would not rise again.

Like a thread snapping, time seemed to contract and the long seconds that had elapsed were gone, lost and fading. Keller scrambled shakily to her feet and ran to Soonir's side.

The rebel leader looked up at her and blinked. "Ah," he wheezed. "That will be the end of me." Pink foam collected at the corners of his lips.

"I need a medical kit!" she called. Allan moved into the lodge, scouring the benches for any of the gear that the Atlantis team had brought with them before the Wraith had arrived.

A shadow covered Soonir. Keller looked up and saw Takkol standing over them. The elder's face was twisted in confusion. "Why?" he demanded. "Why did you do that? You stupid fool, did you think yourself noble? If you had just stood your ground—"

"You would be lying here, yes," rasped the rebel, "and you would die instead of me."

"Soonir, no," said Keller. "Just hold on." Allan returned at a run, and thrust a medical case into her hands. The doctor dumped the contents on the floor and grabbed at bandages and a hypodermic gun.

"Ah, healer. Voyager. You are too late." Soonir blinked slowly. "I did this not for him." He nodded toward Takkol. "I did it for Heruun. Everything I did, I did... I did..." He gave a wet cough and fell silent.

Keller touched a finger to a vein in his neck and felt nothing. She let out a sigh. "He's gone."

"No," insisted Takkol, "he must not die. He has crimes that must be paid for, he must answer for all the things he has done."

"The man is dead," husked Ronon. "If you ask me, you ought to be thankful that it wasn't you." The Satedan turned away and beckoned Allan to him. "We need to secure this building. The rest of the Wraith have to be here."

She nodded. "Roger that. If they call in reinforcements from the hive, we're in big trouble."

Jaaya detached herself from the group of former hostages spoke up. "That way," she said, indicating a carved wooden corridor that led deep into the central trunk of the city-tree. "They took my husband, Aaren and others..."

"Why?" said Keller.

Jaaya's voice trembled. "They said they would give them the cure."

The weight of the towering clone-creature flattened Sheppard's chest and his breath came out in a half-yell, half-grunt.

"John!" Teyla was at his side in an instant. "Are you all right?"

"Get this thing off me!" The Risar was very dead, but it was still damned heavy, and he had trouble breathing. The drone's lipless mouth was pulled back in a rictus grin revealing bony ridges where humans would have teeth, its face scarred with oozy scratches caked with dark fluid. And its eyes; they were ragged holes in the skull. Sheppard's gut twisted as he realized the thing must have gouged out its own eyeballs.

With effort, Teyla and Lorne dragged the corpse off him and the colonel got back to his feet, wincing with the pain of a dozen new bruises.

Teyla studied the clone for a moment. "It must have been trapped inside the craft when Fenrir died. It went insane in there, killed itself."

"Just as long as it didn't smash the controls."

Lorne peered cautiously inside the shuttlecraft, leading with his gun. "It's a little messy in there, but I don't see any structural damage."

Ignoring the new bloodstains streaking his gear vest, Sheppard moved past the major and entered the vessel. The interior mirrored the design of the *Aegis* bridge, replicated on a much smaller scale. There were no chairs, only curved vertical consoles with the familiar control spheres upon them. "Okay. Clock's running. We've gotta move." He found the centre-most console and laid his hands on it. The panel glowed and a deep thrumming sound issued from the walls of the shuttle. "Contact." Sheppard shot Teyla a look. "Hey, you know what the transporter controls look like?"

"I believe so."

"Lorne, help her. I'm gonna earn my pay." He blew out a breath and concentrated on the unfolding hologram in front of him. A web of complex shapes, all circles and rods, shimmered into the air. It was nothing like any flight controls he had ever seen before.

"You sure you can do this, sir?" Lorne said in a low voice. He must have seen the flash of doubt on the colonel's face.

"If I can't," Sheppard said bleakly, "we won't have much time to be sore about it."

Aaren's desiccated corpse collapsed to the floor in front of Errian, a puff of dust issuing from its mouth. He hardly recognized the wizened, shrunken carcass that used to be the elder. Aaren's plump face of tawny skin was now a hollow, pallid thing, the flesh of his cheeks drawn tight over the bones of his skull, knots of blackened matter staring back at Errian from deep inside cavernous eye sockets. Still clad in the rich, heavy robes of his high status within the community, the many golden bangles of his rank clattering against the bony, fleshless sticks that were the dead man's arms, the form that used to be the elder looked as if it were something exhumed from an ancient grave, not a man who had been breathing only moments earlier.

Errian wanted to look away, but he could not bring himself to do so. The horror of what he had seen transfixed him, held him fast. It was more terrifying that the paralyzing touch of the Giants when he had been Taken, because it was his own mind stopping him from motion. He simply could not believe what he had seen; Aaren kneeling before the Wraith warrior, and then the white-skinned monster clawing at the man's chest. There had been screaming; from Errian, from the others who cowered in the corners of the chamber, and eventually from Aaren, who at first had thought he was about to be given some kind of benediction.

Errian had watched it all, shocked rigid as the Wraith sucked life itself from the elder, draining him dry.

And he knew that he would be the next to join him.

Around him, the group of Wraith who had shepherded them down the wooden corridor and into the carved chambers deep within the core trunks of the city-tree pulled at the victims they had chosen. Some of the people had implored the Wraith to let them come with them, those who were their secret worshippers revealing themselves, those desperate for a cure to the sickness or just too cowardly to resist fearfully trailing along with the crowd; and to Errian's shame he counted himself among the latter.

One of the aliens turned a baleful gaze on him and dragged him into a shaft of light falling from a lantern above. All the Wraith seemed agitated, violence in their every motion. Something was awry.

"Please," he managed. "I have a wife and son."

The Wraith cocked its head and hissed. He was unsure if it could actually understand him. It studied the flesh of his throat quizzically; there were welts and lesions there in abundance, the mark of the sickness in its final phase.

"I only wanted to be well… For them…" He blinked. The pain of the sickness rose and fell though him like waves upon the lakeshore, but his terror towered over all other physical sensations. *Perhaps this is for the best*, he wondered. *I will die and the pain will cease, and I shall not burden my family again.* Tears prickled in his eyes. *My dearest Jaaya, my brave Laaro.*

The alien reached down toward his breast and Errian saw a serrated maw opening in the palm of the Wraith's hand, glistening with threads of fluid.

He turned his head away so he would not see it happen, ashamed once more of his own fear.

And without warning a bolt of fiery red light streaked by his face, so close that his skin was singed by its passing. He heard the Wraith give a screaming hiss and it fell away, clutching at its forearm where burned skin trailed wisps of meat-smoke.

"Nice shot," said the lieutenant, hobbling alongside the Satedan. "You winged that sucker pretty good."

Ronon spat angrily. "I was aiming for his head." He cursed under his breath. "These damned shakes…" He glared across at the Wraith, panning his pistol across them. "Give me a fight," he bellowed. "Go on. I dare you."

Keller moved with them, blinking as she surveyed the chamber they found themselves in. Cut into the living heart of the great tree that supported the Heruuni settlement, it was one of dozens of interior spaces inside the great trunk, doubtless part of the community's infrastructure. It made sense that the Wraith would have retreated here to feed; there were few ways in or out, and warm, gloomy atmosphere was similar to the environments aboard their semi-organic starships.

A couple of the Wraith made combative motions and they were killed where they stood, eliciting cries of fear from the cowering Heruuni scattered around the chamber. Keller spotted Laaro's father among them and felt a moment of relief for the boy; but that soon faded when she saw the lesions on his skin. Unconsciously, she shot Ronon a look and frowned.

"Aaren…" Surrounded by a phalanx of his men, Elder Takkol moved to what seemed like a heap of rags lying in the middle of the floor. With distaste, Jennifer realized that she was looking at human remains; whatever it was that was left behind after a Wraith had taken its fill from a living being. Takkol was silent for a long moment. "This was the price of Aaren's weakness," he intoned. "It is a fitting death." The elder spun about and addressed the other Heruuni in the chamber. "You see? Do you see now? There is no cure for the sickness! It is a wound we must bare in exchange for the blessing of the Aegis!"

"Your 'Aegis' is just as alien as they are!" snarled Ronon, stabbing a trembling finger at the sullen pack of Wraith. "Don't you get that yet? No great being hiding in the sky will protect you! You have to fight for yourselves." The Satedan paused and paled, as if the effort of shouting was nearly too much for him.

One of the Wraith—the one Ronon had wounded—saw the moment of weakness and shifted on the balls of his feet. Lieutenant Allan raised her rifle and shot the alien a hard look. "*Don't*," she told it. The Wraith growled and stood still.

Ronon was breathing heavily and he sagged against a wall, blinking sweat away from his eyes. "Damn it…" he mumbled.

"The sickness…" husked Errian. "The voyager is close to the end, as are we all."

All at once, Jennifer Keller felt furious; the emotion came up from nowhere and it engulfed her. Her hands contracted into fists. She had been in this place too many times in her medical career, forced to watch her patients slip away because they were beyond her help, even after they had fought and clawed their way through every last shuddering breath. There was no cure for the nanite infection. The monumental unfairness of it all pressed down on her and her jaw tightened; *No*, she told herself, *I refuse to let Ronon die. I refuse to let these people die.* Keller was not willing to be beaten now, not after all this. *I didn't let Elizabeth Weir die when everyone thought she would. I'm not going to give up here, either!*

There had to be some way to bring Ronon and the others back from the brink, let their bodies heal themselves, some way to fight this slow death with life—

The Wraith take life but they give it as well!

Kullid's angry pronouncement echoed in her thoughts, the import of it hitting her like a wash of icy water. She stared at the knot of brooding, surly aliens. Each of them had fed a short time ago, she could tell by the blush of sickly green across their ghost-pale faces; and the bodies in the chamber attested to exactly how recently.

The doctor's thoughts raced; she had read the reports made by her predecessor Doctor Carson Beckett on the Wraith's unusual abilities, most notably one file that had pulled at her reason with its incredible possibilities. John Sheppard had once been fed on by one of the aliens, but later that same Wraith had somehow returned what he had stolen from the colonel, effectively regenerating his damaged, prematurely-aged tissues. There were even unsubstantiated reports of healthy humans receiving the same regenerative 'gift' from Wraith.

And if that were possible… If Kullid had been right, and the Wraith really could give life as well as take it…

Keller snapped her fingers at the Wraith to get its attention. "Uh, you," she said. "Listen to me. You understand that you're all out of options, right?" She jerked a thumb at the ceiling. "There's a battle going on up there. Your buddies aren't coming."

"Are you certain of that?" The injured Wraith spoke for the first time.

"Are *you*?" Ronon retorted.

The doctor sucked in a shaky breath. "So if you want to get off this planet alive, you better listen to me."

Takkol bristled. "You have no right to offer these monsters any amnesty!"

Allan waved her weapon at the elder. "Hush up, now. Let her finish."

Ronon crossed to her, walking with difficulty. "What do you think you are doing?" he said quietly.

"My job," she told him, then gave the Wraith a level look. "We'll let you gate off this planet."

The Wraith cocked its head. "In return for what?"

She nodded at Ronon and the others. "Make them well. Give them your 'gift of life'."

The Satedan looked at her for a long moment, and Keller thought he would explode with rage at such a suggestion. He hated the Wraith more than anyone else in the room; but Ronon Dex wasn't a fool. Beneath his pride, he had a soldier's pragmatism—and like the Wraith, he had to know it was his only shot at survival.

A slow, cold smile appeared on Ronon's face as he made his peace with the idea, and with care he took aim with his pistol, pointing it at the Wraith's head. "Of course," he husked. "There is the other option. To be honest, part of me is hoping you turn her down." Ronon's smile became a wolfish grin. "What's it gonna be?"

Rodney McKay held on to the console before him for dear life as the computer chamber shook, every loose piece of broken paneling or shattered crystal-glass rattling against the metallic decking. He tried very hard not to think about what was going on outside, about the twisted wrecks of this ship and its Wraith adversary, locked together like a pair of doomed dancers spinning their way into the inferno of re-entry. He kept his eyes glued to the holographic screen, pouring his entire focus into the single task of making the hyper-drive activation program work.

Normally, the staggeringly complex task of collating the trillions of data points needed to make a faster-than-light transition were done by computers, and outside involvement was hardly required. It was all 'point and click'; want to jump from Sol to Barnard's Star? Sure, no problem. Just tap the big red button marked 'Go'. Someone else will do the math for you.

But here and now that someone was McKay, and working in tandem with him several decks above, Sam Carter. The whole thing would have been a hell of a lot easier if they weren't in the middle of crashing to their deaths on an alien starship riddled with catastrophic damage.

Together they had failed three times in a row to correctly compile and initiate the tunneling dimensional reaction, which would soften the barrier between real space and the warped sub-reality of hyperspace. There was simply too much data to handle at once; even with two people as smart at they were in the equation, it was impossible. It just couldn't be done.

"*It's done,*" said Sam, blowing out a breath.

Rodney blinked in surprise. She wasn't wrong. Even while part of him was ticking off the seconds left before his fiery death, something deeper—call it his mathematical subconscious—was on the job. "Wow. I'm even smarter than I thought I was."

The jumble of Asgard text and symbology on the holograph shifted and changed, becoming smooth and even. A countdown rune blinked down toward zero, and the activation of the hyperdrive. Even with the damage the Aegis had sustained, it would be enough to throw it through the subspace portal and across light years. Carter had programmed the vessel to get as far away as it could in the shortest possible time; the de-fold location was in the middle of deep space, nowhere near anything that could possibly sustain life or feed the ravenous reaction of the isa device's detonation.

He released a shuddering breath. Together, they had just saved the lives of everyone on Heruun. And the cost was their own.

Rodney listened to the moaning of the *Aegis* as it inched toward its own ending, and when he spoke into his radio, his throat was dry. "Uh, Sam?"

"*I'm here,*" said Carter. "*Sixty seconds to jump.*"

"Sam, I'm sorry." The words gushed out of him. "I'm sorry you had to be here for this."

"*It's not your fault, Rodney. It's mine. I played this mission wrong from the start. Too many secrets. And look where it took us.*" Regret clouded her words.

McKay blinked and looked at the destruction and the dead around him. He felt more alone than he ever had in his life; but suddenly, not afraid. Not afraid at all. "I-I'm glad I got the chance to know you," he went on. "I know we had our differences early on—"

He heard her smile. *"What, that you thought I was an idiot and I thought you were an arrogant ass?"*

"Yeah, that," he nodded. "I'm glad I got to prove myself wrong. I'm glad I got to know you better."

There was a moment's pause. *"Thanks, Rodney. I was always a little worried you thought I had come to Atlantis to steal your thunder. But I never wanted that. I just wanted to be a part of... All this."* She sighed. *"Thirty seconds. The truth is, I liked working with you. You're the smartest person I know. I feel like I need to run to keep up and that's exhilarating. It reminds me of why I love science."*

He swallowed, touched by the her honesty. "Funny," Rodney replied. "I was just going to say the same thing about you." The rumbling was growing louder by the moment and he blinked as rains of dust cascaded down around him. McKay went to add something more but Carter spoke again.

"Twenty—" Her voice abruptly disintegrated into a humming crackle of static.

Rodney's stomach tightened in shock. "Sam? Sam? Can you hear me? *Sam!*" An answer did not come. "Oh no."

He gripped the radio in his hands as the dying starship's death throes grew deafening; then there was a deep, droning buzz and his senses were smothered with white.

The hyperspace portal formed so close to Heruun's outer atmosphere that it triggered the instantaneous creation of a high-altitude storm cell, the mighty thunderhead sweeping down to bring precipitation to a savannah wilderness that had not known a rainy season for decades.

The ragged-edged rip in space-time yawned open, spilling glowing radiation into the darkness; and together, the *Aegis* and the Hive Ship fell screaming into the shimmering maw, which snapped shut behind them in a shower of spent photons.

The displacement shockwave rode out beyond the collapsed portal, batting away trailing fragments of hull metal and wreckage from the two mighty starships, sending them into new orbits that would decay and immolate them against the planetary atmosphere.

All except one shining sliver of alien steel, a curved shape something like a saucer, or perhaps a manta ray. Swift but unsteady, the object described a wide arc away and down toward the planet's surface.

CHAPTER SEVENTEEN

In the space between stars, in a place where only the light of far distant suns fell, where there were no worlds, nothing but the merest scattering of cosmic dust, there was a brief storm of energy.

From the nothingness came a tear in the fabric of reality, as engines of alien technology sliced open a hole in the black and let glowing streamers of blue-white luminosity issue forth. A jagged collision of metal and bone exploded from the newly-formed portal and tumbled back into normal space, illuminated for a brief instant by the strange fires of hyperspace; then the portal vanished and the battle-scared hulks of the Asgard warship *Aegis* and its Wraith adversary were alone, adrift in the interstellar void, hundreds of light years from the Heruun star system.

The shock of the transition was felt through both craft; each of the ships were mortally wounded and dying by degrees, the few remaining beings that formed their crews mad with rage, or pain, or simple animal panic.

In the command nexus of the Hive Ship, the Wraith scientist who had for so long dreamed of taking the *Aegis* for his clan staggered to his feet. He ignored the burning agony from the bone shard lodged in his shoulder, a fragment that had blown from a nerve conduit behind him in a concussion that had killed a dozen of his cadre's best drone-warriors. Most of the lens-screens before him were dead eyes leaking watery processor fluid, no longer operable. The control surfaces were twitching and writhing as the Hive Ship's crude brain suffered agony from every spot of damage throughout the vessel, the pure sympathetic hurt leaching into the blood-warm air.

The Wraith made it to the panel and hissed through his teeth. His vessel was eating itself alive, reservoirs of acidic bile flooding the lower decks, plasmatic reactors stalled or worse, cycling toward a burning overload; and in the places where the Hive Ship had been violated by the deliberate impact of the Asgard vessel, gelatinous matter gurgled and bubbled as the craft's autonomic antibodies ran wild and uncontrolled. Like an animal that had caught itself in a snare, the Hive Ship was gnawing on its own extremities in a vain attempt to free itself.

Only one set of systems appeared to be working correctly; the external sensors. The Wraith clung to the console, blinking through the caked blood gumming its eyelids and read the stuttering chain of text spilling over the lens-screen. Out there aboard the alien ship, a sphere of radiation was stirring, growing by the second in power and potency. With dawning horror, the Wraith scientist realized what it was he was seeing. Like the others of his caste, the late queen had made him aware of the data she had taken from the humans, and with it the full possibilities of the technology that belonged to these 'Asgard'.

The Wraith watched the energy trace grow and cursed its fate, knowing that his clan's greed was about to kill them all.

Lying amid the wreckage of the computer core, the spinning rings of color around the circumference of the isa device reached a pitch of such speed that they became a solid band of glowing red; and at that moment the countdown ended.

Fenrir's lethal creation reached inside itself and drilled down, through the layers of normal space into unknown, extradimensional realms of energy. Drawing on levels of cosmic power strong enough to cut through the barriers of quantum reality, it twisted gravitation into a lens and blew it outward , forming a sphere of fast-time. In nanoseconds, the orb of altered space ballooned into a perfect globe a dozen kilometers across.

Outside the shimmering edge of the isa effect, time passed normally, second to second, moment to moment; but within the clock ran a million, a billion, a trillion times faster. Monumental ages, lengths of time so vast they could encompass the birthing and dying of entire civilizations, flashed past inside the sphere. Caught at the very epicenter, the *Aegis* and the Hive Ship experienced it at full force.

Every living thing aboard the wrecked vessels became wisps of ash and dust, organic matter, even bone and teeth and claws turning to powder. Unhatched in the Hive Ship's birthing crèche, the cadre's nascent newly-quickened Queen died before she was fully formed, perishing along with her warriors and her scientists. Aboard the *Aegis*, the Risar stopped their mad rampage and died in silence, swept away by the hand of their creator.

Then the ships themselves were ended, as eons passed in milliseconds. Metals and plastics designed to withstand the punishing forces of the stellar void wore thin and became like paper, splitting, breaking, ultimately disintegrating beneath their own weight.

A full ten seconds elapsed before the isa effect dissipated. Without the mass required to create a singularity, it spent itself and faded to nothing. The sphere melted away into the background radiation of the sky and left nothing but a drift of free atoms to mark its passing.

Sheppard pressed down the hemisphere in the middle of the podium with the heel of his hand and behind him the Stargate roared open, sending a plume of energy rushing out and back across the shallow valley.

The unkempt cluster of Wraith standing on the steps to the portal hove closer together, some of them throwing up hands to shield themselves from the sudden wash of silvery light. Many of them averted their faces, the brightness hurting their eyes.

Nearby, Ronon made a snorting noise and folded his arms, the pistol in his hand dangling toward the ground in a deceptively casual grip. He stood squarely, clear-eyed and straight-backed, enjoying the feel of Heruun's hard sunlight on his face. Any lasting trace of the Asgard-inflicted nanite 'sickness' had been banished from him, neutralized by the life-giving effects of an energy transfer from their Wraith captives. It was hard to believe that when all other attempts at a cure had failed, in the end it had been an enemy that had been able to save Dex and all the others. The irony wasn't lost on the colonel. Sheppard caught his friend's gaze and the Satedan raised an eyebrow.

"What?" he asked.

"You feel any… Different?"

In spite of himself, Ronon's free hand wandered to his chest, to a spot over his heart, to scratch at some imaginary itch. The big man didn't seem aware that he was doing it. "No," he said tersely, "Did you?"

Sheppard shook his head quickly. "'Course not. I was just, y'know, checking." In truth, for several days after gaining his freedom from being imprisoned by the militant Genii along with a Wraith he'd nicknamed 'Todd', Sheppard had felt a little strange. The Wraith had made an uneasy ally—one that had crossed the path of the Atlanteans a number of times since—and John had been both surprised and shocked when the alien had healed him after all the times he had preyed on Sheppard during their captivity. It wasn't anything physical, nothing like the strange addiction that Wraith worshippers craved from the touch of their alien masters; it was a sense of invasion, almost a mark on the soul, if you wanted to get metaphysical about it. Even though he had been certified well, it took him a long time to wash off the stain, so to speak.

Sheppard didn't doubt that Ronon felt the same way; but getting the Satedan to admit it would not be likely. He kept his own counsel over that sort of thing. The colonel's gaze drifted over to Lieutenant Allan; along with Ronon and all the rest of the Heruuni infected with the sickness, she had also taken the unusual 'cure', but in her case it had been to reverse the effects of a feeding. She gave Sheppard a respectful nod; there was a look on her face that he had seen in the mirror once or twice, a kind of confused-but-pleased surprise at the fact you were still alive.

He crossed towards the group of Wraith, who stood under the watchful eye of Major Lorne, and a few of the rebels under the orders of Soonir's former second-in-command, Gaarin. A pair of growling lion-cats on thick leashes held them in check, stalking back and forth with paws flexing and claws bare.

The pale-skinned aliens were the sorriest-looking bunch of their kind Sheppard had ever seen. The usual arrogance and swagger he associated with the Wraith was nowhere in sight.

Instead, they stood in a scowling, morose knot, some of them clenching and unclenching their clawed fingers, others moving with difficulty, hobbling. Their weapons and gear had been taken from them, down to the smallest blade; that had been a job that Ronon had taken on with obvious relish.

Every one of the Wraith looked sickly and emaciated, even more so than their typical air of perpetual hunger allowed. They looked, for want of a better word, as if they had been starved, and with good reason. The spur-of-the-moment bargain Doctor Keller had struck with them in Sheppard's absence had been both radical and clever. In return for letting the handful of survivors from the Hive Ship leave with their lives, they had been forced to use their alien physiology to give back what they had stolen—the raw energy of life—and in the process counteract the infection that crippled the abductees taken by Fenrir. Of course, giving it up to so many people had taken its toll. Now it was the turn of the Wraith to understand what it was like to have the flesh go limp on your bones, to have the breath practically stolen out of your lungs. As object lessons went, it was a pretty good one.

Sheppard had to admit that he never would have come up with such an idea, and the fact that a woman like Jennifer Keller *had* forced him to re-evaluate his first impressions of the young doctor. Ever since she and McKay had gone against his orders with Elizabeth and that whole replicator thing, John had kept Keller at arm's length, but now he saw that she wasn't someone who made the hard calls blithely. In the face of certain death, she had saved lives, albeit in a very unconventional manner—something the IOA would be sure to bitch about when his report went back to Earth.

One of the Wraith showed yellowed fangs as he approached. "You will kill us?" he demanded. "Now you have what you want from us?"

Ronon toyed with his pistol. "Hey, that's an idea."

The alien shot him a venomous glare. "I saved your life!"

"And that's why you're still walking and talking," Sheppard broke in. "When we make a deal, we keep our word."

Lorne nodded in the direction of the open Stargate. "That's

your exit. If I were you, I'd take it."

Sheppard mirrored the major's nod. "What he said."

"What about our weapons, our communications devices?" said the Wraith. "We need them."

"No you don't," the colonel replied. "Use your psychic hot-line to dial up a rescue."

"How do we know the place you are sending us to is not a death-world?"

Ronon grunted. "Huh. I should have thought of that."

"You're just gonna have to trust us." Sheppard replied. He gave Gaarin a nod and the Heruuni drew back the big cats, making a path for the prisoners. "Listen, it's last call for you guys. You don't have to go home, but you can't stay here." To underscore the statement, Ronon brought up his particle magnum and gestured with it. John continued. "You healed my people and Gaarin's people, and for that you get a free pass. That's the extent of the conversation that you and me are going to have. Do I make myself clear?"

The Wraith exchanged looks with its kindred, and then without further comment, they shuffled up the steps and began to file through the shimmering wormhole.

Sheppard waited until the talkative one was about to step up and called out. "Oh yeah, there's just one other thing." The alien paused on the threshold, eyeing him coldly. "The Aegis may be gone, but this planet is now under the protection of Atlantis. So if you're thinking of hooking up with some of your buddies and swinging by for a little payback, *don't*. 'Cos we'll know about it, and that's not something you want."

The Wraith paused, letting the others of its cadre pass through the gate and away, until it was the last one on Heruun. "Enjoy your victory while you can, human," it said. "But remember this. Sooner or later, the Asurans will turn their attacks from my kind to yours, and when that day comes, you will wish that you had let us take the Asgard's weapons to defeat them." Without waiting to hear a reply, the alien stepped through and vanished into the ripples.

Sheppard gestured to Allan and the lieutenant severed the wormhole from the DHD podium.

He heard Lorne give a dry chuckle. "Sore losers."

The colonel didn't look away from the silent Stargate, the Wraith's words echoing in his mind. "Yeah. Guess so."

Carter watched the people working around the fringes of the settlement's central oval, clearing the wreckage created in the attack by the Wraith, starting down the path toward setting their lives back on track. The young boy Laaro wandered past and threw her a serious nod, which she returned along with a grin. The youth tried very hard to pretend he was old beyond his years, but she had seen him revert to the child he really was when Sheppard had reunited him with his mother and father. The raw, open happiness Sam witnessed there had brought a lump to her throat.

We did some good here, she thought to herself. *In the end.* For a moment, Carter wondered what she would have done differently, if she could step back to before the mission to M9K-153 had been given the go. She looked away and shook her head. *Second-guessing yourself won't fix anything you do wrong.* General Hammond had told her that the first time she had taken command of SG-1. *Every leader makes mistakes. The real test is if you don't make them again.*

Sam sighed. Command of the Atlantis mission was nothing like she had expected, and in some ways, *everything* like she had expected. Every day was a challenge, and just this short jaunt into the field—and into the grip of certain danger—reminded her with potent force just how much had changed about her life.

No. I wouldn't change the orders I gave if I could. I did what I thought was right, I trusted my people to get the job done. And they did.

"Colonel Carter." She turned at the sound of her name and found Takkol approaching her. His guards remained at a respectful distance, and she noted that there were fewer of them. Sam wondered what message that sent about the changes the man had been through recently.

"Elder," she nodded.

"I wanted to thank you personally for the gifts you gave us.

The supplies and equipment."

"We can spare it," she replied. "It's the least we can do to help." Carter sighed. "I hope you understand, we never intended to bring the Wraith here or upset the balance of things on Heruun…"

"I think… This would have happened sooner or later, would it not? The Aegis…" He stumbled over the word. "This… Asgard being. Eventually he would have left us and the Wraith would have returned. Perhaps it was better it took place now instead of in the future."

Sam felt a pang of sympathy for the man. All the superiority and arrogance he had shown before was gone, and in their place he seemed uncertain and wary. "Change is always difficult," she said, with real feeling. "But we have to embrace it."

"I suppose so. My reticence was a mistake, Colonel."

She answered without thinking, hearing Hammond speak once again. "Every leader makes mistakes. The real test is if you don't make them again."

Takkol accepted this with a nod. "Wise words. In looking back, I find I have made many such errors." He looked away. "I was wrong about the nature of the Aegis. When Aaren and Kullid turned on our ways and went to the side of the Wraith… When Soonir, a man I thought to be nothing but a renegade and dissident, gave his life to save mine… I misjudged so much."

"Things aren't always what they seem. Being a leader can isolate you from that truth, if you let it."

Takkol met Sam's gaze. "Now I look around and all I can do is wonder how many other things I am mistaken about."

"There are worse places to start. But what's important is that you move on, and strive to do the right thing." She was a little surprised by the conviction behind her own words. *Am I talking to him, or to myself?*

"You speak truth, voyager," he agreed. "I allowed my rank and status to close me off from my people. No longer." Takkol bobbed his head. "For that I thank you."

From the blue sky overhead came a humming whine and they both looked up to see the barrel-shape of a Puddle Jumper loop past and fall into a steady hover. The outriggers retracted and the craft settled gently to the open wooden decking.

In the shade of the lodge's porch, Laaro handed the small twists of animal hide and polished stones to Teyla and Jennifer. "These are for you and your friends," he told them. "I made one for each of the voyagers, so that when you return to your great city you will have something to remind you of Heruun."

Teyla turned the gift over in her hand; it was a small bangle, a simple version of the ornate bracelets worn by the elders. She put it around her wrist and Keller did the same.

The doctor paused for a moment, then reached up and tore the Atlantis expedition patch off the velcro mount on the shoulder of her jacket. "Here. This is for you."

Laaro weighed the patch in his hand. "I am honored, Jennifer." He bowed formally. "And I thank you all for making my parents safe."

All eyes turned as the Jumper swept in and landed, the aft drop-ramp falling open. Teyla saw Major Lorne appear in the hatchway and throw her a nod.

"Time to go," she said.

Laaro bowed slightly. "Safe journey to you, voyagers." He stepped off the porch, crossing through the bright, hot sunlight, marvelling at the spacecraft.

Keller reached for the gear bag at her feet and halted. When she spoke again, her voice was low and quiet. "Just so you know. After you came back from the *Aegis*, when I checked everyone over?" She threw a look toward Teyla's belly. "You're both okay, despite the pounding you took."

"The children of Athos are a resilient people." Teyla glanced at the doctor and sensed an unspoken question in the woman's eyes. "As are the Herunni. If Laaro is anything to go by, I believe they will thrive, even without the protection of the Asgard."

The doctor gathered up the bag and the two of them made their way toward the waiting Jumper. "The sickness won't come back," she replied. "I'm certain of that. As for everything else…" Keller smiled ruefully. "Well, we did just completely dismantle their entire belief system in a matter of days."

"We showed them the truth."

"Yes we did. I hope that'll be enough." The doctor paused. "I just wish. There was so much we could have learned from Fenrir. There are so many things we still don't understand about the Asgard, even with the *Odyssey* core."

Ronon was standing on the ramp waiting for them. He caught the last few words of the conversation. "Fenrir paid his debts in full," said the Satedan.

Teyla's eyes widened. "It surprised me to hear you say that. After all that he put us through. After what he did to you."

"I'm not forgiving him, if that's what you think," came the reply. "But I understand why he did what he did. I know what its like to be isolated from your own kind, to be lost, to want more than anything to just go home…" He shrugged. "Can't say I wouldn't have done the same in his position."

The Athosian woman felt a stirring of emotion and swallowed hard. "No being should be so alone."

"Whatever Fenrir did," said Keller, "whatever choices he may have made in the past, he gave the last moments of his life to save others. If that's not atonement, I'm not sure what is."

Colonel Carter was the last one to step up into the Jumper, and as she did so Ronon folded his arms. "So. Can we go home now?"

Glancing back from the cockpit, Sheppard nodded with genuine feeling. "Yeah, I reckon so."

Carter hesitated. "One second, Colonel. There is one last loose end to deal with."

"Oh, right," said Sheppard. "*That*. It's not a problem. I sent Lorne and McKay out to go pick it up."

"Are you sure this is the place?" said Rodney, squinting at the display on the handheld sensor device. "I mean, there's nothing here!"

Major Lorne frowned and surveyed the open span of savannah around them. "I'm telling you, this is it." He pointed. "Look. The grasses here are all compacted. And there's a burn ring where the drives scorched the ground. This is where the colonel put us down."

McKay shook his head. "When Sheppard plucked us off the *Aegis* with that UFO's transporters, we came straight down out of orbit! He could have dropped us anywhere." He sniffed. "And it wasn't his best landing, I have to say."

Lorne gestured at the ground. "No, this is it, I'd bet my oak leaves. I'm telling you, there should be an Asgard shuttle parked right here."

McKay walked forward, waving his arms. "Look, see, nothing! Even if it was cloaked like a Jumper, I'd still bump right into it."

The major was silent for a moment. "You don't think it…left on its own, do you? Can Asgard ships do that?"

"Of course not," Rodney snapped. "We're talking about a faster-than-light spacecraft! You couldn't pilot something like that without a thinking, reasoning intelligence on board!" No sooner had the words left his mouth that he found himself suddenly wondering. "Um…"

Unbidden, McKay and Lorne both turned their heads to look up into the clear sky; and for a second, just for the smallest of moments, the scientist thought he saw a tiny flash of light like sunshine off silver, vanishing into the distance.

ABOUT THE AUTHOR

James Swallow is the author of several books and scripts, and his fiction from the worlds of *Stargate* includes the novels *Halcyon* and *Relativity*, the audio dramas *Shell Game*, *Zero Point* and *First Prime*, and short stories for *Stargate: The Official Magazine*.

As well as a non-fiction book (*Dark Eye: The Films of David Fincher*), James also wrote the *Sundowners* series of original steampunk westerns, *Jade Dragon*, *The Butterfly Effect* and tales from the worlds of *Star Trek* (*Day of the Vipers, Infinity's Prism, Distant Shores, The Sky's The Limit* and *Shards and Shadows*), *Doctor Who* (*Peacemaker, Dalek Empire, Destination Prague, Snapshots, The Quality of Leadership*), *Warhammer 40,000* (*Red Fury, The Flight of the Eisenstein, Faith & Fire, Deus Encarmine* and *Deus Sanguinius*) and *2000AD* (*Eclipse, Whiteout* and *Blood Relative*). His other credits include writing for *Star Trek Voyager*, and scripts for videogames and audio dramas, including *Battlestar Galactica, Blake's 7* and *Space 1889*.

James lives in London, and is currently at work on his next book.

STARGÅTE

SG·1™

STARGATE
ATLÅNTIS™

**Original novels based on
the hit TV shows,
STARGATE SG-1 and
STARGATE ATLANTIS**

AVAILABLE NOW

**For more information, visit
www.stargatenovels.com**

Series number: SGA-1

STARGATE ATLANTIS: RISING

by **Sally Malcolm**
Price: £6.99 UK | $7.95 US
ISBN-10: 0-9547343-5-1
ISBN-13: 978-0-9547343-5-0

Following the discovery of an Ancient outpost buried deep in the Antarctic ice sheet, Stargate Command sends a new team of explorers through the Stargate to the distant Pegasus galaxy.

Emerging in an abandoned Ancient city, the team quickly confirms that they have found the Lost City of Atlantis. But, submerged beneath the sea on an alien planet, the city is in danger of catastrophic flooding unless it is raised to the surface. Things go from bad to worse when the team must confront a new enemy known as the Wraith who are bent on destroying Atlantis.

Stargate Atlantis is the exciting new spin-off of the hit TV show, Stargate SG-1. Based on the script of the pilot episode, Rising is a must-read for all fans and includes deleted scenes and dialog not seen on TV — with photos from the pilot episode.

Order your copy directly from the publisher today by going to www.stargatenovels.com or send a check or money order made payable to "Fandemonium" to:

USA orders: $10.82 ($7.95 + $2.87 P&P). Send payment to: Fandemonium Books, PO Box 2178, Decatur, GA 30031-2178.

UK orders: £8.30 (£6.99 + £1.31 P&P). **Rest of the World orders:** £9.70 (£6.99 + £2.71 P&P). Send payment to: Fandemonium Books, PO Box 795A, Surbiton KT5 8YB, United Kingdom.

Or check your local bookshop – available on special order if they are out of stock (quote the ISBN number listed above).

STARGATE ATLANTIS: RELIQUARY

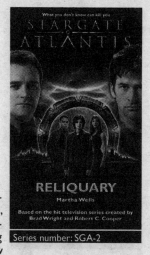

by Martha Wells
Price: £6.99 UK | $7.95 US
ISBN-10: 0-9547343-7-8
ISBN-13: 978-0-9547343-7-4

While exploring the unused sections of the Ancient city of Atlantis, Major John Sheppard and Dr. Rodney McKay stumble on a recording device that reveals a mysterious new Stargate address. Believing that the address may lead them to a vast repository of Ancient knowledge, the team embarks on a mission to this uncharted world.

There they discover a ruined city, full of whispered secrets and dark shadows. As tempers fray and trust breaks down, the team uncovers the truth at the heart of the city. A truth that spells their destruction.

With half their people compromised, it falls to Major John Sheppard and Dr. Rodney McKay to risk everything in a deadly game of bluff with the enemy. To fail would mean the fall of Atlantis itself—and, for Sheppard, the annihilation of his very humanity…

A little knowledge is a dangerous thing

STARGATE
ATLANTIS

THE CHOSEN

Sonny Whitelaw & Elizabeth Christensen

Based on the hit television series created by
Brad Wright and Robert C. Cooper

Series number: SGA-3

STARGATE ATLANTIS: THE CHOSEN

by **Sonny Whitelaw &
Elizabeth Christensen**
Price: £6.99 UK | $7.95 US
ISBN-10: 0-9547343-8-6
ISBN-13: 978-0-9547343-8-1

With Ancient technology scattered across the Pegasus galaxy, the Atlantis team is not surprised to find it in use on a world once defended by Dalera, an Ancient who was cast out of her society for falling in love with a human.

But in the millennia since Dalera's departure much has changed. Her strict rules have been broken, leaving her people open to Wraith attack. Only a few of the Chosen remain to operate Ancient technology vital to their defense and tensions are running high. Revolution simmers close to the surface.

When Major Sheppard and Rodney McKay are revealed as members of the Chosen, Daleran society convulses into chaos. Wanting to help resolve the crisis and yet refusing to prop up an autocratic regime, Sheppard is forced to act when Teyla and Lieutenant Ford are taken hostage by the rebels...

STARGATE ATLANTIS: HALCYON

by James Swallow
Price: £6.99 UK | $7.95 US
ISBN-10: 1-905586-01-9
ISBN-13: 978-1-905586-01-1

In their ongoing quest for new allies, Atlantis's flagship team travel to Halcyon, a grim industrial world where the Wraith are no longer feared—they are hunted.

Series number: SGA-4

Horrified by the brutality of Halcyon's warlike people, Lieutenant Colonel John Sheppard soon becomes caught in the political machinations of Halcyon's aristocracy. In a feudal society where strength means power, he realizes the nobles will stop at nothing to ensure victory over their rivals. Meanwhile, Dr. Rodney McKay enlists the aid of the ruler's daughter to investigate a powerful Ancient structure, but McKay's scientific brilliance has aroused the interest of the planet's most powerful man—a man with a problem he desperately needs McKay to solve.

As Halcyon plunges into a catastrophe of its own making the team must join forces with the warlords—or die at the hands of their bitterest enemy…

Order your copy directly from the publisher today by going to www.stargatenovels.com or send a check or money order made payable to "Fandemonium" to:

USA orders: $10.82 ($7.95 + $2.87 P&P). Send payment to: Fandemonium Books, PO Box 2178, Decatur, GA 30031-2178.

UK orders: £8.30 (£6.99 + £1.31 P&P). Rest of the World orders: £9.70 (£6.99 + £2.71 P&P). Send payment to: Fandemonium Books, PO Box 795A, Surbiton KT5 8YB, United Kingdom.

Or check your local bookshop – available on special order if they are out of stock (quote the ISBN number listed above).

STARGATE ATLANTIS: EXOGENESIS

Global disaster threatens the Atlantis homeworld

STARGATE ATLANTIS

EXOGENESIS

Sonny Whitelaw & Elizabeth Christensen

Based on the hit television series created by Brad Wright and Robert C. Cooper

Series number: SGA-5

by Sonny Whitelaw & Elizabeth Christensen
Price: £6.99 UK | $7.95 US
ISBN-10: 1-905586-02-7
ISBN-13: 978-1-905586-02-8

When Dr. Carson Beckett disturbs the rest of two long-dead Ancients, he unleashes devastating consequences of global proportions.

With the very existence of Lantea at risk, Colonel John Sheppard leads his team on a desperate search for the long lost Ancient device that could save Atlantis. While Teyla Emmagan and Dr. Elizabeth Weir battle the ecological meltdown consuming their world, Colonel Sheppard, Dr. Rodney McKay and Dr. Zelenka travel to a world created by the Ancients themselves. There they discover a human experiment that could mean their salvation...

But the truth is never as simple as it seems, and the team's prejudices lead them to make a fatal error — an error that could slaughter thousands, including their own Dr. McKay.

STARGATE ATLANTIS: ENTANGLEMENT

by Martha Wells

Price: £6.99 UK | $7.95 US
ISBN-10: 1-905586-03-5
ISBN-13: 978-1-905586-03-5

When Dr. Rodney McKay unlocks an Ancient mystery on a distant moon, he discovers a terrifying threat to the Pegasus galaxy.

Determined to disable the device before it's discovered by the Wraith, Colonel John Sheppard and his team navigate the treacherous ruins of an Ancient outpost. But attempts to destroy the technology are complicated by the arrival of a stranger — a stranger who can't be trusted, a stranger who needs the Ancient device to return home. Cut off from backup, under attack from the Wraith, and with the future of the universe hanging in the balance, Sheppard's team must put aside their doubts and step into the unknown.

However, when your mortal enemy is your only ally, betrayal is just a heartbeat away...

Order your copy directly from the publisher today by going to www.stargatenovels.com or send a check or money order made payable to "Fandemonium" to:

USA orders: $10.82 ($7.95 + $2.87 P&P). Send payment to: Fandemonium Books, PO Box 2178, Decatur, GA 30031-2178.

UK orders: £8.30 (£6.99 + £1.31 P&P). Rest of the World orders: £9.70 (£6.99 + £2.71 P&P). Send payment to: Fandemonium Books, PO Box 795A, Surbiton KT5 8YB, United Kingdom.

Or check your local bookshop – available on special order if they are out of stock (quote the ISBN number listed above).

The first victim of warfare is the truth

STARGATE
ATLANTIS

CASUALTIES
OF WAR
Elizabeth Christensen

Based on the hit television series created by
Brad Wright and Robert C. Cooper

Series number: SGA-7

STARGATE ATLANTIS: CASUALTIES OF WAR

by Elizabeth Christensen
Price: £6.99 UK | $7.95 US
ISBN-10: 1-905586-06-X
ISBN-13: 978-1-905586-06-6

It is a dark time for Atlantis. In the wake of the Asuran takeover, Colonel Sheppard is buckling under the strain of command. When his team discover Ancient technology which can defeat the Asuran menace, he is determined that Atlantis must possess it — at all costs.

But the involvement of Atlantis heightens local suspicions and brings two peoples to the point of war. Elizabeth Weir believes only her negotiating skills can hope to prevent the carnage, but when her diplomatic mission is attacked — and two of Sheppard's team are lost — both Weir and Sheppard must question their decisions. And their abilities to command.

As the first shots are fired, the Atlantis team must find a way to end the conflict — or live with the blood of innocents on their hands…

Order your copy directly from the publisher today by going to www.stargatenovels.com or send a check or money order made payable to "Fandemonium" to:

<u>USA orders:</u> $10.82 ($7.95 + $2.87 P&P). Send payment to: Fandemonium Books, PO Box 2178, Decatur, GA 30031-2178.

<u>UK orders:</u> £8.30 (£6.99 + £1.31 P&P). <u>Rest of the World orders:</u> £9.70 (£6.99 + £2.71 P&P). Send payment to: Fandemonium Books, PO Box 795A, Surbiton KT5 8YB, United Kingdom.

Or check your local bookshop – available on special order if they are out of stock (quote the ISBN number listed above).

STARGATE ATLANTIS: BLOOD TIES

**by Sonny Whitelaw &
Elizabeth Christensen**
Price: £6.99 UK | $7.95 US |
$9.95 Canada
ISBN-10: 1-905586-08-6
ISBN-13: 978-1-905586-08-0

When a series of gruesome murders are uncovered around the world, the trail leads back to the SGC—and far beyond...

Recalled to Stargate Command, Dr. Elizabeth Weir, Colonel John Sheppard, and Dr. Rodney McKay are shown shocking video footage—a Wraith attack, taking place on Earth. While McKay, Teyla, and Ronon investigate the disturbing possibility that humans may harbor Wraith DNA, Colonel Sheppard is teamed with SG-1's Dr. Daniel Jackson. Together, they follow the murderers' trail from Colorado Springs to the war-torn streets of Iraq, and there, uncover a terrifying truth...

As an ancient cult prepares to unleash its deadly plot against humankind, Sheppard's survival depends on his questioning of everything believed about the Wraith...

Order your copy directly from the publisher today by going to www.stargatenovels.com or send a check or money order made payable to "Fandemonium" to:

USA orders: $10.82 ($7.95 + $2.87 P&P). Send payment to: Fandemonium Books, PO Box 2178, Decatur, GA 30031-2178.

UK orders: £8.30 (£6.99 + £1.31 P&P). Rest of the World orders: £9.70 (£6.99 + £2.71 P&P). Send payment to: Fandemonium Books, PO Box 795A, Surbiton KT5 8YB, United Kingdom.

Or check your local bookshop – available on special order if they are out of stock (quote the ISBN number listed above).

STARGATE ATLANTIS: MIRROR MIRROR

by Sabine C. Bauer
Price: £6.99 UK | $7.95 US |
$9.95 Canada
ISBN-10: 1-905586-12-4
ISBN-13: 978-1-905586-12-7

Series number: SGA-9

When an Ancient prodigy gives the Atlantis expedition Charybdis — a device capable of eliminating the Wraith — it's an offer they can't refuse. But the experiment fails disastrously, threatening to unravel the fabric of the Pegasus Galaxy — and the entire universe beyond.

Doctor Weir's team find themselves trapped and alone in very different versions of Atlantis, each fighting for their lives and their sanity in a galaxy falling apart at the seams. And as the terrible truth begins to sink in, they realize that they must undo the damage Charybdis has wrought while they still can.

Embarking on a desperate attempt to escape the maddening tangle of realities, each tries to return to their own Atlantis before it's too late. But the one thing standing in their way is themselves...

STARGATE ATLANTIS: NIGHTFALL

A terrifying weapon threatens the Pegasus galaxy

STARGATE
ATLANTIS

NIGHTFALL

James Swallow

Based on the hit television series created by
Brad Wright and Robert C. Cooper

Series number: SGA-10

by James Swallow
Price: £6.99 UK | $7.95 US |
$9.95 Canada
ISBN-10: 1-905586-14-0
ISBN-13: 978-1-905586-14-1

Deception and lies abound on the peaceful planet of Heruun, protected from the Wraith for generations by their mysterious guardian—the Aegis.

But with the planet falling victim to an incurable wasting sickness, and two of Colonel Sheppard's team going missing, the secrets of the Aegis must be revealed. The shocking truth threatens to tear Herunn society apart, bringing down upon them the scourge of the Wraith. Yet even with a Hive ship poised to attack there is much more at stake than the fate of one small planet.

For the Aegis conceals a threat so catastrophic that Colonel Samantha Carter herself must join Sheppard and his team as they risk everything to eliminate it from the Pegasus galaxy…

Order your copy directly from the publisher today by going to www.stargatenovels.com or send a check or money order made payable to "Fandemonium" to:

<u>USA orders:</u> **$10.82 ($7.95 + $2.87 P&P). Send payment to: Fandemonium Books, PO Box 2178, Decatur, GA 30031-2178.**

<u>UK orders:</u> **£8.30 (£6.99 + £1.31 P&P).** <u>Rest of the World orders:</u> **£9.70 (£6.99 + £2.71 P&P). Send payment to: Fandemonium Books, PO Box 795A, Surbiton KT5 8YB, United Kingdom.**

Or check your local bookshop – available on special order if they are out of stock (quote the ISBN number listed above).

STARGATE ATLANTIS: ANGELUS

STARGATE ATLANTIS

ANGELUS

Peter Evans

Based on the hit television series created by
Brad Wright and Robert C. Cooper

Series number: SGA-11

by Peter Evans
Price: £6.99 UK | $7.95 US |
$9.95 Canada
ISBN-10: 1-905586-18-3
ISBN-13: 978-1-905586-18-9

With their core directive restored, the Asurans have begun to attack the Wraith on multiple fronts. Under the command of Colonel Ellis, the Apollo is dispatched to observe the battlefront, but Ellis's orders not to intervene are quickly breached when an Ancient ship drops out of hyperspace.

Inside is Angelus, fleeing the destruction of a world he has spent millennia protecting from the Wraith. Charming and likable, Angelus quickly connects with each member of the Atlantis team in a unique way and, more than that, offers them a weapon that could put an end to their war with both the Wraith and the Asurans.

But all is not what it seems, and even Angelus is unaware of his true nature — a nature that threatens the very survival of Atlantis itself…

Order your copy directly from the publisher today by going to www.stargatenovels.com or send a check or money order made payable to "Fandemonium" to:

USA orders: **$10.82 ($7.95 + $2.87 P&P). Send payment to: Fandemonium Books, PO Box 2178, Decatur, GA 30031-2178.**

UK orders: **£8.30 (£6.99 + £1.31 P&P). Rest of the World orders:** **£9.70 (£6.99 + £2.71 P&P). Send payment to: Fandemonium Books, PO Box 795A, Surbiton KT5 8YB, United Kingdom.**

Or check your local bookshop — available on special order if they are out of stock (quote the ISBN number listed above).

STARGATE SG-1: TRIAL BY FIRE

By Sabine C. Bauer

Price: $7.95 US | $9.95 Canada |
£6.99 UK
ISBN-10: 0-9547343-0-0
ISBN-13: 978-0-9547343-0-5

Trial by Fire follows the team as they embark on a mission to Tyros, an ancient society teetering on the brink of war.

A pious people, the Tyreans are devoted to the Canaanite deity, Meleq. When their spiritual leader is savagely murdered during a mission of peace, they beg SG-1 for help against their sworn enemies, the Phrygians.

Initially reluctant to get involved, the team has no choice when Colonel Jack O'Neill is abducted. O'Neill soon discovers his only hope of escape is to join the ruthless Phrygians—if he can survive their barbaric initiation rite.

As Major Samantha Carter, Dr. Daniel Jackson and Teal'c race to his rescue, they find themselves embroiled in a war of shifting allegiances, where truth has many shades and nothing is as it seems.

And, unbeknownst to them all, an old enemy is hiding in the shadows...

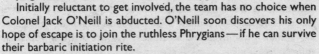

Order your copy directly from the publisher today by going to www.stargatenovels.com or send a check or money order made payable to "Fandemonium" to:

USA orders: $10.82 ($7.95 + $2.87 P&P). Send payment to: Fandemonium Books, PO Box 2178, Decatur, GA 30031-2178.

UK orders: £8.30 (£6.99 + £1.31 P&P). Rest of the World orders: £9.70 (£6.99 + £2.71 P&P). Send payment to: Fandemonium Books, PO Box 795A, Surbiton KT5 8YB, United Kingdom.

Or check your local bookshop – available on special order if they are out of stock (quote the ISBN number listed above).

STARGATE SG-1: SACRIFICE MOON

By Julie Fortune
Price: $7.95 US | $9.95 Canada |
£6.99 UK
ISBN-10: 0-9547343-1-9
ISBN-13: 978-0-9547343-1-2

Sacrifice Moon follows the newly commissioned SG-1 on their first mission through the Stargate.

Their destination is Chalcis, a peaceful society at the heart of the Helos Confederacy of planets. But Chalcis harbors a dark secret, one that pitches SG-1 into a world of bloody chaos, betrayal and madness. Battling to escape the living nightmare, Dr. Daniel Jackson and Captain Samantha Carter soon begin to realize that more than their lives are at stake. They are fighting for their very souls.

But while Col Jack O'Neill and Teal'c struggle to keep the team together, Daniel is hatching a desperate plan that will test SG-1's fledgling bonds of trust and friendship to the limit…

STARGATE SG-1: CITY OF THE GODS

by Sonny Whitelaw

Price: $7.95 US | $9.95 Canada |
£6.99 UK
ISBN-10: 0-9547343-3-5
ISBN-13: 978-0-9547343-3-6

Series number: SG1-4

When a Crystal Skull is discovered beneath the Pyramid of the Sun in Mexico, it ignites a cataclysmic chain of events that maroons SG-1 on a dying world.

Xalótcan is a brutal society, steeped in death and sacrifice, where the bloody gods of the Aztecs demand tribute from a fearful and superstitious population. But that's the least of Colonel Jack O'Neill's problems. With Xalótcan on the brink of catastrophe, Dr. Daniel Jackson insists that O'Neill must fulfil an ancient prophesy and lead its people to salvation. But with the world tearing itself apart, can anyone survive?

As fear and despair plunge Xalótcan into chaos, SG-1 find themselves with ringside seats at the end of the world…

• *Special section: Excerpts from Dr. Daniel Jackson's mission journal.*

Order your copy directly from the publisher today by going to www.stargatenovels.com or send a check or money order made payable to "Fandemonium" to:

<u>USA orders:</u> $10.82 ($7.95 + $2.87 P&P). Send payment to: Fandemonium Books, PO Box 2178, Decatur, GA 30031-2178.

<u>UK orders:</u> £8.30 (£6.99 + £1.31 P&P). <u>Rest of the World orders:</u> £9.70 (£6.99 + £2.71 P&P). Send payment to: Fandemonium Books, PO Box 795A, Surbiton KT5 8YB, United Kingdom.

Or check your local bookshop – available on special order if they are out of stock (quote the ISBN number listed above).

STARGATE SG-1: A MATTER OF HONOR

**Part one of two parts
by Sally Malcolm**
Price: $7.95 US | $9.95 Canada |
£6.99 UK
ISBN-10: 0-9547343-2-7
ISBN-13: 978-0-9547343-2-9

Five years after Major Henry Boyd and his team, SG-10, were trapped on the edge of a black hole, Colonel Jack O'Neill discovers a device that could bring them home.

But it's owned by the Kinahhi, an advanced and paranoid people, besieged by a ruthless foe. Unwilling to share the technology, the Kinahhi are pursuing their own agenda in the negotiations with Earth's diplomatic delegation. Maneuvering through a maze of tyranny, terrorism and deceit, Dr. Daniel Jackson, Major Samantha Carter and Teal'c unravel a startling truth — a revelation that throws the team into chaos and forces O'Neill to face a nightmare he is determined to forget.

Resolved to rescue Boyd, O'Neill marches back into the hell he swore never to revisit. Only this time, he's taking SG-1 with him…

STARGATE SG-1: THE COST OF HONOR

**Part two of two parts
by Sally Malcolm**
Price: $7.95 US | $9.95 Canada |
£6.99 UK
ISBN-10: 0-9547343-4-3
ISBN-13: 978-0-9547343-4-3

In the action-packed sequel to *A Matter of Honor*, SG-1 embark on a desperate mission to save SG-10 from the edge of a black hole. But the price of heroism may be more than they can pay...

Returning to Stargate Command, Colonel Jack O'Neill and his team find more has changed in their absence than they had expected. Nonetheless, O'Neill is determined to face the consequences of their unauthorized activities, only to discover the penalty is far worse than anything he could have imagined.

With the fate of Colonel O'Neill and Major Samantha Carter unknown, and the very survival of the SGC threatened, Dr. Daniel Jackson and Teal'c mount a rescue mission to free their team-mates and reclaim the SGC. Yet returning to the Kinahhi homeworld, they learn a startling truth about its ancient foe. And uncover a horrifying secret...

Order your copy directly from the publisher today by going to www.stargatenovels.com or send a check or money order made payable to "Fandemonium" to:

<u>USA orders:</u> $10.82 ($7.95 + $2.87 P&P). Send payment to: Fandemonium Books, PO Box 2178, Decatur, GA 30031-2178.

<u>UK orders:</u> £8.30 (£6.99 + £1.31 P&P). <u>Rest of the World orders:</u> £9.70 (£6.99 + £2.71 P&P). Send payment to: Fandemonium Books, PO Box 795A, Surbiton KT5 8YB, United Kingdom.

Or check your local bookshop – available on special order if they are out of stock (quote the ISBN number listed above).

Aris Boch is back – and he's after Daniel Jackson!

STARGATE SG·1

SIREN SONG
Holly Scott & Jaimie Duncan

Based on the hit television series developed by
Brad Wright and Jonathan Glassner

Series number: SG1-6

STARGATE SG-1: SIREN SONG

Holly Scott and Jaimie Duncan
Price: $7.95 US | $9.95 Canada |
£6.99 UK
ISBN-10: 0-9547343-6-X
ISBN-13: 978-0-9547343-6-7

Bounty-hunter, Aris Boch, once more has his sights on SG-1. But this time Boch isn't interested in trading them for cash. He needs the unique talents of Dr. Daniel Jackson—and he'll do anything to get them.

Taken to Boch's ravaged homeworld, Atropos, Colonel Jack O'Neill and his team are handed over to insane Goa'uld, Sebek. Obsessed with opening a mysterious subterranean vault, Sebek demands that Jackson translate the arcane writing on the doors. When Jackson refuses, the Goa'uld resorts to devastating measures to ensure his cooperation.

With the vault exerting a malign influence on all who draw near, Sebek compels Jackson and O'Neill toward a horror that threatens both their sanity and their lives. Meanwhile, Carter and Teal'c struggle to persuade the starving people of Atropos to risk everything they have to save SG-1—and free their desolate world of the Goa'uld, forever.

STARGATE SG-1: SURVIVAL OF THE FITTEST

by Sabine C. Bauer

Price: $7.95 US | $9.95 Canada |
£6.99 UK
ISBN-10: 0-9547343-9-4
ISBN-13: 978-0-9547343-9-8

Colonel Frank Simmons has never been a friend to SG-1. Working for the shadowy government organisation, the NID, he has hatched a horrifying plan to create an army as devastatingly effective as that of any Goa'uld.

And he will stop at nothing to fulfil his ruthless ambition, even if that means forfeiting the life of the SGC's Chief Medical Officer, Dr. Janet Fraiser. But Simmons underestimates the bond between Stargate Command's officers. When Fraiser, Major Samantha Carter and Teal'c disappear, Colonel Jack O'Neill and Dr. Daniel Jackson are forced to put aside personal differences to follow their trail into a world of savagery and death.

In this complex story of revenge, sacrifice and betrayal, SG-1 must endure their greatest ordeal...

Order your copy directly from the publisher today by going to www.stargatenovels.com or send a check or money order made payable to "Fandemonium" to:

USA orders: $10.82 ($7.95 + $2.87 P&P). Send payment to: Fandemonium Books, PO Box 2178, Decatur, GA 30031-2178.

UK orders: £8.30 (£6.99 + £1.31 P&P). **Rest of the World orders:** £9.70 (£6.99 + £2.71 P&P). Send payment to: Fandemonium Books, PO Box 795A, Surbiton KT5 8YB, United Kingdom.

Or check your local bookshop – available on special order if they are out of stock (quote the ISBN number listed above).

STARGATE SG-1: ALLIANCES

A failed mission leaves O'Neill dealing with the fallout

STARGATE
SG-1

Based on the hit television series developed by
Brad Wright and Jonathan Glassner

ALLIANCES

Karen Miller

Series number: SG1-8

by Karen Miller

Price: $7.95 US | $9.95 Canada |
£6.99 UK
ISBN-10: 1-905586-00-0
ISBN-13: 978-1-905586-00-4

All SG-1 wanted was technology to save Earth from the Goa'uld … but the mission to Euronda was a terrible failure. Now the dogs of Washington are baying for Jack O'Neill's blood — and Senator Robert Kinsey is leading the pack.

When Jacob Carter asks General Hammond for SG-1's participation in mission for the Tok'ra, it seems like the answer to O'Neill's dilemma. The secretive Tok'ra are running out of hosts. Jacob believes he's found the answer — but it means O'Neill and his team must risk their lives infiltrating a Goa'uld slave breeding farm to recruit humans willing to join the Tok'ra.

It's a risky proposition … especially since the fallout from Euronda has strained the team's bond almost to breaking. If they can't find a way to put their differences behind them, they might not make it home alive…

STARGATE SG-1: ROSWELL

by **Sonny Whitelaw & Jennifer Fallon**

Price: $7.95 US | $9.95 Canada | £6.99 UK

ISBN-10: 1-905586-04-3

ISBN-13: 978-1-905586-04-2

When a Stargate malfunction throws Colonel Cameron Mitchell, Dr. Daniel Jackson, and Colonel Sam Carter back in time, they only have minutes to live.

But their rescue, by an unlikely duo — General Jack O'Neill and Vala Mal Doran — is only the beginning of their problems. Ordered to rescue an Asgard also marooned in 1947, SG-1 find themselves at the mercy of history. While Jack, Daniel, Sam and Teal'c become embroiled in the Roswell aliens conspiracy, Cam and Vala are stranded in another timeline, desperately searching for a way home.

As the effects of their interference ripple through time, the consequences for the future are catastrophic. Trapped in the past, SG-1 can only watch as their world is overrun by a terrible invader...

The past comes back to haunt Jack

STARGATE
SG·1

James Swallow

RELATIVITY

James Swallow

Based on the hit television series developed by
Brad Wright and Jonathan Glassner

Series number: SG1-10

STARGATE SG-1: RELATIVITY

by James Swallow
Price: $7.95 US | $9.95 Canada |
£6.99 UK
ISBN-10: 1-905586-07-8
ISBN-13: 978-1-905586-07-3

When SG-1 encounter the Pack—a
nomadic space-faring people who
have fled Goa'uld domination for
generations—it seems as though
a trade of technologies will benefit
both sides.

But someone is determined to
derail the deal. With the SGC under
attack, and Vice President Kinsey breathing down their necks, it's
up to Colonel Jack O'Neill and his team to uncover the saboteur and save the fledgling alliance. But unbeknownst to SG-1
there are far greater forces at work—a calculating revenge that
spans decades, and a desperate gambit to prevent a cataclysm of
epic proportions.

When the identity of the saboteur is revealed, O'Neill is faced
with a horrifying truth and is forced into an unlikely alliance in
order to fight for Earth's future.

STARGATE SG-1: THE BARQUE OF HEAVEN

by Suzanne Wood
Price: $7.95 US | $9.95 Canada |
£6.99 UK
ISBN-10: 1-905586-05-1
ISBN-13: 978-1-905586-05-9

Millennia ago, at the height of his power, the System Lord Ra decreed that any Goa'uld wishing to serve him must endure a great trial. Victory meant power and prestige, defeat brought banishment and death.

On a routine expedition to an abandoned Goa'uld world, SG-1 inadvertently initiate Ra's ancient trial – and once begun, the trial cannot be halted. Relying on Dr. Daniel Jackson's vast wealth of knowledge, Colonel O'Neill must lead his team from planet to planet, completing each task in the allotted time. There is no rest, no respite. To stop means being trapped forever in the farthest reaches of the galaxy, and to fail means death.

Victory is their only option in this terrible test of endurance – an ordeal that will try their will, their ingenuity, and above all their bonds of friendship...

STARGATE SG-1: DO NO HARM

by **Karen Miller**
Price: $7.95 US | $9.95 Canada |
£6.99 UK
ISBN-10: 1-905586-09-4
ISBN-13: 978-1-905586-09-7

Stargate Command is in crisis—too many teams wounded, too many dead. Tensions are running high and, with the pressure to deliver tangible results never greater, General Hammond is forced to call in the Pentagon strike team to plug the holes.

But help has its price. When the team's leader, Colonel Dave Dixon, arrives at Stargate Command he brings with him loyalties that tangle dangerously with a past Colonel Jack O'Neill would prefer to forget.

Assigned as an observer on SG-1, hostility between the two men escalates as the team's vital mission to secure lucrative mining rights descends into a nightmare.

Only Dr. Janet Fraiser can hope to save the lives of SG-1—that is, if Dave Dixon and Jack O'Neill don't kill each other first...

STARGATE SG-1: HYDRA

by Holly Scott & Jaimie Duncan
Price: $7.95 US | $9.95 Canada |
£6.99 UK
ISBN-10: 1-905586-10-8
ISBN-13: 978-1-905586-10-3

Rumours and accusations are reaching Stargate Command, and nothing
is making sense. When SG-1 is met
with fear and loathing on a peaceful
world, and Master Bra'tac lays alle-
gations of war crimes at their feet,
they know they must investigate.

Series number: SG1-13

But the investigation leads the team into a deadly assault
and it's only when a second Daniel Jackson stumbles through
the Stargate, begging for help, that the truth begins to emerge.
Because this Daniel Jackson is the product of a rogue NID operation that spans the reaches of the galaxy, and the tale he has to
tell is truly shocking.

Facing a cunning and ruthless enemy, SG-1 must confront
and triumph over their own capacity for cruelty and violence in
order to save the SGC – and themselves...

**Order your copy directly from the publisher today by going
to www.stargatenovels.com or send a check or money order
made payable to "Fandemonium" to:**

USA orders: **$10.82 ($7.95 + $2.87 P&P). Send payment to:
Fandemonium Books, PO Box 2178, Decatur, GA 30031-2178.**

UK orders: **£8.30 (£6.99 + £1.31 P&P).** **Rest of the World
orders:** **£9.70 (£6.99 + £2.71 P&P). Send payment to:
Fandemonium Books, PO Box 795A, Surbiton KT5 8YB,
United Kingdom.**

Or check your local bookshop – available on special order if they are
out of stock (quote the ISBN number listed above).